DAY BY DAY ARMAGEDDON

SHATTERED HOURGLASS

J.L. BOURNE

Extraction mission over New Orleans

The locustlike swarm of undead approached from all directions. The knee-deep water seemed to boil with movement. The creatures were closing in fast, hundreds, perhaps a thousand of them. . . .

Praise for J.L. Bourne's page-turning
novels of the zombie apocalypse

DAY BY DAY ARMAGEDDON

DAY BY DAY ARMAGEDDON:
BEYOND EXILE

"There is zombie fiction and then there is crawl-out-of-the-grave-and-drag-you-to-hell zombie fiction. *Day by Day Armageddon* is hands-down the best zombie book I have *ever* read. *Dawn of the Dead* meets *28 Days Later* doesn't even come close to describing how fantastic this thriller is. It is so real, so terrifying, and so well written that I slept with not one, but two loaded Glocks under my pillow for weeks afterward. J.L. Bourne is the new king of hardcore zombie action!"

—Brad Thor, #1 *New York Times* bestselling author of
The Athena Project

"An excellent addition to a zombie section of a library, or anyone's home collection."

—Bret Jordan, *Monster Librarian*

"A dramatic spin on the zombie story. It has depth, a heart, and compelling characters."

—Jonathan Maberry, Bram Stoker Award–winning author of
Patient Zero

"A visceral insight into the psyche of a skilled survivor. . . . Claws at the reader's mind."

—Gregory Solis, author of *Rise and Walk*

Also by J.L. Bourne

Day by Day Armageddon

Day by Day Armageddon: Beyond Exile

Day by Day
Armageddon

Shattered
Hourglass

J.L. Bourne

GALLERY BOOKS
New York   London   Toronto   Sydney

Gallery Books
A Division of Simon & Schuster, Inc.
1230 Avenue of the Americas
New York, NY 10020

First Gallery Books trade paperback edition December 2012.

GALLERY BOOKS and colophon are trademarks of Simon & Schuster, Inc.

For information about special discounts for bulk purchases, please contact Simon & Schuster Special Sales at 1-866-506-1949 or business@simonandschuster.com.

The Simon & Schuster Speakers Bureau can bring authors to your live event. For more information or to book an event contact the Simon & Schuster Speakers Bureau at 1-866-248-3049 or visit our website at www.simonspeakers.com.

Manufactured in the United States of America.

10 9 8 7 6 5 4 3 2

Library of Congress Cataloging-in-Publication Data is available

ISBN 978-1-4516-2881-4
ISBN 978-1-4516-2884-5 (ebook)

For more information about Permuted Press books and authors, please visit www.permutedpress.com.

Author's Note

If you made it this far, you have likely spent some time in my post-apocalyptic world through the pages of the first two *Day by Day Armageddon* novels. Foremost, I'd like to thank you—the dedicated fans—for punching yet another ticket on the train with non-stop service through the bleak landscapes of undead armageddon.

Sit back, settle in, and make ready for what *could* be the final chapter in the *Day by Day Armageddon* saga. This one will be different, you'll see.

Although this story is best enjoyed chronologically, if you are just beginning the *Day by Day Armageddon* saga, allow me to bring you up to speed.

The two-minute version:

The first volume of *Day by Day Armageddon* took us deep into the mind of a military officer and survivor as he made a New Year's resolution to start keeping a journal. The man kept his resolution, chronicling the fall of humanity, day by day. We see him transition from the life that you and I live, to the prospect of fighting for his very survival against the overwhelming hordes of the dead. We see him bleed, we see him make mistakes, we witness him evolve.

While surviving numerous trials and travails in the first volume of *Day by Day Armageddon,* the protagonist and his neighbor John escape the government-sanctioned nuclear annihilation of San Antonio, Texas. They make their way to temporary safety onboard a boat dock on the gulf shores of Texas, and soon after receive a weak radio transmission.

A family of survivors—a man named William, his wife Janet, and their young daughter Laura, all that remain of their former community—take shelter in their attic while untold numbers of undead creatures search for them below. After a miraculous rescue, the family joins forces with our protagonist to stay alive. As they scout the outlying areas for supplies, they encounter a woman named Tara trapped and near death in an abandoned car surrounded by the undead.

They eventually find themselves sheltering inside an abandoned strategic missile facility known by the long deceased former occupants as Hotel 23. Their union may not be enough in a dead world, an unforgiving post-apocalyptic place in which a simple infected cut, not to mention the millions of walking undead, can easily kill them, adding to the already overwhelming undead population.

The situation brought out the worst in some . . .

Without warning a band of brigands, seeing targets of opportunity, mercilessly begin an assault on Hotel 23, intending to murder the survivors for the shelter and take the vast supplies inside. Narrowly pushed back at the end of the first novel, the survivors were able to hold Hotel 23 for the time being.

In the second installment, *Day by Day Armageddon: Beyond Exile,* our protagonist connects with the remnants of military ground forces in Texas. As the last military officer known to be alive on the mainland, he soon finds himself in command. He establishes communications with the acting Chief of Naval Operations onboard a working nuclear aircraft carrier on station in the Gulf of Mexico.

He also discovers a handwritten letter telling of a family—the Davises—hiding out at an outlying airport within prop aircraft range of Hotel 23. The rescue mission results in the extraction of the Davis family—a young boy named Danny and his very capable civilian pilot grandmother, Dean.

After being allotted a functioning scout helicopter from the carrier battle group, he and his men begin searching for resources in the areas north of Hotel 23. Halfway through *Beyond Exile,* our protagonist suffers a catastrophic helicopter crash hundreds of miles north of the facility. Severely injured, he is the lone survivor.

Running dangerously low on provisions, he manages to trek south. He soon encounters Remote Six, a shadowy group with unknown motives, hell-bent on getting him back to Hotel 23. Later he stumbles upon an Afghani sniper named Saien. Little is known about Saien's background, and his cryptic demeanor only adds to the mystery. At the start, neither fully trust one another, but Saien and our protagonist work together and eventually return to Hotel 23 under the watchful eyes of Remote Six.

Remote Six orders our protagonist to launch the remaining nuclear warhead on the aircraft carrier. The order is ignored and a high-tech retaliation against Hotel 23 ensues. A sonic javelin weapon known as Project Hurricane is dropped by Remote Six, attracting legions of undead creatures to the region.

The sonic weapon is eventually destroyed, but it's too late.

A mile-high dust cloud, generated by the approaching undead army, signals the need for an emergency evacuation. A harrowing battle to the Gulf of Mexico ensues, where the aircraft carrier USS *George Washington* waits to take on any and all survivors.

Shortly after our protagonist's arrival onboard, orders from the highest level are issued—a directive to rendezvous with the fast attack submarine USS *Virginia,* standing by in West Panamanian waters.

Destination? China. Mission? Turn the page and find out, but first . . .

Check your doors. Better make sure they're locked.

—J.L. Bourne
JLBourne.com

1

Panama—Task Force Hourglass

Chaos. Pure and complete. The scene below resembled an area following a Category 5 hurricane or aerial bombardment. The many canal structures still remained at the whim of the elements, showing creeping signs of decay and neglect. The jungle was already beginning to reclaim the canal regions, commencing a long bid to erase any evidence that man had split the continents a century before.

Soulless figures walked about, searching, reacting to the firings of dead synapses.

A corpse wearing only a mechanic's work shirt shuffled about the area. The mechanic had met its demise via the barrel of a Panamanian soldier's rifle, back when the national curfew was still being enforced. "He" became "it" shortly after the punctured heart stopped and the body temperature began to fall, letting loose the mystery that reanimated dead people. The anomaly (as it was known) spread quickly throughout the mechanic's nervous system, altering key areas of sensory anatomy. It anchored and replicated in the brain, but only in the sections where primal instinct developed and was stored via DNA and electrochemical switches from eons of evolution. Along its path of self-replication and infection, the anomaly made a quick stop inside the ear canal. There it microscopically altered the physical make-up of the inner ear ossicles, enhancing the hearing. The eyes were the last stop. After a few hours of reanimation, the anomaly completed replication and replacement of certain cellular structures inside the eye, resulting in rudimentary short-range thermal sensory ability, balancing its death-degraded vision.

The former mechanic stopped and cocked its head sideways. It could hear a noise in the distance, something familiar—a nanosecond flash of audible recognition, then it was gone and forgotten. The sound grew louder, exciting the creature, causing salivation. Translucent gray fluid dribbled from its chin, hitting its bare and nearly skeletal leg. The mechanic took a small step forward in the direction of the noise; the open tendons on top of its foot flexed and pulled the small foot bones as it moved. The creature sensed that the increasing sound was not natural, was not the wind or incessant rain noises it normally ignored. The creature's pace quickened as it reached a small patch of dense jungle trees. A snake struck out as the mechanic entered the foliage, slapping dead flesh and leaving two small holes in its nearly gone calf muscle. The creature paid no attention and continued to slog forward, nearly clearing the foliage. The chorus of souls-be-damned boomed out from all directions as the thing broke through to the clearing.

Two hundred thousand undead on the mechanic's side of the Panama Canal bellowed at the sky. A gray military helicopter zoomed over at one hundred knots, trailing the canal southeast. The mechanic reacted instinctively to the engine noise, reaching up as if it might pluck the great bird from the sky and eat it cold. Frenzied with hunger, it followed the whirlybird, eyes locked onto the flying machine. Ten paces later, the creature stepped over the edge into the canal waters.

The canal's twisting form was no longer filled with brown muddy water and transiting ships. Bloated, floating bodies now blocked her once-busy shipping route. Some of the disgusting forms still moved, not yet dissolved by the Panama heat and humidity or mosquito larva—infested waters. The countless hordes on one side of the canal roared and moaned at their undead doppelgängers on the other in a Hatfield and McCoy feud spanning the great divide.

Before the anomaly, the world was fixated on the Dow Jones Industrial Average, phony government U3 unemployment numbers, spot gold prices, currency indexes, and the worldwide debt crisis.

The very few that now survived prayed to go back to a Dow 1,000 and 80 percent unemployment; at least it would be something.

The conditions on the ground had degraded exponentially since the first case of the anomaly was documented in China. Early in the crisis, the surviving executive branch of the United States government made the decision to nuke the major continental cities in a bid to "deter, deny, or degrade the undead ability to eliminate the surviving population of the United States." The cities were leveled by high-order nuclear detonation. Many of the creatures were instantly disintegrated in the process but the tradeoff was catastrophic. The dead outside of the comparatively small blast zones were zapped with so many alpha, beta, and gamma particles that the radiation eradicated any bacteria that might enable decomposition, preserving the dead for what scientists estimated at decades.

A few scattered human survivors remained though, and some military command and control was still in place. An operation was at this very moment underway to uncover the chain of events that brought humanity to the brink, maybe beyond.

Behind closed doors there was talk of possibly engineering an effective weapon of mass destruction against the creatures, as there were not enough small-arms ammunition or people to pull the triggers left on the planet. Behind thicker closed doors, there was talk of other, more nefarious things.

The helicopter pilot screamed back to the passengers, cheek full of chewing tobacco, "Three-zero mikes until on top the USS *Virginia!*"

The helicopter's internal communications system failed to function as advertised months ago. It was now only good for cockpit communications between the pilot and copilot up front.

The pilot was easily in his sixties, as told by his gray hair, deep crow's feet, and old and battered Air America ball cap. The rider in the copilot's seat was not part of the air crew—just another member of what was known on the flight docket as Task Force Hourglass.

Pilots had been in short supply over the past few months, most of them lost on reconnaissance missions. The remaining airworthy military aircraft were constructed of thousands of complex moving parts, all of which needed to be rigorously inspected and maintained, or they would soon become very expensive lawn darts. The old pilot seemed to enjoy the company of having someone in the right seat, someone to die alongside if things went too far south, which was frequent.

The rider appeared jumpy and hyperaware of his surroundings. Wearing an overly tight harness, his hand on the door latch and his eyes on the master caution panel, he nervously scanned the helicopter instruments. The rider risked a glance at the ground; they were flying low and fast. An optical illusion from the cockpit put the helicopter nearly level with the canal banks on either side. The creatures screamed and thrashed loudly as they fell into the water, unable to compete with the deafening engine noise. The rider easily but involuntarily filled the gaps with his imagination, hearing the songs of the dead from below. The permanent PTSD gained from the past year's events pushed forward in his consciousness. He instinctively slapped his side, feeling for his carbine, preparing for another crash.

The pilot took notice and squawked into his headset, "Heard about what happened to you. Chopper went down in the badlands."

The rider keyed the microphone on his headset. "Something like that."

The pilot grumbled, "You just transmitted on the radio. Key down to talk to me, and up to talk to the world."

"Oh, sorry."

"Don't worry about it; I doubt anyone heard it anyway. Only those things around. Lots of fellow pilots walking about down there now. These runs keep getting more dangerous by the sortie. The birds are falling apart, no spare parts . . . What did you do before?" the old man yelled into the headset over the whine of the neglected turbine engines.

"I'm a military officer."

"What branch?"

The rider paused and said, "I'm a navy lieu—uh, a commander."

The pilot laughed as he said, "Which is it, son? Lieutenant is a ways from commander."

"Long, boring story."

"Son, I doubt that. What did you do in the navy before?"

"Aviation."

"Hell, you wanna fly the rest of the way?"

"No thanks. I'm not exactly the best helicopter stick."

The pilot chuckled at this. "When I was running small fixed wings low over Laos before you were born, I didn't know how to fly one of these, either."

The rider looked down at the undead masses below and mumbled, "I didn't think we were flying anything over Laos."

The old man smiled and said, "We weren't. But how do ya think all them Phoenix Program snipers got close and personal with the NVA brass? By humping their bolt guns a hundred miles through the jungle? Shit . . . if you think Phoenix was only active in Vietnam, I've got some oceanfront property in Panama down there to sell ya!"

Both men laughed over the loud thumping rhythm of the spinning rotor blades above their heads. The rider reached into his pack for a piece of gum scavenged from a military MRE, offering the pilot half.

"No thanks, plays hell on my dentures and I'm all out of Fixodent. Who you got back there with you anyway?"

The rider frowned at the old man. "They don't tell you anything, do they? The Arab-looking guy is a friend of mine. The others are SOCOM, or some of what's left of them anyway."

"SOCOM, hmm?"

"Yeah, a few frogs and such. I'm not sure I can tell you much more than that and to be honest, I don't know much more anyway."

"I understand, you wanna keep the old man in the dark."

"No, it's not that, it's . . ."

"I'm kidding, no worries. I had to keep a secret or two in my day."

A few more rotor-thumping minutes passed before the pilot pointed his wrinkled finger forward to the horizon and said, "There's the Pacific. The coords to the *Virginia* are on that kneeboard card. Mind punching them into the inertials?"

"Not a problem."

After the coordinates were entered, the pilot altered course a few degrees starboard and maintained heading.

"What's your name, son?"

"My friend back there calls me Kilroy, Kil for short. What's yours?"

"I'm Sam. Pleasure to meet you, even though this may be the first and last time."

"Well, Sam, you sure know how to keep spirits high."

Sam reached up, tapped the glass on the upper gauge panel, and said, "You know the risks, Kilroy. There ain't no tellin' where you're goin' in your little black submarine. Wherever it is, you can bet it will be just as dangerous as right below us. There ain't no safe zones anywhere."

2

A United States aircraft carrier, one of the last fading symbols of American military might. There were others, but those had been anchored offshore months ago, abandoned. One carrier was even reserved as a floating nuclear power plant, providing gigawatts of electricity to withering military island outposts and some remote coastal airstrips. Previously known as USS *Enterprise,* she was now officially renamed as Naval Reactor Site Three. A small contingent of power plant engineers was all that remained of her former five-thousand-sailor crew. Not all of these behemoths were accounted for. A handful of the steel giants had been trapped overseas when the alarms sounded and society collapsed. The USS *Ronald Reagan* sat at the bottom of the Yellow Sea with most of her crew undead, still floating through the black compartments of Davey Jones's locker. In the beginning, there was blame to cast and throw about like blacksmith anvils—that is, while men still lived to cast it. There was chatter via classified cables that the USS *Ronald Reagan* had been brought down by simultaneous attacks from several North Korean diesel submarines in the days just after the anomaly. No one really knew for sure. The USS *George HW Bush* was last seen dead in the water near Hawaii. Visual observers from a nearby American destroyer reported that the undead creatures swarmed her decks—she was now a floating mausoleum and would remain so until a rogue wave or super typhoon sent her down to Poseidon.

Some of the surviving crews from the remaining carriers had been recovered and consolidated onboard the USS *George Washington,* still on active service in the Gulf of Mexico. The U.S. military diaspora continued.

· · ·

The twenty-thousand-ton USS *George Washington* cut through the Gulf waters, maintaining a patrol box ten miles off the infested Panamanian coastline. The Continuity of Government still remained, its primary orders clear and concise. *Recover Patient Zero by any means necessary.*

Admiral Goettleman, Task Force Hourglass commander and acting chief of naval operations, sat in his stateroom eating breakfast, watching the ship's cable TV network. A loop of *The Final Countdown* had been playing over and over again for the past week. He'd need to call someone about that, or maybe he'd let it go. *Perhaps the crew enjoys watching an aircraft carrier travel back in time with the opportunity to change history.* A loud knock on his door signaled Joe Maurer, a CIA case officer and his aide since the beginning of this mess.

"Good morning, Admiral," Joe said cheerfully, but somewhat insincerely.

"Mornin', Joe. Our boys make it to the *Virginia*?" Admiral Goettleman asked, chewing his final bite of powdered eggs.

"They will shortly, sir. The radio room reports that they are over the Pacific and zeroing in on *Virginia*'s beacon now."

"I wouldn't be an admiral if I didn't worry about the weather. The helo reporting any bad chop?"

"No, sir, smooth waters, good air. Got lucky today, I suppose."

"We're going to need to save some of that luck. Hourglass has a long way to float. I'm deeply concerned at how all this is going to play out. Despite that I've asked you a hundred times, what are your thoughts? Ground truth, no bullshit."

"Admiral, they'll need to get there first. Assuming they survive the transit to Pearl, the Kunia operation in Hawaii, and the long transit to Chinese waters, the worst will still be in front of them. The lights are out around the world and we've received no communications from any of the Chinese Military Regions since last winter. The country has gone dark. We don't have the HF radio operators to monitor the band. We could have missed their transmission a dozen times and not known. We're short on Chinese linguists. If our people did receive their transmission, we have maybe five folks onboard that could interpret. Let's say it's a given that the team makes it across the Pacific to the Bohai and up the river. Then what? You know how bad it is in the continental United States. We had maybe three hundred twenty million people a year ago. Kinetic operations up to this point have attrited some creatures, but the nukes didn't exactly help the cause."

Listening to Joe's commentary, Admiral Goettleman went back in time for a moment, to the decision to nuke the population centers. At the time, even he had agreed with that decision. From the bridge of his ship, he had heard the cheers from the crew as the nighttime fireballs lit the sky and rocked the targeted coastal cities. Hell, he'd clapped and yelled, too. The great mushroom plumes differed vastly from old nuclear-testing stock footage. All colors of the rainbow coursed through the pillar below the massive mushroom cap. Great blue lightning beamed and zapped throughout the thrown vertical wall of city debris, dust, and human remains.

"How's our research into the New Orleans specimens progressing?" asked Goettleman.

"Well, sir, you read what happened on the Cutter *Reliance*. We have SIGINT cuts from overhead with good geolocs of hundreds of radio transmissions out of New Orleans and other nuked cities I can brief you on. The transmissions originated after the detonations occurred. All intelligence indicates that those bastards are just about unstoppable in moderate numbers. Higher cognitive function, agility, speed. It's not only their bite or scratch that can kill you—it's the radiation from those high-yield nukes shooting from their corpses. The Causeway and Downtown specimens are no different."

"I was hoping for a little good news, you know," Goettleman said, almost sadly.

"We still have propulsion, fresh water, and some food, sir."

The admiral forced a smile. "I guess that's something."

Joe took a drink and coughed, saying, "The men on that chopper getting ready to bungee into the drink don't even know what they're going after."

"They soon will. The intelligence officer on *Virginia* will see to that."

"Sir, I know we've discussed this but my stance has not changed. Telling them everything could complicate things on some level. Patient Zero, if they can even locate it, may not be worth retrieving to them. They may perceive it as a waste of time and resources."

"Joe, Patient Zero may be the only key to unraveling this mess. I'm willing to sacrifice a multi-billion-dollar sub and every man on it for a chance at that . . . and then there's the tech."

Joe walked over to the bar and poured himself another finger. "We've had tech for seventy years with no vast leaps forward except maybe solid state, some low observability, primitive maglev, and lasers. It took decades to reverse engineer our laughable and oversized jury-rigged versions. Besides, what good is the tech against seven billion walking predators?"

"Those are compelling points, but what else is there?"

"Admiral, we could gather survivors and head for an island. Secure it and live out our days at least a little safer than we are here."

"Abandon the U.S.? Leave it for those creatures?"

"Sir, with all due respect, there is nothing left on the mainland but millions of those things. Many are radiated to the point of a zero decomposition rate. Even if none of them were exposed to the radiation, the analysts predict they'd still walk around for another ten years or more and be a threat for even longer than that. There is truly no guess on how long they might last. Some are saying thirty years or more."

The admiral looked through Joe to the wall behind him. He appeared to be in a trance repeating to himself . . .

"Thirty years. Thirty years, my God."

Joe continued: "Unless we launch a coordinated pincer assault on both coasts and give 'em what for with every man, woman, and able child, we will not take back the continental United States anytime soon, if ever. So that's it. We are dealing with something that not only infects the dead, but the living as well. We all have it. The only humans left not carriers of the anomaly are the poor bastards on the ISS. We haven't received burst comms from the station in weeks."

The admiral's eyes moved away from Joe to a lit corner of his cabin, where a very old painting of General George Washington prominently hung on the bulkhead. "What would General Washington do?"

"Probably defend Mount Vernon by cutting, shooting, blasting, and cursing. Fisticuffs, if it came to that."

"Exactly, my boy. Exactly."

3

Task Force Phoenix

A four-man special operations team sat in the back of the C-130, flying angels twenty-two over southeast Texas. The men stared at the light near the cargo door, tugging at their chute straps, willing the light to turn steady. They sucked on pure oxygen through the aircraft's O2 system, attempting to remove nitrogen from their blood and maybe avoid potentially deadly hypoxia. They were five minutes out.

The men were not strangers to jumping out of airplanes, but there was something to be said about doing it in the cold dark of night, twenty-two thousand feet over an infested area, with no ground or close air support. You just never convinced yourself that it was a good or worthwhile endeavor. Every man's extremities shook so hard they could barely connect to the static line. It wasn't the jump; it was what happened after their feet, knees, ass, back, and then shoulders absorbed the impact of their twenty-foot-per-second descent after hitting the ground. Many of their comrades had completed similar essential jumps to retrieve items or information deemed crucial to the survival of the remaining U.S. civilian population and infrastructure. Some jumpers extracted items like insulin formulas, manuals, and machinery; some were sent into big-box hardware stores looking for lithium battery–powered hand tools. Some went into abandoned fields. Some landed on the roofs of buildings in high-density infested areas. Many jumped into the waiting arms of the dead or incurred a simple broken leg on impact—forcing them to take homemade suicide capsules, pills that didn't always work as intended.

According to airborne infrared cameras, many were still alive when the creatures found them, although stunned and slowed by the poison. Ironic . . . every jumper packed their own chute and every jumper cooked their own capsules. Better not to think about that sometimes.

His fellow operators called him Doc. A year ago he was eating sand and 7.62mm in the mountains of Afghanistan, hunting high-value targets. That was before the worldwide troop recall. Only 35 percent of the military forces spread across the globe made it back to the mainland before things went stupid. Doc and Billy Boy, his longtime friend and fellow SEAL, were the last men out of the southern Afghan provinces. They fought hellishly south across Pakistan to the Arabian Sea, where they caught a ride back stateside onboard the supply ship USNS *Pecos* waiting offshore. It was a long swim that day.

Doc sat swinging on a cargo net near Billy Boy and the C-130 shitter curtain. Wearing a puke-green David Clark headset, he listened to the pilot chatter up front.

The pilot keyed the mic and said to the copilot, "These guys have some balls jumping out into the shit below in the dark."

"Ain't no fucking way I would volunteer for that shit. Hell, flying this deathtrap is dangerous enough. How many we lost in the past three months? Four? Five?"

"Seven."

"Shit, seven? We never recovered even one downed aircrew. I wonder if any of those poor bastards are down there somewhere, alive and on the run."

"I hope so."

"Me too, man."

Doc interrupted the chatter: "Can I get an inertial position check?"

The internal communications system from the flight station crackled, "You got two minutes to go time, Doc."

"Roger that, flight. You guys have a safe RTB, we'll catch you on the flip side."

With the lack of available personnel, the four-man SOF team had to hit the wind with no jumpmaster. As each of the four checked the others' chutes, Doc punched the actuator on the cargo ramp, allowing the icy medium-altitude air to rush into the cargo bay.

After checking his watch, Doc looked directly at Billy Boy just before the light above turned steady. The air was thin and cold as Billy Boy pulled himself out the door into the open sky over Texas. The two other members of Task Force Phoenix, Hawse and Disco, were next. Hawse joined the team after surviving a particularly harrowing escape from D.C. Disco, a Delta operator, was the newest member, reassigned after Doc lost a man in the highly radioactive zones of New Orleans.

Doc saw Hawse disappear out the door and keyed the mic to the flight station. "Last man out in ten."

He tossed the headset to the front of the tube and shuffled back to the door, his portal and one-way elevator to hell. Looking down at the landscape miles below, he saw the pinpoint evidence of fires, but no clear sighting that the power grid ever existed; it was that dark. While he jumped from the cargo door into the night, he thought of the unstoppable waves of gruesome creatures below. Doc's parachute deployed, jolting him into focus.

He checked his throat mic and yelled over the wind, "Billy?"

"Right here, Doc."

"Disco?"

"Check, boss."

"Hawse?"

"I'm fuckin' here."

Doc grunted into the mic, "All right, everyone snap two-ninety, gogs on, IR beacons, too. Let's try to find each other."

Through the night-vision goggles, Doc could see the curvature of the earth below. He was well above ten thousand feet and could feel the subtle onset of hypoxia as he descended. Under normal circumstances, jumping out this high, he would be on a portable oxygen bottle. But that was a luxury of the past. Doc hoped that because his team had sucked a little O_2 in the aircraft before the High Altitude–High Opening jump, they could avoid some of the side effects.

As Doc shot a glance down to the compass mounted on his wrist, he saw a faint flash below him, then another in a different location.

"I see two fireflies—is everyone flashing?"

"Disco flashing."

"Billy flashing."

Breathing a sign of annoyance, Doc said with disdain, "Hawse, goddamn it. What's the fucking problem?"

"Uh . . . I . . . uh, can't find my firefly."

"Did you bring your compass, dumbass?"

"Yeah, I'm on two-ninety. I'm gonna flash my torch a couple times. If I burn you out, you'll know it's me."

"That's cute, Hawse."

"I thought you'd like it."

Doc scanned his field of view and checked his altimeter—eighteen thousand. "I see you, Hawse. Turn off the torch—you're fucking up everyone's gogs."

"Check, man . . . what's your angels?" Hawse asked Doc.

"'Bout seventeen, why?"

"I got seventeen and a half."

"Go fuck yourself, Hawse."

The men continued their parachute glide descent. The temperature was getting noticeably warmer, at the rate of about 3.5 degrees Fahrenheit per one thousand feet. At angels 15, Doc called for a hypoxia check.

"Pox check."

"Disco up."

"Billy up."

"Hawes up."

"Good to go, guys. We've got about twelve minutes until we hit dirt. Intel says that the swarm has moved west a bit, in the direction of what's left of San Antonio. That doesn't mean that we're dropping into a tropical resort down there. You can bet that those dead claws will be reaching for your ass before you touch your harness release. Get 'em ready. I want M-4s tapped, racked, quiet, and lasers on."

The men didn't speak it aloud but they were petrified as they fell to earth, pondering the worst-case.

What if we're dropping into a swarm? Smack dab in the middle, undead for a mile in all directions.

No amount of training and operational experience would prepare them for that.

When their boot soles hit angels 10, Doc again transmitted, "Pox check."

"Disco still awake."

"Billy up."

"Hawse cold."

"Say again, Hawse."

Hawse said slowly, "I'm gold, er, I mean cold."

Doc began to ask the standard medical questions. "Hawse, we have eight minutes till feet down. Start saying the alphabet backwards."

With a bad slur Hawse throated, "C'mon, man."

"Do it," Doc insisted.

"Rogerrr. Zee, Y, double U, Vee . . . Shit man, sorry. I can't."

"Hawse, you're getting hypoxic. We're below angels 10—you should be okay by the time we're on deck. Disco, Billy, rally on Hawse as soon as you click out of your chutes."

Disco responded quickly, "Wilco."

Billy muttered, "I'm on it. Wait, how are we gonna know where to rally? Hawse forgot his firefly."

Doc snapped back, "Good point. Hawse, turn on your IR laser. It's the only way we're going to find you. When you hit the deck, wave it around as soon as you're out of your harness."

No response.

"Hawse, goddamn it, acknowledge!" screamed Doc.

A faint, slurred voice uttered, "Raaajer."

Angels five.

"Pox check."

"Disco fivers."

"Billy up."

Nervously, Doc relayed over the radio, "We better be on Hawse ASAP. We're just below five thousand and I can smell them already. Four minutes!"

Both Disco and Billy simultaneously transmitted, "Roger that."

They strained to look for any sign that creatures might blanket their landing zone. They were not yet low enough to see the ground in any detail with their optics.

The goggles provided only the illusion of depth perception. The rules were: keep your eyes on the horizon, knees slightly bent, don't anticipate the impact. Variations of this were repeated subconsciously as they fell the last hundred feet. The stench of the

15

creatures was nearly overwhelming as they plummeted down into the dark well of the undead badlands.

Disco was the first operator to hit the deck. He immediately recovered, scanned for threats, and unhooked from his chute. They all suspected that Hawse was likely unconscious or dazed from the hypoxia. Hawse annoyed the shit out of the team most of the time, but they generally respected him—he did escape Washington, D.C., in one piece. More important, none of them welcomed the idea of being one man down on a four-man team. Especially now.

As Disco reached up to adjust the intensifier on his goggles, Billy Boy hit the ground twenty feet to his left with a curse and a soft thud. Doc impacted ten seconds later. They regrouped on Disco and scanned all sectors looking for Hawse's IR laser. They saw nothing until the flash of a suppressed carbine drew them west to a finger of terrain.

Hawse had blacked out at some point below a thousand feet, not realizing he was headed fast toward a large spruce tree. His chute had caught a branch with a loud crack. He hung there for a few minutes, dazed, until the creature started chewing on his left steel toe boot. Both of the corpse's bony hands were gripping his foot. His carbine was hanging at an odd angle, forcing Hawse to take a shot with his weak side. After nearly shooting a hole in his foot, he scrambled the creature's brain on the third shot, crumpling it to the ground like a bag of wet leaves.

Hawse activated his IR laser and started waving it around. After a minute, he discovered that his earpiece had fallen out during the descent. After feeling for the coiled clear wire, he pushed the mic back into his ear.

Doc was transmitting, "I see his laser. Looks like he's on a hill. Everyone spread out, twenty meters, I'll take the front with Disco; Billy, you take our six."

Disco gave the verbal thumbs-up on the order.

Billy replied via radio with only "Six."

Comm brevity was king in this dead world. Hawse wouldn't break in on the chatter unless it was absolutely necessary. The men could hear the crack of underbrush telling them they were not alone. They quickly closed the fifty meters to where Hawse hung in his spruce.

Doc's radio crackled with Billy Boy's voice. "Tango seven and nine, thirty meters, strength five."

There were five undead thirty meters behind the three.

Doc gave the order, "Kill 'em, Billy."

The sound of Billy's suppressed carbine throwing lead down range was soothing to their ears.

"Tangos down," Billy reported.

Topping the terrain finger, they could see Hawse hanging in the tree, straining to keep his legs pulled up to his chest.

Shaking his head, Doc said, "What the fuck, Hawse?"

"Man, I blacked out in my chute and woke up to *that* chewing on my boot," Hawse said, gesturing to the corpse. "What do ya want from me?"

"Disco, cut him down," Doc ordered.

"My pleasure."

Disco climbed the tree high enough to slice through the lines, dropping Hawse to the ground with a thud. He landed only a few feet from the corpse.

"Disco, you fuck! I could have fallen on that thing's face! Quit fuckin' around!"

"You're fine. Don't be such a bitch."

"Disco, you're a little outnumbered, man," Doc added jokingly.

"I guess so, but one Delta equals three frogs any day," Disco sarcastically retorted, believing it.

"Okay, enough grab-assing, let's get our chutes and take a fix on the terrain to see how far out we are," Doc ordered.

Three acknowledgments resonated simultaneously in their earpieces.

Billy pulled out his map and compass. He marked the jump point on the map and noted the wind during his descent by the direction of the smoke from the areas that still burned. He refined and pinpointed their position off of nearby terrain features before they all agreed on the fix.

"Doc, we gotta hump three miles north by northwest to ballpark the access doors," Billy said.

"Better than I expected."

They gathered their chutes and stored them in a large trash bag from each of their kits, marking the location on their maps. The chutes would come in handy later, but they were not worth stuffing into their packs and humping the extra weight right now. Time was of the essence. Being caught in daylight was a very bad thing in these parts.

4

Tara lay in her bed, looking up at the ceiling. It was not unlike the way she would look through a boring professor back in college, a lifetime ago. The rectangular-shaped fluorescent lights were switched to red. Her bunk rolled slightly as the ship made its way through the churning seas.

The loud bells from the PA speaker mounted above her door forced her attention back into focus. Some of the crew called it a *one MC*. It was on her list of things to learn. So much to absorb. Her boyfriend had been gone for only a few days. They evacuated Hotel 23 a week ago—seemed like much longer; it was all such a blur.

She could still hear the noise beacon in her head. The lot of demons in hell couldn't have frightened her more. She didn't believe in hell in the sense in which it was portrayed in churches and horror novels, but knew only the real hell she had seen with her own eyes the day they fled Hotel 23.

Tara had been ushered onboard a helicopter with Dean, Jan, Laura, and the others. Laura clutched John's little white dog, Annabelle, tightly out of fear. No one knew what was ahead for them as they evacuated the last place they had briefly called home.

Saien had pushed her onboard, reassuring her, "Don't worry, I'll take care of Kil for you. He'll be safe with me. Go on!"

Scarred into her consciousness and fueling her recent dreams were the snapshots of the battle from Hotel 23 to the Gulf just a few days ago. The helicopter hovered over the compound and Tara began to see what seemed like millions of undead come into focus. Pure death converged on the nexus, Hotel 23. The survivors convoyed out in military vehicles, as well as in cars and trucks, and even on foot. Only the women and children were airlifted to safety.

She vividly remembered the marines blasting away at the hordes, instantaneously disassembling masses of them, gunfire tossing rotting limbs in all directions. Some of the bullets looked like laser beams, she thought, as the marines swept down thousands on the undead front. Even so, legions more advanced beyond the gun's sweeping lines.

There were just too many to stop.

The helicopter flew south and she caught her first look at the USS *George Washington,* a speck on the horizon growing by the second as they flew quickly inbound to the ship.

A man named Joe Maurer debriefed her yesterday. She was politely asked to start from the beginning—months ago, the car where she was found and rescued. She had felt a small hint of embarrassment when Joe asked her how she survived so long inside the vehicle.

Her blushing intensified when he asked, "How did you go to the bathroom?"

It wasn't just embarrassment, but fear that struck her like a bolt when he asked that question. She remembered the creatures. They watched her inside the car as she slept, watched her as she cried, watched her as she cursed and spit at them, and even watched her as she relieved herself in a large McDonald's cup. Thank goodness they were not strong or intelligent enough to break the glass using rocks, like she had seen before. They kept pounding on the glass with bloody, pus-filled stumps—what was left of hands. They even used their heads as rams, trying to get at her. One of them pried its own teeth out of its rotting mouth attempting to bite through the glass to reach her through the cracked window. *They are primally driven,* she had thought.

She had been in the early stages of heat stroke when he rescued her. Kil was not her only savior, but it was Kil whom she saw first as her eyes focused from the brink of death. Now he was gone, ordered away on an assignment that probably wouldn't make a difference. The mission really didn't matter to her—she just wanted him here. Tara now understood how her grandmother had felt when Papa had been ordered away to Vietnam.

At least she had John and the others.

John was what held the group together. He had stood by them all during their darkest times—the day at Hotel 23 when the helicopter never returned. She cried for days after that. Never giving up, she lived near the radio. Every waking moment she monitored the distress frequencies; every sleeping moment she made John promise to do the same. John did so without complaint or question. It was very likely he'd have been dead if it had not been for Kil.

Truth be told, they'd all probably have been dead if it had not been for John himself. His network engineering and general Linux computer savvy were what had enabled the survivors of Hotel 23 to take advantage of at least some of the complex and classified systems. His ability to control the security cameras, satellite imagery feeds, and communications gear was crucial to the group's situational awareness.

Tara heard the bells again and wondered what they meant this time.

John had made it a point to keep himself busy since Kil's departure. He was still somewhat angry, and maybe a little hurt, but he understood the reasons for Kil's decision to choose Saien. Putting that behind him, he was quick to volunteer to help the ship's communication division keep the critical communications circuits up and running. The ship's email systems were useless, as there was no World Wide Web with which to connect. There was, however, a robust radio communications network established between the USS *George Washington* and several other information nodes still active both at sea and on the mainland. Although John hadn't been given access to the circuits, it was only a matter of time before the shipboard communications technicians became familiar with him and let their guard down, granting him full access. His knowledge of basic RF theory and computer systems made him a crucial asset in the carrier's skill pool.

• • •

A few decks below and aft of the communications shack was the ship's sick bay. Before the anomaly, it had resembled a general outpatient clinic, but now looked much like a war zone trauma center. Most of the doctors had been killed in the line of duty since the anomaly had been detected in the United States. This wasn't hard to imagine, as the doctors onboard were often the first exposed to the infected. The ship had five doctors before the anomaly. Reanimated corpses quickly infected the first two—ironic how the same doctors pronouncing death were killed by the creatures that had fooled them. A third was killed after an infected sailor blew his own head off, sending splattered blood into an open shaving cut on the doctor's face. The doctor's own preference was also a bullet to the head, followed by burial at sea. The fourth doctor went the nonviolent route via morphine overdose. At least he had been decent enough to his corpsmen to strap his lower body to a gurney before injection. His suicide note was so disturbing that it had been confiscated and destroyed by the ship's security officer, fearing it would prompt further suicide attempts or even mutiny.

The last doctor standing was Dr. James Bricker—a consummate professional and a Naval Academy graduate, as well as a lieutenant commander. Anyone who has spent time in the navy will tell you that doctors are a different breed of military officer. Many high-ranking doctors don't give a damn if you call them sir, ma'am, rank, no rank. They just care about their job—about making you better.

Bricker had been near the point of insanity, or possibly even the old reliable morphine drip himself, when Jan arrived fresh from Hotel 23. Upon arrival and after debriefing, the new passengers were instructed to fill out a practical skills form. The screeners knew whom to look for and knew what the top priorities were at any given time. When the screening staff reviewed the forms and noticed a fourth-year med-school student, they practically ripped Jan out of her seat and away from her husband and daughter, rushing her to the sick bay.

On arrival, Jan immediately felt as if she had walked into bedlam. Infected but living patients screamed in their beds, struggling deliriously against their restraints. Volunteers hovered between the hospital beds like bees. A lone mad doctor with wild, unkempt hair hunched over a microscope, cursing at whatever it was he saw between the slides.

The screener interrupted, "Dr. Bricker, I have—"

"Not now."

The screener waited a few seconds, seemingly deciding whether or not to interrupt again. "Sir, I have a—"

With eyes still in contact with the microscope eyepiece, Dr. Bricker lashed, "Let me guess, you have an Eagle Scout with a medical merit badge, perhaps a CPR class graduate, or hmmm . . . how about a mail-order medical records transcriptionist?"

"Sir, she's a fourth-year med student."

Bricker paused for a moment, still fixated on the microscope and the secrets underneath it. "Are you certain?"

"Sir, she's right here. Go ahead, interview her, give her a um . . . I don't know, a doctor's test? Whatever you want to do. I have others to screen so I should get going. She's all yours."

Jan looked over at the screener, annoyed by his candor.

"Ma'am, I'm sorry. I don't mean to talk as if you aren't here. It's just been a long day."

Jan's expression eased from one of annoyance to understanding. "Don't worry about it."

The interview began immediately and went on for some time.

"Where did you attend . . . What is your experience with viral . . . Do you have any theories as to the origin . . . How fast have you seen them . . . What are your personal thoughts on where they derive their . . ."

Jan was exhausted when Will tapped her on the shoulder, interrupting Bricker's inquisition-style interview. Murder board was more like it.

"Who's your friend, Miss Grisham?"

"It's Missus and that's Mister Grisham. He might let you call him William, though," Jan said.

Bricker reached out awkwardly to shake Will's hand; Will gripped it like a vice. Jan took notice, giving him a facial expression to tone it down.

"Pleasure to meet you, doctor. Want to tell me why you were

questioning my wife as if she were a terrorist in an interrogation room?"

"Uh . . . well, I mean you must understand . . . understand that I'm the last doctor left onboard. It's beyond triage now, Mr. Grisham."

"You can call me Will."

"Thank you, Will. We are lucky to have Mrs. Grisham, or Jan if I may?"

Jan nodded in agreement.

"I am in limited contact with doctors abroad via the ship's radio networks. Unfortunately, as I told you, I'm the only medical doctor on this floating city. I'm afraid your wife, Jan, has stumbled into a critical position onboard. She's now a member of the priority-one, protect-at-all-cost, and kill-to-defend list. She, along with myself, the senior leadership, the nuclear engineers, the welders, communicators, and a handful of other personnel, are absolutely critical to the success and survival of this station."

Jan let that set in for a moment before asking, "What exactly are we doing here, doctor?"

"My orders are as simple as the line officers that command this ship. Find out what is causing the dead to rise and find a way to stop it. At least stop new infections, perhaps."

"What about the health of the people onboard now?" Jan asked, as the patients' screams underscored her point.

"Secondary, I'm afraid," Doctor Bricker said, sighing. "By my calculations, we are far beyond the point of no return. Mankind is on the edge of abyss; good science is our only chance. A hundred ships at sea, armed to the teeth and well provisioned, would make little difference. It's not a secret that we're outnumbered by millions of those things in the U.S., billions worldwide."

5

USS Virginia—Task Force Hourglass

Six coils of thick rappelling line dropped from the helicopter doors nearly simultaneously. The intense rotor wash whipped the team about as the lines uncoiled like mamba snakes, hitting the deck of the USS *Virginia* just behind her sail. The boat rolled from side to side, obedient to the randomness of the Pacific. The submarine's hull was not designed to sit on the surface; she was much better suited to black-ops commando insertion or delivering quiet death to the doorsteps of enemy subs.

A few seconds after the ropes slapped the deck, the six passengers followed. The first four descended with timing and comfort that only came from years of special-operations experience. The two that followed seemed sloppy and uncoordinated in comparison. Halfway down, one lost his balance and flipped about in his harness like a snared animal, nearly hitting his head on one of the masts as he flailed in the lines.

After some period of hot rotor wash and clumsy rappelling antics, Kil and Saien joined the other four already on deck. The lead operator stood there, wash from the powerful engines above blasting their clothes about. His sea legs and feet gripped the steel deck like magnets, and he effortlessly kept his balance. He gave a hand signal up to the crew chief in the helicopter. A few seconds later, five large black canvas duffel bags full of weapons and equipment slowly descended to the deck. The men gave a thumbs-up to the hovering pilot and the crew chief started pulling up the black lines. The pilot saluted the men on the submarine deck and immediately pulled the cyclic controls. The helicopter bolted north.

The noise and rotor wash quickly faded into the distance. The men were now at the mercy of the Pacific. The operators said good-bye to the surface and moved up the spine of the boat along the rough nonskid walkway to the sail.

Kil and Saien followed, one saying to the other under his breath, "When in Rome."

They made their way what seemed like a good distance, down the ladder, through the hatch, and into the belly of the boat. They descended down into the control area of the submarine, the light from the sky fading and the red internal lighting of the submarine intensifying. The four operators disappeared aft into the complex internal organs of the submarine, leaving Kil and Saien standing on the bridge among strangers.

A man wearing wrinkled blue coveralls, tennis shoes, and a Navy ball cap approached, extending his hand to one of the men. "I'm Captain Larsen, commanding officer of the USS *Virginia*."

One of the new arrivals reached out and firmly gripped Larsen's hand. "We are—"

"I know who you are and why you are here," Larsen interrupted.

Kil tried hard to hide a reaction before Larsen continued.

"The admiral transmitted a personal message three days ago. He graciously included information on the team you arrived with, as well as information on you and your friend, Mr. Saien. We've heard about you and we've heard about the strange goings-on with whatever this Remote Six might be."

"Well, I guess the admiral saved me some time," Kil responded.

"That he did. Master Chief Rowe will show you to your stateroom," Larsen said, starting to walk away.

"Quick question, sir?"

"Go ahead, Commander."

"What's in China?"

"We'll brief you in the SCIF. Be ready for read in at eighteen hundred."

"Aye, aye, Captain."

• • •

Larsen departed in a hurry, speaking something that Kil couldn't understand into a brick-shaped radio before disappearing into a tiny adjacent passageway. Master Chief Rowe maneuvered in front of the two, inspecting them with eyes likely calibrated by years at sea. He was a short man, maybe five foot eight, stocky, with a hell of a mustache. *I've flushed more salt water than you've sailed on* was a common saying among senior navy sailors. Somehow it seemed to Kil that this maxim might have started with Master Chief Rowe.

"Well, I'm told that one of you is a commander. It's probably you," Rowe said, pointing at Kil. "Do you want a uniform? We have extras, though none of 'em have wings."

Kil knew instantly that the master chief had done some homework.

"I'd appreciate a set of coveralls or two if you can spare them, Master Chief."

"No problem, sir. You know my name, who are you?"

"Kil."

"Suit yourself, Commander Kil."

Saien laughed, not meaning to.

"And your name, Ali Baba?" Rowe said to Saien.

Kil bit his lip.

"My name is Saien."

Rowe looked at them both with critical eyes as if he had both judged and sentenced them on the bridge of the *Virginia*. "Commander Kilroy and Mr. Saien, welcome aboard *Virginia*. Follow me."

Saien and Kil stayed behind Master Chief Rowe as he navigated the maze of passageways and ladders. Kil was already beginning to notice that time and space were peculiar and fluid things onboard a submarine. He didn't think the boat had looked this big from the outside. They arrived at their new home. It consisted of canvas tarps thrown up against the bulkheads forming a deformed square with racks for sleeping and footlocker storage.

"Enjoy the new apartment, guys. It's a bit drafty, but with some duct tape and zip ties, she'll fix up nice. I'm the chief of the boat; you can call me COB if you want. Shorter than master chief."

Kil nodded at Rowe. "Thanks, COB."

"Very good, sir." Master Chief Rowe bolted away with purpose, screaming something about coveralls and cleaning stations down the passageway.

Saien and Kil had met under interesting circumstances. Kil learned some time after they met that Saien had tracked him for days, observing him make his way south after surviving a nasty helicopter crash. In the process of tracking him, Saien discovered his handwritten note along with a cache of discarded weapons and supplies in the refrigerator of a long-abandoned home.

Kilroy was here.

The nickname stuck just before the swarm.

Kil's stomach sank even now as he thought of that day. They had been attempting to get the car started while thousands of creatures closed fast on their position. Three hundred meters, two hundred meters . . . dust, moans, closer. In a fit of panic and confusion Saien called him Kilroy, from the note he'd left. Kilroy evolved over the days ahead to just simply *Kil*.

They unpacked and stowed their gear in every nook and cranny they could find. Their racks were small and space was limited. They placed some of their personal belongings under their mattresses; there simply wasn't enough room for what they had brought over from the spacious carrier. Neither had ever lived aboard a submarine, a fact made glaringly obvious by the way they misallocated precious space.

Kil sat on his rack and listened to the boat. It was designed for silence and felt like a public library compared to the carrier's montage of dragging chains, noisy ventilation, and cycling solenoid valves. He heard *dive, dive, dive* right before the bow of the boat dipped a few degrees, sending *Virginia* into the deep. Kil knew what he was up against and that he would most likely not make it back alive. It was simple numbers, logic. There were just too many. He was now up against over a billion, not millions.

It was four hours until the men were briefed on the perilous mission that lay ahead.

This marks my first journal entry onboard USS *Virginia*. It's been two hours since I boarded the submarine. The sea was a little choppy before we dived. The skipper informs me that we'll stay in the area for the next twenty hours to prepare for the voyage to Pearl Harbor. Saien and I are bunked in one of the berthing areas onboard converted into sort of a pseudo-stateroom. I'm lucky we were not stuck sleeping in the tor-pedo compartment, as is the treatment of most outsiders and non-submariners, NUBs.

Although I had served many deployments onboard ships in the navy, I had never thought I'd hear this being announced over 1MC: "Now muster all available personnel for nuclear reactor maintenance training."

It made perfect sense. We were not making anymore nukes—nuclear-trained naval personnel—in the navy, so it was either train new people or eventually we would run into a problem where the maintenance required on the reactors could not be performed.

Nuclear-powered boats were made for this sort of world-ending event. I can remember serving onboard a conventional carrier. Every few days we would need to pull alongside a re-fueler. Those types of boats would never make it in this new world. There are no refineries up and active to meet the massive fuel requirement.

The only real weaknesses to the *Virginia*'s mission are general hull maintenance, food supplies, and reactor repairs. The training being carried out in the reactor spaces could abate one of those weaknesses. The *Virginia* generates her own water and scrubs her own air using onboard equipment powered by the reactor. There is no shortage of electricity. Just as some of the carriers with active reactors are being used as power plants, the *Virginia* could power a small town with little trouble.

I'm told that Saien and I are meeting with the boat's intelligence officer for briefing on the operation. The only hint about the op that I have received came from Joe before this morning's helicopter ride.

Joe yelled out over the rotors as we left the carrier's bridge island, walking to the helo across the steel and nonskid deck. "You're not going to believe it, Commander. Keep an open mind."

I still wasn't used to being called commander. I wasn't a real commander. I wasn't even getting paid, not that currency matters anymore, I guess. Either way, as of right now, I have no idea what could possibly surprise me after what I've been through the past eleven months. It feels like my first night of boot camp. I'm out of my environment, a little scared, and have no idea what's going to happen next.

6

Hotel 23—Task Force Phoenix

"Hurry up, Doc!" one of the men screamed out from the darkness.

"This little plasma ain't as speedy as the cart; I'm going as fast as I can."

"They are on us, man . . . Get the door open or we're screwed! I can see them in my gogs. They look pretty bad."

"You ain't helpin', man. Focus up."

Doc concentrated through the eye shielding on the white-hot starburst of the plasma torch. He traced the previous weld, slowly cutting through. He heard the undead footsteps and groans behind him while he worked, but would not pause. Either he was getting through the heavy access door or he would be stopped by the cold claws of the undead, ripping him off the entrance. The creatures approached, drawn by the bright light and noise from the cutting torch and the action of the suppressed carbines.

Excitedly, Billy called out over the firefight in progress, "Doc, hurry. I'm serious. I can smell their breath!"

"Dude, I'm moving. Just a few mikes," Doc responded.

"No time. Disco, frag 'em!" Billy hissed.

Disco pulled a grenade from his vest, yanked the pin, and tossed it out into the growing mass of creatures that approached.

"Frag!" Disco yelled as the grenade rolled to a stop under the canopy of walking undead corpses.

All four men hit the ground. Seconds ticked like minutes before the blast rocked the immediate area, scattering bits of rotting meat and bone everywhere. The blast took out a large number of the undead, or at least rendered them immobile.

Hawse went to town with his suppressed carbine, blasting at

the stragglers. He screamed at Disco, "You're on laundry detail, asshole!"

"What?" Disco responded, pulling a foam earplug from his right ear.

Hawse kept firing and lecturing, "Jesus, man, toss those things. You're gonna get bitten on the ass and won't even hear it coming."

"Whatever, man. You know what happened here. When the sun comes up you might be able to see the rest of it sticking out of the ground," Disco responded.

The undead flowed through the tree line from the woods beyond, drawn to the explosion. Wouldn't be long before the team would be beyond the help of a hundred frag grenades—minutes at best.

Doc and the rest had been briefed before the jump. Some time before they arrived, a large, javelin-shaped device, designed to generate devastating barrage noise, had been dropped on this facility. The remnants of the intelligence community concluded that the weapon had been designed to sterilize the area of all life by attracting a mega-swarm of undead by blasting intense omni-directional noise. It was known only by its codename given in a classified intelligence report—Project Hurricane. It took a flight of A-10 Thunderbolts and their 30mm guns to disable the device.

Doc listened to Disco and Hawse banter back and forth as he continued to inch through the welds on the thick steel door that led inside. Disco and Hawse continued to talk shit to each other, taking shots in between, giving themselves enough time to think of better insults. It was all show, Doc knew. The men were actually terrified.

"Halfway there," Doc said to himself out loud.

He called out to Billy Boy, craning his neck over his left shoulder, "Billy, just to be sure, intel did say that it *is* empty inside, right?"

Billy replied while he scanned the area for leakers—undead that made it past the defensive line. "Yeah, the marines cleared it before welding the door shut. Nothing inside but maybe a few dead rats and some cockroaches."

"Roger."

Doc thought about undead rats for a second and dismissed the idea as nonsense. *They'd be too slow anyway, unless . . .* Better not to think about it. He concentrated again on the torch.

Doc's cutting tool continued to advance around the steel door while the gunfight intensified behind him. Disco and Hawse ran their weapons until the heat from the gas system began to break down the oil inside. The smell of burning lubrication reminded Doc of the long war against terrorism that had defined his adult life. A war that was ended in just a few short days by the rise of the undead. Disco and Hawse fired relentlessly at the advancing creatures; bone and brain exploded, sending pieces scattering all over the growing ranks farther away in the darkness. They were drawing a crowd now.

The intelligence reports were very detailed about this place. Not long ago, this area had been overrun with hundreds of thousands of creatures. The previous tenants barely made it out with their lives. Some of the undead had remained after the noise device was destroyed. The rest wandered off to parts unknown in a self-perpetuating death march—locust swarms that devoured the living.

Doc finished the last few centimeters of weld and dropped the searing torch to the ground near his feet. "We're in, guys. Billy, watch our six; we're moving."

"Roger."

Their goggles automatically adjusted for the IR-filtered weapon lights shining brightly into the dark compartment ahead. Doc walked through the open door and passed Billy the notice to follow.

"Last man," Billy said.

"Roger, close it up," Doc replied.

Billy secured the thick steel door and tried to seat the bolts, making the door as strong as a bank vault. Most of the bolts seated but some didn't. *Good enough,* Doc thought.

Hawse reached up to the front of his weapon. "Lighting up."

The men pushed their goggles up and off their eyes and adjusted to the new light. The other three flipped off the IR filters of their lights while Doc grabbed his map of the facility.

"This was hand-drawn by the former commander during his debrief on the carrier. He marked an *X* where he stowed a bottle of whiskey in the ceiling vent of the environmental room. Should be incentive enough to clear the place."

"You know it," Hawse said with a smile.

"Okay, here's the plan: Hawse, you take the living quarters and the halls leading to them. Disco, you take environmental. Billy, you cover me while I work mission control."

Hawse moved quickly down the dark passageway. His first impression aligned with the intelligence reports. The facility had been abandoned in a hot hurry weeks ago. Hundreds of thousands of creatures converged on this position as a result of a weapon designed to attract them to its payload. Clothing, trash, and personal effects were scattered about. A dusty family photo album sat open in one of the rooms, random blank spaces telling a story; select pictures had been removed from the pages posthaste. There was no sign of life or death.

Hawse continued his sweep just outside the living quarters. A mechanical sound startled him, causing a flash of starbursts as his blood rushed into his eyes. He walked slowly, managing his breathing, trying to identify the sound. There were footsteps on the floor leading around the corner.

Hawse called out into the darkness, "That you, Disco?"

He rushed the corner, readying his gun as he rounded it. Expecting to face a corpse head on, he was met with only a dead end. The footsteps were from before, when the facility was still occupied. Hawse continued on to his primary objective, the whiskey bottle hidden in the ventilation. It was there, just as the map had indicated.

The place was completely abandoned, but this didn't matter to any of them. They stood watch and patrolled the facility as if danger were in every room. They were all friends and refused to be responsible for any of their teammates' demise at the jaws of undeath. They had seen more undead than living humans in recent months. It was not really hard to imagine.

During their last intelligence brief, it had been disclosed that they might be outnumbered in the United States by two hundred and ninety-five million and rising daily. There were some survivors holding out in attics and basements around the U.S., but not many, the analysts estimated. Their numbers were diminishing hourly, adding them to the enemy's collective.

Doc transmitted out, "Hawse, how close are you to the generator room?"

"Uh, ten meters, I think."

"Think you can get it going?"

"Depends on how much diesel we got in the tanks."

"Do what you can, man, I'll need some juice."

"Okay, I'm workin' it."

Billy continued to scan. "Doc, you hear that?" he said.

"Nope."

"Those things are already thrashing on the door we used to come in."

"Fuckin' relentless. Think any of them are hot, Billy?"

"One in ten in this area, according to intel."

Doc listened to the radio crypto sync in. "I'll have the genny up in a sec, man; we got an eighth of a tank of fuel, though. Recommend we run it only a couple hours a day, at least until we find more," Hawse reported.

"Agreed. The marines left us a sketch of the area with the few locations worth checking. We're gonna need to snatch a tanker, or at least figure out a way to move some fuel here."

Doc could hear Hawse switching the main breaker off and priming the generator; the sound traveled down the steel corridors as if Hawse was in the room next door.

Hawse cut in again. "Found the checklist, beginning the sequence."

The battery must have held enough charge since the evacuation; it cranked the generator to life on the first attempt. The pungent fumes filled the spaces until positive pressure took over and sucked the exhaust aboveground through the ventilation ducts. Doc heard the main breaker actuate again.

"We're good, Doc," Hawse yelled down the corridor.

"Okay, bringing up the mainframe."

They all returned to the control room to observe the systems as they came online, one by one.

Doc started the half-hour process of waking the facility in priority order. The mission would be a failure if he could not restore the mainframe and connect with the aircraft carrier. Every password had been memorized by all four men and also written down in a waterproof notebook as extra insurance. The system was synched and encrypted to the previous commander's common access card. Doc removed the card from the protective sealed case and looked at it for the first time. A navy lieutenant? He had been told the man was a commander. He had heard of some spot promotions here and there since this started.

He rubbed the gold chip at the bottom of the card with his thumb to make sure it was clean before inserting it into the reader. A log-in screen flashed, requesting a pin. Doc had it memorized but still consulted the notes to be sure. Too many unsuccessful log-ins would result in system lockdown. He carefully keyed *7270110727.* He could hear the system's RAID drives spinning in response. The pin was accepted and the mission systems status began to display.

Although they didn't need the card for most facility functions, the card gave the team full access. Doc clicked on the security icon. A display of eight screens appeared on the desktop. Only five were operational. The screens marked *SE, SILO,* and *ENTRY B* were blacked out. The others appeared operational as he could see dark outlines of terrain and fence lines. Doc clicked the icon to change the operational cameras to night-vision mode and then to thermal mode. The camera labeled *MAIN DOOR* failed the thermal test but functioned under night vision without issue.

Billy glanced down at his watch. "Boss, sun is up in two hours. We're gonna need comms."

"Disco, make it happen, I'll watch you here. Hawse, go with him. No one is alone outside the wire."

As the designated communications officer, Disco was charged with humping the medium-sized pelican case from the drop zone all the way here. Before the undead walked, SOF teams used this particular system to establish a covert communications station deep behind enemy lines. When closed, it was a typical hard composite case. When opened, a small high-gain antenna was released via button mechanism and the low observable black solar charging panels were then exposed under the lid. The transmitter device connected via encrypted and cloaked 802.11n Wi-Fi signal to the laptop in the facility control room, wired to an existing surface antenna.

When properly deployed, the device was weatherproof, self-contained, and durable, and would provide secure two-way text and file-burst communication with the command node elements onboard the aircraft carrier. It was also resistant to RF interference as the transceiver hopped frequencies ten times per second. Designed to thwart savvy first-world hostile-signals intelligence collection, this type of security was overkill, meant for a more civilized and technologically advanced enemy.

Hawse brushed past Disco in the passageway and looked back over his shoulder, saying, "I'm on point."

"I was hoping you'd say that. Have fun with the salesmen at the door."

"Shit, I forgot about that. I'll pull, you shoot?"

"That works. They'll have to walk past you to get to me."

The men rounded the corner. Their boots clicked on the tile floor. The sound was gradually dampened by the increasing sounds of the undead thrashing against the steel door outside.

"This could be bad."

"I know, point man."

Hawse went over the plan with his trademark absurdity. "Okay, I'm gonna tie this line around the wheel. When I spin the wheel and pull, you start sprayin'."

"Hawse, why don't we go dark? Lights off, gogs on. They can't see in the dark, idiot."

"I was gonna say that. It goes without sayin'."

"Whatever, let's get this over with so we can get back inside. I don't want to be up there in the dark one second longer than need be."

The men doused the lights and pulled down their NODs. The darkness seemed to intensify the thrashing and howling sounds of the creatures. The undead noises competed against sounds of slapped mags, carbine press checks, nervous breathing, and heartbeats. Disco imagined what pure evil might walk beyond the heavy steel barrier at this moment. He prayed to himself it wouldn't be enough to rip the door from its vault-like frame.

Hawse tied the line securely to the door.

"Ready?" Hawse yelled.

"Spin it!"

Hawse hit the wheel, disengaging the heavy door leading to the savage and unforgiving world beyond.

7

Three loud raps on the bulkhead broke the silence.

"Come in."

A young enlisted man parted the curtain leading to Kil and Saien's makeshift stateroom and entered. "Sir, the intelligence officer will see you now. Please follow me."

"What about my friend here?" Kil said, gesturing at Saien.

"Sorry, sir, I was ordered to bring you to the N2, no one else."

"He's coming or I'm not going."

Nervously, the petty officer agreed to let his superiors sort it out, and all three departed for the ship's sensitive compartmented information facility, known to most onboard as simply *the SCIF*.

As they moved through the submarine, Kil took notice of the details. Passing an exercise area with treadmills and other machinery, he saw that all the equipment was mounted on rubber shocks. The same was true with the pipes that riddled the overhead. Nothing was permitted to rattle onboard, no erroneous sounds to give away their acoustic position to the Sino or Russian frenemies of days gone by.

Tapping Kil on the shoulder, Saien asked, "Where are the nukes?"

"No nukes here, Saien; this is a fast-attack boat. No idea where the nearest boomer might be or if there are even any left on patrol."

Frame after frame passed by as they marched aft. After some snaking through very tight passageways they arrived at what the escorting petty officer dubbed as the green door.

The young man picked up the phone and waited a few seconds.

It rang audibly through the handset; an answer came after three rings.

"Sir, I have them both at the green door and—"

The yelling from the obnoxiously loud handset blasted across the passageway.

"Yes, sir. He insists that they both—yes, sir."

After replacing the handset the scorned petty officer said, "A SCIF escort will be here shortly, sir. Sorry to leave you here in the passageway but I'll need to be on watch in two hours and I haven't slept in twenty-four."

"No problem, hit the rack and have a good watch," Kil said, mostly to send the young man off on a positive note.

"Aye, aye, sir. Thanks."

Just as the man left their field of view, Saien asked, "What's aye, aye mean?"

"It means . . ."

The green door flew open and out of it sprang an older man wearing thick birth-control glasses, tennis shoes, and a blue set of coveralls with navy commander rank on his collar. His nametape said *Monday*.

I hate Mondays, Kil thought.

The man approached Kil nearly toe to toe and seemed to scan him with his massive convex lenses.

"What's this I hear about you insisting your foreign national friend come with you into my SCIF for mission briefing?"

"Sir, Admiral Goettleman allowed me one partner from the USS *George Washington* for this mission. I chose Saien and if I'm going to potentially trust my life to him, I damn sure want him to know the score. Besides, I'm going to tell him what you tell me anyway, so what's the difference?"

Monday chewed on that for a second. "I figured you'd say that. I was ordered by Captain Larsen to read you and your man into what we are up against. Knowing what you are about to be exposed to, I wanted to see if I could somehow persuade you to come here alone. It just goes against my grain having him inside the SCIF. I'm sure you understand."

"Saien, would you mind stepping around the corner for a minute?"

"Sure, Kil. Don't be long, I have a massage appointment."

Kil laughed and then proceeded to use his best diplomatic candor to express his point to Monday. "Yeah, I understand, but you gotta understand, too. I've vetted him. True, he's a foreigner, but he's come through for me, and he's the only one on this ship I trust at this point."

"Okay, Commander. We're square. I just want you to understand the sensitivity and the severity of what you are about to hear after we go through that door. The four operators you arrived with are also waiting inside and about to be briefed. It's never pleasant to reveal information of this nature."

Skeptically, Kil blurted, "How goddamn crazy can it be? The dead started walking last winter and now they try to eat anything that moves."

Monday replied rhetorically, "How far down the rabbit hole can you fit?"

Saien returned to the hallway and stood alongside Kil.

Monday continued his sermon. "This shit is heavy. This is far beyond flying around in your little spy plane during the war, listening to enemy phone sex and making up SIGINT reports. Before I go on, I gotta ask you both one final question."

Both Kil and Saien said almost simultaneously, "What?"

Licking his lips, eyes squinting behind his Hubble glasses, Monday began, "Once we go through that door and I tell you two what I'm about to tell you, I can't un-tell you. Is that clear? We don't have Men in Black mind erasers. It will affect you for the rest of your lives."

"I'm ready," said Kil.

"Me too," muttered Saien, although not sounding as cavalier.

"Okay, gentlemen. Follow me."

Monday turned to the green door leading into the SCIF and reached his hand into the cipher lock housing that covered the keys. Five button clicks resonated. After a brief pause the sound of magnetic locks releasing cued Monday to push the green door into another world of possibility. All three men walked through and from there things became more and more curious.

8

"Was that you?"

"Me what?

"Did you throw something?"

"No, what's wrong with you?"

"Never mind, probably flies."

"Not this far out, not this time of year."

A chorus of giggles resonated from the passageway outside the ship's combat control center.

"Those fucking kids. I want to throw them over the side. You wanna scare them straight or should I?" said one of the men sitting at his radar operator chair.

"It's my turn, let me do it," his colleague replied, grinning. Reaching into a cardboard box near his radar terminal, the sailor removed a gruesome Halloween mask, resembling the face of a corpse. He placed it over his head, adjusting the fit so that he could see through the mask's small eye openings.

"Watch this!"

He stepped over to the open door and jumped through the threshold, roaring like a banshee. The small group of children screamed for their lives and began to scatter . . . all but one.

A swift front kick from the child to the radar operator's groin brought the man crashing to the floor. The other radar operator broke out in hysterical laughter that was cut short as the child advanced, moving with a visible intent to kick the man's head in with all his small might. Just in time, an older woman with curly red hair entered the space, drawn by the screams and the commotion.

"What is going on in here, Danny?" the woman asked with authority.

"Granny Dean, I thought he was a . . ."

The man slowly pulled off his mask and remained in the fetal position moaning in pain.

Embarrassed, the little boy said, "Sorry, mister, I didn't know. Thought you were dead."

The woman walked up to the man on the floor and helped him to his feet. "What is this about? Do you spend all your time scaring children or just while on duty?"

Struggling and still dazed by the pain the man replied, "Ma'am, I'm sorry. The kids were being loud and driving us crazy and I thought it'd be funny to . . ."

"Funny until someone accidentally shoots you in the head! Give me that thing, I'm going to throw it overboard this instant. Consider yourself lucky I don't speak to the admiral about this."

The man quickly handed over the mask. Dean snatched it from his hand like a striking snake.

"You better get used to the kids, too. I'm teaching class up the hall and they'll be coming through here on the way to and from."

"Yes, ma'am. Sorry."

"While we're on the subject of apologies, Danny, care to say anything?"

"Sorry for kicking you in the nu . . . I mean, between the legs. You scared me good."

"Sorry, kid."

"S'okay," Danny said regretfully.

Dean boomed again with authority, "Danny, gather up the kids and get them back to class. One of the doctors will be teaching first aid in fifteen minutes."

She didn't have time to explain to Danny the difference between a hospital corpsman and a medical doctor.

"Okay, Granny. Just like hide and seek. Bet I can find Laura first!"

A little girl's voice echoed, "No way!" from behind a fire hose down the passageway, and the chase was on.

Dean shot a disapproving look past the radar operators and followed Danny to the classroom.

"Youth is truly wasted on the young," she said.

9

Disco tugged the rope tied securely to the door. Nothing happened.

"Hawse, the door opens outward. You're gonna have to kick it."

"All right, stand back, I'll . . ."

The door began to rattle and creak on its heavy hinges. It opened slowly; white bony fingers rounded the dark steel edges like hermit crab claws protruding from a shell.

"Fuck, get ready, get on the radio!" Hawse said frantically.

While Disco relayed the situation to the control room he brought his carbine to his shoulder—one hand on the weapon, the other grabbing for another full magazine.

The door opened wider and wicked faces appeared in the darkness just beyond the cold steel door.

"I'm shooting," Hawse proclaimed.

"Kill 'em."

"They're already dead!"

Hawse began blasting the undead, aiming above the eyes. Disco knew the plan as they'd practiced it before. Hawse intended to drop the creatures quickly to construct a makeshift barricade of bodies, blocking the things from opening the door wider.

"This ain't fucking worth it, man!" Hawse screamed.

The report of the suppressed carbines temporarily deafened both of them, ringing their bells in the confines of the steel hallway. Suppressors don't actually work like they do in movies. Hawse pulled the trigger in controlled fire until he ran out of rounds; instinctively Disco stepped in front of him and handed him his full mag. Hawse slapped the mag in and pulled another one from his pouch to hand to Disco when they had to change over again.

The system seemed to work well. Disco had cut his teeth on tactics like this, seeing action during Operation Enduring Freedom in the Philippines. Based out of Camp Greybeard on Jolo Island, he had advised (and assisted) in his share of gunfights against the Abu-Sayaf Group terrorist organization. Often they'd change mags like this after firing all twenty-eight rounds at ghosts in the jungle just outside the wire. These creatures were no Abu-Sayaf terrorist group, but they were just as deadly.

The team's fear of running out of rifle ammunition was ever present. Without ammo to feed their carbines, they'd be limited to shorter-range pistol calibers. When that ran dry, they'd be forced to go hand to hand. Every man knew what that likely meant.

Disco counted fifteen rounds before the creatures no longer presented their rotting faces through the partially open door. They waited, guns at high ready, ears still ringing from confined shooting. Disco used up a few seconds of time on a tactical reload, topping off his gun with a fresh magazine.

They both nearly jumped out of their boots when Doc and Billy exploded into the room from behind with guns and knives drawn, ready to fight.

"Nice timing, assholes!" Hawse whined.

"You fuckers called us crying like a bunch of babies, so here we are. What's the problem?"

"I think we got 'em all," Disco said.

"It was pretty fucked up . . . I saw lots of fingers grip around that door," Hawse said nervously. He jerked his weapon about the room as if the area were crawling with manhole-sized spiders.

"Okay, well since we're all down here, lets get the comm gear set up. Billy, take your mirror and have a look out the door."

A faint rustling noise came through the small gap from outside, causing all of them to grip their rifles a little tighter.

Billy reached into his pack and pulled out a small signal mirror, attaching it to the end of his suppressor with a thick rubber band. Walking slowly and quietly to the door, he extended the mirror out into the blackness. His goggles were constantly and electronically adapting to the darkness. Through the small mirror he observed at least three dozen bodies scattered about outside.

One creature still twitched on the ground. Billy had seen this happen more than once before.

"I don't see nothin', Doc. A twitcher a few meters out and lots of rotters piled up against the door. Gonna need a couple shoulders to push it open."

"Okay, let's put our backs into it. Billy, you stand behind us in case you missed one in the pile."

"Roger."

"Okay, on my mark . . . one, two, push."

The door surged open a foot or so, moving the pile of rotting corpses enough for them to squeeze through, barely.

The four carefully spilled out the door into the dark night made bright by technology that Billy suddenly realized would probably never advance beyond its current state.

"Straggler," whispered Billy, almost inaudibly. He brought his carbine up to high ready, mesmerized for a millisecond by the way the unholy thing stalked them.

It moved with hungry purpose, arms clenched, claws gripping. Billy noted that it lacked lips. Its stained teeth shined brightly with reflected and intensified moonlight. He smoothly squeezed the trigger. The magnified muzzle flash illuminated the bullet impact. Billy was so close he felt the earth thud under his feet when the creature hit the ground.

That was a big one, Billy thought.

"Thanks, man," Hawse said a little too loudly. Hawse was closer to the creature than he was.

Billy gave a hang ten sign with his support hand, in a *You're welcome* gesture. "Who's got the comms?" he whispered.

"Fuck."

Disco ran back to the door; Billy followed without being told. No one went anywhere alone—that was the most important rule. A few minutes passed before the men returned with the heavy communication equipment.

They went to work quickly, choosing a spot out of the way so the gear would not be accidentally rendered inoperable by the undead. Using some debris, they constructed a makeshift enclosure out of a section of damaged fencing. Disco worked inside the small confines. He opened the comm box and arranged the power panels so that they would have maximum southern exposure. Booting up the system on battery power, he connected to the ruggedized laptop within seconds.

He then sent out a burst message to the USS *George Washington*: "GW DE TFP, INT ZBZ . . . k/disco."

Again he sent: "GW DE TFP, INT ZBZ . . . k/disco."

After a few minutes the laptop beeped loudly, indicating a new burst transmission had been received from the ship: "TFP DE GW, you are spittin' nickels . . . Admiral wants your status . . . k/IT2."

Disco responded, "DE TFP, Hotel 23 up and online, systems green, confirmed zero one (01) bolt in the quiver . . . k/Disco."

"DE GW, be advised sun up in 58 mikes . . . this station req you check back in 24 hrs . . . AR/IT2."

Disco shut the clamshell on the computer and slid it into his pack. "Comms are full up, Doc."

"Good to know. Let's get below before sunup and lock the place down. No one goes out during the day. Those things plus the other event that happened here make it too dangerous. No RF transmissions unless it's burst. I doubt we were lucky enough to go undetected but we'll keep trying to stay out of sight and mind, if able."

"Good fucking plan. Don't want one of those huge lawn darts dropping on us," Hawse said half-jokingly.

No one gave an approving laugh. They all wanted to deny the possible deployment of what the intelligence briefers referred to as Project Hurricane, as there would be no convoy or helicopter evac for these men. The carrier was still far to the south, near Panamanian waters.

Billy was again last man as he spun the wheel securing the door to the world outside. They would all now live as vampires.

10

Doc lay in his rack, drifting somewhere in a world just before sleep. Since the fall, most of his dreams had involved the undead. His special-ops team had been haphazardly thrown together by national command authority after he and Billy escaped Afghanistan. When their ship finally arrived in U.S. territorial waters, a giant swarm of undead stood fast on the eastern shore to greet them.

Before it got this bad, Doc heard stories of people burning money to stay warm, and using two-hundred-thousand-dollar sports cars as road barricades. Hawse told a tale of a Washington, D.C., street vendor trading candles and antibiotics from an armored car in exchange for ammunition and bottled water. That was before the undead population exploded to the point that it wasn't even safe to look out of your boarded-up windows.

Hawse joined them sometime after he fled Washington, D.C. Disco showed up after they lost Hammer. Doc moved slowly toward sleep as he recalled Hammer's last mission.

A helicopter screamed up the Louisiana coastline, well inside the New Orleans hot zone. Doc knew Sam, his pilot, as this was not their first ride together.

"I want to make this quick, Doc," Sam said into his headset.

"Me, too, I don't like going overland these days anymore than you do."

"We lost another bird last week. A friend of mine, Baham, was the pilot. Hope he's okay."

Knowing that he was very likely not okay, Doc said comfortingly, "He's probably trying to get back home on foot."

"Yeah, if you say so." Sam wasn't buying it. "I see those steel cages back there and I know what we're after but I gotta tell you right now, Doc, I don't like this shit. The first sign of trouble, you toss those cages out the door, and we are gone, got me?"

"Yeah, you won't have to tell us. Hawse said the same thing. He doesn't want any part of it either," Doc said. "Besides, our job is to grab 'em and secure 'em. We don't know where you're taking them. Want to tell me?"

Sam looked over with a conspiratorial grin and said, "You're gonna find out anyway when we get there. As a reward for delivering those radioactive pus sacks, I've secured you boys one night living in the lap of luxury. After we pick 'em up, we're takin' 'em to the carrier. The researchers want to poke and prod 'em. See what's makin' 'em run."

Doc sat up in his seat. They could see the outline of Lake Pontchartrain now.

"Sam, I don't think me or the boys will want to stay on that carrier with those things onboard. I don't care how soft the beds are or how nice the air-conditioning is or how hot the showers might be."

"No choice. We gotta stay and get fuel and maintenance on this bird so I don't end up like Baham down there somewhere . . . okay, we're getting close. You guys check your HAZMAT suits and put those hoods on, for fuck's sake. Intel says it's hot enough to melt your face off down there. Don't get too close to the cars and trucks or anything metal. They'll be throwin' out the radiation. Who's staying up here to work the winch and tend the cage?"

"Hammer volunteered." Doc looked back at Hammer just in time to see him give a thumbs-up.

"Roger that. I'll keep you steady when Hammer drops the hook. Our recon photos show a small group of them trapped on the causeway. We'll be cruising over in a minute or two. Get ready."

"Roger." Doc began to unstrap and head back. Sam stopped him, grabbing his arm.

"Be safe and have a good 'un."

"Have a good 'un," Doc replied.

Doc scanned the team, checking all harnesses. "Billy, good to go. Hawse, tighten your shit."

Hawse reached down and yanked his harness tight. Doc looked over to Hammer, no harness. He wasn't going to the ground today.

"Hoods on!" Doc yelled. "Sam is taking us low. The dust won't be breathable. You'll end up one of those vets with cancer lawsuit commercials in thirty years when things get back to normal."

"Ha ha fucking ha," Hawse said as he slid his mask on.

Billy and Hammer followed suit.

"Radio check," Doc ordered.

Everyone came back with a good check, their voices muffled by the HAZMAT hoods. The chopper was hovering high over Lake Ponchartrain and the causeway bridge that spanned the large Louisiana estuary. The helicopter jerked a little. Sam flew the aircraft with his knees while he put on his hood. The helicopter began its descent. The causeway grew larger below them as Sam carefully adjusted altitude, starting his hover. Looking out the door below, Doc could see that Sam had picked a good spot. There were three creatures on a hundred-meter section of the causeway, plugged on both sides by multi-car pileups. The helicopter hovered between the roadblocks. On either side of the wrecked cars were hundreds of excited creatures looking up at the hovering helicopter, attracted by the noise, hands reaching for the sky.

The creatures began to crawl over the cars to get to the section of causeway directly below the chopper. Streams of undead converged from both directions. The corpses moved swiftly.

The team wouldn't have much time.

The three men hooked up to the helicopter deck and began to descend with their gear. Even as they lowered themselves down, the three creatures contained between the wreckage began to trot over to their landing area. The rotor blast threw radioactive dust particles in all directions. Without the suits, the operators would no doubt be dead from exposure in hours, and reanimated shortly after. Their orders were surprisingly simple. *Extract two undead specimens from two different radiated zones: one exposed to medium-level radiation and another exposed to ground-zero radiation.*

The second their boots hit the ground, they unhooked their lines. Hammer was fifty feet above, working the controls on the winch line; it slowly descended, bringing the hook down to ground level.

The three creatures moved closer.

Hawse shot the runt of the litter and Billy shot another. They wanted the best specimen—they didn't wish to risk a mission repeat if the specimens were found wanting.

The remaining alpha didn't seem to notice that the other two were no longer part of its pack. The three had likely been trapped on this same section of crumbling causeway since the nuke destroyed New Orleans almost a year ago. Doc aimed his gun at the last creature and pulled the trigger.

The Kevlar net blasted forward from the high-pressure pneumatic gun at over a hundred feet per second. It hit the creature, violently knocking it to the concrete. The creature squirmed about, angrily tearing at the Kevlar netting. Hawse ran over to the net searching for a spot free from the creature's teeth and hands. He found one and quickly dragged the thing over to the winch line and hook. The rotor wind continued to whip them about. Sounds of radioactive sand and dust particles ticking at their hood visors were audible, even over the helicopter wash. Making sure the hook was grounded, Doc attached the winch line to the Kevlar netting and backed away, raising his thumb to Hammer high above. Hammer returned a thumb and the winch line began to raise the netted and furious creature up to the bird.

Hammer soon radioed down to Doc. "It's secure."

"Roger, lower the winch. Do not descend. You'll just get more dust in the chopper."

Hammer lowered the winch and pulled the three operators back up into the aircraft. Inside the bird, the caged monster jerked about, gnashing its teeth on the metal. Its white, hollow eyes followed the men while they prepared for the next specimen extraction.

The helicopter lurched toward the ruins of New Orleans to the south, to ground zero. No building or cell tower taller than twenty-five feet remained. The nuclear blast ordered by the government as a last-ditch effort had decimated everything—including the levees. New Orleans was now a decayed, radioactive swamp. Moving south along the shore, Sam and the team scouted a place to extract the next and final specimen.

"Interstate 610 is just below. I won't go as low as we did over the causeway. It's a lot hotter down there," Sam told Doc.

"I don't blame you, Sam. Check out that on-ramp," Doc said, pointing through the cockpit glass.

Sam lowered the helicopter down, closer to the I-610 on-ramp. "Yeah, that'll probably work. You're gonna have to take care of that business down there first."

"Hawse is already on it," Doc said, pointing back to the cargo area where Hawse lay in the prone at the open side door, with a LaRuc Tactical 7.62 sniper rifle welded to his cheek. The 10x optic would provide Hawse a crystal-clear magnified view of the situation on the ground. Sam began to orbit around the LZ like an AC-130 Spectre gunship. Hawse went to work. Billy had a shoulder bag full of twenty round 7.62 mags ready to feed the gun.

Looking through the binoculars, Billy started calling out targets and estimated range. "North side of black Subaru Forester, near hood, two-hundred."

Hawse exploded the creature's neck and face, sending the head flying on a volleyball-serve trajectory. White fragments of bone sprayed the hood of the Subaru, resembling artwork that might have sold at auction years earlier for thousands. Hawse slowly exhaled just before taking the next shot. Billy kept calling them out and Hawse kept popping their heads, missing some as the helicopter pitched and orbited. This wasn't easy shooting.

The undead were now attracted to the helicopter noise and most had moved away from the target area.

The team needed to be fast, as the helicopter noise would draw the creatures back to the extraction point quickly. Hawse stowed the 7.62 gun and unslung his orange-stripe-painted M-4 carbine. It was easy to lose your carbine in the crowd when everyone carried them. Sam nosed the bird forward and the men once again made ready to rappel into hell. Masks were secured in place for the descent as they hovered one hundred feet above the radioactive mess below.

"Okay, hook up, let's get this over with!" Doc screamed loudly into his radio over the rotor noise.

"Hell yeah. Let's do this. Warm shower here I come!" Hawse yelled as he hooked up and stepped off the helicopter into the wind.

The other two followed, leaving Hammer behind. Their descent was twice as far this time, a prudent precaution based on the radiation levels they were dipping into. The rotor wash wasn't as bad when they touched down, but the deadly particles still swirled in lethal dust devils around their faces.

Billy was looking over at the Big Easy, what was left of her. Most of it was covered in water and radioactive sludge. He could see thousands of creatures slogging through the shallow muck in their direction, waves of them, all converging on the noise epicenter of the rotor blades and helicopter engines. The creatures left a V-shaped wake behind as they waded through the slimy, disease-infested, and radioactive water. All wake tips pointed in their direction.

"Fucking wasteland," Billy said loudly as he readied his AK-47.

The radiated creatures were closing fast.

Hawse raised his carbine, aiming through his ACOG optic. The optic's bullet drop was calibrated for military 5.56 ammunition and the crosshairs were graduated for the appropriate drop. No math required. Just match the width of the ACOG reticle to the creature, aim high for the head, pull the trigger, and down goes the body on the other end—in theory. Hawse neutralized four. Billy went to work with his Afghan-liberated AK-47 war trophy and took out three more.

No one was running suppressed for this mission—there was no need. The helicopter noise eliminated that possibility. Doc took down four more with his carbine, leaving two. He slung the M-4 over his back and reached for the pneumatic net gun, ensuring the capture net was properly loaded and positioned on the gun. Both Doc and Billy shot at the same time. Billy took out the creature that was closing on Doc, and Doc netted his target specimen. Mission accomplished, almost.

They stood in a low stance with their backs to the netted creature and watched as the locust-like swarm of undead approached from all directions. By gust of wind, the winch hook contacted the netted creature, shocking it fiercely. Its eyes bulged, and it bellowed and clawed in anger. The built-up static from the helicopter would have knocked one of the men off their feet if not grounded before contact. Now that the electricity was discharged from the hook, Hawse connected the corpse to the net and watched the captured creature spin about and rise the hundred feet to the helicopter door. The NOLA swarm was building and getting closer, the moans overpowering the rotor blades above. The knee-deep water seemed to boil with movement two hundred meters out.

Billy started to engage with the AK-47. The 7.62x39 round had a bit more punch than Doc's or Hawse's M-4 carbines, but the AK was somewhat less accurate. You couldn't tell with Billy behind the gun—he was dropping them at two hundred plus meters with iron sights.

The creatures were closing fast, hundreds, perhaps a thousand of them now.

Billy noticed a shadow flash by in front of him and jumped

away from the group. Both Hawse and Doc were knocked to the ground, the wind pushed out of their lungs—the creature they had just captured and sent up to the helicopter had fallen one hundred feet to the ground, free from the netting, with Hammer in its grip.

Hammer's left arm was clearly broken, a piece of bone jutting from his forearm. Doc couldn't tell if the break was from the fall or the creature's grip. The thing had bitten him severely. His neck was leaking blood in cadence with his rapid heartbeat.

Hammer reached down to his waist to retrieve the only weapon he had on him when he fell—his tomahawk.

The radiated creature wrestled with Hammer.

The NOLA swarm was a hundred yards out.

Tears of fear and rage flashed in Hammer's eyes when he gripped the Micarta scales of the handle and swung the hawk, driving the spike deep into the creature's cranium, dropping it instantaneously. Hammer's mask had been torn off by the creature before he fell—mortally wounded, already exposed to lethal doses of New Orleans radiation.

As Doc and Hawse recovered and pulled themselves off the ground, Billy grabbed clotting agent from his med kit and quickly slapped it on Hammer's neck. He applied a bandage to put some pressure on the wound. It would at least buy him some time.

Before anyone asked, Hammer laboriously held his neck wound and said, "They're strong and fast. Ripped . . . right through the net."

Some blood dripped from Hammer's mouth as he spoke.

Hammer looked over to Billy. "Trade me." He handed Billy his bloody tomahawk and Hammer took Billy's AK. "We still got a mission. I'm not gonna last long. I'll let one through so you can bag it. Reload that net gun and let's go."

Doc was shaken by Hammer's ghostlike appearance. He had no clue as to how Hammer kept conscious. Doc compartmentalized the horror of seeing his teammate's life force fade in front of his eyes. He'd somehow save the emotions for later.

The three hugged Hammer and shook his hand before saying good-bye. There was no time for more. Hammer nodded to all three and turned to engage. He managed to get to the nearest front of undead and began shooting.

Doc reloaded the net gun and radioed up to Sam, "Bring her down or we're all dead!"

Sam didn't bicker. Inside of thirty seconds, the helicopter was hovering ten feet above the team, kicking dust, debris, and walking dead everywhere.

Hammer fought with everything that was left in him, emptying his magazine, allowing one creature through to attack the others near the hovering helicopter. Doc bagged the creature and all three men hurriedly dragged it inside the flying machine. Hammer *was* right—these radiated abominations were stronger than anything he'd encountered. It nearly breached the fresh net in the time it took the three of them to throw it in the steel cage. It was now no mystery how the second specimen got through the net; it had a hundred feet of winch ascent to rip and claw before getting to Hammer. Doc estimated that the strength of the second specimen must have been many times that of the first from the causeway.

The rest was a blur. They had both their snarling, powerful specimens securely stored in the hardened, partitioned steel cages. The helicopter gained altitude. Doc asked Sam to hold at two hundred feet. The team watched the scene below as Hammer was making his last stand against the undead with only his knife. He stabbed and slashed and killed three more before they rushed him. Doc moved to the rack, grabbed the scoped LaRue 7.62 and went prone. Through the glass, he confirmed that Hammer was dead, the creatures viciously feeding on his warm, radioactive remains. Anger shot through Doc's body and he cursed them all to hell before paying final respects to Hammer with a sniper round through his skull. Hammer would not become one of those things down there. He hoped that Hammer would have done him the same courtesy. Doc looked out over the decimated and decaying NOLA skyline.

Doc sat up in his rack and checked his watch out of habit. It was 1400. He was confused for a second. *Is Hammer alive? Where am I?* he asked himself until the total recall made a retreat back to the dark nook of his mind. Doc was back in his Hotel 23 bunk, where Hammer was dead and the undead still ruled.

11

Kil, Saien, and Monday stepped into the secure compartmented information facility. There was nothing special, no supercomputers whirring in the corner, no real-time video satellite feeds for an army of analysts to sift through. The equipment was old and overengineered. Kil entered a room marked *SSES*.

The four men that had fast-roped onto the sub with them were inside.

"I know this place," said Kil.

"How so?" Monday asked.

"Transmitted a few messages to SSES in better times," Kil answered reluctantly.

"Well, we're not exploiting many foreign signals in here these days. We still have a linguist spinning and grinning in the corner over there when we need him, but no one seems to be transmitting much of anything anymore."

"What's he speak?" asked Kil.

"Chinese."

"I guess that'll come in handy in a few weeks, huh?" Kil probed.

"Yeah, maybe sooner. Sit tight—you'll be happy to know that the navy still runs on PowerPoint in the apocalypse. We'll need to boot up our systems and log in to the standalone JWICS computer before we start. Might take a minute."

Leaning over to Kil, Saien whispered, "What's JWICS?"

"It's another Internet, one you've never seen and likely never heard of. It wasn't a secret that the government had it before this went down. It's just a secret what information is shared on it. Nothing too conspiratorial; back in the days before this, you could get most of it from mainstream news or other online sources."

"Like who killed Kennedy and all that?"

"No way," Kil said, briefly reminded of his mother. She'd had a habit of asking him about those kinds of conspiracy theories, considering his vocation. "Nothing like that, just regular old sensitive information. The good stuff was on the White House Situation Room LAN or on some intranet in some unmarked Northern Virginia building. I never wanted access to that. Fewer fingernails I'd lose if I got shot down somewhere."

Monday stepped to the front of the room, interrupting Kil. "Good afternoon. For those that don't know me, my name is Commander Monday. I'm going to talk to you for a bit before you go through the formal read-in process. I can count the number of times I've given this brief on one hand. For the four of you from our special-operations community—I want to thank you for your service."

One of the men nodded a response from the back of the room.

Monday gestured to Kil and Saien. "Also, for those of you that don't know . . . these two survived on the mainland for almost a year. Pretty remarkable, considering the odds."

"Bullshit," one of the other men muttered.

Monday continued. "Let's get to business. It may seem a little unorthodox for a naval intelligence officer to just come out and ask, but please raise your hand if you believe in God."

Neither Kil nor Saien raised their hands; only one from the other group broke from the majority. Kil wanted to, he just wasn't quite ready.

"I see. I suppose that might make this at least a little easier in some ways. You see, what I'm about to tell you cannot be untold. I'm going to be saying that again in the next few minutes. You must understand that from childhood to adolescence to adulthood many of you were raised on certain paradigms and unshakeable principles—established cultural norms. The sun rises in the east and sets in the west, what goes up must come down, the house always wins, etcetera, etcetera. Sometimes when we are exposed to template-altering data that cannot be refuted, it has odd effects on the mind. Do any of you remember the day you discovered that there was no Santa Claus?"

Everyone in the room nodded that they remembered, even though Saien didn't.

"Well, imagine that multiplied a few dozen times." Monday paused for a long minute, looking at each and every man in the room. "This may be the last time I say it or I may say it a hundred more times, it depends on if I think you need to hear it again. Once you are told this, you cannot be untold. Do all of you understand this?"

They all nodded as if they might, but Monday didn't seem so sure.

"Okay, that's it. You're about to get punched in your philosophical gut. I've reviewed your records, all but yours, Saien, but we've already discussed that. You're only seeing this by the direct authorization of the admiral, and subsequently, this boat's captain. If it were up to me, you wouldn't be here, I want that to be clear."

Saien gave no reaction to Monday's statement. The four special operators whispered back and forth. Kil couldn't understand what they were saying.

"All right, here goes."

Monday activated the display. A yellow banner at the top and bottom of the large, wall-mounted LED screen showcased numerous warnings.

"The overall classification of this briefing is top secret, SI, TK, G, H, SAP Horizon, and everything else you can think of. I'd like to welcome all of you to the Horizon Program." Monday clicked to the next slide.

08 JUL 1947—Recovery Activity

Uintah Basin, Utah

T O P S E C R E T // CRITIC CRITIC CRITIC

YANKEE 08 JUL 1947

FROM: SECRETARY OF WAR

TO: PRESIDENT OF THE UNITED STATES

SUBJECT: RECOVERY ACTIVITY

VESSEL RECOVERED. FOUR IN
CONTAINMENT. ONE ALIVE, EN ROUTE,
WRIGHT FIELD.

DECEPTION OPERATION UNDERWAY. DEBRIS
STAGED, ROSWELL, NM.

. . . PATTERSON SENDS . . .

T O P S E C R E T // CRITIC CRITIC CRITIC

12

Somewhere Inside the Arctic Circle—Outpost Four

Minus 70. Cold enough to freeze a man's bare face in seconds. Life existed here at U.S. Research Outpost Four at the mercy of technology and fifty-five-gallon diesel drums. Nearly a year had passed since the dead broke the known laws of nature and physics. The remaining survivors of the outpost were now inside their second wintering over without resupply. Most of their forty-five-man crew had abandoned the outpost last spring, choosing to hike a hundred miles south to the nearest thin ice and what they hoped might be pockets of surviving civilization. Most of them were never seen again. A few did wander back to the outpost, perhaps out of instinct or habit. They looked the same as all the others: milky white and frosted eyes, heads frozen forward, hungry.

Outpost Four experienced the fall of civilization one high-frequency transmission at a time. High frequency was the only semi-reliable means of communication this far north. The sat-phones had worked in the first months after the anomaly, but they eventually failed as satellite orbits decayed with the rest of technology dependent upon a complex and fragile infrastructure.

There was only one advantage to the brutal and unforgiving winters of the Arctic—they encountered far fewer of the ravenous creatures than those outside the big, cold circle. At first, the dead seemed to be a distant problem—something one heard about over the shortwave or watched in horror on satellite TV. It was not yet a concern or cause for worry here at good ol' Outpost Four.

In the spring after the anomaly began, one of the researchers passed away from diabetic complications. The shrinking crew fast realized that the anomaly had arrived; it now assaulted their climate-controlled safe haven. It took a swift ice axe to the head to put the creature down for good, but not before it claimed another life. They tossed the bodies over a two-hundred-and-fifty-foot drop near the outpost. That's where the dispatched corpses all now went—many bodies, broken and frozen, lay at the bottom of what the survivors nicknamed Clear Conscience Gulch.

Farther south in the real world, people were fighting and dying for their lives against lottery odds of survival. Up north, inside the Arctic Circle, the survivors waged war against low body temperature and constant darkness. They had not seen the golden glow of the sun for weeks and some had private thoughts that they might never do so again. They rationed heating oil and diesel as if it were water on a life raft lost in the Pacific. Everyone knew that they were as good as dead if they didn't get off this ice rock inside of sixty days. That put them into January—deep winter. No aircraft (if there were any left) would risk the flight, and no man could make the journey south on foot. They had dogs and sleds, but even then, it wouldn't be enough. They were too far north.

Crusow Ramsay was the unofficial station chief of Outpost Four—leader of what few survivors remained. He wasn't the oldest or most senior outpost crewman, but he was the most respected. Crusow had an old-sounding name, older than 1950s names like Dick or Florence; it belonged to his grandfather. Thirty-five years ago his father had passed the name on to Crusow without much deliberation. He came from a long line of strong Scottish immigrant men, alpha males who made their own way in life.

His father's spartan way of showing affection had made Crusow tough, harder than most men. His father had always given the girls leniency, but not Crusow. His sisters had enjoyed the benefit of money when they needed it, free cars, monthly allowances, but not Crusow. It was off to the sawmill at the age of seventeen for him.

Needing money to support his expectant wife, Crusow interviewed for a job that eventually put him where he was now, the cold embrace of the Arctic. There were not many choices during that dark economic time. They told him that he would only be gone five months per year if he got the job. The cryptic minimum eligibility requirements intrigued him.

Mechanical Engineer with three years machining experience / experience with diesel engines. Single scope background security clearance eligibility a requirement . . .

Outpost Four had its secrets. Most of the research that required an Arctic base camp had been completed decades ago. Officially the outpost had been established to study electromagnetic wave propagation in the northern extremities. Crusow wasn't a part of the search teams and before everything went to hell, he didn't give a damn what they were looking for out on the ice. He always thought it strange how they would pack up for a three-day trip, brief the (now dead) outpost commander on where they were headed, and then disappear into the snow, dogs and all.

The story that the outpost members were told was that the teams were looking for Martian rocks. The experts say that Mars was bombarded by countless meteors ages and eons ago and this Martian ejecta eventually found its way to Earth, reentered the atmosphere, and landed somewhere in the Arctic ice.

The team never returned with anything interesting that Crusow knew about. They'd always stow their gear, clean up, and report to the boss. Same story, every time. Crusow never became acquainted with the searchers; they always rotated out every time the military airlift made its rounds.

It didn't really matter anymore what the teams were searching for out on the ice.

Even before the anomaly, Crusow had believed that the world was on the brink. The economy was on the edge of collapse; unemployment was at 15 percent. Gold was approaching two thousand dollars per troy ounce and collapsing countries were the talk of mainstream news. His goal in the Arctic was simple. If he could just survive one, maybe two wintering overs here he could purchase his retreat out west and raise his family there, free from societal corruption, decay, and full-blown collapse.

Crusow looked up at the stars, a rare waste of time for him since the world ended. He'd lost as much as anyone to this unholy blight. Wife, unborn child, home, everything.

The only things he owned worth anything to him were worn on his belt or slung across his back—a good stag-handled Bowie knife, a 9mm Smith & Wesson M&P pistol, and a well-maintained M-4 carbine. Possessions really didn't matter anymore, as the world to the south belonged to whoever could survive its challenges. Rolex watch? Sure, if you wanted to risk getting infected crawling around in some mega mall somewhere. Bars of gold? Fort Knox was over-run, but if you could blow the vault, all the gold-plated tungsten you wanted was yours. No one would try to stop you. Money? If you had it, you used it to start fires or you kept it in your wallet to look at and pretend things were normal. It was tough to pretend when the dead walked and tried to eat you, a very frequent occur-rence far south, back in the real world.

Crusow did what he could to remain on this side of sanity. He read books, wrote letters to people who were probably already dead, and sometimes prayed. The cold slowly drained energy from the outpost, energy that would not be replaced. Outpost Four was a dying star, about to be cold and void of all things. Crusow's soul was already approaching absolute zero, closer every time he thought of her.

News of his wife's fate had come over satellite phone months ago. Things had already devolved worldwide into anarchy. Out-post Four survivors watched the news feeds and listened to the HF broadcasts. Utter chaos filled the airwaves. Rioting overwhelmed the major cities first. People rushed past the massing undead, looting TVs and tablets, bringing them to homes that didn't even have power.

Under normal circumstances, spouses and next of kin were given Outpost Four's satellite phone number in the event of fam-ily emergency. The survivors took turns at standing watch with the satphone as part of their rotation on the operations center watch bill.

Under world-gone-to-shit circumstances, people still stood the phone watch along with their normal duties, but incoming calls were extremely rare. The reliability of the United States phone network was sporadic in the weeks following the new year and the rise of the undead. It was midnight in February when Crusow's roommate and best friend, Mark, received the frantic call.

"Hello, it's Trisha, I need Crusow."

"Trish, my God, the phones are working there?"

"Goddamnit, Mark, I don't have time! They're at the doors and the house is on fire!"

"Okay, okay, I'm running to get him . . . Just wait on the line."

By the time Crusow made it to the radio room all that remained were Trisha's screams echoing on the other side of the line and on the other side of the world. She was being torn apart. Crusow collapsed to the floor at hearing his wife's last words. He lay there long after the fire severed the connection, sending a pulsing tone through the handset. Crusow didn't move for hours. He wished for death, hoping that the searing pain of grief would take him. It didn't.

13

Crusow sat in the operations room with Mark, a close friend he'd made when first starting his career at the outpost. They rationed generator time, as clean diesel was quite literally a non-renewable resource, but they saw limited success with biodiesel. It was dirty, it smelled, and it made Crusow's job even more arduous, but it helped keep core body temps at or above 98.6 degrees Fahrenheit.

Crusow grew tired of tearing down, rebuilding, and maintaining the diesel engine that the outpost had designated for biofuel, but he knew that without him, the whole station would be a block of solid ice right about now. The small sense of worth and accomplishment that came every day he kept the station alive gave him purpose—reason to live. He now felt painfully alone. The last person he truly loved was dead, and he hoped she wasn't walking now. He often wondered if the fire had finished the job, but it hurt thinking about that nearly as much as imagining Trish being one of *them*.

He and Mark had recently completed repairs on the station's high-frequency array after one of the support cables snapped in the high Arctic winds. They used the Sno-Cat to pull the cable taut and attach it to the new anchor point in the ice. Without HF, they had no ears as to what was happening on the mainland. The HF tuning process was very operator-intensive and required at least some basic knowledge of radio frequency theory. Some frequencies didn't work at certain times in the Arctic and some did. This process was already complicated under normal atmospheric conditions, but problems increased exponentially this far north. When atmospherics were right, sometimes they picked up a BBC shortwave signal still operating on a loop from some far-off transmitter likely powered by alternative energy.

"Stay in your homes—all known rescue facilities have been overrun. If you have been injured or know someone that has been injured by the infected, quarantine them straightaway . . ."

Mark had been manning the HF headset when communications with USS *George Washington* were established. The link was cut off by the wind-damaged array. Now that the array was repaired, they began to scan the spectrum looking for the ship again, or anyone else that might be listening.

Although a carrier would have little chance at effecting rescue this far north, perhaps the ship was in contact with units that might have the capability to reach Crusow, Mark, and the other survivors.

The only thing anyone at Outpost Four was hoping for now was the viable means to stay warm, to maintain core temperature. Crusow knew that winter was raging and there was no way off this hell short of a miracle.

Besides himself, Mark was the only one he trusted out of the five that remained. There were very few military left in the group. Crusow was friendly with them, but couldn't bring himself to trust them. *They're like cops,* he often thought. They would protect their own, by any means necessary.

Crusow kept Mark company as he tuned to 8992 on his planned transmit schedule. "Any station, any station, this is U.S. Arctic Outpost Four, over."

Static filled the airway right before a very strong HF signal canceled out the white noise, as if the transmission originated from the next room.

"Outpost Four this is USS *George Washington,* have you weak but readable, great to hear you again."

Crusow and Marked cheered, filling the room with whistles and shouts in a brief flash of optimism . . . one that soon faded.

14

The military leadership wandered into the briefing room for Admiral Goettleman's morning update. With the carrier running on a skeleton crew, the senior officers were all able to fit inside the small shipboard auditorium, a place typically reserved for formal briefings. The admiral maintained the morning tradition of keeping full situational awareness of fleet status, what was left of it.

John sat in the back row holding a newly issued hardback green military logbook. He was a recent addition to the morning meeting. His attendance was not by choice; he was now deemed essential to operations. When the admiral wanted answers regarding the status of the ship's communications systems, he didn't want excuses. In his short time onboard, John had already mastered many of the complex computer networks and radio systems, as well as the links and nodes between the two.

His notes included proprietary information on frequencies, tuning, and circuit diagrams. Since most of the newer breed of technicians had lost the fine art of radio theory, it was John's task to return this skill set to the carrier communications department. SATcom circuits were tied up and dedicated to task force missions and could not be used for lower priority ship-to-ship communications.

John studied his notes as he sat in the back row overlooking the auditorium. He traced a diagram with his fingers and thought to himself, *Romeo circuit or . . .*

He heard someone in the front yell out, "Attention on deck!"

Everyone stood, including John. He had learned of this particular military custom at his first morning meeting a few days earlier.

Admiral Goettleman marched over to his seat at the front of the auditorium. John was one of only a handful of civilians in the room. Joe Maurer, one of the men he recognized, sat in the front at the admiral's side.

"Good morning," Admiral Goettleman said.

The room murmured, "Good morning, Admiral."

The admiral glanced over to the current battle watch captain, nodding for him to proceed with the briefing.

"Good morning, Admiral, COS, staff, and crew. This morning's update brief has the USS *George Washington* position of intended movement a hundred miles north of Panama and steaming to an area farther north and off the coast of Texas in support of Task Force Phoenix."

"How are they holding up?" the admiral interrupted.

"Last communication with Phoenix was eight hours ago. All secure, systems green. Radio informed me this morning that they intend to scout the area tonight, after sunset. Phoenix reports that there has been no sign of unusual activity and no indication of any aircraft in vicinity of Hotel 23."

"Very good," the admiral said, rubbing his chin. "Continue."

"Hourglass is well underway and steaming west to Oahu. They are reporting all systems green, moderate supply of food. They are on three quarters rations as a precaution."

"Gonna have some grumpy submariners by the time they see Diamond Head," Goettleman joked.

Some laughs rounded the small auditorium; they were heard less frequently of late.

"That being said, let's keep them all in our prayers. They are on the most dangerous mission in military history."

The room's small amount of positive energy depolarized as if a blanket of seriousness had fallen from the ceiling.

The briefer continued: "Admiral, pending your questions or further comments, that concludes the task force update for today."

Goettleman's non-response seemed to indicate that all was acceptable. The briefer continued calling down the list of departments, asking if they had anything to add to the briefing.

"Weps?"

"Nothing to add."

"Air?"

The acting air boss chimed in, "We're still working on a plan to restore carrier operations, but only a reconnaissance capability at this point. Fuel and aircraft are a problem. The jet's maintenance schedules can't be met; we only have a handful of mission-capable Hornets, and we need to reserve those for any possible incoming UCAVs. We still have a respectable number of helicopters, but we're short on pilots. The catapults and arresting gear all need depot-level maintenance and we're down to our last four cross-deck pendants. That's all I got, sir."

"Reactors?"

"Both are fully mission capable. No change in status."

"Engineering?"

"We are having a little trouble machining parts. Nothing critical, but we're out of some metal stock that we need. Recommend we put the metal on our scavenge list for the mainland runs. Nothing else to report."

"Supply?"

"Admiral, we have ninety days of food onboard for current crew strength. Situation critical. No change."

"Always bad news from Supply. Since the Air Boss can't seem to get fixed wing in the air, why don't you two start a garden up on the flight deck?" Goettleman teased. "Keep going."

"Yes, sir. Communications."

A few seconds went by before John noticed that the COMMO was not in the auditorium.

"Communications?" the briefer prompted again, nervously annoyed.

John stood and opened his green notebook. "Admiral, uh . . . as you know, SATcom is up and stable with Task Force Phoenix. I've been working on transmitter theories and different high-frequency RFs to hail the Arctic station again. I have my people trying to contact them in radio right now. We are close to figuring out the wave propagation to allow for signal bounce with that station. Networks are up and stable for local LAN email traffic. I know that was not a priority but it is fixed. I guess that's all, sir."

Admiral Goettleman raised an eyebrow and nodded in approval.

Today is going to be a good day, John thought to himself as he stood at the top of the auditorium with his green, dog-eared notebook.

"Admiral, this concludes the morning brief pending your questions or comments," the briefer added.

As if timed with the ending of the brief, one of the radio clerks entered and passed off a paper message to the table of senior officers.

Goettleman slid on his glasses and began to read aloud. "'HF radio contact established with Arctic Outpost Four.' Good brief. I need senior leadership to remain and all others to carry out the plan of the day. That is all."

John had renewed feelings of confidence as he departed the small auditorium. He had a little more pep in his step as he made his way to radio to fix more impossible problems and to look into the Arctic dispatch. *Good job, radio. Today is going to be a good day,* John again thought, as if trying to convince himself . . .

15

December was close at hand. It had been nearly a year since the creatures started showing up in the mainland United States. The air was now cold at night and the sounds were unlike anything that Doc or Billy Boy had heard a lifetime ago in the mountains of Afghanistan.

The Taliban didn't moan, announcing their position. They did not sit idle or dormant until you passed an open car window at night, inviting their clutch. Although the Russian 5.45-caliber rifle round was dubbed the poison pill by many in Afghanistan, it had nothing on the poison of an undead bite. Nothing could save the infected. The best medical minds on the planet were at a loss. Even top surgeons at the ready to amputate an infected arm or leg could not stop the fever, eventual death, and subsequent reanimation.

The dead didn't hide in caves or plant roadside bombs. Doc thought about this for a brief moment: *At least the undead were fair.* They never deceived purposely. Like the fable of the Scorpion and the Frog, it was just a matter of their altered nature; they were killers, destroyers of souls.

Doc recalled the days after he and Billy had made the decision to bug out of Afghanistan. Their journey from the southern Afghan provinces across the vastness of Pakistan and eventually to the sea was fraught with peril. It could have been much worse, but the low population density of the region compared to the first world gifted them some small advantage. They didn't face a hundred thousand creatures—at least not yet.

That did not stop them from racking up undead kill counts

that might rival some operations at the beginning of Operation Enduring Freedom. The two laid waste to undead Taliban the whole way south, running out of M-4 ammunition halfway. They liberated three AK-47s as they continued their escape, fighting through thickening waves of undead, for weeks.

The terrain and sometimes thin air gave them no quarter. They dared rest no longer than a few hours between movements; any more and the undead would stumble in pursuit from behind a boulder or a finger of terrain. Not since BUD/S training had they been so exhausted. They force-marched for hours at a time over the cold moonscape.

At one point along the way, Doc remembered falling asleep while running. It took a face-plant into rocky terrain to jolt him back into the fight. He and Billy killed intensifying waves, stopping to scavenge magazines from creatures that had died days or weeks earlier, with their AKs still slung across their backs. The numbers of undead increased to dozens and in some cases approached a hundred or more.

The closer they moved to the coastline, the denser the hordes. The anomaly was so new that the creatures had not yet spread out from the coasts; most of the world's population lived in the littorals, and now the dead ruled these regions.

Fueled by rumors that the fleet might be anchored off the coast of Pakistan in the Arabian Sea, Doc and Billy pressed south. It was not until the day before they reached the coast that radio chatter began to break in on their handsets. They eventually made contact with the USNS *Pecos*—their ticket home.

Doc adjusted course based on the ship's transmitted position and they continued to pay their toll in lead to the undead for the last miles to the sea. The sun was setting and their scorched rifles were out of ammunition by the time their boots filled with seawater. They sidestroked away from the massing thousands of creatures that churned the surf with undead footsteps.

The *Pecos* was the last ship remaining at anchor to take on American evacuees. Billy and Doc soon found that the *Pecos*'s master was pleased to have the added security of two special operators aboard. After arriving, eating, and taking a shower, Doc and Billy received a current situation briefing.

• • •

Doc learned of deadly piracy taking place on the high seas. The pirates were capitalizing on the lack of maritime security, and ruthlessly attacked all vessels on sight. Chinese, American, British, all were falling prey to Somali warlords and other vile sea vermin. The pirates were cold-blooded in their attacks, using stolen military hardware to sink vessels that didn't explicitly comply with their demands.

On their way stateside, steaming south, deeper into the Arabian Sea, they verified the worst of the reports. The GPS navigation network was failing. This, combined with a lack of sea charts, forced the *Pecos*'s master to adjust course west and visually hug the African coastline. Pirates had been a problem in the Horn of Africa region long before the undead, and now they were a force that rivaled them.

Pecos was under attack long before they saw Africa.

The faster pirate vessel approached quickly through the choppy blue waters. As the vessel maneuvered into range, it began firing at *Pecos* with crew-served machine guns, aiming for the stern just above the waterline. Fortunately for *Pecos* and her crew, the pirates were not trained marksmen.

Doc, Billy, and the ship's master-at-arms took down the pirate vessel in a flurry of accurate sniper shots. Anytime a head popped up above a catwalk to man a machine gun or peek through a porthole, Billy put its lights out. The ship soon surrendered to *Pecos* and her superior firepower and was boarded.

Doc remembered when he and Billy had boarded the ship all those months ago. It was one of those things that would be difficult, if not impossible, to forget.

"Doc, look at that," Billy said, pointing to the pile of shoes six feet high, near the pirate ship's bow.

"Let's take a look down that hold," Doc said, hoping his first instinct was wrong.

"Chief, you open that hatch, me and Billy will be ready to spray whatever's down there."

"Aye, sir."

The chief master-at-arms jerked the hatch open, exposing a

putrid and hellish pit to the East African sun. The stink was so intense that the chief dropped the hatch cursing and gagging. He poured canteen water on his face and covered his mouth with a bandana before making a second attempt.

Doc stepped up to the edge.

The hold was filled with barefoot, half-naked creatures. They reached up to the light seemingly asking for help, just a hand. Doc felt the heat from the open hatch radiate from the baking and bloated corpses. The men examined the pulley boom and tackle mounted over the hatch; it stank, covered in sun-scorched human remains. Its purpose was clear.

The pirates lowered victims into the pit after robbing them of everything from gold fillings to the very shoes on their feet. The brigands likely used the pit as intimidation to force their victims to tell them where valuables were hidden. Doc, Billy, and the chief tried and executed the remaining pirates. A burial at sea was held before they opened key valves belowdecks, eventually sending the pirate vessel to the bottom.

Months had passed since, but time would never fade the horror of that dark hold.

There was no moon when Doc and Billy rolled out into the Texas badlands. Disco and Hawse stayed back to provide security and monitor the radio while the others were outside the wire. During their mission brief before they boarded the C-130, Task Force Phoenix had been provided copies of maps indicating the positions of air-dropped equipment originally intended for Hotel 23's former commander.

Based on what had been recovered from the other drops, Doc thought this equipment would prove useful to his team and possibly shed some light on what the intelligence reports did not reveal—the identity of the organization responsible for the airdrops, and for wreaking utter mayhem on the former occupants of Hotel 23.

According to the briefing, the previous equipment recovered consisted of some rather advanced hardware. This hardware was described in reporting as "surpassing current technology by ten years" and "things you might find in an agency directorate of operations back room inventory."

The Task Force Phoenix operation orders were clear:

Primary mission objectives: Secure Hotel 23, verify her systems are in the green, verify remaining nuclear warhead viability in support of Task Force Hourglass.

Avoid detection.

Secondary mission objectives: Recover abandoned hardware for exploitation, assess the origin of Remote Six, recover supplies for ongoing support of Hotel 23 launch activity.

There was not much left for ambiguity. His primary tasking had been met. Hotel 23 had been secured, secure communications had been established, all networks checked green, and the nuclear payload had passed all function bit checks.

Although unclear as to what exactly the mission objectives of Task Force Hourglass might be, he knew it was something big and something far above his snake-eater pay grade. No matter what the mission of Hourglass, he still had his team's remaining objectives to meet. Doc never fell short of tasking.

Their target for the evening, an airdrop eight and a half miles east of Hotel 23, was the closest drop identified on the maps. Working east they moved wall-line abreast of one another. No point man, no straggler. They knew they didn't have enough people to run this excursion safely, so they evolved tactics to mitigate the extreme threat.

Their sleep cycles and circadian rhythms had already adjusted to night operations. Normalizing their bodies to their new living conditions was necessary before heading out. They needed maximum awareness and attention for night reconnaissance like this. Their night observation devices were functioning literally in the green, with fresh lithium batteries as well as back-ups tucked in their packs. Neither Doc nor Billy observed anything out of the ordinary in the night sky. They scanned overhead from time to time, always aware that there might be air assets collecting on them from above.

They hadn't brought enough water, as they hadn't wanted to hump it sixteen miles round-trip. The iodine tablets they carried would kill any bugs in the stream water they collected along the way.

They were only five hundred yards outbound from Hotel 23 when they had their first encounter.

Billy whispered to Doc, tapping his shoulder. "Three tangos caught in the fence about a hundred yards."

The field was shaped in such a way that the men had no choice but to pass close to the creatures to stay on course. The other option was to avoid them by taking the adjacent path through the woods. Not a choice, since both men knew that option would be much more dangerous than just engaging these immobile undead. Leaving them flailing about in the fence would draw too much attention—quick kills were the only option.

Approaching cautiously from the west, they switched on their lasers and each took to their targets. Billy Boy took the two on the left and Doc took the right. There was no real need to count down and execute a time-on-target kill, but they did so anyway out of habit.

Doc whispered back, "Three, two . . ."

Thunk, thunk.

The first two shots occurred simultaneously; Billy had an extra shot for the remaining third creature. Clockwork. All three lay caught up in the barbed-wire fence and would stay that way until they decomposed to dust. Strange, but wild animals wouldn't generally eat the dead.

Doc held down the bottom wire with his boot and pulled the second wire up with his fabricator-gloved hand—no point in risking tetanus or even a simple infection. Billy quickly ducked between the sharp wires and held them wide for Doc. They both continued to move.

"What's your pace count, Billy?"

"About six hundred, you?"

"Yeah, about that."

Moving east they noted possible shelters and egress routes in the event they were swarmed or stalked by any foe, dead or otherwise. Thinking back to the briefing, Doc remembered, *Stay off the roads. It's okay to use them as a guide but remain offset at least twenty-five meters. The roads just aren't safe. The dead congregate there.*

The intel report from the former Hotel 23 commander was useful as hell. Some of it was common sense but Doc was fine with that. There was valuable intel in the reports that he was glad to have for his team, like the detailed written account of the base commander's helicopter crash and subsequent journey back to the compound. In reading the reports, Doc could not help but notice interesting patterns of thought in the man's mind-set and methods of survival.

It was nearly midnight. They stuck to the preplanned route. Doc didn't want to risk detection by whatever it was that had attacked Hotel 23; this meant that radios were out, no omnidirectional RF communications. The burst unit set up back at Hotel 23 would evade detection if proper comm discipline was observed, but their Motorola brick units could easily be intercepted and were subject to direction finding (DF) by the most rudimentary SIGINT collection capabilities.

This was Doc's reasoning for religiously sticking to the planned route. If Doc and Billy didn't return by daybreak, Disco and Hawse would lock up and search for them at next nightfall, following the trail.

Doc wasn't thrilled about being clueless about the contents of this airdrop or the other drops marked on the map, but mission was mission.

"Shhhh!" Billy said.

Using hand signals he told Doc to take cover behind a huge pile of storm debris. Doc did so without hesitation and Billy followed, walking backward in a crouch. The instant they were hidden, the howling and moans commenced. Like a night chorus of demons on Halloween night, they bellowed.

Billy whispered to Doc, "At least a hundred."

"No way, Billy, I'd say about a hundred and four."

Without thinking, Billy punched Doc hard in the arm, causing Doc to bite his tongue to keep from yelping out.

"Thanks, asshole."

"No problem, prick."

"We're about a mile from the drop," Doc said.

Smiling, Billy replied, "Naw, more like a mile and a quarter."

They remained behind some cover until the mini-swarm of

creatures passed by. When they were far enough out, Doc broke cover and crossed the road where the creatures had just been. The wind blew fading sounds of the creature's hunger about.

USS *Virginia*

The only man onboard who is aware I keep a journal is Saien. Even so, I feel apprehensive in documenting some things, in the event my journal is lost or stolen. Not long ago, Saien and I were told of certain historical facts as well as current events that if true, at least for me, forever change everything. I'm told that the United States has in its possession a large portion of a space vehicle recovered in the forties as well as the cadavers of four extraterrestrial beings. First thought, total and complete bullshit. Second thought, pretty clever to stage the weather balloon debris at the Roswell crash site to divert attention away from the true crash site in Utah.

The vessel was allegedly held and studied by government scientists until they reached a technological barrier in the 1950s. They were unable to exploit the tech beyond basic circuitry, lasers, and low-observability characteristics. Knowing that they had only unlocked a small fraction of what the hardware's true capabilities might be, they turned to the military-industrial complex.

According to what I've learned today, Lockheed Martin has possessed the vehicle wreckage for over sixty years and made quantum advancements in the technology, resulting in the development of a particularly secret U.S. aircraft known as *Aurora*. I remember hearing about flying triangles in the newspapers and all over the online video-sharing websites before all of this. It wasn't often, but every now and again someone would catch a triangle flying silently through the night sky on their night-vision cameras and upload it to the Internet.

Although no one could prove this was *Aurora,* the aircraft's existence was almost an open secret in the halls of the Pentagon. Despite *Aurora* being disclosed to me today, no one was to ever know or would ever even believe that this Skunkworks project was a result of Lockheed Martin's reverse engineering of advanced alien technology.

Intelligence obtained from *Aurora* is what led to the formation of Task Force Hourglass (the operation that Saien and I are now in the middle of). Since before the anomaly in January, *Aurora* had overflown China forty-seven times conducting sensitive reconnaissance operations. She had taken thousands of extremely high-resolution photos of a crash site discovered by the Chinese military only weeks before the anomaly took its first communist Chinese victim.

In the very early days of crash-site reconnaissance executed by the U.S. intelligence community, *Aurora*'s hypersonic propulsion and extreme altitude saved her from being shot down by the still-operational Chinese SA-20 Gargoyle surface-to-air missile battalions.

The HUMINT reports coming out of the PRC combined with *Aurora* imagery and SIGINT capability gave the U.S. intelligence apparatus a pretty good picture of the situation on the ground around the Mingyong glacier crash site.

The Chinese had discovered their own "Roswell" crash site and were well into the process of excavation by December of last year. The information is incomplete (or withheld) as to the relationship between the *anomaly* (that's what everyone keeps calling it) and the Mingyong crash site. Commander Monday purports that we're headed to China to study the source of the anomaly to see what might be done about stopping it. I'd be a liar if I said I trusted him and I still don't believe half of what was briefed to me today.

The government and its elected representatives have had their fair share of diplomatic flaps as a direct result of being caught in bold-faced lies. The Gulf of Tonkin, Operation Northwoods, Watergate, WMD in Iraq, and other blatant Constitution burning brought on by the Patriot Act are a few examples from memory. Hey, I don't have the benefit of a Google search to dig up the hundreds, maybe thousands more. Guess what, the lies were the same after all this shit went down.

"Stay in your homes, the situation is under control."

Same story, different lie.

If this *ancient Chinese secret* turns out to be true (a long shot), I can safely add it to the long list of conspiracy facts.

—A cynical naval officer

16

U.S. Outpost Four—Somewhere in the Arctic

"I read you Lima Charlie. *George Washington,* where are you?"

After a minute of static the ship responded, "Sorry, OP4, we can't disclose our exact operating location on this net. I'm authorized to tell you that we are operating somewhere in the Gulf of Mexico, over."

Both Mark's and Crusow's hearts sank. The ship might as well be light-years away. They were using atmospheric bounce to communicate, a phenomenon that was intermittent at best. Mark continued his dialogue with the first living Americans he had spoken to since Crusow's wife last winter. He didn't know how long the atmospheric HF bounce might last.

"GW this is OP4, understood. We are an Arctic scientific research station. Our situation is dire; we have less than sixty days of fuel and food. We have five souls onboard, some are not in good health, over."

"OP4 this is GW, roger that, I'll be passing your situation report up the chain to the highest levels immediately, over."

"GW this is OP4, you do that, please. What is the situation on the mainland, over?"

"OP4 this is GW, situation really bad. The mainland United States has been deemed uninhabitable. Nuclear detonations have destroyed many overrun cities to no measurable advantage. The undead continue to dominate in the lower forty-eight. No word on Alaska."

"GW this is OP4, roger that. Winter has set in here pretty hard and heavy. The worst of it is in front of us. You might like to know that the creatures don't fare too well up here. The cold freezes them up pretty good. They can't move if exposed longer than a few minutes, over."

"OP4 this is GW, acknowledged. There will be folks interested to hear that. Before we lose connectivity, recommend we set up a radio contact schedule with times as well as primary, secondary, and tertiary frequencies, over."

"GW this is OP4, sounds like a damn good plan."

Mark continued his back and forth with the ship, exchanging common High Frequency Global Communications System frequencies as well as contact schedule times based on Greenwich Mean Time. Mark had finished establishing his comm schedule and started exchanging news when the transmission faded to garble.

"Damn it," Mark said angrily.

"Buck up, little camper, this is the best news we've had in months. If that boat is up and running then maybe more might be. Maybe something that can help," Crusow replied.

"Don't even try to be optimistic. We're well over a hundred miles from thin ice and even so, the weather is so fuckin' bad, no ship captain in his right mind short of an icebreaker skipper would risk it. Even if they did, how the hell are we going to hike a hundred miles over chasm-filled and unforgiving terrain in negative-fifty conditions, Crusow?"

"We have the Cat, right?"

"Yeah, I guess we have that."

"It's something. I am not giving up. If anything this makes me at least a little more hopeful. I'm not dying at the top of the world. I'm staying at ninety-eight-point-six degrees and you are, too. Neither one of us is headed to the bottom of the gulch and I'll be damned if I'm not off this ice cube before I die. We will see the sun again. There's a lot of work to do. Write out three copies of that schedule you just made with the ship. You keep one, give one to me, and post one at the desk, under the glass top. We need to call a meeting to let the others know."

"All right. Okay. I'll start now," Mark said as he sat up straighter in his chair, with just a little more focus, a little more hope.

17

It wasn't long before Tara and Laura found their way down to the sick bay, and to Jan. Laura missed her mother and wanted to know why she was down with the sick people all the time. The moment Jan saw Laura, she peeled off the blood-stained lab coat and gloves, removed her face shield, and picked Laura up, squeezing her tight.

"I'm sorry, baby, Mommy's got to be here, it's important."

"Mommy, I miss you. Can't you leave? You're gone *all the time.*"

"I know, baby, Mommy is trying to figure out a way to stop the bad people. Mommy is tired of the monsters and wants them to go away."

"I want them to go away, too," Laura said, frowning.

Putting Laura down with a grunt (she was getting bigger), Jan asked Tara how she was holding up with Kil being away.

"I'm all right," Tara said. "To tell you the truth, being able to babysit Laura keeps my mind off of him being gone. I'm helping out Dean with school lessons and that keeps me busy during the day. Did you know that Dean has nearly one hundred students now? It's practically a full-time job."

"Yeah, you won't believe this, but Dean came down to sick bay after teaching classes yesterday and helped to get this place back in order. I have no idea where she gets her energy to teach kids all day and then volunteer down here."

Tara laughed at this and without warning, broke down into tears.

Jan comforted her. "It's going to be just fine, he'll make it back, I promise."

"It's not that, Jan. It's something else."

"Well, honey, do you want to talk about it?"

"I'm pregnant," Tara blurted out as more tears started to meander down her cheeks.

"Oh boy," Jan said with eyes wide open.

"Yay!" Laura appeared from under the lab table.

Danny hated the monsters. All the grown-ups looked at it much differently than he did. His whole family except for his granny had been murdered by the monsters—that's what his friend Laura called them. Being a little older, he knew they weren't real monsters, but it didn't matter. They acted like monsters and they chased you like monsters and they ate you like monsters. The grown-ups treated them like snakes or spiders—avoiding them and smashing them and shooting them only when they needed to. For Danny, it was personal. Danny knew that he wouldn't be alive if it were not for his Granny Dean. She flew them both away as far as she could.

Danny had been trapped on a water tower and peeing off the top of it onto the monsters' heads when Kil found them months ago. Before the tower he remembered the propeller incident. His Granny had to land to get gas for the plane. They were running on fumes when she touched down at the airfield. He thought he might have remembered the engine sputtering. They were about to be taken by monsters just before Granny decided to chop them up like vegetables with the plane. *She took out a whole bunch,* Danny thought. The monsters trashed the plane, sending Danny and his grandmother to the tower in exile and away from the safety of flight.

Then Kil came for them.

Danny was done with school for the day and had permission to roam about until dinner as long as he stayed on the 03 level, off the catwalks and out of the way. Danny loved to hide and listen to everyone as they passed by. He thought he needed the practice. He hadn't spied on grown-ups since before his parents became monsters. That didn't bother him much anymore unless he thought about it too long. No one but him knew how tough his granny was. She saved him and smashed them. He never heard Granny tell anyone about that so he didn't either. She was tough, *maybe tougher than Kil,* he thought.

Danny was in one of the less-populated parts of the O3 level; he noticed the painted number on the wall was 250. Hearing someone stomping over a knee-knocker up ahead, Danny hid beside a firefighting storage locker and behind an open hatch.

As the sound grew louder, he overheard one of the men say, "How long are we going to hold those things onboard? They creep me the fuck out."

"I'm with you. I want to jettison the things ASAP. We are not getting a damn thing from them. We don't have the equipment. The admiral wants to hold on to them until . . ."

Their voices faded quickly after they passed Danny's hiding spot. He thought about following them for a moment but then decided against it and headed down the passageway from where the men had come.

There were benefits to being small; it was a lot easier to hide. Danny had shown Laura all the secrets behind hiding like a boy. After being found a few dozen times when it was Danny's turn to seek, she had picked up some tricks of the boy trade.

Danny would tell her, "El, you gotta pick less easy places. I found you in two seconds."

Laura would pout and stomp off and begin counting to thirty, a bit faster than was fair. She was tired of being *it.* Danny was a hiding ninja and was rarely found, unless he was trying to boost Laura's self-esteem.

Danny had just overheard a curious conversation between what he thought were two soldiers—not knowing the difference between soldiers and sailors—about holding *things* onboard. His eavesdropping was abruptly cut off as the men kept moving down the passageway. Danny had never been farther aft than where he was hiding now.

. . . "Things onboard . . . creep me out . . . jettison" . . . The conversation between the two men kept repeating in his mind. Danny hadn't yet learned what *jettison* meant, thinking it might mean to fly away or something like that. He would ask his English teacher at the next class. *She is the best,* he thought to himself. He kept moving to the back of the ship, scouting hiding spots, jumping at every sound of footsteps.

He was far back in the ship when it came time to make a decision . . . go down the ladder or go back to his room. Danny didn't even think. He quickly and quietly scurried down the ladder. It was dark and unfamiliar, and it smelled funny. Reaching the last step, the sterile smell intensified. As his eyes slowly adjusted, he recognized the red night-lights that were sometimes on in the sleeping areas of the ship.

He could see a fan room just up ahead—his healthy young eyes could make out the label on the hatch clearly. Adjacent to the fan room was another door marked *Restricted Access*. There was a little box next to the door where he had seen soldiers enter codes before—not here, but where John worked—in the radio shack. With no one in sight he sprinted for the fan room. His heart thumped faster as he closed the distance . . . only one knee-knocker to hurdle before reaching the door.

In midair jump, he heard the metallic sound of the door handle from the other door turn. Quickly, he slung open the fan-room hatch and dived in under the air circulator; he didn't have time to shut the hatch behind him.

The mold was a quarter-inch thick under the circulator; the rapid transition from the hospital-like aroma to the mildew stench caused his stomach to turn just a bit. The light from the passageway spilled into the fan room but was broken by a silhouette of legs. He could see only the outline of boots from his vantage point.

"Has maintenance been here today?"

"No, but we've hit some heavy seas in the last few hours. The hatch probably flew open in the chop."

The hatch slammed shut, leaving Danny in darkness; the voices slowly trailed away just like before. Inside the black of the cool steel around him, Danny's mind wandered into equally black parts of his imagination. He thought of the monsters and for a second imagined that they might be in this dark place with him. Rolling into the fetal position, he squirmed in fear on the damp and moldy floor until he was certain no one or thing was near.

His fear faded after his senses told him that there was no immediate threat. He lay there listening to all the ship noises—sounds he had started to tune out after his time onboard. Someone above him dragged chains across the deck and then some distant valve opened somewhere and the sound of steam escaping drowned out the chains. This duel of noises continued for a few moments, nearly hypnotizing Danny . . . and then silence. The fear he had shaken flooded back as the sound of something familiar, distinct, and terrible came through the vent above him.

Looking up, he followed the vent. His eyes were adjusting to the darkness. The vent connected to the wall and then into the adjacent space—the restricted area. Danny was a boy with a wild imagination, no disputing that, but he had definitely heard that sound. The hair standing stiff on his neck confirmed it.

18

Kil couldn't sleep. The USS *Virginia* had been underneath bad weather seemingly since they hit the blue water of the Pacific, leaving the Panama coast. They stayed submerged, cut off from the sun and all radio transmissions.

His watch was set to GMT time and he'd forgotten how that corresponded to where the sun might be at the moment. Sliding out of his rack, his feet hit his shower shoes perfectly. He grabbed his shower kit and scooted down the passageway, bumping his shoulder on one of the thousands of pipes and junction boxes jutting out from the bulkhead. This served to wake him up a little before hitting the showers. The *Virginia* had less than half the walk space of the carrier and two people couldn't walk side by side in most areas.

The head was already packed by the time he arrived. He recognized some of the crew members, mostly enlisted. Addressing him as a commander, they offered to let him have the head of the line. He declined, fighting off the urge to tell them that he had been only a lieutenant until a recent and bizarre spot promotion. He brushed his teeth while moving forward along the line of sinks to the shower. As a long queue of sailors coming off watch formed behind him for the showers, he decided to put the soap in his hair before getting in, a time-saving measure.

"Hollywood" showers would make you the target of hate and discontent onboard any submarine. They had plenty of fresh water (they made their own onboard), but the *Virginia* was 105 percent manned at the moment with Kil, Saien, and the special-operations team onboard. As an officer, Kil thought it best to stay extra humble and quiet until he figured out how things ran onboard.

It was soon Kil's turn anyway. He quickly hung his kit on the hook outside and stepped in. The water was hot—better than the 50/50 hot shower he had had at Hotel 23. He sang "The Star Spangled Banner" in his head; by the time he reached "home of the brave," he knew he should be reaching for his towel.

On his way out of the head, Kil noted that one of the submariners wasn't wearing shower shoes and thought to himself, *nasty bastard*; he'd rather get in the wrestling ring with one of the undead than go barefoot in a U.S. Navy submarine shower—almost.

Back in his stateroom, he was careful not to wake up Saien—still sawing logs and saying something to himself in his sleep. He threw on his coveralls, ball cap, and sidearm and headed for the galley. The officer's mess was shut down in an effort to pool resources. For better or worse, officers and enlisted men dined together onboard.

Kil pulled his coffee cup off the hook on the wall. He was very happy to see that his cup was starting to grow a pretty respectable coffee residue on the inside. Since you did your own dishes onboard there was no risk of his coffee cup being accidentally washed. Most officers made fun of him for this but Kil was prior enlisted and liked his cup with a full coat of old coffee on the inside. Better for the flavor, and this boat's coffee needed all the help it could get. They were operating on low rations and the coffee tasted on par with dirty dishwater most of the time.

He ordered a powdered egg and cheese omelet from the kid working behind the grill. While his omelet cooked, he scooped himself some oatmeal into a chipped bowl. He'd noticed the cooked weevils in his oatmeal from the first breakfast he'd eaten onboard but decided it was best to imagine they weren't there. He sat alone at the table, watching the boat's TV feed. The movie playing on the screen hanging above the dining area was *Logan's Run*. Kil remembered watching it years ago and laughed to himself at the shiny robot flailing around on the screen, 1970s style.

Captain Larsen—commanding officer of USS *Virginia*—walked into the dining area with his tray of food just as Kil shoveled a spoonful of powdered eggs into his mouth and began to chew.

"May I join you?" asked the captain.

"Yes, sir," Kil replied, trying to talk and eat at the same time. "How's it going, Skipper? Anything happening?"

"You know better than calling me skipper—this isn't a ready room," the captain said, smiling. "But to answer your question, the ship is still fully mission capable and we're only a week out from seeing Diamond Head from the sail hatch. The only negative to report is that our communications with the carrier are spotty. We can only connect for a situation report when the fickle HF wave from our radios decides to bounce the right way."

Kil thought for a moment before asking, "What's the main objective in Hawaii? I've heard the crew rumors about resupply but it seems like a pretty risky thing to attempt."

"Go on, tell me why you think that," the captain said.

Reluctantly, Kil began. "Well, for starters, it's an island. Oahu and especially Honolulu were highly populated when the dead started coming back, and because it's an island, there would have been no escape from the creatures. It will be very risky to attempt resupply with that many of those things massed in the areas we'll be operating. Also, I overheard the cooks talking in the passageway. If rationed, *Virginia* has six months of food onboard; that's more than enough to make it to China and back to Panama, or wherever our port call might be."

Nodding, the captain said, "Very good. Although this would be classified top secret at one time, I suppose that there is very little security risk in discussing it at the table. Resupply is an objective, but only a secondary priority. We are going to need the ability to monitor the situation as we transit west from Hawaii. We are going to need indications and warnings. We have no idea who or what survived. There may very well be a fleet of Chinese warships operating in the green water off the coast of China. If that's the case, we don't know their rules of engagement and without the ability to monitor their intent ahead of time, we could be at a severe disadvantage."

"What does Hawaii have to do with this?" asked Kil.

"You should know. You're the former airborne SIGINT guy," Captain Larsen said sarcastically.

After hearing that, Kil knew instantly. "Kunia?"

"Yeah, you got it. There is a Chinese linguist onboard who will soon find himself as the last resident of the RSOC Kunia facility. Our spook was stationed there two years ago and knows systems. He will be providing support to Task Force Hourglass after we clear out the cave facility."

"How exactly are we going to clear anything? There are probably eight-hundred thousand creatures on that island, and I bet that underground facility is no different."

The captain took a long sip of coffee and said, "Last intelligence estimates have Oahu very sparsely populated, maybe two hundred thousand on the whole island."

Kil replied skeptically, "Where exactly did you come by that number? I'm no census worker, and I know it was outside tourist season back in January when this went down, but that seems just a little on the low side."

Larsen sat back in his chair and pulled a map from his shirt pocket. "I guess they never told you? Take a gander at that."

Unfolding the map, Kil saw the answer to his question.

As the captain took the map from Kil's grasp, he said, "As you can see, a strategic nuclear weapon pretty much ended the tourist season on Oahu forever."

At that moment, Kil didn't feel like finishing his powdered eggs.

19

The stretch of highway near where Doc and Billy trailed was overgrown with tall grass jungles in the median and on the sides. They were deep into the Texas wastelands now, on their way to retrieve a mysterious supply drop, represented by nothing more than a small symbol on a cryptic map. They could see the road every now and again in places where debris stunted vegetation growth. The seasonal freeze and thaw and complete lack of maintenance had converted some sections of the road into gravel pits. Doc recalled the faded remnants of old railway tracks from the 1800s around his hometown. *It won't be long until the highways go that way,* he thought.

Doc had a map in a clear pouch attached to his left forearm, folded to the area they now traversed. He kept pace count, checking their position every hundred meters.

Doc quietly updated Billy: "One thousand meters to target."

"Roger," Billy whispered in response.

They moved along an old cattle trail very close to the highway. There was no sign of the undead; only the night wind and partial moonlight accompanied them.

"Billy, we got an overpass up ahead. We need to get on the road and take it across, man."

"I don't like it, boss. Bad call."

"Well, what are you thinking?" Doc asked, putting Billy on the spot for an alternative. He often did this with his men, pushing them to make quick tactical decisions on the move. He thought it made them better leaders.

"Let's stay offset from the road a few meters, and get as close to the overpass as we can, and look down below. If it's infested, we take the overpass. If it's not, we take the low ground."

"Fuck that. Didn't you see *The Rock*? Never take the low ground," Doc replied jokingly.

Laughing together at a whisper, they approached the overpass at an offset. Doc was in charge, but he wasn't stupid; he listened to his people, especially Billy Boy. Billy was Apache Indian and his instinct was uncanny. Billy was cautious like a wolf; if Billy ran, raised his carbine, or hit the deck, Doc would do the same, and fast.

Doc took a look across the overpass with the magnifier on his carbine. The span was packed with cars both above and below. He carefully studied the details through his optic; Billy instinctively covered him. Panning back and forth, Doc could see only a few undead corpses hibernating inside cars or stuck between pileups.

Billy abruptly smelled a wisp of rot on the wind, slapping Doc's shoulder in warning. Billy clarified the alarm with a silent signal by pinching his nose. Within seconds, they both saw the leading edge moving down the road around a bend in the distance.

"They're coming. I smell 'em strong now. There's a lot of 'em."

"Let's sit here for a minute and see what's up. We don't want to haul ass right into their arms," Doc replied.

A few stressful minutes later, the choice became obvious. A large, bellowing swarm approached from the north and moved directly at them along the highway running under their overpass.

They had little time.

"Billy, we need to move, now. We don't want to get trapped on this side of them—we'll never reach the drop if we do."

Both operators sprinted, the sixty pounds of kit seemingly light as a pillow as the adrenaline pushed them to the west side of the overpass. They ran perpendicular and above the road. The moans of the approaching horde jolted the creatures nearby out of hibernation.

Billy turned his head over his shoulder to Doc. "Engaging."

Billy's suppressed carbine dropped three creatures on the crumbling overpass. Doc followed with shots on two more; he aimed low on the second one, the round passing through the creature's neck, missing the spine and slinging dead muscle and fat onto an overpass guardrail. Doc quietly scorned himself for not remembering his gun's point of aim, point of impact. Like most red-dot optics, his Aimpoint Micro was mounted a few inches above the bore of his M-4, resulting in a low point of impact if not compensated higher at close ranges. He took another shot at the top of the dome, hitting the creature's switch.

Timers and switches, Doc recalled. The human body was composed of several kill timers but few kill switches. Hitting a femoral artery was a timer. Hitting the heart or brain was a switch. But that was on a *living* human. The rules were different now—only one switch mattered. The undead didn't respect timers.

The SEAL accuracy bar had been raised since the dead began to walk. A center-mass switch hit was now a miss; the only valid hit was above the nose and below the scalp.

Doc and Billy quickly moved across the overpass like thieves in the night. Through their NODs, they saw a pileup of cars thirty meters out. They'd need to negotiate this Jenga pile of steel in order to reach the other side.

The first leading edge of the swarm began to trickle beneath the overpass. The main river of corpses approached rapidly. The smell sickened Doc when the wind shifted, pushing those rotting molecules into his nostrils.

Doc knew that the unforgiving and lethal thing about a swarm like this was that the head of the undead snake could be led and altered by anything. Stray dog, deer, a still-functioning car alarm—anything.

"Doc, we might wanna hold here at the middle of the bridge and see where they go. I don't want to pick the wrong side. Could be really bad," Billy suggested.

Doc thought for a moment about the worst-case scenario. *What if the swarm split and they spilled onto the overpass from both sides? No factor.* "We need to get over those cars and a few hundred meters ahead. We have about two hours before we have to head back to arrive home before sunup. We'll wait a few, but I don't like it. Take a look."

Both men peeked over the guardrail up the river of undead. Although visibility through the NODs didn't give them long-distance resolution, they still knew they were looking at a mile-long and thirty-foot-wide mass of creatures. Neither of them wanted to do the math on that one.

The flow rate of the undead river increased from trickle to stream. Just over halfway across the overpass, Doc and Billy began to low-crawl, not because they needed to, but because they were so goddamned scared. It was like ducking when getting out of a running helicopter—unnecessary, but not really a bad idea either.

They reached the vehicle wreckage. The walking river below was at peak flow, causing the overpass to vibrate. Doc again risked a peek over the side and saw at least a half-mile of moving corpses on either side of the bridge. The things didn't seem to suspect that potential prey was spying on them from above. Some of the ghouls tried to break away from the pack, but returned quickly, again attracted to the loud rumble of the swarm.

"Let's take a break and have some chow," Doc suggested.

"Sounds good. We got at least twenty minutes."

They tore into expired energy bars and drank the wine of iodine as the bridge shook underneath and the oblivious dead river ravaged down a derelict road to nowhere.

20

Arctic North

Crusow, Mark, and the other three outpost survivors met in the conference room adjacent to the control center. The station's military consultants, Bret and Larry, as well as He-Wei Chin, the outpost scientist, stood together, still wearing heavy, ice-crusted cold-weather gear. He-Wei spoke very broken English and was sometimes a source of politically incorrect comedic relief for the rest of the survivors. Before posted in the Arctic, He-Wei was a Chinese national applying for U.S. citizenship status. He had volunteered for duty at Outpost Four to speed up his application process. Expedited citizenship was one of the incentives of arduous duty while serving in the U.S. Arctic research programs. Everyone called him Kung Fu, or just Kung, because of his passable resemblance to Bruce Lee.

Even though Crusow, Mark, and Kung had spent the past several months living with Larry and Bret in a place barely bigger than a modern space station, they didn't know much about them except that they were military men and part of the mission here before the shit hit the ice.

Many American operatives who were alive before the undead rose up suspected that there were hundreds of covert facilities around the world, many using missions to conceal their true purpose. Outpost Four had been publicly drilling for core samples before the fall of man, but so had every other outpost on the ice—facilities owned by a dozen other countries.

Larry and Bret never discussed their military status but their haircuts and demeanor gave it away upon arrival. Just like all the other fresh meat before, the new crew members would touch down in a modified C-17 aircraft outside the wintering-over season. There were new faces every time, but the same haircut and attitude remained.

Now Larry was very ill, his condition worsening over the past few weeks. Mark thought that Larry might have come down with a bad bout of pneumonia. They used up half of the outpost's remaining antibiotics on him with no measurable effect. Larry could barely stand most of the time and Bret was often observed helping him to and from the different areas of the outpost. At least Larry was considerate enough to wear a face mask.

They couldn't risk anyone else getting sick, especially Crusow. They'd all likely be frozen inside of eighteen hours if Crusow was killed or incapacitated. He was the one who kept the generators running on schedule and also somehow formulated rudimentary biofuel using the dwindling chemicals and surplus food fats on hand. He wasn't one of the expendables, to be sure.

"Okay, thanks for showing up," said Crusow, addressing the small group. "I won't waste time in telling you that we've made contact."

"With who?" Bret asked excitedly.

"The USS *George Washington*."

"We're fuckin' saved!" Larry exclaimed, coughing loudly inside his mask.

Crusow frowned, saying, "Not really. They're in the Gulf of Mexico and couldn't make it here even if they wanted to. We're on the Pacific side of the Arctic Circle and even if it were spring and if they had an icebreaker ship, it would take them too long. We'd run out of supplies by then and be in the solid state, literally. We need to start thinking about contingency plans."

Larry coughed again, shooting crud inside his face mask. After a spell of cursing and changing masks, he asked, "What plans? We might as well be on a Martian outpost. Without a rescue party, we'll be blocks of ice in a month or two."

"Yeah, maybe so, but I ain't giving up either," Crusow replied, a little louder than he wanted. Taking himself down a notch, he continued: "It's true we're low on fuel, but I have a plan that might work."

"We're listening," Bret said.

"I've modified the Sno-Cat to run on biodiesel. This means that more of the remaining regular fuel can be used to keep this place at least warm enough to support life, say fifty degrees. We'll need to start sleeping in our cold-weather gear to conserve fuel and we'll need to start chopping off the outer limbs of this facility. We're spread out now as it stands and that wastes a lot of juice. Larry, you and Bret are going to need to suck it up and move into the crew wings and seal off your areas of the outpost."

"Wait a goddamned minute!" Bret yelled. "Why do we need to move here? Why not the other way around?"

"Listen! Either you two move in with us, or you freeze! I control the heat, the darkness, and the light, and I'll be shutting you down in forty-eight hours. It's nothing personal—I need to be near the equipment and I'm not moving to the military wing with you and Iron Lung here."

Neither Larry nor Bret responded. They knew the hand they were dealt. Crusow could see their eyes shift. They were both military and both were likely calculating a way to regain some leverage. Crusow didn't trust them, and probably never would.

After a moment, Larry coughed and asked, "We're lower on biodiesel than we are on the regular stuff. How are you going to make enough to keep that Sno-Cat full?"

"This is the part that gets a little weird and maybe dangerous. We've been brewing the biodiesel with old cooking oil up to this point. We're getting low because I've been running one of the generators on it to conserve the good stuff. I think I may have found a source of animal fat that might give us enough fuel to run that Sno-Cat a hundred miles, inside thin ice, and maybe, if there are any out and about and within portable radio . . ."

Bret interrupted, "If you're talking about killing the sled dogs, I'm all for—"

Crusow cut Bret off mid-sentence. "No, we're not killing the dogs. We might need them. Stop worrying about food, Bret—we have enough stored here to last us a while with everyone gone or dead. There's not really enough fat on those dogs to get us enough fuel needed to make any sort of difference anyway."

"Well, what is it then?" Larry asked impatiently.

Crusow made eye contact and said, "We're gonna have to rappel down the gulch and have a reunion with some of our old friends. Some of them were overweight. The fat on them has been frozen and preserved. There's probably a few hundred pounds worth at the bottom. We'll be able to make enough diesel to get the hell out of here and, if lucky, some to spare."

"You *are* ape-shit crazy, Crusow," Larry said.

"Maybe so, but unless you can think of a goddamned better way to keep these generators running with enough fuel in reserves to run that Sno-Cat off this ice shelf, I'd keep your mouth shut. Besides, you're too weak to make the trip down the gulch and back up even once, so you have no say. It's over two hundred feet, mostly straight down. We'll need two people at the bottom to rig the bodies to the ropes and two up top with the dogs to pull them up."

They all looked at each other, waiting for someone to say something about the plan. Crusow didn't give them any time to think about it.

"Okay then. Which one of you bastards is going down there with me?"

One week from Oahu

Saien and I have learned at least some of the routine of submarine life. We understand the hierarchy of privilege and although I had sea legs from my time serving onboard navy ships, it is a culture shift serving onboard a submarine. I have been helping out in the radio room, mainly for selfish reasons. I have used the access to dispatch communications back to the USS *George Washington,* letting my Hotel 23 family know I'm okay. So far, no one onboard has voiced opposition.

The most recent message from John:

"Tara sends love"

Although only three short words, even these brief dispatches really help. I've been gone less than two weeks; it seems like longer. Without email, it takes me back to a time where communication was more personal, more valued.

I wonder how many young adults of the "me generation" died during the outbreak while checking the signal on their smartphones or posting an inane update to their social network pages?

It probably went something like:

OMFG, they're breaking down the door!

As self-centered as those kids were, I still wish they'd survived. I've unfortunately put a lot of skinny pant–wearing creatures into the dirt from whence they came since all this started.

A few days ago, the captain briefed me on our mission on the island of Oahu. I'm honestly not surprised at the details, just at the risk we will be taking for limited return on our investment. According to military intelligence, the nuclear strike on Honolulu was successful, resulting in a total annihilation of the city and outlying suburbs.

Larsen seems overly optimistic that the nuclear strike on Hawaii was somehow more effective in exterminating the undead than the one on the mainland United States. He's betting that the mass of creatures was in Honolulu at the time of detonation. In my professional opinion, this is a careless assessment. He is the captain of the boat and I'm only a consulting guest, but I was not shy in offering my dissent on the matter.

It is my personal opinion that we should keep our Chinese interpreter on board and task him to operate the boat's onboard SIGINT collection gear in order to provide self-protection and any warnings of Chinese military activity. There is a high probability that, if we leave him on the island, we might lose our interpreter to the creatures while we transit west to China. Also, there is no guarantee that Kunia's sensors are still viable this long after Hawaii went grid-down and dark. The biggest gamble is that we have no idea the current status of Kunia. Most of it is underground and it could be flooded, overrun with radiated dead, or caved in by a stray nuclear warhead. We just won't know until we go boots on the ground on the mainland; a plan I'm not willing to endorse right now, or ever.

Maximum pull-ups: 5

Push-ups: 65

1.5 mile treadmill run: 11:15

I hope the treadmill keeps working. I am spoiled by the luxury of running for exercise instead of for life and limb.

21

Southeast Texas

"Billy, is that what I think it is?"

"What?"

Doc activated his laser and pointed it a few hundred meters out, into a field. "That."

"Looks like someone took a plow and just started pulling. I can't really tell through the NODs."

"The map says the drop should be there. Let's break off and hit the field. Stay close."

"Roger."

Both men hopped the fence and stayed low, heading for the scarred terrain ahead. The wind shifted and they caught a foul whiff from the swarm in the distance.

"Goddamn that stinks and I'll never say it doesn't," Doc said under his breath. "One hundred meters out. Looks like our drop hit there and was dragged away by the chute. Let's see where it goes."

"I'm following you—let's spread out a few meters though, okay?" Billy said.

"Okay, spread out, stay in visual, and get eyes on me every few seconds. I'll do the same."

"Sounds good, moving."

"Move."

They followed the gouged trail for a quarter mile to the top of a shallow ridgeline. As they moved closer, they heard what sounded like laundry flapping on a summertime clothesline. Peering over the top of the hill, they observed the target. A pallet wrapped in packing plastic sat tipped over on its side with a ripped chute streaming out in a straight line like a crazy comet tail.

The flapping noise must have drawn the creatures in the days and weeks since the drop came to a rest here. A couple dozen of them stood below the ridge in hibernation, waiting for anything alive to set off the primitive trip wires. Doc knew this by the way they stood like stone sentries. They arrived expecting food, only to shut down in order to conserve whatever energy source they utilized. This mystery was perplexing. Doc suspected that they derived energy from something other than the dwindling food source they hunted and consumed.

"How do you wanna handle this, Billy?"

"Well, we could stay back here and start dropping them in a certain order that will keep them sleeping. I'll start on the east group, you start on the west, and we'll meet in the middle. With any luck, we can have them all dropped before they hear anything much louder than that flapping parachute. Our cans should muffle us this far out. We can even take a few steps back if we need to. At this distance point of aim and point of impact will be the same. Aim for the forehead anyway."

Doc knew Billy was pimping him about his point of aim.

"Okay, I like it," said Doc approvingly. "It's dark, they can't see us, but we can see them. I say we go for it."

"Just give the word."

"I'm west, you're east, engage after me."

"Roger."

Doc looked down the length of his carbine through the optic, noticing the glare of moonlight off his suppressor. He slapped the magnifier over, enlarging his sight picture. Sure enough, they stood like terrible gargoyles in the night. He thought that they might sway ever so slightly in this condition but could not be sure. No one spent enough time close enough to test the theory.

Deep breath, slow release, both eyes open, kill.

Bam.

As soon as Doc dropped his first creature, Billy Boy followed. Billy already sighted his first target and was just waiting for the suppressed sound of Doc's before he put the ghoul to the ground.

FUMP, FUMP, FUMP were the noises of the rounds hitting

the rotting skulls. They slowly and deliberately took their shots. One Mississippi, *FUMP*, two Mississippi, *FUMP*. Their plan was working; the creatures were staying in hibernation. They were down to only six remaining when Doc took his next shot. Pulling the trigger, Doc knew instantly something was different. A strange sound resonated, as if he'd just shot a street sign or a car. Doc had heard of this before, but never had it happen. Some creatures had metal plates implanted from previous injuries before the world went to hell. The creature was thrown to the ground. Doc used his magnifier to get a better look. It was returning to its feet.

Doc turned to continue shooting his targets. *FUMP*.

The creature, now back on its feet, was very irritated. It began to call out, moaning, waking the others. It moved quickly, reacting to sound, even the suppressed sounds of their carbines. It started moving up the ridge toward them.

"Keep on yours, Doc, I'll keep dumping lead into this one."

"All right, Billy, handle it! It's fast!"

The creature continued to advance up the hill at a startling speed. Doc was right—it was faster than the others. Billy continued to take shots at the creature, missing most of them.

"Reloading!"

"I gotcha, do it," Doc said.

Billy dumped his empty mag and reached behind him for his fresh one. In high-stress situations, Billy always performed well because he told himself what to do, based on his training.

"Push, pull, rack, bang," he whispered aloud, executing what he was thinking.

After *pushing* the mag into the mag well, he *pulled* it to verify it was seated. He *racked* his M-4 charging and pulled the trigger. A *bang* sent the titanium cranium tumbling permanently down the hill in an awkward and tragic pose.

"Close one," said Doc. "That thing would have been up here with us, hanging out and telling jokes, if you'd have waited another few seconds."

"Yeah, I know, freaky. Not used to seeing them so aggressive."

"Me neither. Let's stay here at the top and watch for a minute

or two. Might be some more down there. Don't want any ankle bit-
ers, know what I mean?" Doc suggested.

"Yeah, I know."

They waited. Minutes went slowly by with no movement. It
was always like this after an encounter with them. Man wasn't
meant to see the dead walk. Man wasn't meant to fight them either. Post-traumatic stress disorder was something that everyone
suffered from these days, like the common cold. From the two-
year-old that witnessed her mom being eaten by her father right
before a SWAT rescue, to the old man that locked his wife in the
basement because he didn't have the heart to end her—they all
suffered now, if they mustered the courage to remain living.

"Looks clear down there," Billy said to Doc.

"Yeah, let's get down. We have thirty minutes until we need to
start humping back to Hotel 23 and before the sun gets us."

As they walked down the ridge, Billy asked, "What do you
think would happen if we didn't make it before sunrise?"

"I think we'd get made and might find ourselves the recipient
of a five-hundred-pound warhead. We're obviously not welcome
at Hotel 23."

"I still don't understand why this group would want the carrier
nuked."

"I have no idea, Billy, but I do know they can hurt us during
the day. And don't get Disco and Hawse worked up, but I'm not so
sure they can't go high order on us at night."

"Yeah, I was thinkin' it, just didn't want to say."

The pile of corpses at the bottom was a gruesome sight, with
some still twitching. Both were careful to avoid getting too close—
a bullet to the brain didn't always mean the threat was eliminated.
Even after trauma to the brain, the biting reflex was sometimes
still present. Whatever caused the dead to rise didn't give up easily; even severed heads required extreme caution.

Doc pulled out his blade and cut the strings holding the flapping chute to the drop. The fabric fluttered up into the darkness on
the whim of a night wind. Doc thought of a man o' war jellyfish as it
drifted over the ridge area, dangling its stinger-like paracord strings.

There were white letters painted to the outside of the plastic
wrap that held the drop together, but the elements and the wear-

ing of time had made it unreadable. The drop rested on its side against a wedge of dirt. Doc swiped the plastic wrap with his blade, spilling the black hard cases onto the ground.

"Billy, get on perimeter while I check this out."

"I'm on it."

Doc started the unpacking process one box at a time, carefully, as if there might be booby traps in the containers. He listened for the action of Billy Boy's carbine as he opened the containers—all quiet.

The first box contained a weapon that Doc thought curious, marked *swarm control gun*. The instructions were written in a simple manner, resembling the pictorial directions that one might find on how to operate a seatbelt in a commercial aircraft. The gun was somewhat cumbersome, requiring the user to literally wear it; an illustration depicted a man wearing the gun attached to what resembled a harness.

The other boxes that Doc inspected contained the compounds that were required to fuel the gun. According to the documentation, two different bottles attached to the gun. When the gun was actuated, it was supposed to expel a stream of foam at ranges of up to fifty feet. The two compounds mixed when exposed to the air and the foam would harden within two seconds. Doc read the cautionary note on the documentation:

WARNING: FOAM COMPOUND WILL HARDEN
COMPARABLE TO CURED FIBER CEMENT/FIBER RESIN.
USE EXTREME CAUTION WHEN AIMING.
THIS FOAM WEAPON IS LETHAL.

As Doc continued scanning the instructions, he noticed a section mentioning the possible uses of the weapon.

—*Immediate temporary immobilization of large groups*
—*Immobilization of moving vehicles and heavy armor*
—*Freezes doors and other access points*
—*Chemical bonding of any material to another*

Doc estimated the gear weighed about eighty pounds in all. There was nothing else in this drop. Doc called Billy over to discuss the cost versus benefit of humping the extra weight back to Hotel 23.

After looking over the gun documentation, Billy commented, "Man, if this thing can do what it says, I'll hump it back myself. Our M-4s are good for running and gunning and the surgical wet work and all, but this thing might help against the likes of what we saw on that overpass. I wouldn't mind having a fire hose that can shoot instant concrete on demand, would you?"

"Yeah. We'll split up the gear and hump it back. But we'll test it out another night. We're losing night cover."

After rigging the gear to their packs, they headed back to Hotel 23. Doc marked an *X* over this particular drop on the map, crossing it out. As they crested the ridge heading back, Doc paused.

Was that the sound of an engine in the distance?

He intended to ask Billy if he had heard it, too, but the wind shifted and the sound vanished like a fleeting thought.

22

USS George Washington

The carrier briefing room buzzed with brass. Admiral Goettleman and Joe Maurer sat at the table in front of the auditorium, facing the small group of officers and a handful of senior enlisted.

The admiral leaned over to Joe. "Make sure the doors are secure. There's already scuttlebutt circulating about the deck plates."

"Yes, sir."

Joe sat up and told one of the officers in the front row to check the starboard doors before personally verifying the port and returning to his seat alongside Admiral Goettleman.

"All secure, sir."

"Very well. Let's get started."

The admiral tapped the microphone button in front of him. "Thanks for coming today—not like you really had anywhere to go."

Some tired laughs ebbed around the room.

"The reason I have called this meeting is to provide an update on Task Force Hourglass. As most of you are aware, they are currently underway, onboard the submarine USS *Virginia* and a week from Oahu. As the TF commander, I'm privy to information relating to all phases of the Hourglass mission. All of you are read into the special-access program known as Horizon and what likely occurred in China, or at least what we think happened. Phase one of Hourglass has so far been a success, as *Virginia* continues steaming west with a team of special operators and consultants aboard. Phase two of Hourglass is about to commence—that is the reason we're here today."

The admiral paused for a moment, surveying the small crowd while he took a sip of water. "Phase two involves the Nevada specimens. The Continuity of Government has decided to run a test, exposing one of the specimens to the anomaly. We don't know if CHANG is of the same species as our specimens, but we still may learn a great deal from the experiment. At the very least we may find out why all of our HUMINT assets went dark not long after CHANG was moved to the Bohai region; at most we may find some way to return the contents of Pandora's box."

The chatter in the auditorium began to roll in waves and thunder about. One of the officers in the back raised his hand.

"Go ahead, Commander," the admiral prompted.

In a cautious tone, the commander began. "Sir, we have no idea the effects this might have on the Nevada specimen's physiology. The Mingyong anomaly was measured by the Chinese at over twenty thousand years old. Our specimens were recovered in the nineteen forties. Was this plan really thought out by the COG or was this only a plan to throw an idea at the wall to see what sticks?"

The admiral glared at the officer. "Well, Commander, I think you make good points, but COG folks with brains larger than ours and that are in power as the result of laws passed by officials elected long ago have decided that this is the best way ahead. Besides that, I propose to you the following: What if Hourglass fails to succeed? What if the *Virginia* never makes it to China? Then what? These are all reasons we will conduct these experiments. Hourglass may *not* succeed."

The admiral scanned the room, surveying reactions. "Right now as we sit here onboard the USS *George Washington,* preparations are being made to extract one of the damaged specimens from long-term cold storage. I'll circle back to you on the findings."

Wild chatter erupted throughout the auditorium.

Breaking through the noise, another officer asked, "Admiral, what if exposing the Nevada specimen is the catalyst that causes the anomaly to jump airborne? We just don't know. It's uncharted territory!"

"So is the dead walking. That is all!" Goettleman barked.

"Attention on deck!" Joe called out, before the admiral stood and abruptly departed the room.

23

Arctic

December. Outside was a relentless bombardment of snow and ice. Crusow opened the heavy hatch to the unforgiving atmosphere. Not quite whiteout weather but close. No matter, it would be this or worse the rest of the year and into the next, until spring. If they waited on perfect conditions they'd die hungry and frostbitten. They were well into the long night; probably ninety days of dimness remained before the sun resumed its familiar arc.

Bret arrived from behind Crusow. Kung and Mark would begin readying the dogs to pull up the frozen bodies from the bottom of the gulch soon. It would take Crusow and Bret at least an hour to get to the bottom and secure the bodies to the lines. Crusow left his rifle behind in his quarters and wore only his Bowie knife and ice axe on his hip. They didn't have moving parts and would not fail him in fifty-below-zero conditions. All the bodies at the bottom of the gulch were frozen solid. Perhaps the polar bears would have a go at them.

Crusow spun around in his snow shoes to face Bret. "You ready for this? Gonna be brutal. Hope you had a big breakfast."

"Fuck you, Crusow. I'm in no mood for your . . ."

"Good morning to you, too, bitch tits," Crusow prodded.

Bret didn't cave on the harassment as Crusow hoped. Their packs were stuffed with rope and rappelling harnesses. Crusow brought a small amount of water and even some food along for energy. With the cold and the moving around in this fur, a man could burn hundreds of calories per hour out there. For good measure he also brought a firelog of compressed wood, an insurance policy if something went wrong and they had to wait on Mark and Kung.

They reached the edge of the gulch; Crusow wondered why they called it that and not a cliff. He leaned over the steep lip and looked down, flipping on his headlamp. Visibility was about thirty feet below the edge—they would be blind most of the way down.

"I'd feel safer tying up to the Sno-Cat for the climb down instead of pounding ice anchors for a top rope," Bret said to Crusow with some concern in his voice.

"That'd be a great idea if she wasn't nearly out of juice. It would cost us a quarter-gallon of diesel to get the Sno-Cat started, warmed up, and moved over to the edge. Plus, we don't know how stable the ice is out here. We could end up falling into that abyss with the Cat chasing us down to the bottom."

With that, they began hammering their top rope anchors into the solid ice. Three anchors per line were secured in different areas to reduce the chance of losing a line. With all anchors secured, both Crusow and Bret threw their lines out over the edge. They could hear the line slap and tumble down the face. They had a difficult time getting the harnesses out of their packs as their Arctic gloves diminished their dexterity. It was like trying to open a door with your elbows. The wind picked up as the two slipped on their harnesses. They checked each other over, ensuring that their gear was secure for the trip down. Crusow yanked off his snow shoes and tied them to his pack with a bit of cordage. He then clamped the sharp steel snow spikes to his boots and stomped a shelf of ice to see that they were fastened tight.

Crusow reached for the Motorola radio in his coat, fumbling for the transmit button. "Mark, me and Bret are about to start heading down. It'll probably take about thirty minutes or more to get to the bottom and get set up, over."

Crusow was accustomed to the HF radio and caught himself closing the transmission by saying *over* instead of just letting the automated beep do the job.

Mark keyed his radio. "Roger that, man. Kung and I are at the dog paddock and we're prepping them now. We'll throw down fresh ropes when you say the word. Our end will be attached to the dogs, your end to the . . . you know. I don't think we should use the ropes you just rigged to pull them up."

"Why not? They'll already be down here."

"Because the dogs might weaken your anchor points or the friction over the ice could fray the ropes. Bad day if that happens."

"Good point, thanks. Okay, we're headed down. Talk soon."

Mark doubled-clicked the transmit button in acknowledgment.

Crusow didn't risk his life out of want; things had degraded into dire need. If they could not harvest enough body fat from the corpses below, they would never reach thin ice. Fuel was more valuable than water in this harsh, frozen world.

Crusow reached down to his sides to make sure his tools were secured tightly. Even though his gloves were too thick to feel the texture, just knowing his twelve-inch stag Bowie knife was safe in the leather sheath on his hip made him feel somewhat better. It did any job he asked of it, every time.

"You ready, Bret?"

"Yeah, I'm ready."

"Let's go."

They leaned over the edge, paying out slack, and down they went into the void of Clear Conscience Gulch, one of many graveyards of man.

24

Kil sat in his stateroom reading a book. *Tunnel in the Sky* by Robert Heinlein. John had passed him a copy before he boarded the helicopter and told him not to lose it. He remembered that John had an extra copy of the book, identical cover and all. Kil had been immersed in the novel since he learned the fate of Oahu, as it was an escape from what the mission might be up against. It was a tale of a group of young students, dropped off in a strange land, trying to survive. The scenario depicted in the book was bad, just not nearly as bleak as what Kil saw during his time in exile after the helicopter crash. He reached up to feel the scar on his head as he thought about this for a moment between paragraphs.

Saien was beneath Kil's rack in the bunk below playing solitaire with an old deck of Afghanistan's Most Wanted playing cards on top of his sheets. Saien had made efforts to absorb the happenings onboard since his arrival. He told Kil that he'd never thought he would find himself a member of the crew of a fast-attack nuclear-powered submarine, and he'd even taken on work during his time onboard, standing engineering watches. He wasn't responsible for much, just to monitor gauges to make sure they were inside normal parameters. This allowed some of the overworked engineers to get some much-needed sleep and also made him a few friends in the process. He wasn't just the awkward and out-of-place foreigner anymore.

Kil turned the page to the next chapter and lost his grip on the paperback, dropping it to the deck below. He swung one leg over the side of his bunk, then he heard Saien.

"I'll get it, Kil."

"Thanks."

Picking up the novel, Saien took a glance at the synopsis on the back before handing it to Kil.

"Why the hell are you reading about this, man? You crazy? Have you not lived this long enough?"

"I know we've been underway for a while but are you already getting cranky, Saien? We aren't even close to getting a beer day."

"What's a beer day?" Saien asked.

"It's when you've been underway so long you get to drink a couple beers."

"I don't drink, so I don't care. How about a fresh air and sunlight day?"

"Sorry, Saien, they don't have those on these boats, I'm afraid. I'll put in a request to the captain for you if you want," Kil said, laughing.

"Thanks. I hope you dream about those creatures tonight."

Kil ignored Saien's hexing and went back to reading his book. After five pages, Saien interrupted.

"Sorry, I didn't mean that. I don't really want you to dream about those things tonight. That wasn't nice. I'm just not familiar with these conditions."

"Don't worry about it, man. We all get cabin fever. It's just how things roll onboard the boat."

"Cabin fever? Never mind. I was thinking about what you told me, what the captain mentioned to you about our next destination," Saien said.

"Yeah, what about it?"

"Well, it's been exploded to bits by a nuke. You and I both know what that means. There may be hundreds of thousands of those things running around there. Yes, Kil, I did mean *running*."

"I don't like it any more than you. You and I are consultants, and so far I've been doing just that. I made my case to the captain, but this is his boat. I personally think he's crazy for even thinking about making landfall in Hawaii. If it were my decision, I'd pick one of the smaller non-radiated islands and order all surviving warships to set course for it. We could secure it and start over. The surviving leadership doesn't agree, so here we are, onboard a floating nuclear reactor heading for a nuked paradise, facing nuked corpse armies."

Saien looked up at Kil with a tinge of disdain on his face. "Now it is you that will give me the nightmares I cursed you to endure. Stupid pig eater."

Kil laughed at Saien and leaned back down to continue reading his book. "Just don't make any noises crying for help—I'm trying to read up here."

A hard thud on his mattress from below indicated Saien's acknowledgment.

25

Friendships were no longer forged via social networks; they were not born in churches, at parties, or during happy hours. Staying in touch in this time of undead reign harkened back to the dawn of radio. A handful of families still survived, those prescient few that had prepared for calamity. Unfortunately, none had prepared for anything resembling the current state of affairs. Most were concerned about terrorist attacks or financial collapse—a source of mainstream hysteria right before the dead started to walk. Europe and the Middle East were ablaze with civil unrest. The euro had already collapsed; the streets of Spain, France, Ireland, and even Britain were among those littered with police barricades and burning cars, even before the undead filled them.

The survivors huddled quietly in their boarded-over or underground shelters or hidey-holes in Idaho and other non-radioactive places. They tuned their shortwave radios to any frequency that still carried signal—any sound or modulated static that might give temporary reprieve from the permanent terror they endured. This was the new normal.

The majority of the dwindling living U.S. population didn't enjoy the safety of life onboard an aircraft carrier or inside a strategic nuclear missile silo—they lived in attics, abandoned FEMA centers, prisons, rural cell-phone tower perimeter fences, small coastal islands, and even boats. Some even tried their luck in abandoned rail cars or banks on the outskirts of what was once civilization. From handheld walkie-talkies to citizens band radios to HAMs, they attempted contact with each other, with anyone.

Every now and then, it was established, even if only for a fleeting moment—sometimes the sound heard over the airwaves was splintering wood or screams or the sound of a lonely gunshot. The last social networks were falling, node by node.

USS *George Washington*

John was now considered the official USS *George Washington* communications officer, bestowed full access to the ship's communications arrays. He had a small contingent of civilians and junior enlisted to keep the ship's meager capabilities up and running. His primary orders were to maintain secure over-the-horizon contact with Task Force Hourglass due off the coast of Hawaii in five days. His secondary mission was to keep a secure laptop SATcom link with Task Force Phoenix, embedded at Hotel 23.

He'd been informed that TF Phoenix's main objectives were to secure the remaining nuke and attempt to salvage some of the Remote Six airdrops. On top of his duties as the ship's communications officer, John had been dubbed caucus leader by the Hotel 23 survivors, a title he tried to downplay, but secretly loved.

John made his rounds daily, checking on Tara, Laura, Jan, Will, Dean, Danny, the marines, and others whom he had befriended during his time at Hotel 23. Annabelle, his Italian Greyhound, was still at his side happy and content when Laura wasn't borrowing her. Her hackles had not risen since she evacuated on the helicopter under the death grip of little Laura. Laura told John that she was *sooooooo afraid* that she would drop "Annie"—that's what Laura called her. It was sometimes inconvenient letting her out to do her business, walking all the way down to the hangar bay, where a dog-loving crewmember laid sod over some topsoil for the animals onboard. Annabelle wasn't the only shipboard canine. A few military working dogs found their new home on the *Washington,* treating Annabelle like one of their own, as they sensed who the common enemy really was. Any of the undead on the mainland would take down a dog and reduce it to a wet mess if the chance was presented.

John had no shortage of irons in the fire, but there was room for more, he thought. One of his enlisted men, Petty Officer Shure, was a particularly good radio operator. He was having regular luck making contact with Arctic Outpost Four. Last communication was about their fuel supply status and plans to expand it. The rumor going around the radio shack was that the Arctic outpost survivors were actually planning to refine biofuel from the frozen undead they had previously killed and discarded down a cliff, leaving them to freeze solid in the Arctic ice last spring and fall. John had been present during the transmission and knew it was no rumor. The admiral asked that he keep that information confidential; the admiral didn't fancy the prospect of talk circulating around about their Arctic friends behaving like mad butchers. It was too reminiscent of Kil's debriefing after his return from the crash; he had run into a band of cannibals that were using the undead as food—actually cooking rotting flesh—somehow neutralizing whatever caused the things to reanimate in the first place.

The shortwave radio link between the *Washington* and USS *Virginia*/Task Force Hourglass was becoming very unreliable. The ship's SATcom worked fine, but many of the satellites required to bounce the signal back to the Gulf of Mexico footprint had already burned up in reentry, their orbits left to decay without National Reconnaissance Office support and orbital adjustment. The SATcom birds that still functioned in orbit were operating under access codes that no one had, or knew how to get. Shortwave was the main game in town for the military and the rest of the surviving populace.

John called a long overdue but impromptu meeting in the radio room. In attendance were all of his enlisted communicators as well as the civilian HAM operators who had volunteered their knowledge of shortwave communications.

The purpose of the meeting was simple—to establish and improve on the communications plan. John rolled up the projector mat that concealed his white board and began listing all priority circuits and their individual statuses.

> *Actively maintained circuits in order of precedence:*
> *Secure HF voice circuit with TF Hourglass—PMC*
> *Secure HF teletype circuit with Nevada facility*
>   *(UKN)—FMC*
> *Secure SATcom burst circuit with TF Phoenix—FMC*
> *Non-secure HF voice circuit with Arctic Outpost*
>   *Four—PMC*

"Now, as you can see here on the board, we have some problems to solve," he began. "Our top priority circuit is only operating in a partially mission capable, or PMC, status. We have been unable to reach Task Force Hourglass for some time now. We're going to have to offset this problem. Any ideas?"

One of the HAM radio operators in the back of the room spoke up. "We could try a relay."

"That's not a bad idea at all," John said, returning to the whiteboard.

Picking up his black marker, he drew an out-of-scale map of the world, outlining where the different task forces were operating and where the other facilities were roughly located.

"Task Force Phoenix is a no-go. They don't have HF capability up and working. They're using a discreet burst SATcom transceiver with a laptop configuration to send the text to that terminal over there." He pointed his hand at the corner where an operator was monitoring the two-entity mIRC chat room. "Besides, Phoenix can't transmit during the day and is under strict emission control conditions anyway. They won't be transmitting unless absolutely necessary. I'm not privy to what is going on in Nevada. Those circuits pipe directly into a KG-84C crypto box sitting in this ship's signals exploitation space. They only call down here to have us check our patch cables and recycle crypto for their circuits. Those two circuits are out of the running for any relay help. This leaves only one viable option: Outpost Four. I've been listening to the shortwave spectrum and our choices are limited. Rarely do we receive any shortwave coming from the mainland, just some troposcatter bounce and old news relays playing in a loop, probably up on solar power."

The HAM spoke up again. "We can adjust our frequencies for time of year. Use the higher frequencies during the day and the lower frequencies at night. The old sun up, freq up rule. Might have more luck."

"Now we're getting somewhere," John replied. "Let's get a solid plan on paper and in a few hours during our next scheduled contact with Outpost Four, we'll drop the request. Hopefully they have enough manpower left up there to help us out with our relay. One thing to keep in mind is that the outpost is in darkness and will be for some time. I'm not sure how this might affect the frequencies."

Petty Officer Shure, John's sharpest enlisted man, raised his hand.

"Yes, what's on your mind?"

"Well, right now we're using our KYV-5 crypto boxes to go secure voice with Hourglass. How are we going to relay sensitive data over shortwave to Hourglass and back using the Arctic station as the middleman?"

"We're going to have to go old school and use paper encryption and onetime pads," said John.

"No one remembers how to do that, boss. The last real radioman in the navy that could do that probably retired twenty years ago. We're a bunch of IT computer geeks."

"We're going to have to relearn the lost communications knowledge and forget what's advanced since it's become obsolete. You all have your marching orders—let's make it happen."

The small crowd dispersed, all except those who manned a radio watch station. John pondered for a moment as people began to clear out of the space. Walking back over into tech control where all the circuits were patched, he thought to himself, *We issue the crypto to SSES, so how hard could it be?* The theory floating around in his mind was not one of complexity. In the span of minutes, he figured out how to access the circuit that was fed directly into the SSES from the still-active facilities in Nevada. He would splice the encrypted circuit and run one splice to SSES and run the other splice through his extra KG-84C encryption device loaded with the same crypto that SSES used—crypto that his office had issued.

He would tell no one, as the penalty for network intrusion at this level would be swift and severe. He rationalized it by telling himself that he wasn't doing it to satisfy childlike curiosity—he was doing it for Kil.

26

Somewhere Inside the Arctic Circle

"Slow down!" screamed Crusow.

"What's the fucking problem? We're a hundred feet in the air above a sharp ice floe. I don't want to slow down. I want to get off this goddamned rope!" Bret yelled over the wind whipping through the darkness.

"Take it slow, you're going too fast. You break your leg or arm, the dogs will be pulling you up the side of this face at their speed, not yours."

The men descended somewhat slower now. The snow curled in horizontal whirlwinds against the ice face. Their spikes dug deep into the ice as they walked backward, traveling deeper. They wore green glow sticks attached to their ankles via the elastic material sewn into their cold-weather pants. They didn't want to risk using their headlamps just yet as the battery supply at Outpost Four was running low with no chance of replenishment.

Crusow thought about the fire log in his pack and how it was so damn dark that they might actually need it to see. He tried to think about little details like this but the real subject on his mind was the dead below. He counted them in his head. He thought there might be about ten, maybe fifteen of them, most of them overweight—two of them three-hundred pounders. Fat was real energy and if done right, with the right chemical additives, one could convert those stored food calories to combustible liquid fuel. He thought about what they might look like and what they might—

"Watch where you're swinging!" Bret whined loudly. Crusow accidentally banged into him during his short daymare about the dead. *Focus, Crusow,* he chanted to himself.

They descended slowly for well over one hundred feet. Neither of them knew for sure if that was the real depth, though; they just knew that the ropes were longer than the gulch was deep—at least that's what Franky had told them last spring when he rappelled down the face at the other side of the outpost. The other face was higher.

Now Crusow and Bret approached Franky's final resting place at the bottom of the gulch. Crusow remembered that night. One of the researchers—Charles, Crusow thought his name was—had died of diabetic complications in his sleep and woke up hungry. He tore Franky's throat out before both were shut down by an ice axe to the head and tossed down into the abyss below.

"How much longer you think it is?" Bret asked.

"It's over two hundred feet, or somewhere thereabouts, from top to bottom. I'd say we're now probably close to it."

Just as Crusow finished talking, his feet hit the beginning of the bottom. The ice face lost its vertical grade and began to incrementally angle out away from the wall. The grade continued to angle farther out until both men walked backward down a steep but manageable hill.

"Found one," Crusow said.

"Where?"

"You're standing on its chest."

"Shit!" Bret exclaimed, jumping to the side, nearly tumbling down the hill.

The outline of what was once a man lay half buried in the ice, its face glowing green by the shine of Bret's chemlight. It was Franky. The body was twisted and broken from the fall, and the gash in his head from Crusow's axe could clearly be seen just above the forehead.

"I'm still sorry about that, Franky," Crusow said loud enough for Bret to hear.

"Sorry for what? That thing wasn't human when you killed it."

"You may be right, and you may be wrong, but I'm still sorry."

They both paused and looked at Franky for a moment before Bret broke the silence.

"How many we bringing up, Crusow?"

"All of them. I'll start digging Franky out of the ice and you start looking for the others farther down."

"Roger," Bret said, fading into the darkness deeper down the angled ice face.

Crusow checked his gloves to make sure the drawstrings were tight. He didn't want any exposed skin while swinging his axe. Although he tried not to look at Franky's corpse, he found himself fixated on its gaping mouth filled with red ice. He forced back laughter when he thought of Han Solo frozen in carbonite. Franky's forearms were protruding in front, perpendicular to its body, as if frozen during struggle. Crusow began to hack carefully at the ice that gripped the corpse. He did so for minutes, missing on occasion, knocking frozen flesh bits into the white powder around his dim sphere of green. Crusow didn't have a weak stomach, but the thought of butchering Franky made him sick enough to take a short break. He pulled the radio out of his vest pocket where it was tied to a button hole to keep it secure if dropped. Hanging at an awkward angle, he turned it on with his teeth.

"Mark, we're down here, man. Bret is at the bottom and I'm about fifteen feet above him cutting Franky out of the ice."

"Franky? Hardcore, man. How does he—"

"Don't ask, man. Just don't."

"Okay, well, Kung is at the dog paddock and I'm above you at the ledge. The dogs are rigged and we are geared up. I think the most we should lift at once is two or three bodies."

"Yeah, I think so, too. Looks like we'll be down here for a couple hours. My temp says fifty-five below. That's warm for this time of year." Crusow thought he could hear Mark laughing in response from the ledge above. "In a bit, I'm going to flash my headlamp and you mark the spot on the ledge so you know not to drop them on us. Might hurt from up there."

"Okay, Crusow, we won't drop 'em until you say it's cool."

"All right, talk soon. Out."

A double click on the transmitter indicated Mark understood the plan. Crusow called out to Bret.

"Bret, where are you? Find any?"

A faint voice cut through the wind. "Yeah, I found three. Chopping them out. It's fucked up."

"I know. Let's pile them in one spot. Careful to stay away from their mouths or anything sharp," Crusow yelled out to Bret below.

"No shit, Captain Obvious."

Prick, Crusow thought.

After a few more minutes, Crusow swung his axe down and dislodged the last piece of ice holding Franky to the steep face. The corpse slid down the hill for two or three seconds before hitting something with a thud.

"Goddamn it, Crusow! That was close."

"Sorry, where is it?"

"It hit the pile," Bret replied bitterly.

"Well, that's good then. How many are piled up now?"

"Four, including that one," Bret said as if somehow it mattered that he had gathered more corpses than Crusow. "Listen, I'm getting cold. We're gonna be down here for a bit and we have enough bodies to call down the ropes and rig a few to go up. Why don't we use that fire log I saw you put in your pack and warm up a bit?"

"I was going to save it until we really needed it, but all right, I'm coming down."

Crusow descended another fifteen feet before the face leveled out to the point that he didn't need to be in a harness. Clicking out of the carabiner, he walked over to the glow of Bret's chemlights.

"I'm switching on my lamp for a sec."

Crusow flipped the red filter over his light lens and switched on the LED. He could see the half-naked corpses piled on the snow as if the creatures were frozen while playing Twister. *Goddamn that's sick,* Crusow thought as he dropped his pack onto the ice.

He placed the fire log on the ice. Crusow moved over to the corpses to scavenge a makeshift fire mat. He didn't want the log sinking into the ice, putting itself out. One of the corpses in the pile wore a pair of house shoes. He couldn't recognize the face, probably crushed by the fall. He pried the shoes from the corpse and placed them underneath the log. Crusow started the fire quite easily despite the snow and wind that bore down on them. The bright light from the small fire burned patterns into his sight.

Crusow turned to Bret. "Okay, we dig, pile them here, and take shifts resting, sound good?"

"None of this sounds good," Bret said as he stood up and began the search for more bodies.

Crusow used the time to stand near the fire and warm his extremities. The temperature out here would kill you in a few hours, even when wearing cold-weather gear. The heat would slowly slink out of you and soon your core temperature would creep below ninety-five degrees into hypothermic levels, causing shakes, confusion, fatigue, and eventually death.

The radio crackled. "Crusow, you guys getting close to being ready for the first run? I think I see a fire down there."

Crusow pulled the radio from his pocket. "Yeah, Mark. We're freezing solid down here. Needed the fire. Tie a chem stick to the end of the ropes and throw 'em down. I'll let Bret know they're on the way. Give me thirty seconds before you drop."

"Okay, you got it."

Putting the radio back in his pocket he called out, "Bret, the ropes are coming. Get back to the fire so you don't get hit."

There was no response.

"Bret, you out there?"

Faintly—over the wind—Crusow could hear Bret's voice.

"I'm okay, drop the rope. Be back to the fire in a minute. Almost got one."

Crusow looked up in enough time to see the three green chemlights phase into view as they plummeted toward him. They hit the snow near where he'd dug out Franky and slid down the face fifteen feet off to his left.

Keying the radio, Crusow said, "I see them. Going to grab them and pull the slack over to the bodies and tie them up."

"Okay, man, just pick three light bodies for the trial run. Don't hook up any heavies, all right?"

"No worries there, mate. Three corpsicles coming up to you in ten minutes."

Mark was a dog lover, which was why he asked Crusow to make the first trip a light one. He didn't want the dogs to get hurt pulling the weight.

Crusow swung his axe, slamming it into the ice, climbing up the face to the ropes. He grabbed the bitter ends of the rope and tossed the slack down. Back at the pile, he tied the three bodies using a bowline under their arms, carefully avoiding their mouths even though their brains were destroyed. He could feel the warmth of the fire and was happy he'd thought to bring the fire log. Just as he'd finished securing the bodies, Bret was returning, dragging a corpse through the ice behind him by the tip of his axe.

"Mark, you there?"

"Yeah, I'm up here. Kung is on the sled. You ready?"

"Yeah, three bodies secured to the ropes. Go ahead and pull 'em up."

"Okay, say good-bye."

"Very funny, Mark."

"I try."

Five seconds later, both Crusow and Bret could hear the ropes take slack and slap against the ice face. The bodies began their journey up the sheer face and slowly out of view. The corpses seemed to move on the ropes as if some great spider had slung massive webs, pulling the bodies up into its spindly legs.

"My turn to warm up. Another fifteen minutes digging those bone sacks and I'd be looking at frostbite."

Crusow nodded, leaving the safety and security of the small but warm fire. Even with the fire's radiant energy, the area around it remained frigid. Nonetheless, the fire helped to ward off the creeping death of the Arctic. As Crusow moved away from Bret and the fire, the temperature plummeted quickly, a reminder of where he was. He removed the ice axe from its sheath, gripping it tightly in his gloved hand. He moved into the darkness for a bit, seeing nothing. Crusow peeked over his shoulder back at the fire—only a pinpoint of light now—deciding it best to turn on his headlamp and find more bodies. He was far from the cliff face; the ground transitioned from hard ice to snow. He pondered whether or not he needed to retrieve his snowshoes hanging on his pack, back at the fire. After a few more meters, the snow was much deeper. He was far away from the face and the fire. *Time to turn around; I'm too far,* he thought.

He turned and started to walk back to the fire and tripped over a leg, falling to the snow. He lay there for a while and lost track of time.

He looked up and caught a glimpse of a break in the clouds above. The vastness of the Milky Way peeked through the overcast sky for a moment, bright and majestic.

The cold eventually jolted Crusow out of his meditative state and he sat up. He realized his headlamp was still on, and panned it over to the body part he'd tripped over. He began the laborious work of removing the corpse from the ice. Crusow hacked and hacked until the half-naked thing was free from the ice. He dug his axe into the creature's armpit, wrapping the paracord tether around his wrist, and began to make his way back to the firelight, dragging the miserable block of muscle, fat, and bone behind. The light grew larger as he slogged toward the makeshift corpse camp.

How long was I gone? he thought.

The body was heavy and the thin paracord hurt his wrist even through the thick anti-exposure gear. He was fifty yards out when he saw the green glow of chem sticks. Crusow wasn't sure if Mark had sent the rope down again, or if the glow belonged to Bret's stick.

He called out to Bret for help with the heavy corpse.

The wind howled. *He can't hear me.*

Crusow would need to drag it a little farther. The body was heavy, probably two hundred and fifty pounds. Forty yards out he could see Bret, still standing near the fire. It looked like he held one of the creatures upright as if inspecting its condition. At twenty-five yards, Crusow called out again. This time Bret responded.

"Bret, this fucker weighs a ton. Drop that thing and help me pull this to the pile."

Bret slowly turned to face Crusow. The frozen creature that should have fallen to the ice did not—it remained upright. Crusow stepped back, turning up his headlamp to the brightest setting. Bret's throat and face were torn open, and his Adam's apple lay flapping to the side. Bret's eyes—not yet milky from death—locked on Crusow, and his undead body moved forward.

Crusow reacted, yanking off his left glove, grabbing for his Bowie knife. With the Bowie in his left hand, and the ice axe in his right, he went for the thing that was once Bret. The searing cold shocked his exposed hand as it gripped the frozen stag handle of the Bowie. Using his large knife to keep the creature at a distance, he came down with the ice axe like a great thunder god. He dug deep into the creature's left shoulder, spattering fresh blood to the ice below. The creature, feeling nothing, attempted to grasp Crusow with its right hand but could not gain purchase; it still wore the thick Arctic gloves. Crusow reamed the axe free from the creature's shoulder and tried again, this time swinging the axe on a haymaker trajectory. The blade penetrated the temple, immediately and forever switching off whatever synapse lights remained in Bret's brain.

The creature collapsed, and the momentum pulled the embedded axe—along with Crusow—down to the ice. Snow from the impact flung up into Crusow's face, blurring his vision. His left hand was frozen around his Bowie knife when he saw the other undead creature approach. With his axe embedded deep into Bret's temple, Crusow had to engage his attacker with his knife. There was no time to de-glove and switch hands. Crusow stood up quickly and moved in, slashing and pushing the terrible thing back away from the fire.

As Crusow's vision cleared, he saw evidence of what had gone down. The thing's brain was obviously intact, the fire warming it enough to thaw its long-dead appendages. As he parried with the wraithlike thing, he noticed no evidence of head trauma; only a small bullet hole in its chest told the story of the creature's original demise. *Must have been early on, before we knew for sure,* Crusow thought.

The half-frozen creature lurched forward—mostly naked—flailing about in tighty-whiteys. Crusow slashed at the creature's chest, digging in deep enough to feel the frozen flesh at its core. The Bowie was razor sharp, a gift from his father twenty years ago on his fifteenth birthday.

A dull knife is far more dangerous to its owner than a razor-sharp blade, Crusow recalled his father preach time and again over the years.

With his numb left hand, he thrust forward into the naked creature's eye. It wailed in protest as Crusow shoved the blade deep through the splitting eye socket, striking the back of the skull with force. Lights out. Bret's killer took Crusow's weapon to the ice with it.

Though there were no more undead foes hiding in the darkness, Crusow began to panic. At the very least, he always had his knife for protection. He frantically went for the precious Bowie, bracing his boot on the creature's head, giving him leverage as he yanked it from the skull. He cleaned the blade as best he could, stropping it on the creature before sliding the heirloom back into its custom leather home.

With his anxiety and feelings of defenselessness temporarily abated, he sat down on the ice, warming his numb left hand on the flickering fire. He would need to rig two more loads of bodies before beginning his dog-powered climb back to Outpost Four.

With Bret gone, Crusow planned to strip his corpse and leave him down here at the bottom of the gulch. He didn't have it in him to butcher Bret for fuel, and didn't really think anyone else would be up to the task either.

He clumsily took the radio from his pocket and keyed the transmit button while he looked up into the sky, toward the top of the gulch. "Mark, we have a situation here."

There was no answer.

Crusow's fear swiftly returned. His thoughts ran wild about the creatures that Mark and Kung pulled topside on the first load. Ice-climbing the sheer face in front of him would be a death sentence without a top rope. *What if their brains were not completely destroyed, like the thing that tore Bret's up? What if—*

The radio crackled. "This is Mark, what's going on, you okay?"

"No, man, I'm pretty damn far from that. Bret's dead. One of the frozen things down here killed him. I had to finish the job."

Mark keyed his radio but said nothing for a few seconds. "Uh, how in the . . . I'm sorry. Are you okay, man? You ain't bit, are you?"

Crusow blasted back, "No! Let's just get these things up topside. I'll explain it to everyone when I get back. Let's just get the job done. I'll strip Bret, throw his shit in his pack, and send his gear up with two more bodies. The temperature is dropping and I can only handle another hour or so down here. That's enough time for two more loads, not counting myself."

"Okay, I'll radio Larry and tell him to have some tea and hot soup ready. He'll need it, too; he ain't getting any better. Listen, I know this isn't the right time to bring this up with what happened to Bret and all, but we have a request for support from the ship."

"I can't imagine we'd be able to do much of anything for them. We'll talk about it topside. One more thing," Crusow said.

"Go ahead?"

"Don't get those bodies near heat unless you're damn sure they're full-on dead, got me?"

"Yeah, I got you. We'll make sure."

Crusow began to follow his plan, checking all the bodies at the bottom for head trauma before sending them up the sheer ice face to Mark. He gave most of them a hard chop to the head for good measure, taking out some anger on them. Still deeply shaken, his hands vibrated almost uncontrollably as he rigged the bodies and Bret's kit to the ropes. It was nothing a half dozen rations of whiskey wouldn't fix. Bret wouldn't mind.

One day from paradise.

We will have Oahu in sight tomorrow evening. Hard to believe I have been writing in this journal since the beginning. Sometimes I go back to the first pages, because on those pages are remnants, hints of what things were like before. Sometimes I need to remind myself of how things were so that I can hold on to some of it. It would seem foolish to most.

Saien and I have decided that we like it better when the submarine is submerged. The damn waves knock the hell out of the boat, rocking us back and forth as if we were sitting in a kayak during a hurricane. One of the crew members tells me that submarines were not designed to cruise on the surface, their shape is not conducive to surface stability. We surface only when we need to transmit on shortwave, which is daily, sometimes twice per day.

I've put in some time in the radio shack and have been successful at establishing comms with the flagship and John on occasion. John told me yesterday via shortwave that another station might be coming on line to help with relays, somewhere in the Arctic. He'll pass a frequency list and schedule soon.

We have a complement of Scan Eagle UAVs onboard and will be launching them tomorrow to recon the island before the team goes in; that is, after the techs set up the launch and recovery gear. I've spent a combined one hour in the same room as the SEALs and don't even know their names. Don't really care either. They stick to themselves, go to the gym, eat, and hang out exclusively, like a fraternity. They seem to look down their noses at Saien and barely notice I'm here. Probably just another officer getting in the way as far as they are concerned. I can't say that I envy them going feet dry in Oahu. I think the plan is to patrol the island coast and park the boat off the North Shore. From that point, the team will ingress along Highway 99 to Wheeler Army Airfield and then to the Kunia facility, where they'll secure it, bring up the systems, and drop off the resident expert before exfiltrating to the sub. Two days of operations sitting off the coast of Oahu, then we're headed farther west to Chinese waters.

Maximum pull-ups: 8
Push-ups: 68
1.5 mile treadmill run: 11:15

27

"They're back," Hawse told Disco as he reached for his M-4.

Although he was pretty sure it was Doc and Billy, Hawse didn't take a chance. While escaping Washington, D.C., he'd witnessed the undead open doors and climb stairs.

Hawse was the only special operator to make it off the North Lawn alive. He vividly recalled the day he'd escaped.

Hawse had been forced to go full auto on White House grounds, fighting waves of creatures, clearing the way for the vice president and first lady to escape to the helicopter. He shot everything he had from the door of *Marine Two,* just before the dead toppled the black iron perimeter fences and overran the White House. Flying over D.C. with some of the last remnants of national command authority, he looked upon the nation's capital for the last time.

The creatures looked like maggots crawling over cars and through houses, over the corpse of D.C. Weeks before the creatures took the North Lawn, FEMA had raised the Woodrow Wilson drawbridge and demolished the other links that spanned the Potomac, cutting off Virginia from D.C. and Maryland. Despite these extreme initiatives, the anomaly eventually crossed the Potomac. From the affluent homes in Northern Virginia to the ghettos of Suitland, Maryland, the undead reigned. No more Republicans, Democrats, or other ineffective factions. The politics of death ruled America now. Virginians fared far better than those in Maryland; the draconian gun laws in place before the anomaly assured Maryland's quick decimation. The dead were gifted the benefit of so-called gun-free zones, the same benefit that lunatic gunmen and thugs enjoyed before the undead walked the streets.

Doc and Billy were now at the door, bringing Hawse back to reality.

Hawse held his carbine up to the low ready as the door wheel spun around from the other side to the open position.

"What's the secret pass phrase?"

"Fuck you, Hawse," Doc said, stepping through the door to the control center.

"Correct, you may enter," Hawse pronounced with a terribly fake British accent.

Both Hawse and Disco noticed the extra gear the returning men packed in.

"Well? What happened out there? Sun is coming up in an hour—we were starting to get a little punchy in here thinking about going out there after you two assholes."

"We missed you too, ol' chap," Doc said in his own horrible fake accent.

Doc and Billy debriefed the other two on the happenings on the way to the drop, including the mile-long undead river that flowed beneath them on the overpass.

"You guys must have had to change your diapers after that one," Disco said.

Billy was never much of a talker—when he had something to say the team listened. "I've never seen so many in one place. This was worse than New Orleans. You weren't there for that, Disco. You never knew Hammer, we lost him there. Good operator. One lapse in noise discipline and me and Doc would be part of the river right now, coming for you." As usual, there was no emotion in Billy's voice, but the words hit their intended target.

"What's that gear all about?" Disco asked, changing the subject.

Doc pulled the documentation from his leg pocket and tossed it at Disco as he began his explanation. "It's sort of like that crowd control foam that they were going to give us in Afghanistan before the shit hit the fan. The only difference is that this stuff cures to concrete hardness in a couple seconds, instead of just being sticky. There is a compound that *de-cures* the foam, and here it is." Doc held the bottle of clear liquid up so everyone could see.

"What are we going to do with it?" Hawse asked. "I guess I mean, what good is it? What can it do that my M-4 won't?"

"Can your M-4 stop a hundred of those fucks in less than ten seconds and create a concrete wall of bodies in the process?" Doc said.

"Well, if it works. I don't want to be the one in front of a swarm trying this thing out for the first time," Hawse added.

Billy glanced down, checking the action on his M-4, and said, "I hope we don't have to use it at all. Doubt it would have stopped that river we saw. Maybe slowed it down."

The words set in with Hawse for a few moments before anyone spoke.

"What's the plan now, Doc? From the sounds of things, it took all night and a near-death experience to bring back a gadget that we might never use," Disco said.

"You may be right, but me and Billy grabbed some intel from the drop that we'll all need to analyze. There was documentation in the equipment boxes and another drop map that we can cross-reference with the one we have. My point is that we got more than the gadget."

Doc pulled the recovered documents from an outside zipper pocket on his pack. "I've only had a second to look at this stuff, but check this out."

Doc pointed to a map with a transparent overlay showing all the previously executed drops. "When you compare this new map to ours, we see some pretty big differences. This new map has quite a few more local drops listed than the one we jumped in with. There seem to be a couple places within twenty klicks, mostly north of Hotel 23. Disco, you and Billy send the SITREP to the ship. We only have a few minutes before sunup. Make it happen."

"You got it, boss man," said Hawse.

Hawse and Billy left the conversation and headed over to the SATcom burst terminal to transmit a short report on last night's mission.

Doc continued, "So when we look at the date stamp of both maps, we see that the drop we reconned last night happened right before the noise device was dropped on Hotel 23. So the question remains: Why would the same organization that brought a swarm down on Hotel 23 drop a prototype weapon that could be effective, at least short term, against a swarm?"

"I'm not sure we'll ever find out or if it even matters at this point," Hawse said, placing the map back down on the desk.

"It may not matter, but these maps can tell us something. The drops seem to occur around the same time of day every time. If the aircraft that drops the gear takes off at the same time from the same airfield for every sortie, we might be able to find the originating airfield, at least within a few hundred miles using some basic math, a map of the U.S., and a straight edge."

"SITREP transmitted, boss," Disco said.

"That was quick."

"Well, I only say what needs to be said. They'll ask a dozen questions no matter what I send. Might as well put the basic SITREP down and wait on the flood of questions. I shut down the circuit though. Don't want any RF tempest leaks giving us away."

"Good call," Doc said. "We've been lucky so far, but don't count on that to last. The next item on our checklist is to spin up that nuke, run the diagnostic program, and make sure we're ready for the new coordinates. Don't ask because I don't even know where they'll be."

"What if they're U.S. coordinates?" Hawse asked seriously.

"Depends on the target. I hope they're not, but if they are, we'll cross that bridge when we come to it."

Hawse briefly thought of the Constitution, displayed in its bulletproof case in downtown D.C., surrounded by the undead.

28

USS George Washington

They were closing fast. Danny attempted escape by scurrying under the air circulator in a large fan room; he wasn't sure exactly where, as things were foggy and seemed to move at an odd pace. The creatures were unrelenting and pursued with determination. Danny's knees were raw and bloody; it seemed to him that he had been crawling for miles.

He felt the cold grip of death on his heels. The creature's meatless claw closed around his foot and squeezed like a vice. Danny could no longer move forward; the thing was dragging him back for the kill. A peculiar-looking rat watched him with glowing red eyes from a dark corner.

Danny thrashed, screaming loudly, saving himself from the landscape of nightmares—the clutches of the sandman.

Someone shook him, tugging him the rest of the way back to reality, to the safety and security of a grandmother's arms.

"Danny, wake up, hon. You're dreaming, just dreaming. Wake up."

Danny struggled under his blanket until sure it was his grandmother that had him.

"They're on the ship, Granny!" Danny exclaimed, still visibly shaken from the nightmare.

"No, hon, they're not onboard. They're far away on land. We're safe—just try to calm down and breathe."

"Granny, I heard them before. I was on the back of the ship, hiding. I heard them," Danny said, sobbing.

"No, honey, they're not here. Just calm down and try to go back to sleep," Dean said, petting down Danny's cowlick.

"Yes they are, I know what they sound like. I remember. I remember the water tower. I remember Mom, Dad—"

A knock on the door interrupted Danny before he could go down that dark road of memory. Dean tucked him back in bed, kissed him on the forehead, and went to the door. She cracked it to see who was calling at such a late hour. Tara stood outside in her nightgown.

"Is everything all right, Dean? I heard Danny."

"Yes, another nightmare. He's had them for over a week now and I don't know what to do."

"Can I help?"

"No, it's all right. Thank you for offering. He'll just have to work through it. He really believes they're onboard."

"Those things?"

"Yes, he's convinced. He thinks he heard one of them."

"Where? When?" Tara asked, a flash of fear moving over her face.

"Over a week ago, farther back on the ship on this floor, in the restricted area. He didn't tell me he'd been back there; I found out during the first night of nightmares."

"What do you think?"

"About Danny?"

"No, about what he said about *them* being here."

Dean tilted her head to the side for a moment, choosing her words carefully. "I think Danny has been through a lot, let's put it that way."

"You're a pretty strong lady from what I've seen."

"Thank you. I may seem like a cast-iron old bird at times, but every now and again it sure helps to hear that."

"I mean it. Goodnight, Dean."

"Goodnight, hon. You and Laura be sure to let me know if you need anything. I know her momma is busy these days with the doc."

"Thanks," Tara said, leaving for her adjoining stateroom.

Dean closed the door behind Tara, and turned to check how Danny was doing. The blanket moved slowly up and down in the rhythm of the boy's breathing. Tara's voice must have soothed him enough to ease him back to sleep. Dean turned on her reading lamp and scanned her bookshelf. She decided on a random paperback to help her nod off. She started somewhere in *Freakonomics,* learning about why drug dealers still lived with their mothers . . . a time not so long ago when there were still drug dealers and their mothers, anyway. Dean eventually grew tired and drifted off to dreamland. Her final thought before the book dropped to her lap—*stay alive for him.* The creatures had thus far failed to sever their bond—Dean swore she'd not outlive Danny. He was the last of her line.

29

USS George Washington

At about the same time Dean found sleep, a loud rap on the door woke Admiral Goettleman from his own rest, prompting a deluge of cursing as he pulled his legs over the side of the bed into his slippers. On his way to the noise, he looked up at the time—0300 hours. He cracked the door open to see his two guards standing like stone sentries next to Joe Maurer.

"Sir, I have a priority-one communiqué for you from the facility. I'm the only one onboard that has seen this and you are going to want to read it right away."

Joe moved past the sentries and inside, closer to the admiral's desk, and handed him the locked bag containing the message just received via secure wire.

"Close the door, Joe."

After whispering something to the sentries, Joe did what he was told.

The admiral pulled the key out of his desk and unlocked the bag. Inside was a briefing folder with numerous classification markings. He put on his reading glasses and began to scan the cable.

BEGIN TRANSMISSION

KLIEGLIGHT SERIAL 205

RTTUZYUW-RQHNQN-00000-RRRRR-Y

T O P S E C R E T//SAP HORIZON

SUBJ: NEVADA SPECIMEN ALPHA REACTION TO MINGYONG ANOMALY

RMKS: BY ORDER OF COG AUTHORITY,

THIS STATION EXTRACTED ONE OF FOUR
DECEASED SPECIMENS FROM DEEP AND
LONGTERM CRYOGENIC CONTAINMENT.
THIS STATION EXPOSED SPECIMEN ALPHA
(FIRST SPECIMEN RECOVERED FROM 1947
CRASH SITE) TO AMBIENT AIR INSIDE
A CONTROLLED AND SECURE TESTING
FACILITY ON OUTBREAK D+335.

BACKGROUND: HUMAN TEST SUBJECTS
REANIMATE ON AVERAGE AT + ~60 MINUTES
FROM TIME OF DEATH BASED ON ROOM
TEMPERATURES—LOWER TEMPERATURE
LENGTHENS REANIMATION TIME—AND
NATURAL CAUSE OF DEATH (NO EPIDERMAL
BREACH). REANIMATION FOR HUMANS WITH
UNDEAD INDUCED EPIDERMAL BREACH NEAR
MAJOR ARTERIES HAS BEEN NOTED ON MANY
OCCASIONS AT LESS THAN ONE HOUR. LESS THAN
THIRTY MINUTES FOR SMALLER SUBJECTS.

SUMMARY: UPON RELEASE FROM THE
CLOSED CRYOGENIC CAPSULE STORAGE
ENVIRONMENT, SPECIMEN ALPHA
IMMEDIATELY REACTED TO THE MINGYONG
ANOMALY, BEGINNING REANIMATION
PROCESS INDICATED BY ERRATIC MOVEMENT
AND VOCAL NOISE FROM A MOUTH ORIFICE.
FULL REANIMATION WAS NOTED BY
OBSERVATION TEAM AT FOUR MINUTES,
TWELVE SECONDS. SPECIMEN ALPHA WAS
SELECTED FOR TESTING BASED ON BODY
CONDITION. MOST OF THE SPECIMEN'S
LOWER TORSO WAS MISSING FROM INJURIES
SUSTAINED IN THE 1947 SHOOT DOWN.

THIS EXPERIMENT RESULTED IN TWO
CASUALTIES.

SPECIMEN ALPHA—DESPITE MISSING
LOWER EXTREMITIES—WAS ABLE TO
COMPROMISE THE STEEL DOORS OF THE
ENGINE TESTING FACILITY AND KILL TWO
SPECIAL OPERATIONS PERSONNEL BEFORE
AUXILIARY TEAMS WERE ABLE TO DEPLOY
COUNTERMEASURES ON THE CREATURE

AND THE NEWLY REANIMATED OPERATORS.
SMALL ARMS WERE NOTED AS MOSTLY
INEFFECTIVE. ALTHOUGH DIFFICULT TO
EXTRAPOLATE THE REANIMATED STRENGTH
DEMONSTRATED BY SPECIMEN ALPHA, THE
DESTROYED STEEL DOOR WAS RATED TO
WITHSTAND PRESSURE FLUCTUATIONS OF
EXPERIMENTAL ENGINE TESTING.

IT IS TACTICALLY SIGNIFICANT TO NOTE
THAT SECOND ORDER MEDICAL EFFECTS
WERE EXPERIENCED BY EXPOSED
PERSONNEL IN DIRECT LINE OF SIGHT TO
SPECIMEN ALPHA. THEY INCLUDE MIGRAINE
HEADACHES AND EXTREME FATIGUE
SYMPTOMS IN ALL PERSONNEL IN VICINITY
OF THE CREATURE DURING THE TWELVE
MINUTES OF REANIMATION. THESE MEDICAL
EFFECTS SUBSIDED IMMEDIATELY AFTER
SPECIMEN ALPHA'S BRAIN WAS DESTROYED
VIA FLAME THROWER.

IT IS ALSO TACTICALLY SIGNIFICANT TO
NOTE THAT THE REANIMATION OF THE TWO
DECEASED SPECIAL OPERATIONS PERSONNEL
OCCURRED ALMOST IMMEDIATELY. THE
TWO REANIMATED OPERATORS DISPLAYED
CHARACTERISTICS SIMILAR TO BASELINE
UNDEAD THAT HAD BEEN EXPOSED TO HIGH
LEVELS OF RADIATION FROM THE CITIES
THAT WERE DESTROYED BY TACTICAL
NUCLEAR WEAPONS. THE REANIMATED
OPERATORS WERE ORDERED DESTROYED
ALONG WITH SPECIMEN ALPHA.

SPECIMENS BRAVO, CHARLIE, AND DELTA
REMAIN IN SECURE COLD STORAGE AND
UNEXPOSED TO THE MINGYONG ANOMALY
AS OF THIS TRANSMISSION.

T O P S E C R E T//SAP HORIZON

END TEXT TRANSMISSION

BT

AR

• • •

Admiral Goettleman spoke, eyes still fixated on the cable. "Looks like our theories were flat-out wrong. Our best minds bet on the Mingyong anomaly having no effect. The two creatures were at least twenty thousand years apart in evolution. The Office of Naval Intelligence is the originator of this report?"

"Yes, sir. One of their analysts drafted this up immediately after the experiment."

"Who else knows?"

"The surviving COG, of course, the Nevada facilities, the remnants of the intelligence apparatus, myself, and now you."

"Very well. Some of the senior officers onboard will be inquiring soon. We'll need to tell them that the experiment was never carried out due to cryogenic complications. There is no benefit that I can see of informing them of this outcome."

Reluctantly, Joe dissented. "What about Task Force Hourglass? It would increase mission success if we were to let them know what they might be up against. The creature in that report didn't have legs, and was still able to wreak havoc—it killed two highly trained military personnel. Although not twenty thousand years old, the Nevada specimen was soaked and infused with preservative and flash frozen for decades before being reanimated by whatever is causing this. The creature inflicted massive damage—there is no question about that."

Admiral Goettleman sat for a minute, staring down at his desk, before speaking. "Let's hold off on this. *Virginia* is due in Hawaiian waters tonight and there's no need to raise the alarm bells quite yet. Before we tell them what we know, that is *if* we decide to tell them, we'll need to take that report and turn it into actionable intelligence. Case in point—fire may be the only way to neutralize CHANG, or whatever it is. Although fire didn't kill Specimen Alpha instantaneously, it is the only validated means to destroy a reanimated gray—we've just confirmed that. I'm also a little puzzled by the psychological effects mentioned in the report. We'll need more information. No need to go off half cocked without analyzing the data."

"Very good, sir."

"Get some sleep, Joe, you look like shit. It's three in the morning, take what you need. Thanks for stopping by with this. When you get the chance, not now but later, brief me on the things we're holding back aft. What are they calling them? Was it Bourbon or something like that?"

"Causeway and Downtown. They were named after their capture points. The Downtown specimen received hundreds of times the radiation of Causeway in the blast. The eggheads are measuring the effects. Soon, they'll be in final phases of experimentation. They'll alter brain function—surgically. Also, they are suspicious that this, whatever it is, causes some type of vision enhancement."

"Yes, well, more about it when you wake up. Better turn in."

"Will do, sir, see you in a few."

Joe departed the room under a different mind-set. He felt more concerned than ever for the members of Hourglass. Also, there were whispers onboard. Talk of a young boy and his claims that he heard the moans of the undead—likely Downtown or Causeway—in an area aft through a fan room bulkhead. Rumors that he'd need to brief the leadership about after getting some sleep. Joe's boot heels clicked on the glossy blue tile as he made his way back to the SCIF to destroy the compartmented report.

30

USS Virginia

Captain Larsen sat in his chair at the conn. All navigation instrumentation indicated that USS *Virginia* was off the northern shore of Oahu. It was 2300 hours local Hawaii time, full dark.

"COB, up periscope. Let's have a peek."

"Aye, sir."

The master chief proceeded to use the night-vision capability of the periscope to reconnoiter the coastline.

"What do you see?"

"Sir, there's fire in the distance. I'd switch to another spectrum, but I don't think it would help. I see palm trees bent and blasted in our direction like an explosion snapped them over. I'll scan the shore a bit."

"Very well."

The master chief slowly panned along the shoreline. What was a mile offshore seemed like only a few feet with the sub's powerful periscope optics. Except . . .

"There's something wrong with the scope, Captain," said the COB, still glued to the eye shields.

"What do you mean?"

"The shoreline is grainy. I can't focus on it."

"Move aside." The COB stepped down from the periscope, allowing the captain to have his first look at Oahu in the three years since he was last in port on another boat—the one before he took his current command.

Captain Larsen peered through the optics, out at the shoreline, allowing his eyes to adjust. "I can't see anything, COB, what do you mean?"

"Captain, the shoreline is grainy. Like something is wrong with the software."

"Well, I missed my eye appointment this year, so my prescription may not be up to date. Remind me to make that appointment if we ever get back to the mainland."

Some laughs spread around the conn between the sailors.

"I'll do that, sir."

The captain looked around the conn for younger eyes and saw Kil standing there in coveralls, holding a cup of coffee.

"Commander, why don't you have a look with those aviator eyes of yours?"

"You got it, Skipper," Kil said to the captain, attempting to pull some humor from the old man.

"I thought I told you this wasn't a goddamned ready room."

"My apologies, Captain, force of habit," Kil replied with a half smile as he approached the periscope.

Kil leaned down to the eye shields just as the COB reached over to adjust the height. Kil nodded a thanks and had a look.

"Oh shit."

"What's the situation?"

"Captain, there's nothing wrong with your periscope . . . those are mobs of creatures on the shoreline. It might look like static to those of you not fortunate enough to have twenty-fifteen vision. Looks like thousands of them."

"How could they know we're here?! We came in at the dead of night on a goddamned fast-attack nuclear submarine!" the captain said angrily, addressing the whole conn.

"Captain, I don't think they did."

"Then how can this be?"

Kil stepped up to the grease board and began to illustrate.

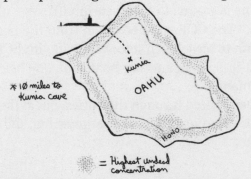

"Captain, this is a rough representation of Oahu. Although not quite a circle, it is obviously an island. To understand why the dead are on the North Shore is to understand why they move, and the rudimentary way in which they *think*—so to speak. I, of course, don't mean they think in the same way we do, but in the way one of those automatic robot vacuum cleaners might move, or perhaps a child's toy. Do any of you know the term *diaspora*?

One of the sailors raised his hand and said, "I'm Jewish—I've read about it."

"Well, then you'll likely know what I'm getting at. In all my travels in and across undead-infested areas, I have learned their priority of movement. The number one influence to undead migration is sound. The number two is visual stimulus from something they identify as alive. If sound is not present, I think they may spread in much the same way as a good break in a game of pool: outward."

The captain had the appearance of a student in a college classroom, suddenly interested in the subject matter being presented. "Are you saying that the dead have spread to the shore all the way around?"

"With Oahu being a relatively small landmass with a relatively large population per square mile comparatively, I think what we see on the North Shore is not an anomaly. I'd be willing to bet that if we steamed around the entire island, we'd see creatures on every open beach. They have spread out as far as they can go. There may be inland pockets but the majority of the undead, based on what we've seen, are likely spread out around the edge of the island. Strange that they're not in hibernation like many I've come across, but it could be that the sounds of the waves are keeping them moving."

"All right, Commander, if what you hypothesize is true, what are your tactical assessments for the incursion?"

Kil answered without much hesitation. "If the SOF team can punch through this belt of undead, they may experience a lighter density as they move closer to the center of the island. This of course assumes they don't gather too much attention on their way in."

"You're starting to earn your place around here instead of just taking up good bunk space and drinking our coffee."

The crew in the conn murmured a few laughs again at the captain's humor.

"Yes, sir, I've already started my submarine qualification. Looks like I'll earn my dolphins before we get back to CONUS."

The captain nearly spit out his coffee. "Like hell!"

Kil suspected that his respectful banter with the captain might be good for crew morale. The submarine had no executive officer, and the old man had his hands full cracking the whip and managing the health and welfare of his crew.

"COB, order the Scan Eagle crew to unpack their gear and get ready for UAV launch at sunup tomorrow. We'll get a look for ourselves."

"Aye, aye, Captain."

Kil took another look through the periscope and adjusted the focus. There was no doubt: the North Shore crawled with creatures forming a dense barrier of death. It reminded him of playing Red Rover as a child.

Red Rover, Red Rover, send the warm bloods right over, he imagined the creatures saying with raspy dead voices while he watched them mill about on the beach.

31

Crusow sat shaking from the blood-freezing cold he had endured at the bottom of the gulch—the place where Bret had met his fate a few hours earlier. Crusow wore insulated long johns while he sipped hot tea. Mark and Kung sat beside him. Larry stared from across the metal research table, wearing a face mask to protect the others from the serious illness he continued to endure. Everyone heard Larry's labored breathing; his lungs sounded as if they were full of rocks.

Coughing violently, he flamed at Crusow. "What the fuck happened? Were you settling a score down there?"

"No. Why don't you simmer down a minute before you get yourself worked up—it'll just make you worse off than you already are. We can all see the shape you're in."

Larry slammed both fists on the table, leaning over into Crusow's face. Larry was a tough read, as the mask concealed everything but his cold, bloodshot eyes. "I was there when Bret said those things about your wife. I saw how pissed you got. You sure some of that didn't come out down there at the bottom?"

"Larry, my wife is gone. And yeah, I hated Bret because he's a military asshole, just like you're a military asshole. That doesn't mean I'd murder him like an animal, no matter what he said about Trish."

Larry leaned back and sat down on the cold bench. Although his face was mostly hidden, everyone noticed him slowly spinning down from his rage over Bret's unexpected death. *He's probably delirious,* Crusow thought.

"Larry, we're not military like you. I know you guys don't talk

157

much about yourselves, and none of us really know why you are really up here anyway, but I think you're still human despite all that training. For example, if you were a selfish prick like Bret, you wouldn't be wearing that mask."

Larry adjusted his mask, tightening the straps. "Well, if we lose your sorry ass, we're all dead anyway."

Mark jumped in to defuse the situation. "Larry, that's the most I've ever heard you talk to anybody here, except your military buddies. They're all gone now, pal, so you're going to have to start opening up some if you want to work together."

Even though none of them could see Larry's face, his eyes acknowledged that Mark was onto something.

"What were you guys looking for out there before all this shit happened?" Mark asked.

Larry looked down at his hands, tracking them as they reached for the teacup. "Ice cores. We were drilling goddamned ice cores. We have a rig set up a few klicks southwest."

"What's so damn Secret Squirrel about that?"

"I haven't spoken about this to anyone because I signed an agreement that would put me in prison if I did," Larry said, coughing heavily into his mask. "Remember back before all this shit, some asshole on that watchdog site leaked those government documents? He got his, but not before the economy started coming apart. I don't know exactly why we were drilling for the cores, but I do know a few things. I suppose since I've confirmed that the whole world is fucked, there is no reason why I can't talk." Larry was pale, looking as if he might need an IV bag, and twenty hours in his bunk.

"So what the hell are you waiting for? Go on," said Mark.

"Me, Bret, and the others weren't told much, just that there might be something of national security interest in the ice. Not just anywhere though." Larry hesitated for a moment, standing up and limping to the other side of the room to remove his mask and take a sip of tea.

He put his mask firmly back in place and walked back to the table. "Me and the other military folks were here for security and to make sure there were no leaks if we found something strange down here. We were told to expect anything. We were also informed that the core drillers were ordered to take the bit down twenty thousand years into the ice.

"Our chain-of-command was pretty specific. They wanted the ice from twenty thousand years back. Give or take a few hundred. The orders came down from the White House NSC, directly from the intelligence community. Apparently they were searching for something there right before all this shit went down. I got nothing linking any of this together, but me and the other cleared people suspected there was some sort of link. The timing was too suspicious. Half of this facility's military and civilian crew jumped ship last spring. I think a few of them knew more about all this than I did. That's all I know."

"Damn," Crusow said, spitting a stale sunflower seed shell into an empty Solo cup. "You don't think that something out of that ice did this?"

"I don't see how—the world was crawling with undead and we didn't drill anything out of that ice but a few core samples. We didn't have time, everything happened so quickly. Those useless cores are locked in that shipping container, ready for transport. That'll never happen. I'm not saying that anything we were after caused all this shit, I'm just saying that the timing is strange. I've never seen orders like this." Larry's cough was getting worse.

"You sound bad, like cat with hairball," Kung remarked. "Get rest. I take you."

Larry nodded in agreement. Kung led him back to his quarters and made sure he was settled in as Crusow and Mark finished up the conversation.

"What about this ship business?" asked Crusow.

"Well, while we were pulling up those bodies, Larry was monitoring the shortwave and wrote down a request received from the ship. They want us to help them relay information to one of their boats on a rescue mission in the Pacific."

"That's good for us, Mark. I think we should play ball. They're the only lifeline we've been able to reach. They may be the only game in town with the effective transmit power to reach us all the way up here."

"Yeah, I was thinkin' the same thing. They'll be passing us

another frequency schedule next comms cycle, and the relays could start soon," Mark said.

"This is good news all around, man. If the navy is running rescue operations, that means the whole world isn't totally gone."

Mark came back with his standard negativity. "No, not the whole world—just us poor fucks trapped well inside the Arctic circle and in darkness."

"I can always count on you, Mark. Keep it up, and I'll nominate you to help me with the corpse fuel."

"Fuck that noise."

"Hey, it's either you or Kung."

"Kung will do it. He's lucky he's not part of a *Bodies* exhibit somewhere anyway, being as where he's from."

"Damn, that was bad even for you."

"I try."

One kilometer off the north shore of Oahu

The final planning phase is underway. The target is over nine miles inland and roughly south. Saien and I will be standing by to support via the SOF team voice net. We should at least be able to provide some insight even though we're stuck back here in the rear with the gear. Knowing what I know about the creatures, I do not envy those men. They are going in at night but because of the distance this will likely be a two-day round trip. Another factor is the radiation. Before they head out, I'll formally introduce myself and brief them on the radiated creatures—if they'll listen. They haven't spoken ten words to me or Saien since we arrived on the helicopter.

As a former radioman, I have found my way into the radio shack and also back into the groove of setting up rudimentary radio networks. They are very understaffed in the shack so it wasn't hard to convince the acting COMMO, a LTJG, that my help might be needed. We had the HF circuit up in no time and were communicating with a station I hadn't expected to be a functioning relay.

An Arctic outpost, a man named Crusow, was providing

assistance in the form of comms relay from the carrier to our boat. The carrier had not been lucky with direct communication and the outpost to the far north seemed happy to provide assistance. Aside from the normal communications that I expected relayed from the carrier (general operating area, etc.), I also received some personal communication from John. He'd asked to start a chess game and offered his first move over the relay. I wrote the move down and will set up the game board and send my move out with the next transmission. It's good to hear from home.

32

North Shore of Oahu

"COB, sun?" asked Larsen.

"Low on the horizon, sir, won't be long now," Master Chief Rowe replied.

"Very well, bring us up."

The USS *Virginia* quickly surfaced, half a nautical mile from the beautiful Hawaiian beaches of the Oahu North Shore. There was no question about the situation on the shore from this distance.

The hatch was opened, allowing the sea air to rush in. The Hawaiian undead were now more than an image on the boat's sensors. Their moans traveled the distance, fighting through the surf to the ears of the crew. The submarine seemed to amplify the noise like a soup can on the other ond of a piece of string.

The sound was beyond unsettling.

"Shut it, shut the damn thing!" a sailor yelled, holding his hands over his ears.

"You secure that mouth!" Larsen barked.

The moans were unrelenting. Kil and the captain climbed up the ladder, through the sail, into the sea air above. They used binoculars to survey the situation, taking advantage of the last remaining rays of light shooting in from the west.

"Think they know we're here?" asked Larsen.

"Probably. They can see—I don't know how well, but they can. That's probably not what gave us away though. They can hear pretty damn well, don't ask me how I know. I imagine that we made some noise surfacing, right?" Kil said.

"Not much, but some."

"Pass those over please," Kil said, reaching for the binoculars.

Kil scanned the beach slowly, watching the creatures. Although not funny at the moment, if he concentrated long enough and squinted a little he thought he might be able to see a few Hawaiian shirts in the crowd. Suppressing a laugh, he passed the binoculars back to Larsen.

"Well, as a consultant I am counting on you to actually consult," Larsen jabbed.

"Captain, I've expressed my position. It's about ten miles in a straight line to the cave entrance, a few hours at the facility for setup, and ten miles back. There is no way that I can tell you that a twenty-mile round trip to secure an underground facility that may not help the mission is worth the potential loss. The *Virginia* has sensors that can provide what we need."

Larsen weighed that for a moment, and said, "Wheeler Air Base and Kunia are not what I consider near the coast. You said yourself that those things might spread out away from the center of the island, with more of them congregating along the beaches."

"Might," said Kil. "If I'm wrong, then our SOF team *might* have their hands full with a few thousand radiated creatures. I have been wrong before."

"Noted."

"Were you briefed on exactly how many nukes slammed down here nearly a year ago?"

"The reports say one. Air burst over Honolulu. Fallout should be moderate. Because of today's sea state we were unable to surface and launch the Scan Eagles. We'll launch the IR-capable bird tonight when the team reaches shore."

"I'm going out on a limb and assuming that they will be wearing suits, right?"

"Correct. They'll also be wearing dosimeters and checking their exposure regularly. The nuke detonated on the south side about thirty miles southeast of here, over city center at five hundred feet. The wind likely scattered most of the radiation eastward, out to sea."

"The EMP from that air burst is going to make it tough trying to secure transportation. Might have fried some car electronics," Kil said.

"You *are* a negative son of a bitch, Kil."

"Maybe, but I survived on the United States mainland for nearly a year while you were sitting safe on this boat."

"I'll give you that," said Larsen.

"I don't want anything *given,* Captain—I ask for no quarter and I *give* none."

The four-man team stood on the rocking deck of the surfaced submarine, looking out over the moonlit Hawaiian waters. The waves were typically higher this time of year; they were fortunate that the night's sea state was manageable. Also on deck was the UAV crew setting up the equipment for launch.

Rex, Huck, Griff, and Rico were their names. Not their real ones per se, but some military customs never went away, even during Armageddon. Names didn't matter much these days, and even so, they'd still hail each other by their call signs.

The boat's Chinese interpreter climbed out of the hatch with his backpack of classified manuals on the cave facility. He gave a friendly nod to the team, already staging their gear. Although his real name was Benjamin, the team quickly dubbed him Commie, even though he was a twenty-four-year-old white boy from Boston that had never even set foot on Chinese soil or any other communist country for that matter. He had learned his Chinese in Monterey, California, after being selected to serve as a linguist for the navy's cryptologic services.

Before coming topside this evening, the operators sat down with the officer they flew in with and his partner, a Middle Eastern man.

"First and foremost I'd like to say that I'm not trying to tell you all how to run your mission. I'm simply going to go over some of the problems I encountered and pass along some of the basics on how I survived my time on foot in the undead Louisiana and Texas badlands. Some of this stuff will be second nature to you, because of who and what you are. Even so, I took a few notes in the solitude of my travels that might be helpful en route to the cave facility."

Kil was careful not to hint that he kept a detailed journal of his accounts, referring to his scribbles as notes.

He began to recite some of the main lessons learned, some of which were literally written in blood.

"Move at night—obviously you all know this one, but I need to stress it, as it is at the top of my list. Like us, they can't see well at night and your NVGs will give you the advantage. Press check your carbines. I won't elaborate on that one. Sleep well off of the ground. Unless you have a platoon of people standing guard around you, it's dangerous to sleep anywhere within reach of the creatures. They'll find you. Stop and listen often. Parallel the roads and stay off any highway. For some reason, these creatures are drawn to main roadways. Store water inside your body, meaning drink it if you have it. Keep your weapons lubed as if you will be in a firefight any minute. I had to use motor oil on my gun, escaping from a helicopter crash. It was all I had and believe me, I used it. Move fast in the open. Protect your eyes—face splatter probably means infection."

The team listened politely, but Kil felt as if they were humoring him to an extent.

"If you have no choice but to take shelter on the ground level, do so on top of a hill and inside of a car or truck with your hand on the e-brake. That way if you get overrun, you can pull the brake and roll down, away from the threat. In small numbers they're no challenge, but when you start looking at numbers over ten, they can bash a car in and pick you out of it like lobster meat from a shell. Now I can't explain the reason for this, but some of the things I've killed required two shots to the head."

One of the guys on the team cut in with a question. "How many did you say you encountered at once?"

Kil was annoyed at the question; the man obviously hadn't thoroughly read the reports. Kil drew a breath and said, "Huck, was it?"

"Yeah, that's me."

"Well, Huck, me and Saien over there encountered a swarm on our way back. The organization we were in contact with at the time relayed to me that the swarm was over five hundred thousand in strength."

"How the fuck did you survive that?" asked Huck skeptically.

"Long story. It involves an Abrams tank, Reaper UCAV with

five-hundred-pound laser-guided bombs, a bridge, and luck. Another time."

The incursion team was suddenly attentive to what Kil was saying. The magnitude of trouble that he and Saien survived on the mainland rarely yielded survivors.

"A few more minor things. All dogs are likely now feral. I'd avoid them. I've seen them attack the dead on sight. They may attack you, too, I don't know. If they do, you could get infected by the rotten flesh they carry in their jaws. Last but not least, and pay close attention to this, Honolulu was hit by a nuke months ago. Captain Larsen thinks the Hawaiian weather cycle might have washed some of the radiation particles into the Pacific. I'd still avoid anything large and metallic like school busses or tractor-trailers if they were in line of sight of the nuclear blast. They'll likely be hot like a Chernobyl fire truck. That's really the least of your worries. For unknown reasons, radiation has a profound effect on the creatures."

Huck interrupted again. "We have read the intel about them being a little faster. We can deal with that."

"Okay, Huck, since you have this thing suitcased, why don't you just head out on the mission? My work here is done—good luck."

"Huck, shut the fuck up and let the man speak," one of the other men said. "I'm taking notes and I don't give a damn what you think about the intel. I'm listening. Sir, please stay and finish."

Kil expected that and turned around to continue as if nothing happened. "All right, as I was saying, radiation makes them very fast, and smarter. It's not just the speed you'll need to worry about though. Call me crazy, I don't care, but on the night of . . . wait a second, let me find it."

Kil flipped through his notes, looking for the specific encounter that might turn on the lightbulb for Huck. "Here it is. I was on the run, taking shelter in an abandoned house. While scavenging the downstairs, I dropped something out of my pack, alerting a creature outside to my presence. The thing began using a hatchet on the door to get to me. I escaped out the upstairs window that night. The next day I was climbing on the hood of a school bus to stow my gear when the same creature took a swing at me with the hatchet. I knew it was the same corpse because I risked a look through the peephole inside the house the day before. It was definitely different from the others. I've seen them run and sometimes reason, at least on a rudimentary level. I've seen them play dead after being shot, too. I lost a marine to one of them onboard a coast guard cutter, a ship that was taken down by only a few radiated undead. I call the ones with skill the talented tenth, because I've found that one in ten are different. I'd also like to add something that I can't really prove but might come into play. This island was nuked at its population center. I'd be willing to bet that my mainland talented tenth theory does not apply here on the island; the ratio is likely much higher in favor of the radiated creatures. Maybe as many as three or four in ten could be radiated here."

The same man who had defended him against Huck minutes earlier jumped in with his own question. "I'm Rex, you may not remember. I'd like to ask you about your experience with movement and evasion. Is there anything different about moving that we'll need to know about?"

"Good question. A ten-foot bubble around me was the best way to avoid surprises. You know, the kind of surprises that pull you into an open car window or the kind that bite your hand off from inside a freezer in an abandoned convenience store."

"Huh?" Rex uttered, confused.

Kil went on, "This might be counterintuitive to what you did before the dead walked. You might be inclined to stick close to cover, walls and such. That might get you killed against these creatures. What kind of NVGs are you running?"

"We're running PVS-15s and PVS-23s. We also have a scope that's sensor fusion capable, night vision with a thermal overlay. Good for getting a visual ID on warm bodies. Why?"

"You probably know this already, but the eyes of the undead don't reflect in your goggles like living eyes. Just a little something for you guys not running thermal."

"Gotcha."

Kil walked closer to the men and shook their hands. "Good luck, men. I mean that."

"Thanks, Commander."

Their gear had already been taken topside and the RHIB was

ready to take them to shore. The chaplain entered the SOF staging area and asked to speak to the men before they departed.

"I know that some of you don't believe in God anymore, but some of you still do, and I know I do, and I'd like to lead a prayer for you men, if you don't mind. A prayer of safe return."

"Go ahead, Chaps," Rex said.

"Let us pray." The men bowed their heads. The chaplain continued, "Lord, though these men will soon walk through the valley of the shadow of death, please give them the strength to fear no evil. Please guide them on their mission and see them safely back to the USS *Virginia*. We know that if it is in your will, they will succeed. In the name of Jesus Christ, Amen."

There were a few scattered *amens* in the group, but even those were feeble. Seeing the dead go after everyone you ever loved had a tendency to ruin your religious perspective and convert you quickly to the Flying Spaghetti Monster religion. Even so, military chaplains were always given the time they requested; you might be wrong about God, after all. Best to humor the chaplain and avoid any stray lightning bolts.

"Okay, men, godspeed," said Larsen.

After a nod to the captain, Rex led his men to the dive locker to suit up in their protective garments before going topside.

Kil knew that these men were probably not coming back alive, at least not all of them. *There must be another motive,* he thought. Although his duties kept him off shore and safe inside the sub, he still eyeballed the small armo rack. He caught Saien doing the same thing. *You never know.*

"Rico, how's the RHIB?" Rex said, his voice muffled through his protective hood.

"It's loaded, fueled, and ready."

"Get it in the water."

Rico and Huck shoved the front of the RHIB from the submarine deck into the ocean. Behind the sail, the UAV ground crew launched their small surveillance aircraft into the night sky from a temporary catapult system. The sound of the tiny gas engine was barely audible over the thundering creatures on the shore. The UAV climbed away into the Oahu skies.

Rex moved back behind the mast to speak to the UAV crew. "Thanks, guys, we appreciate it. Give the pilots below our best and our thanks as well for keeping an eye on us."

"Will do, sir, good luck."

"You, too. Have a good 'un."

Rex boarded the RHIB. It started on the first pull, a good sign.

33

Hotel 23 Facility—Southeast Texas

Task Force Phoenix slipped into a comfortable rhythm. This was not necessarily a bad thing, just something that Doc felt might prove dangerous if they became complacent. Their current location was secure and there was no sign that Remote Six knew of their occupation. No one in Task Force Phoenix had much knowledge about Remote Six; they all read the reports, noting the huge gaps in the intel.

A week ago, Doc had started the launch drills. At first the exercises were very unpopular to the other three men—Doc woke them up at all hours for a practice launch against a notional target. They were starting to get acclimated to the drills and understood the reasons behind them. Doc was right all along—they could have very short notice to strike.

Last night, Disco and Hawse headed outside the wire to check the launch doors. On arrival, they observed that the doors were overgrown with foliage, and covered with weathered and cracked camouflage netting.

"Hawse, rip that shit off the doors. I'll cover."

"What? You think I'm gonna trust an army guy to watch my ass while I play minimum-wage landscaper?" Hawse said, laughing.

"Whatever, swabby meat-gazer. How happy are you that don't-ask-don't-tell was abolished before the shit hit the fan?" Disco said.

"Pretty fuckin' happy—leaves me more women. As long as it

doesn't scare the horses, I don't give a damn what another dude does in his house."

"Just clear the launch door so we can get the hell—"

Both men heard a noise—something too loud to be wind.

"What was that?" Disco said in a near whisper.

"Shit. Get 'em up, Disco, I'll take east, you take west."

"Yep."

They scanned their areas for any movement.

"Not too far, stay near the missile doors," Disco said.

Minutes passed as the wind picked up some, swaying the trees back and forth ten meters out.

"I got something," Disco said quietly over his shoulder to Hawse.

Hawse was instantly shoulder-to-shoulder with Disco. He brought his carbine up and activated the IR laser. "Where is it, man?" he asked.

Disco brought his own carbine up to high ready and activated his laser. "There, that. What the fuck is that?"

A cloud passed, revealing a full moon, illuminating the expanse. Minds of men have a tendency to degrade and flounder in stressful situations like this. So naturally, Hawse's first instinct was to pull his trigger.

FUMP, FUMP, FUMP.

The rounds struck meat; the sound was tragically too familiar. The creature came at them from the darkness of the tree line. Disco and Hawse instinctively put three rounds into the creature's skull; its head exploded, sending rotting chunks of the top third into the night sky. It fell to the ground ten feet from them, the sound of skull pieces falling through the foliage coming shortly after.

"Holy fucking hell!" Hawse exclaimed.

"Dude, don't. Want more coming? Save it."

"Sorry, man, that was way fucking close. Was that thing stalking us? That sound—and I only took the shot because I felt something looking at me."

"I heard it, too," Disco said.

"Okay, fuck. Cover me again. I'm gonna clear the launch doors and then we'll haul ass. It might be nerves, but I feel like I'm being watched again."

"Look at that thing. Looks fresh," Disco commented, staring at the corpse.

"Concentrate. Keep your distance; it might be hot. Intel said that the bombs preserved 'em—twisted."

Hawse cleared the door, removed the brush and the camouflage netting, and tossed the rubbish aside. The two double-timed it back inside Hotel 23, ignorant to the dead that might be watching from the tree line, and the evidence they left behind—a cleared launch door that could be seen by anyone or anything that spied from above.

Remote Six
Two Weeks Post-Outbreak

"Status?" a voice called out from the shadows.

"Well, um, the cities are now what I would consider uninhabitable."

"Elaborate."

"God, what the fuck do you want me to tell you? D.C., New York, Atlanta, Los Angeles, Seattle . . . nothing to elaborate. They are all dead!" The operator hit a sequence of buttons on his touch screen and a satellite view of an island metropolis appeared. He manipulated the zoom while the ominous figure over his right shoulder looked on.

The operator panned and zoomed to Manhattan.

Scattered debris and sporadic fires defined the scenery on the screens. Slow figures lumbered through smoke, moving about in the streets. Faster movement caught their eyes as a small group of survivors armed with baseball bats were weaving around the creatures and between abandoned cars.

The orbital mechanics of the reconnaissance satellite above New York caused the viewing angle on the screens to skew oddly.

Both men silently watched the survivors. *Doomed.* The phenomenon was spreading too quickly and there was nowhere to run. The Lincoln Tunnel billowed smoke from both ends. Fighter aircraft had already destroyed the bridges in a failed attempt to keep the contagion from spreading, locking the barn after the horse had bolted.

It was being reported by remaining news feeds that even those who had died from natural causes were turning. The men at Remote Six had no answer for this phenomenon. The data analyzers could only propose one solution: Everyone exposed to the open air must contain a dormant rendering of the anomaly.

The dark figure standing over the status screens was known as God. Real names were a useless and forbidden taboo here. The codenames that were given in the tank were used to loosely represent the positions of the people to whom they were given.

God began his career in the Central Intelligence directorate of operations, developing and executing black-ops programs inside the United States. He had been trained by the best, the nastiest. His long-dead mentor had the dubious but extremely classified honor of creating the playing rules behind Operation Northwoods—a plan to execute false-flag attacks inside the U.S., murdering civilians and blaming it on radicals in order to garner American backing for the military invasion of Cuba.

God was the prodigy of true tyranny. His shadow organization had fronted the startup money that gave birth to Google and other DARPAnet giants. At the highest levels of compartmented intelligence, his agency, in partnership with NSA, had pure and unadulterated access to all—private email, individuals' Web searches—everything. God's old identity had been erased and replaced with a star on a wall somewhere in Virginia. Shortly after erasure, he was ordered to command what only very few inside government officials knew as Remote Six. God only knew the rest.

Many covert think tanks in and around the Beltway region dealt only in information. Remote Six did that, of course, but they were also an executing entity. They could make decisions, carry out kinetic operations with the resources and power granted to them by fearful elected officials—people that didn't want to get their hands dirty and didn't want to know the details. This covert decision node was not located anywhere near the District of Columbia—it existed far from the political radar and influence of any Beltway bandit or dreamy-eyed, newly elected politician. Remote Six, established before World War II, had been a variable in everything from dropping the atom bomb on Japan, to assassination of key NVA leaders in the Phoenix Program, to similar and more recent destabilizing operations in the Middle East. Remote Six made the big decisions. The three branches of government ensured the balance of power and illusion of Constitutional leadership, but covert entities like Remote Six pulled the strings behind the wizard's curtain.

Twin advanced quantum computer systems existed deep underground inside Remote Six, under God's control. Multiple and redundant quantum hologram storage drives held every piece of the human knowledge base from how to make fire to the technical details of the Large Hadron Collider, and far beyond.

Every song ever written and every movie ever made was stored and archived here. The entire Internet was regularly crawled and chronicled on the quantums' storage as well. When humanity fell, precious scientific knowledge and art would not.

An incoming message indicator flashed on the flat panel, addressed to Chief of Station. God walked over to the flashing screen and ordered an aide to print the document. As the message spun off the printer, God began to read.

Situation dire and unrecoverable. Request R6 option package, uploaded all viable options to Pentagon II Situation Room LAN.

God laughed out loud, imagining the president on the other end of the transmission at the alternate site in the Shenandoah Mountains sweating fucking bullets. He would do what was asked of him, for now. God would feed the quantums.

Possibilities of viral origin: 90.3%
Possibilities of other origin: 9.7%
Error of +/- 2.4% lack of data input.
Would you like another analysis? Y/N
—

INPUT US population: 320,520,068
INPUT infection Rate: 100%
OUTPUT based on infrastructure conditions, national supply inventories and archived weather data.
Possibility of undead majority within thirty days: 100%
Possibility of undead majority within fifteen days: 94.3%
Would you like another analysis? Y/N
—

INPUT US population by city|top fifty
INPUT interrogative: How many cities in order of high population will need to be destroyed to hold undead minority at day thirty?
OUTPUT based on 55.2% conversion day twenty.
Cities destroyed to maintain undead minority at day thirty: 276
OUTPUT based on undead density in vicinity of city center and accurate deployment of thermonuclear weapon(s).
Would you like another analysis? Y/N

God had his calculations—the quantums were never wrong. Every time they went against the automated output, it bit them in the ass, hard. Even in situations when dissenting against the quantums seemed the only viable choice, time eventually proved the computer's AI prescience. At the first decade of the twenty-first century, the quantums advised against going to war with Iraq, and later, warned against any stimulus injection into the collapsing economy.

The twin bastards were tied into the Internet, SIPr, JWICS, VORTEX, NSAnet, and every foreign network on Earth, even if brute force decryption on the fly was required. They crawled information in real time and could make frightening assessments on problems that no one knew existed. The quantums even tied into the RF spectrum, analyzing cellular and other radio traffic. They were designed to understand human speech and output based on normal speaking syntax. It was rumored by some inside Remote Six that the two quantums working in tandem might accurately predict the future out to six months by crawling the various nodes, connecting key subconscious phrases in high numbers of Internet user text input.

Another report would soon arrive on God's desk, subject line *Horizon*. Oh, yes, God knew everything about this little skeleton. His directorate had been in contact with the Mingyong scientists via encrypted correspondence. All Horizon Program intelligence would later be analyzed and assimilated into the quantums despite the best efforts of Chinese Central Military Commission cyber-defense agents. Not now, though. He had cities to destroy, by proxy.

One klick off Hawaii

It's go time. The special operations team just departed. The Scan Eagle UAVs are airborne, and Saien and I are monitoring the IR feed. Although gyro stabilized, the picture isn't even close to the quality of Predator. The upside is that these little UAVs can be launched from the deck of a submarine with little maintenance and fuel required to keep them running.

I received a relay from Tara earlier today with some updates regarding the goings-on onboard the ship. She was also nice enough to send John's chess moves along with her message.

I love her, and I realize it now more than ever. I wish I could get over whatever it is that keeps me from expressing it more outwardly, even on this piece of paper.

Being away this long only magnifies my feelings, as there is a gaping hole in my chest where I left a piece of myself back on the carrier. I will be doing everything I can to make it back in one uninfected piece so that I may hold her again.

Although I'm not typically the emotional type, seeing those men leave for the mainland made me feel for them. They might not be as lucky as I've been. I almost feel guilty, as if there is a finite amount of luck in the world, and I used it all up. To clear my mind, I'm going to sneak back to my quarters and enter John's chess move and strategize my next move until I'm needed. His most recent chess move looks strange. I'll have to try and figure out what John meant. In his other moves he would send something like:

John to Kil: K to 3C

His latest move was a series of combinations that looked like:

John to Kil: W&I p34 w34 BT p34 w55—and the combination goes on for quite some length.

I'll need to spend some time looking at the board to see what he meant. He sent too many combinations to be only one chess move. Maybe something was garbled.

Maximum pull-ups: 10

Push-ups: 90
1.5 mile treadmill run: 10:58

Ninety thousand feet over Chinese airspace

High above the Earth, a triangle-shaped aircraft was moving at Mach 6, its sensors tuned to the situation on the ground in the People's Republic of China.

"This is Deep Sea checking on station, Bohai, over."

The transmission sounded mechanical and muffled as the pilot spoke into his oxygen mask.

"Say angels, Deep Sea."

"Deep Sea is angels ninety, Mach six point one."

"Roger that, Deep Sea, moving a little slow today. How's the view?"

"Cameras are slewed, no changes since last mission. About twenty percent of Beijing is still on fire, no sign of unconventional detonation in sensor range. She's still intact, Home Base."

"Roger that, think you'll have time to make a Moscow run today, Deep Sea?"

"Home Base, that's thirty-two hundred nautical miles as the crow flies. I can be there in thirty-eight minutes. Priority one?"

"No, Deep Sea, not pri one at this time."

"Roger Home Base, I'll stay on COG pri one tasking here."

"Understood, Deep Sea, just seeing if you had the time."

The black aircraft continued its hypersonic patrol of the Bohai regions of China. The pilot pointed the multispectral camera at Tiananmen Square for optic calibration and began to switch from electro optic to thermal. The hundreds of thousands of moving and walking undead registered cold. The pilot then began to enter the passkey on his multi-function display to access the coordinates of the facility—a place known by the pilot to hold something deep in its bowels so classified that the mere unauthorized knowledge could get him killed—even pre-anomaly.

Soon, perhaps in a week, Task Force Hourglass would be entering the Bohai, and subsequently Chinese waters. The pilot would be tasked with one final priority, one mission in this area during the incursion, in support of Hourglass. After that it wouldn't be safe, considering what he knew might be planned for their exfiltration.

Continuing on its reconnaissance track, the bird took thousands of digital photographs and high-resolution video that would be analyzed and transferred to the remaining COG. That in turn would be trickled down through military leadership to Joint Task Force Hourglass for mission planning. Knowledge of this aircraft's existence and even its capabilities was buried away inside its multi-trillion-dollar black-budgeted special-access program, from a time when government acronyms and codenames mattered.

34

USS George Washington

Dr. Dennis Bricker wiped the sweat from his face with his smock, adding another stitch to the child's elbow. Jan assisted, as she knew the patient well.

"Danny, you need to be more careful. The ship is a dangerous place. You could have just as easily split your head open."

Danny wouldn't meet Jan's eyes. Jan had become an aunt to him during their months of survival together at Hotel 23. "I'm sorry, Ms. Jan. I was just havin' fun and playin' zombie."

"Playing what? Why would you do that?" Jan asked as Dr. Bricker looped another stitch, causing Danny to wince in pain.

"Ouch!" Danny jerked a little. "Well, we play it because it's fun. Makes my friends not as scared at night." Bricker listened, analyzing Danny's words and mannerisms.

"Scared of what, Danny?"

"Scared of the zombies on the ship."

"Danny, honey . . . look, they're not here. They're far away, on shore."

Bricker looped the last stitch and said, "Okay, young man, we're all done. I don't want to see you down here for stitches again; we're almost out of thread and I'll be using staples on you next time. Got it?"

Danny's eyes widened at the thought.

"Thanks, Dr. Bricker. Thanks, Ms. Jan. Can I leave now?"

"Yes, honey, we're all done," Jan said reassuringly.

Danny hopped off the table and pulled his T-shirt back over

his head before walking out the door. The rhythm of his feet indicated he was running as soon as the door closed.

"He'll be back," Bricker predicted.

Jan sighed. "Yes, I know."

"You know, Jan, that's not the first talk I've heard of those things aboard. This ship is over a thousand feet long, over two hundred and fifty feet wide, and goes nearly seven stories underwater. Lots of room. There are places I've never even seen."

"You don't seriously believe that the military is keeping them here? For what purpose?"

Bricker removed his face shield and glasses, looking over at Jan. "Every now and again, before you arrived, I received strange requests to do abnormal things, and then shut up about them. You've been here working for me long enough so I don't feel remiss in telling you. Every once in a while, one of the crew might bring brain samples down and ask me to analyze them. I have some of the samples in storage. I told them I had destroyed them, post-analysis. I can't do much beyond normal cellular study as we're not equipped with a transmission electron microscope, but we're working on that. They only ordered a cursory medical examination, but I completed tests beyond that."

Jan slid off her stainless metal stool and stood up. "Like what?"

"Well, for one, I used the medical Geiger. The brain material registered significant spikes of radiation. Not enough to harm anyone, as the brain sample was too small, but it was enough to let me know a few things. Enough to let me know that the piece of brain was a part of a frontal lobe that likely belonged to one of those creatures. Not the ones that move like a sloth—one of the radiated. The most alarming thing was that no one had conducted a mainland reconnaissance or salvage operation in the two weeks prior to me receiving the sample. It was very cold when I took possession—refrigerated. Much cooler than room temperature; I remember documenting that."

"Well, what do we do?"

"Nothing, Jan. We do nothing and go on about our business. There's no point in rocking the boat."

Disgusted, Jan walked out of the infirmary without taking off her lab coat or saying good-bye.

Bricker shouted down the passageway, "Jan, that's between us. Okay?"

Jan thought for a moment that she might put up her hand and flip Bricker the bird on the way, but her better judgment told her that wouldn't help anything either way.

35

The RHIB hit the Oahu sand at twenty knots, jarring the operators from their positions onboard the small craft. Rico wiped the water spray from his hood and NODs and took the shot. Other suppressed carbines followed. Shooting accurately proved difficult through the hood's distorted view, but the undead didn't know the difference, dropping to the sand, surf washing over them.

They fought inland, using darkness to avoid many of the creatures. They used weapon-mounted IR lasers to designate targets, avoiding the engagement of the same creature twice. The men systematically killed in teams. Commie reloaded magazines when he could.

Slogging inland, they saw the wreckage of a large sailboat sitting in their path, the victim of a tsunami or rogue wave. Badly decomposed creatures hung from doors, hatches, and torn sail rigging. They still moved.

The UAV above their heads reported that there were no hordes in wait behind the boat, but the concentration of undead remained high. Not quite as Gucci as Predator, but it would have to do. Even if they did have Predator, it required massive manpower and a full-up airfield for launch and recovery—not something they enjoyed on the stern yardage of a fast-attack nuclear submarine. The Scan Eagle flew low, and the men could hear the comforting hum of the small engine. So could the undead.

Griff called out the heading: "One-five-one degrees to target. Nine miles."

"Roger that, Griff, keep us on track line," Rex said.

Another transmission keyed in—Kil's voice came through.

"Scan Eagle has you one mile inland. High density for another two miles until you break through the creature belt. We see only four glint tabs. Anyone have glint covered up?"

Rex stopped the group, forcing an instinctive defensive formation where all operators faced outward, backs to one another, protecting their high-value asset: Commie. "Okay, guys, you heard the boat. Check your glint. They need to see us to mark the threat."

All five men hit their IR weapon lights, and green light filled their NODs. They looked for a one-by-one-inch piece of IR reflective tape that each wore to indicate their positions to the UAV orbiting above.

"Shit, man, it was me. Sorry." Huck ripped the velcro American flag patch off his protective suit sleeve, revealing the glint tab beneath.

"Karma for being a prick, man," Rico replied, never missing a chance to put Huck in his place.

"*Virginia,* how many do you see now?" Rex asked over the radio.

"That's it, I see all five now, break."

"Be advised, recommend you move heading one-eight-zero for a klick. Massive group up ahead at one-five-zero, three hundred meters your position."

"Roger, avoiding," Rex replied.

The men adjusted their course farther to the south to steer clear of the mass of undead. Rex looked down to the portable radiation sensor on his belt. The levels were high, but not outside the protection capabilities of their suits. Kunia was less than nine miles inland and, according to the blast modeling, should be within radiation survivability parameters as long as suit integrity held.

Hopefully.

"Tangoes thirty meters, engaging," Rico said to the others. Rex shot a round, dispatching an undead child. He forced this fragment of horror out of his head to kill the next in line.

Click.

Goddamned double feed, he thought. Rex dropped the mag, yanking the bolt back, and jammed his fingers inside the magazine well. He fumbled with his radiation gloves for a bit before the two dented rounds fell from the weapon to the ground. Rex slammed in another magazine right before Rico blasted, spraying radioactive fragments of flesh over the face of Rex's hood. Rex passed Rico a nod as he wiped the material from his mask. *Better to be filthy and alive.*

The ammunition weight alone in their packs was staggering, but lessened by the minute as they engaged viciously and broke contact. The theme was rinsed and repeated most of the night. They slogged over the hilly, warm Hawaiian terrain for hours—killing when they had to, evading most other times.

Not wanting to risk a suit breach, they were careful not to touch their rifles' front sight posts; the barrels were blazing hot when they punched through the two-mile belt of undead that circled the island.

At midnight, they reached the home stretch of the nearly ten-mile march to the tunnel facility. Only the speed and maneuverability of their short, suppressed carbines and the security of the night saved them from being torn apart. The UAV support also saved their lives half a dozen times along the way. Rex marveled at the speed and ferocity of the creatures, flinching at every sprint attack attempted against the team. Weary with fatigue and sweating inside their exposure suits, they finally arrived at Kunia.

The tunnel parking lot was as packed as any typical workday, another lost relic of a dead world. The dusty cars sat unevenly on the paved parking surface. Some of them had burned down to the ground long ago, the intense heat melting paint and rubber and cracking the glass on nearby cars. The parking area was fairly clear of undead, except for a few stragglers that wandered around the steps leading up to the cave.

The team formed up near one of the boulders that marked the parking boundaries, preparing to make an assault on the tunnel.

"Okay, Commie, go over it again," Rex demanded.

"Yes, sir. Those doors at the top of the stairs there lead to a one-quarter-mile tunnel that goes under that hill there. At the end of the tunnel, there are sets of turnstiles to the right. We'll need a way to get through those; they are full-body revolving doors. If the place were still under power, my IC badge would get us through. After we make it through the turnstiles, the generators are right up from the target. Bottom line: quarter mile into the tunnel, take a right, take a left. The place we need is on the left. Generators are farther down on the right."

They consulted their hand-drawn maps and compared target locations. They all had laminated copies provided to them on-board the *Virginia*. A suppressed shot interrupted the silence—it was Commie.

A creature hit the parking lot with a thump a few meters away behind a parked car.

The radio crackled with the *Virginia* crypto sync tone: "Hour-glass, be advised, we see movement outside the gates. Small flow of creatures, strength fifty, stirring. I'll let you know if they become a factor. Check in before you enter the tunnel, we'll be lost comms while you're inside."

"Roger that, *Virginia,*" Rex replied. "Commie, we're gonna move on the tunnel right now. Stay between us, and for Christ's sake don't die. Larsen will crush us all if you do."

"Aye, sir."

The men moved to the long staircase that led up to the guard shack. Bodies littered the steps on the way up, some of them still writhing about, disabled. The Geiger was giving a low audible alarm. The stairs were covered with metal roofing, likely absorb-ing large amounts of radiation in the Honolulu blast event. The five ran quickly up the stairs to escape the radioactivity cooking their suits.

Reaching the top, Commie pointed over a few meters to a small building in front of the tunnel doors. "That's the guard shack."

An undead sentry stood inside with an assault rifle still slung across its chest. Its lips had long since rotted away from its mouth. It seemed to grin at the men through the ballistic glass, but it was only an illusion; the creature could see nothing and had no hint of their presence. They could barely see the thing through the layer of death sludge caked on the guard-shack window. The Hawaiian heat had been slow-cooking the creature over the months.

Commie looked through the glass and said quietly, "Visitor IC badges. A whole stack of them in the corner over there. The visi-tor badges had full access and I doubt they changed the four-digit visitor codes. I had to escort VIPs inside this facility—senators, generals, admirals, everyone. You'd be surprised at how many couldn't work the security doors and just gave me their visitor codes and badges so that I could badge them in and out. The even badges use codes 1952 and the odd badges use codes 1949. The power is no doubt off inside but we may need a couple of them for when we restore limited power, if only to prop some of the security doors open."

"Roger that. Rico, kill that guard and swipe those badges."

Rico nodded his head and kicked the door jam with a loud thud. It didn't budge, but the creature stirred, striking the door. The smacking sound of putrid flesh slapping the door caused Commie to double over, dry heaving inside his suit.

"Master key?" Rico asked.

"Not yet. Commie, how do we get the cave doors open?"

"Hold on a sec," Commie said between dry heaves. "There's a manual access there near the doors that requires a hand crank. It's secured with a padlock. The key and crank handle are inside the shack."

"Are you fucking sure?" Rex said, his voice filled with tension.

"Yes, sir, I'm sure. I stood this watch when I was the new guy. It's under the desk on the floor. Had to check it for power-failure drills."

"Rico, master key!" Rex exclaimed.

"Everyone back, get ready to move!" Rico pulled his sawed-off Remington shotgun from the leather holster on his back, flipping off the safety. He always kept a round in the hole. He pulled the trigger and shredded the wooden guard-shack door around the lock. Only a hole remained where the doorknob once was. Rico kicked the shit out of the door again.

The door flew inward and knocked the creature to the floor, onto its face. It attempted to get back up, but Rico pulled the knife from his belt, stabbing it in the back of its soft, half-rotted skull. He was careful not to thrust too hard as he didn't want to damage the tip of his blade by going too far through the head into the concrete floor. With the bottom of his boot, he yanked the knife from the skull and wiped it on the guard-shack seat. The smell would have been overwhelming if it were not for the suits.

"Okay, five badges in here, no hand crank!" Rico yelled out the door. He knew there was no point in being quiet after the shotgun blast.

Huck glanced away from his sector of cover and risked a look down the steps. "Rex, they're on us, man, bottom of steps," he said calmly.

Rex ran into the guard shack to help Rico look for the hand crank. "Rico, grab 'em. We gotta move. They're coming up the steps."

Both Rico and Rex ran out of the shack and looked at Commie, flashing anger in their eyes. "Commie, what the fuck?"

"I don't know; that's where it was!" Commie said nervously, adjusting his NODs, looking around the area.

Griff was at the top of the steps, weapon ready and pointed down at the creatures stumbling up the stairs. Griff watched while the others dashed to the door, attempting to gain access using their fingers—the steel door was fifteen feet tall.

Commie moved to the other end of the huge door, hitting his shin hard on something. "Fuck! That hurt," he shouted, looking down. "Found it!"

The hand crank was already inserted into the hydraulic panel. Commie quickly turned it as fast as he could; the door creaked and strained. It opened one quarter of a centimeter per full turn—a slow undertaking. Bits of rust flaked from the hinges of the massive doors as they slowly creaked outward.

Griff yelled back to the group from the top of the stairs a few meters away. "I'm engaging, there's too many! Thirty seconds!"

That was all they had left before all hell broke loose and undead would start their advance up the steps to rip them all apart. It was only fifteen meters from the top of the stairs to the doors that Commie was feverishly working to open. The door was a few inches wide now. Griff kept shooting, stacking them up on the stairs below. Surgical with his shots, he neutralized creatures he felt might fall a certain way to block the flow behind, buying a little time.

Commie turned the crank to the point of muscle failure. "My arms are toast—someone else jump in."

Huck jumped in on the hand crank and started spinning for his life. The door was now open nearly a foot wide.

Griff yelled back, "Commie, get your ass over here and start shooting!"

"Moving!" Commie replied, mimicking brevity he'd heard along the way to the cave.

"Be damn careful, Commie, fall back if they get closer than ten feet!" Rex reminded him, covering Huck.

Commie and Griff blasted away with their suppressed carbines. Some of the rounds passed through the creatures and ricocheted off the concrete steps, hitting the metal roof and parked cars. The creatures continued their relentless march up the steps at them.

The undead got so close that Rex witnessed Griff brand them with the end of his gun, pushing them back. His suppressor was so hot from expelled gas that the creature's skin would sizzle just before Griff pulled the trigger, scattering brain all over the steps below, toppling corpses back down the stairway to hell. If not for the darkness, all of them would already be dead. The creatures were that fast.

"Commie, take two steps back. They're advancing."

Commie complied and kept gunning.

"It's open enough," Rex said from nearby the doors. "Get your asses in here!"

Both Commie and Griff walked backward, shooting the whole way to the door. One by one they dropped their packs and threw them through the opening. Rex had just cleared the immediate area inside the cave doors but had no idea what lurked farther back in the tunnel. Relying on moonlight and NVGs, it was pitch-green beyond fifteen meters. He didn't have time to turn on his IR weapon light to sweep it further, revealing the blackness.

Commie squeezed through the door into the cave. It smelled of death and mildew inside. He thought creatures might be close. "How are we going to close the door behind us?"

The dead were screaming now.

All five were in the tunnel now, the door frozen at eighteen inches open. Rex looked outside, seeing those things throng about. They already filled the guard shack and Rex knew that they would soon be flowing to the cave entrance.

"Any ideas?" Rex solicited.

The radio crackled. "Hourglass, Scan Eagle is indicating a swarm event developing in your area. Looks like the creatures are beginning to rally on your posit," an unfamiliar voice said over the net.

"Roger," Rex answered rolling his eyes. "No shit."

Rico began firing his carbine out the door at the creatures—they were getting curious. Because the door was open at an unfortunate angle, he had to hang his torso completely out to control his carbine shots.

Looking around the tunnel with his IR light, Huck found a pillow-top mattress sitting against the wall on top of a box spring. "Rex, give me a hand with this."

They slid the mattress vertically into the eighteen-inch gap of the open door just before a creature was about to poke its head in. It was a snug fit, but only a temporary fix.

"We need to stack a load of shit here to keep the mattress in," Rex said to the others.

Everyone fanned out in the immediate area, looking for debris or anything that might be used to barricade the door. Commie began to walk deeper into the tunnel.

"Not too far, Commie—the old man ordered me not to let you out of my sight," Rex said.

"Yes, sir, you got it. I see something up ahead."

A golf cart. Rex followed Commie for a closer look. The small battery-powered cart was used as a shuttle to transport VIPs back and forth to each end of the long underground tunnel. It was marked with a removable sign that displayed a blue background and four white stars.

"Looks like a four star was the last to ride on this. Let's push it to the door," Rex suggested as he stomped on the pedal, releasing the brake.

They both moved quickly, pushing the cart to the opening. All five men grunted, lifting the cart, placing it parallel to the door. It was tight against the mattress that plugged the undead leak. Rex reengaged the braking mechanism, holding the car in place. The sounds of bony fists were loud against the steel while the men stood in a circle to gather their thoughts.

"*Virginia,* this is Hourglass. We're inside—keep an eye on the door. If you see them getting in, give us a shout. One of us will stay near the entrance to keep comms up with your station," Rex transmitted.

The reply came in a bit weak, but readable. "Roger that, Hourglass. I'm on it." It was Kil's voice this time; Rex's eyes did not roll.

The very fact they'd even made it to the cave was remarkable. There they were, a mattress and a golf cart between them and certain undeath, on a radioactive island wasteland inside a defunct top-secret facility. Easy day.

Kil was in the control room now and ordered the UAV pilots to adjust orbit over the cave door as requested. One of the men gave attitude regarding the order, causing Kil to hammer him back in line by threatening to personally send the man to the cave entrance to watch the door. Kil was nervous about the situation on the ground ten miles away, but made sure to project confidence on the radio. He had read books on the Apollo 13 mission and remembered how important it was for mission control to keep their cool with the astronauts. Although he was safe on the submarine, he still understood the value of projecting confidence to those that needed it.

Fifteen minutes went by before Kil gave an update. "Hourglass, the creatures are not concentrating on the door. No increase in activity or intensity right now."

"Roger that, Kil, good to know. Thanks for the overwatch," Rex said, briefly letting his comm discipline slip. "Griff, you stay near the door and relay any radio traffic down the tunnel to us. We won't be able to pick up *Virginia*'s transmission as we move farther down this tunnel."

Griff nodded in compliance.

"I'll lead. Commie, you stay between me and Rico. Huck, you are welded to Commie. Rico, you have our back." After he was certain that everyone understood what was happening, Rex began to advance. "Have a good 'un, Griff."

"You all too," Griff replied without looking back, fixated on the door and the undead outside.

The creatures had been screaming since the group entered the tunnel. The men blocked the noise as best they could. There was no getting accustomed to it. Moving deeper into the tunnel, Commie began to remember his time stationed here at the cave.

The walls were covered in artwork on either side, all created by military personnel stationed here over the years. One mural depicted a skeleton marine sitting in a chair, wearing a headset in front of some radio equipment. It seemed to listen to some unknown transmission. The quarter mile of murals was an odd visual representation of the loose history of this facility. Some of the details depicted in the art could only be understood by a former spook like Commie. Some renditions were hints of highly classified real operations that occurred here. Commie smiled as the team moved by pieces of art he had contributed to before being transferred to his next assignment.

"We're about halfway down the tunnel now," Commie told the others.

"Shhhh! I hear something up ahead," Huck whispered.

The men brought their weapons up to their shoulders in anticipation.

"Commie, stay back here with Huck. Rico, you're with me."

Rex and Rico moved ahead a few meters.

The slight curvature of the tunnel straightened, revealing the last-stand barricade. There were dozens of the creatures, mostly in hibernation, standing on both sides of the makeshift barrier. A few of the undead moved about, triggered awake by the noises made near the cave entrance.

"There's too many for just us to handle—they'll wake up any moment and fuck us up," said Rico.

"Yeah, let's go back and get the guys," Rex said.

The two hoofed it back to the others, relaying what they had just witnessed.

"Okay, we're gonna need everyone. There are maybe fifty of

them sleeping near a barricade a hundred yards up the tunnel. Some of them are waking up."

A crashing sound in the darkness interrupted the silence. A creature must have knocked something over near the barricade.

"Let's go take them out. Walkers first, then the sleepers. Commie, I don't want you near them. If they start rushing us, you run your ass back down the tunnel to Griff, understood?"

"Yeah, I guess. I have a gun you know." Commie's ego was clearly stung a little in being told to flee.

"Yeah, you may have a gun, but none of us know Chinese," said Rex. "What happens if you get infected and we're forced to kill your ass? Ever think about what might happen if we can't communicate with the Chinese when we reach their waters? What if part of the Chinese General Staff and civilian leadership have survived and we can't tell them that we come in peace? One submarine versus the Chinese North Sea Fleet? Get the picture?" Although Rex couldn't see Commie's eyes behind his goggles and mask, he could tell by the body language that Commie understood.

After taking a Geiger reading, Rex gave everyone the option to remove his protective hood before laying out the plan. "This is how it's gonna happen. We're moving up just enough to start taking shots at the ones that are active. Then we'll start picking off the sleepers. No one shoots unless in self-defense or until I shoot first. These carbines are going to be loud in this tunnel, suppressed or not. Be ready for that, Commie."

Commie nodded at Rex.

"Okay, let's move."

The four advanced down the tunnel until Rex held up his fist to stop the group. Rex readied his gun and took the first shot, signaling everyone else to start dropping the undead.

They began with the active creatures first, missing some; the shots sparked off the concrete walls, jolting the sleepers. The entire barricade area buzzed with movement, making the follow-up shots more difficult. The tunnel distorted the sounds, sending the creatures in all directions. Some of the undead walked at the group, but were quickly destroyed. The team managed to drop all of them except for a few stragglers on the other side of the barricade.

The radio crackled: "Guys, things are degrading fast back here," Griff said, as the others were taking care of the creatures on the other side of the barrier. "*Virginia* says that they're massing at the front of the cave and I believe it. The doors are buckling."

"Hold the fucking line!" Rex radioed to Griff.

The four jumped the barricade, gunning down two more creatures before advancing on the turnstiles ahead. Without power, the badges were useless for accessing the secure areas of the cave.

Rex thought he could hear the suppressed action of Griff's carbine a quarter mile down the tunnel—it sounded like a real gunfight. Rex pushed Griff's problems out of his head and pulled out his pick set for the side handicapped access that bypassed the electrically dependent turnstiles. Without graphite lube to spray into the lock, he knew it might give him some trouble.

A suppressed shot rang out five meters away.

"What the fuck, Rico?!" Rex exclaimed, dropping the pick on the floor.

"One of them was still moving, man, crawling! I had to dust it before it crawled over here and bit your ass!"

Rex nodded his thanks in response, felt for his lock pick, and went back to work on the lock. He used the tweezers from his Swiss Army knife, bending them into a torsion wrench, and began to rake the pins. He worked the lock for five minutes; drops of concentration sweat hit the floor as he struggled. The lock finally gave and Rex wondered if he had bested it or actually stripped out the internal pins. He pushed the door open and moved a nearby corpse in place to prop it open, careful to avoid the creature's slack mouth.

They were now technically inside the secure area of the cave.

Rex herded everyone in and keyed his radio. "Griff, we're in! All tangos down. Move your ass!"

There was no answer on the other end. Rex repeated his broadcast down the tunnel.

"Maybe we should go back and check?" Commie suggested.

"It's too risky," Rex snapped. "Once I shut that goddamned gate, we're secure inside here. A lot can happen on the half-mile round trip getting down to the door and back. I saw a lot of maintenance access doors on the way here. There could be dozens of them inside those unsecured rooms. Not all of them were closed." Rex was shaken at being forced to leave Griff to his own fate. This was not something acceptable in the special-operations community.

The gate shut with a metallic clank and the four men waited. Ten minutes passed before the radio keyed again.

"They broke through and I'm nearly out of ammo," came Griff's voice. "If I don't go out there and close those doors we're all dead. Now or never, man, about to be too many outside to reach the crank. Good luck . . . out."

Rex stood for a few seconds frozen in shock at what Griff had just said. He was sacrificing himself to save the rest of them. "Griff, thanks. SAR dot bravo, twenty-four hours, IR strobes. Make it if you can. Good luck."

There was no response.

Onboard *Virginia,* Kil focused intensely on the Scan Eagle UAV feed. He'd transmitted warnings in the minutes leading up to Griff's decision to leave the cave and secure the door by way of manual hand crank. He'd heard Griff's radio message to Rex a minute before and watched the IR signature of his carbine shooting out the large steel doors.

The UAV cameras detected something small fly out of the open steel doors and into the mass of undead that congregated nearby. About four seconds later an explosion, likely a frag grenade, rocked the gaggle of creatures, sending them in all directions. Chunks of flesh flew against the steel doors and the guard shack in black splats. Immediately following the explosion, Griff sprinted through the opening and to the manual control crank to close the massive steel doors. Kil panned the UAV camera out a bit and noted the creatures' reactions to the explosion. The parking lot below the stairs was teeming with undead activity, polarized like iron on a magnet, all converging on Griff. Panning back to Griff's immediate area, Kil called in the SITREP.

"Griff, strength fifty, about twenty meters right behind you. I'll call out when danger close."

No response.

Although Kil could not be sure from the feed, it appeared that Griff was ignoring everything and resigned to the prospect that nothing mattered but getting the door closed. Kil watched the video feed as if it were a rerun; he had seen this play out before, but not in the black-and-white monochrome of the IR video on screen before him—he'd witnessed it in living color. It never ended well. The creatures moved, frenzied—they didn't know where Griff was in the darkness, exactly. He zoomed in on the door, just as the UAV orbit shifted to allow a good look angle. Six inches of gap. Too small for any undead to fit.

"Griff, danger close, danger close! That's enough! They can't fit through that gap!" Kil exclaimed.

Griff gave the crank another full turn and looked over at the door, verifying Kil's report. Jumping to his feet he pulled his back-up weapon, a Glock 34 pistol. His rifle sat empty, propped on a wall inside the cave. Griff began working the crowd. With only a single magazine remaining, he thought of saving one round for himself.

His decision was made when he slammed the full magazine into his handgun, slapping the slide forward. His ears rang from 9mm reports. The final round from his last magazine dropped the nearest threat—but there were hundreds, possibly thousands more coming. He re-holstered his sidearm, reaching for his tertiary weapon. In his right hand, wrapped with a paracord lanyard, was a large, razor-sharp, fixed-blade knife; in his left was another frag. This was Griff's life-insurance policy, payable in death to any undead thing within fifteen meters.

Another frenzied creature wandered too close and sensed Griff in the darkness. Swinging his knife from far right to left he beheaded his attacker, dropping the severed head and body to the ground at his feet. He reached over with his knife hand and pulled the pin on the grenade in his left, leaving the spoon in place—dead man's switch.

Hundreds more poured up the steps like a bizarre reverse-flowing waterfall. There was nowhere to flee, and Griff was so tired of running anyway.

"Griff, I'm sorry, man," Kil transmitted, watching the last stand play out from above.

Griff looked up into the sky, waving his knife, and then did what only a few men had the fortitude to do in past wars fought over land, freedom, or money.

He charged.

Griff picked the largest group and ran screaming and slashing at their heads in a bid to kill every creature on the island. Kil could not see what was happening beneath the maelstrom of flailing undead appendages, but many of the undead fell before Griff's insurance policy was paid out in full. In a white flash of frag and guts, Griff held the line to the very end.

36

Making biofuel was a gruesome and nauseating effort. With Kung's help, Crusow hacked away at the half-frozen bodies, removing the precious fat. The skin was freezer burned and blasted by the Arctic wind. Kung was at first confused by what Crusow needed during the butchering process; he had too much muscle in his first lops of flesh.

Crusow explained what he needed by grabbing what little fat he had on his midsection and pointing it out to Kung.

"This here, Kung, not this," Crusow said, now pointing at his bicep.

After harvesting a couple hundred pounds of fat from the bodies, Crusow began the tedious chemical process of converting the fat into biofuel. The smell was abhorrent and took some getting used to. Careful heating of the fat was required to properly process the fuel. Crusow wore a mask and goggles to protect him from the boiling fat. His first few batches turned out well and seemed to work fine when tested indoors.

Crusow brought a small amount outdoors, away from the heated lab, to test it on one of the generators modified to accept alternative fuel. After leaving the fuel in the generator shack for half an hour, he returned to find that it had solidified to a gel-like consistency inside the container.

Crusow brought the fuel back in, placing it near a heating vent. The fuel eventually returned to a liquid state. Crusow's solution to the solidification problem was to use the Sno-Cat's primary diesel tank to start the engine and mount a secondary tank near it. He installed heating coils on the secondary tank to keep the fuel in a liquid state. It wasn't ideal, but he didn't have access to a full-on refinery or the luxury of complaining about it.

Crusow and Mark had kept a close eye on Larry the past few days. He was bedridden, teetering closer to death since Bret was killed at the bottom of the gulch. Despite the encouragement of the other three, Larry was giving up. They moved Larry's quarters near the radio room, where he could be monitored more conveniently. As a countermeasure, they leaned chairs and other things against his door—they would not be surprised if he returned from death. This made the watches interesting, when their improvised warning devices fell unexpectedly.

The odd-hour radio watches were necessary, resulting in several successful communications relays from USS *George Washington* to USS *Virginia* and vice versa. Arctic Outpost Four was now an information nexus between the warships.

Via shortwave radio, Crusow was becoming more familiar with John as well as his friend Kil. He even started his own chess game with John after learning of the ongoing matches. It was a good way to pass the time; Crusow was anxious to make radio contact at every opportunity. With the extra chessboards from the outpost game room, Crusow was able to follow John's game with Kil while he played his own game. It was surprising the lengths a man went to in the attempt to fight boredom.

Crusow had already seen every movie at the outpost several times; at least the ongoing games were fresh content. If you included the players, these radio-broadcast games would have the highest per-living-capita Arbitron ratings in broadcast history.

Chess and military communications were not the only things being passed via shortwave. News from the outside was always good to hear, no matter how bad. In the past week, Crusow learned that Oahu, Hawaii, was a nuclear wasteland, that America still had aircraft flying in limited capacity, and that the *Virginia* was continuing her rescue operation west after leaving Hawaii. Some of the military brevity made the messages unclear in meaning but Crusow and Mark were able to put most of it together when it wasn't encoded.

Now that the Sno-Cat had been modified with dual tanks, they could make the trip to the thinner-ice zones to the south, where an icebreaker might be able to rescue them.

Eventually, Crusow distilled fifty-five gallons of biodiesel, a convenient amount, as the modified heated tank installed on the

Cat was a fifty-five-gallon steel storage drum salvaged from the outpost dump.

In Crusow's dealings with Larry, Kung was a valuable ambassador. He felt bad for Kung, realizing that he had been dealt a bad hand. Although he was improving, English was still a distant-second language for him and he found it difficult to communicate his thoughts and feelings to the others. He was truly a stranger in an odd and unforgiving place.

The stress from the encroaching cold was causing a group mental breakdown. There was a clock ticking down to the date they would run out of fuel and freeze. This date could not be slid to the right, rescheduled, or put off any longer that the time the generators would run dry. To Crusow, spirits seemed to be crumbling fast.

Since his horrible but necessary trip to the bottom of the Gulch, Crusow's nightmares had returned in full force. The long darkness of the winter north only fueled the feelings of fear and hopelessness that heaved him into torturous and unrelenting dreamscapes. He would not soon forget the hand-to-hand combat with Bret or the other creature with a face that was familiar but forgotten—wiped from memory by the horrors endured since his incarceration on this ice rock.

USS Virginia—*Hawaiian waters*

I'm off duty for the moment. The shore element of Task Force Hourglass is still inside the cave facility. I've instructed the watch to wake me if they hear or see anything on the Scan Eagle picture. Another UAV launch is scheduled soon to relieve the bird that is airborne. We haven't heard from the team in six hours since Griff—

Well, since he fought to the death; I suppose that's the best way to put it. Saien and I have been discussing the current situation on the ground and thinking of all possible outcomes.

One possibility: We never hear from the team again and proceed to China without a SOF team, or Chinese interpreter. Saien and I know the second and third order effects of that; neither of us are fans of that outcome.

Another more favorable possibility is that they make it out of the cave, reporting that it's secure, well stocked, and operational. Saien and I have already given a warning order for a ready boat.

With the sun high in the sky earlier, we went topside with the binoculars to check the beach.

I could see the creatures standing in and around the team's RHIB, seemingly waiting for them to return. A large percentage of the landmass had been nuked. The effects of large-scale radiation on the creatures is likely still not understood by anyone, or at least anyone I know of.

I received another cable from John today—more chess moves. The first pair of numbers was intuitive, but the second series was like another I received a few days ago—strange.

Along with the mystery numbers was a question. "Read *Tunnel in the Sky*?"

Actually I had. I sent Crusow (the man running the Arctic Outpost relay operation) a reply, and we talked a bit afterward. Crusow was my usual contact when I conducted the relays.

Late one night, Crusow and I switched to a higher alternate and clearer frequency and had a conversation about our past and the events that led up to now. Crusow told a harrowing story of recent capers at the bottom of a cliff near the outpost, and how they lost another man as a result of a thawed corpse. The story was disturbing, but did give valuable insight on the undead. Crusow was beginning to seriously worry about his survival up there. His fuel states were running low but he'd taken gruesome measures to produce more. Only four souls remained at Outpost Four with one very sick and close to death as Crusow described.

John seems in good spirits, Crusow informs me. Crusow passes that John says Tara is well also. Even though the vast distance has disabled voice comms in all but the most perfect atmospheric conditions, this is still better than nothing, and keeps me going.

About to catch some shut-eye, Saien is already sawing logs in the bunk below.

37

Hotel 23 — Southeast Texas

The four-man team had been out twice since Doc and Billy's encounter with the river of undead. They were lucky on the first excursion; they didn't encounter more than a dozen creatures, easily enough for two men to handle under the cover of darkness. The team hadn't seen the sun since the days before parachuting into the Texas wasteland. Despite that Remote Six had not shown itself thus far, the broken bee stinger of Project Hurricane still remained where it originally impacted, partially destroyed by Warthog GAU-8 cannons weeks ago. This was a daily reminder to the team, an obelisk of warning that they were not alone.

Hawse and Disco grew restless, prompting Doc to let them have the second outing. They followed the same procedure—no radio calls, and stick to the planned route.

The coordinates were a bust, and the drop was gone, or had never even existed. Hawse and Disco decided to scavenge the area on the way back so that the mission wouldn't be a total loss. They recovered a twelve-volt battery charger, a twelve-volt air pump, some painkillers, and a crossbow with ten bolts. That was it.

They ran into trouble during one of their stops, forcing the mission to go a little longer than expected. Hawse convinced Disco that they should scavenge a home that sat a quarter mile off the main road. The damaged home had visible solar panels and expensive SUVs parked in front—probably rookie preppers with money. Through their optics, they observed that one wing of the home was burned, indicating abandonment or possibly siege. They hopped the fence and approached cautiously, intending to verify abandonment before entering through the damaged McMansion wing.

They both hoped that this would be a rescue operation instead of justified theft.

Approaching the wing, they saw charred skeletons scattered about. The corpse nearest the house was also burned, but some flesh still remained. It lay facedown, wearing a military surplus flamethrower. The fuel reservoir on its back was damaged; jagged parts of the tank pointed outward. They neared the corpse.

It began to move.

The creature's head cocked sideways at the two. Its eyes were burned out, but it somehow sensed their presence. It tried to crawl but what was left of its lower body was buried in rubble and ash. Hawse approached close enough to kill it with his knife. He saw that the creature wore a leather bandolier of ammunition across its chest.

"Looter?" he said.

"Not sure, maybe. Let's get this over with," Disco said.

"The walls aren't as damaged as I thought, we'll need to get in somewhere else," said Hawse.

They walked around to the front. The home was much larger than it appeared from the road. There were bullet holes in places, concentrated around the window frames. The front porch was littered with tarnished brass, most of it 7.62x39. *AK-47 or SKS,* Hawse thought. The screen door sat near the front door, torn from its hinges, covered in grime. A sign hung on the front door.

Insured by 1911

"Looks like they needed a better insurance policy," Hawse said.

"Yeah, something like that."

Hawse reached for the knob and began to turn. The door was unlocked. He paused, listening.

Nothing.

Hawse turned the knob and pushed the door inward. He caught a glimpse of something, a small wire, just as the door swung open.

Ping

A familiar sound. Both men instinctively dived from the porch onto the ground, and covered their ears before the explosion.

Booby trap.

The ground was two feet below the plane of the grenade detonation. Disco suffered only minor splinter injury from the damaged porch. They both heard the moans as soon as their ears stopped ringing. The sounds came from behind the house. There must have been dozens, maybe a hundred back there.

Hawse and Disco hoofed it back to Hotel 23, pursued by a respectable horde of undead. They beat the creatures, and the sun, barely.

The third outing was an operational order coming from the carrier, and required vehicle transport. Doc and Disco were to acquire transportation and meet another team for supply pickup and intelligence exchange. The other team was stationed at Galveston Island, ninety miles east of Hotel 23. Both teams would split the mileage and meet at midnight at a bridge on a county road spanning the Brazos River. They would each bring high explosives as a precaution, providing them the ability to deal with a sizable undead mass. If a swarm pursued either team, they would rig the bridge and call it even on the safe side.

On the night of the mission, Doc and Disco checked and rechecked their gear. They had a fully charged car battery—heavy but essential in starting a long-dead vehicle. They also had two gallons of good stabilized fuel that Hawse had scavenged on the previous mission.

Forty-five miles on foot would be a death sentence; there was no doubt that a vehicle would be an absolute requirement. There was only one type that would give them the speed and power they needed with two gallons of fuel—a motorcycle.

Both men said their good-byes to Billy and Hawse and closed the hatch behind them. They moved east to the nearest road, eyes open for vehicle possibilities. The weight of the car battery and fuel pulled heavily on their backs as they tried to keep a good pace. Their NODs had fresh batteries, and the stars lit the cool December night quite well.

The first prospect they found appeared to be a winner. A black Kawasaki KLR 650 sat parked on its kickstand between two cars. There was no undead movement in the immediate area, so the two decided to make a move on the bike. Doc led and kept his carbine high, adjusting his optic brightness to his NODs. The bike's tires were low. The men modified the twelve-volt air pump with alligator clips so that they could connect it directly to the car battery they had with them. There were drawbacks, as the modified battery-powered air pump made a hell of a lot of noise.

There was no point in pumping the tires if the engine wouldn't start. They checked the oil via the window on the right side of the engine. Probably old, but it would work. The keys were missing but these bikes didn't have overly complicated ignition systems. Disco was able to defeat the ignition and the gas cap with his multi-tool and some ingenuity. The bike battery was confirmed dead—no surprise to Doc. He was a motorcycle rider and every time he returned from deployment, he would need to charge the damn battery, even after some of the shorter, ninety-day detachments.

Reaching under the headlight, Disco snipped the wires for light discipline. He did the same for the brake lights and turn signals as they were often accidentally activated while riding. They poured a quarter gallon of fuel into the tank and shook the frame, sloshing the good gas in with whatever was left in the tank. Looking inside, Disco could see that it was about half full. They'd need more at some point in the night. Disco checked the tank switch, verifying it was switched on.

They ripped the plastic side panels off, revealing the dead bike battery, so they could quickly attach the alligator clips from the charged battery. The bike had a choke, so Doc preemptively pulled the lever; it would need it after sitting out in the elements this long. They decided to air the tires and start the engine simultaneously. Both would make noise, so they might as well save time. Before they began either, Disco took point and started the watch—they would definitely attract undesirables now. The tires were not completely flat but would need a lot of air to support their combined weight and keep the motorcycle stable.

"Okay, Disco, here goes," Doc said quietly, attaching the clips from the charged battery to the dead motorcycle. *Nothing happened,* Doc thought. Then he remembered—*gotta push the starter button.* He depressed it and the engine cranked over but didn't start. He repeated for a minute or two, adjusting the choke lever. He also managed to air both tires in between attempts.

The engine started to show promise. Doc was not startled by the sudden sound of Disco's suppressed carbine—the dead were near. The engine finally started fully, prompting Doc to remove the clips and stow the car battery in the side pannier compartment of the bike. The dead were still blinded by the darkness, reacting to Disco's carbine. What Doc wouldn't give for a huge pack of Black Cat firecrackers to toss down the highway. He adjusted the choke lever and the bike began to sputter, but soon adapted to the new setting, growling with health.

"Get on, bitch!" Doc said to Disco.

Disco didn't seem to care; he worried more about the approaching mob. They jutted forward as it began to get crowded on the road. Doc called back to Disco to go over the memorized directions again. They had forty-three highway miles to clear with a fuel stop somewhere in between.

The road was as they expected, cluttered with debris and abandoned cars and the undead. They had to move at least thirty miles per hour, or the engine sound would draw the undead to the road ahead of them. All along the way they noticed the details of desperation. SUVs that had attempted to go around traffic jams and were stuck in medians; cars flipped over, burned out, and filled with undead. Ambulances sitting, back doors wide open, with undead strapped to gurneys. Huge, unserviced potholes were also a menace to them on the motorcycle. If they had been riding a sport bike, they would have already dumped it in the numerous foot-deep holes in the road.

At the top of a hill, they saw a fuel truck jackknifed at ninety degrees with mostly flat tires. There were bullet holes in the cab, but the tank trailer appeared undamaged.

Doc remained on the bike, keeping it running. Putting the kickstand down would activate the engine cutoff, and Doc didn't trust the battery. Not worth it to take any chances.

"Disco, knock that tank and let's see if there's any juice. I'll cover."

Doc fought the bike into neutral—a difficult task while the engine ran—activating the bright green light on the display panel of the bike. The light burned out his NODs for a moment. Doc covered the light with his glove while Disco checked the tanker.

"She's got gas, man!"

"Okay, what are you waiting for then?"

Disco started the transfer process. Hopefully the fuel sitting in the tanker had not gone bad. The bike didn't have a gauge on the panel so they were guessing at this point. Doc reached down to the reserve lever to make sure it wasn't actuated. He wanted a failsafe.

Using a piece of hose he cut from the trailer, Disco was able to siphon gas from the tank access. He filled the fuel can up, topped the bike off, and then filled the can once more. The markings on the tanker did not indicate whether or not the fuel was mixed with ethanol additives, important for the shelf life. Disco closed the access and suggested that Doc mark this wreckage on the map. Slightly relieved, and with fuel concerns out of the way, they reset their odometer and kept riding to the bridge between them and Galveston Island.

38

USS *George Washington*

"How far along am I?" Tara asked Jan.

"Well, hon, it looks like you're fast departing your first trimester and everything is looking great," Jan said, presenting her most positive tone as she examined the ultrasound image. Onscreen, the baby was deceptively large. Its actual size was a little larger than a grape.

"I'm going to tell him."

"You sure about that? He probably has a lot going on right now. He's not expected back until February. Tell you what, why don't you sleep on it tonight and then, if you think you need to tell him, ask John to send the message tomorrow. Whatcha think?"

"I think that sleeping on it is always a good idea. I'm just so excited. It's that, well, this is the most positive thing to happen to me since before. Since before . . . you know."

"I know, honey. You don't have to say it, I know. I'm excited for you, too. Can I ask you something personal?"

"Sure, I mean of course," Tara said, almost annoyed that Jan would even need to ask.

"Why didn't you tell him before he left? You knew already. Maybe it wasn't official, but you knew. Why not then?"

"I don't know; it just didn't feel right. With so much loss, so many gone—I felt that if I told him, we'd lose the baby. Don't ask me why. I know it's a terrible thing to say, but the only thing we have left to hold on to is life, what little is still out there. I didn't want to jinx it, I guess." Tara frowned and then started to cry.

"It's okay. Let it out. You're pregnant, this is allowed. You'll be in your second trimester when he gets back. Here are some prenatal vitamins and this book to read up on in the time being. Get excited, you're going to be a mom. Believe it or not, you're the only one onboard that's pregnant. At least the only one I know of."

"Jan, I can't thank you enough."

"Don't, I'm here. We've been through a lot. I'll be here for you when you need me. I mean it."

"Thanks, anyway."

"I want to see you every week to monitor your progress and make sure you're okay, got it?"

"Yeah, I got it," Tara replied with a Mona Lisa smile.

39

Southeast Texas

The road was a desolate, unforgiving place. Doc and Disco rode the long curled highway as if on the back of a giant black eel. The continuous potholes, debris, and hulks of abandoned cars and trucks caused near-accidents at every turn. They were not far from their rally point now—a bridge named by the Galveston Island team as the halfway point. Keeping an eye on his odometer, Doc realized that Galveston might have gotten the better end of the deal. The bike trip meter read fifty-five miles when the two men crested the hill that overlooked the bridge spanning the Brazos River.

Doc squeezed the front disc brake, stepping on the rear brake simultaneously, jerking the dual sport bike to an abrupt stop. Both men looked down the hill to the bridge, where they could clearly see muzzle flash erupting from unsuppressed weapons. The flash was like lightning, revealing a hundred creatures clearly engaging the gunmen on the bridge. Doc hoped that the men down there were not the men they were supposed to meet, but he knew that their luck had run out back at the fuel truck.

"Let's ride up and shoot at two hundred meters," Doc said over his shoulder to Disco.

"Yeah, two hundred meters, and lean the bike against something to keep it running."

Doc rode the bike down the hill, turned it around, and leaned it in neutral against the sandbag barrier of an old pill box from a time when the living outnumbered the undead and men were still fighting, not hiding.

"Okay, Disco, fire at will. Check your six every five rounds and I'll do the same, staggering on your count."

"Roger, boss, engaging."

Both men began to surgically target the heads of the creatures below, using the other group's muzzle flash to avoid fratricide. It was a game of timing and speed. If both teams hurried, they could neutralize the mass of dead before more replaced them, responding to the unsuppressed report of the weapons on the bridge.

Suppressors dramatically reduced undead response radius, meaning less reaction on Doc's position. Unsuppressed weapons extended the response radius exponentially, reducing the ability to escape before undead reinforcements arrived to replace the fallen. It paid to be fast, and they were.

It took seven minutes of constant shooting by both the hill crest and bridge valley teams to clear the hundred or so undead. After the last creature dropped, Doc and Disco sprinted down the hill to a scene of carnage. Only one man remained standing out of the three-man bridge team. The others were dead or dying from mortal wounds.

They had also arrived on motorcycles.

"Let's get this over with. Those were my friends," the survivor said to Doc right before moving over to his mortally wounded comrade, administering his last rites.

He whispered a good-bye and took a bloody piece of paper from the dying man before shooting him in the head at point-blank range. He didn't face them for a moment, but eventually turned in their direction, face flooded with tears.

"You guys are from the silo?" the survivor asked.

The sounds told of more dead approaching.

"Yeah, listen, we're sorry about . . ." Disco offered.

"Save it, I don't want to hear it. Those bikes were theirs," the man said, gesturing over to the dirtbikes leaning against the guardrail of the bridge. "Take 'em. They're full of gas."

Doc looked at the dead operators in disbelief. When their teammate, Hammer had been killed in New Orleans, it was devastating to the team. Doc still thought of Hammer often and wished he could have done something, anything that day. Hammer's life ended in much the same way as the man bleeding and lifeless on the ground; a bullet from the barrel of a friend.

Doc saw the man's AK-47 underfolder slung across his chest

on a single-point sling, a paratrooper model. "Here bud, take this; you'll need it," Doc offered, handing over his suppressed M-4 carbine.

The man looked down at the rifle and said, "Thanks. I'll take you up on it. I hope that your side of the river will treat you better than mine. One of my men flipped his bike off an overpass on the way here, broke his neck avoiding those fucking things. We lost our only silent rifle with him. Take my AK—I don't want to leave you in the same boat I was in."

"Thanks, brother," said Doc. "Here's my ammo and three mags, got any seven-point-six-two?"

"Yeah, six mags. Here. Also, this is what I was ordered to bring you."

The man handed over a military radio with a frequency written on the outside of the case in silver Sharpie. Attached was a small notepad of waterproof paper.

"The radio is tuned to talk to our A-10 drivers at Galveston Island. We've converted the road to an airstrip there and cleared the dead. Some seem to get in anyway though. The notepad is our weekly flight schedule and brevity codes. We've been ordered by the COG to support your missions. You transmit your scouting plan to the boat and they'll notify us of our strip alert times. If you run into trouble that you can't shake, our Hog pilots will be on scene inside of twenty mikes for the troops in contact. They'll literally be sitting in the ready room geared up at the times your teams are out. I'm ordered to tell you that the Hogs are carrying air-to-air IR missiles in their loadouts, too, whatever that's supposed to mean to you."

Doc quickly thought of the Reaper mentioned in the previous Hotel 23 commander's report, but decided not to mention it.

"One last thing, I'm sure you know that transmitting is a bad idea in your keypad and especially killbox. I wouldn't use that radio unless the devil himself started coming out of the ground with hell behind him."

The dead drew nearer and Disco took shots, thinning them out with the smaller noise radius of his carbine—the only suppressed rifle between the two, now that Doc had donated his.

"Do you have anything for me?" the survivor asked Doc.

"Yeah, here are our reports and copies of some equipment we recovered a week ago, and some other intel." Doc handed over the package.

"Thanks." The man took possession and slid it into the leather messenger bag slung across his chest.

"You got a name?" Doc asked the man.

"Galt. Yours?" he replied as he mounted his bike.

"I'm Doc, and that's Disco. Good luck."

"Thanks. You too, thanks for the gun."

"Least I could do. I'm really sorry about your friends. Thanks for the Warthogs."

Galt didn't say a word. He slung his leg over his motorcycle and his M-4 over his back and was out of sight before Doc and Disco departed.

"Doc, it's time to go," Disco reminded him apprehensively.

"Yeah, I know. Take that bike and scout up ahead where we left ours."

Disco mounted one of the dirtbikes that belonged to the fallen Galveston Island team; it started without trouble. Doc jogged behind, trying to keep up with Disco as he rode up to the other bike, which was still running. Disco's gunshots told Doc that the undead had been attracted to the running engine while the two were down at the bridge. By the time Doc made it up the hill, Disco had already dispatched the creatures, littering the ground with more corpses.

"We gotta roll, man. That AK caused a major ruckus. I wouldn't doubt it if every creature for five miles is headed for our pos." Disco revved his engine, heading back in the direction they came, with Doc trailing.

They made good time back to the tanker, refilling without incident. The undead density was higher on the way back, remainders from the dead attracted by their motorcycle on their way to the bridge, causing more swerves and weaving. The vampires of Hotel 23 once again beat the winter sun.

Remote Six—Eve of Project Hurricane

God stood on the watch floor, deep inside a covered facility, staring at the Global Hawk UAV picture of a particularly high-interest area in Texas. He remembered the day, more than ten months ago, when he shut the doors, securing himself below ground—the day the president was declared dead.

At that time, the vice president was still alive somewhere in the mountains west of Washington, D.C., issuing logic tree orders to Remote Six via secure cable. Logic trees were made of complex responses, as they required more than a simple yes or no finding. They were basically a prediction market, something that the intelligence community had experimented with prior to the fall of man. The logic tree response demanded a chain of yes or no answers and probability annotations for each option. This was no trouble for the quantum's mind mapping and reasoning algorithms. To complement the quantums, Remote Six boasted a small team of nuclear experts on site for the human reasoning input on the decision to deploy tactical nuclear warheads on U.S. soil. Strange, Charm, and Top were their codenames—Remote Six did not use real names, only those that represented the expertise of its personnel. Over nine and a half months ago, the quantums, as well as nuclear weapons experts Strange and Charm, all agreed that the full destruction of a majority of cities was necessary to regain control of the United States. The lone dissenter was Top. Top believed that more research needed to be conducted on the second- and third-order effects of radiation and on the true origin of the anomaly.

God looked down on the facility that the pathetic squatters called Hotel 23. His database had another name for the place, but that really didn't matter anymore. Under most circumstances he'd leave them for the undead—sooner or later they'd leave the safety of the compound looking for food, water, antibiotics, whatever. The creatures would pick them off slowly but ever so surely.

Now, God was forced to devote time and attention to the miserable pimple and its squatters below, because Hotel 23 still contained a viable nuclear warhead. The quantums ran the numbers, informing his think tank that there was now only one way to destroy the USS *George Washington,* the COG's military right hand. Remote Six had a squadron of Reaper UCAVs armed with five-hundred-pound laser-guided bombs and even a small number of Global Hawk UAVs with a prototype weapon. None of those weapons could so much as dent the hull of the carrier. The LGBs would fall straight down and possibly damage the flight deck but would have no chance at sinking the ship.

There was only one working nuclear weapon inside the United States that God had a shot at controlling. That warhead was secure inside the closed silo beneath his Global Hawk—an unmanned aerial vehicle that orbited at sixty thousand feet over Hotel 23. It monitored the area equipped with an advanced optics suite and one other prototype payload—Project Hurricane.

God grew tired of helping him along. The man, according to Remote Six SIGINT intercepts, held control of the warhead launch via an encrypted Common Access Card. He nearly had a heart attack the day he learned that the man had been in a helicopter crash, fearing that his chance of neutralizing the USS *George Washington* had evaporated. Remote Six designated the man as Asset One, or just *the asset*. The asset had been doing a fair job of evading the creatures, but God took no chances.

He ordered full Reaper and air-drop support the instant that Remote Six intercepted and geolocated the distress beacon from the asset's survival radio. God would have dispatched a small extraction force, but he was very short on air-breathing aircraft pilots and couldn't risk losing an extraction team in a mishap onboard one of the prototype C-130 UAVs. Technology was not a problem for Remote Six, but personnel was becoming a big limiting factor.

The fully functioning twelve-thousand-foot runway co-located above Remote Six was increasingly difficult to secure, despite its location—a secret basin far away from what many would consider a densely populated area. A ten-foot-high, double-layered, K-9 patrolled chainlink fence buffered the runway from the straggling dead near the facility.

But some got through.

There had been casualties since January, since going underground. The most valuable resource in Remote Six was people—those still loyal to the charter of the facility anyway.

The strength of the facility was her drones, DARPA prototype weapons. Though formidable, there were things darker, blacker. Things known only by a whisper between the highest elected and appointed officials before the fall. Things reverse engineered from technology secured in a Lockheed Martin laboratory vault since a time when the government hit its own technological impasse in the 1950s and thereby signed the hardware over to the military-industrial complex.

God grew impatient. He'd thought that the asset would have been more appreciative; after all, he'd saved him from certain death more than once. The asset had made it back to Hotel 23 a few days ago, and had been unresponsive to God's iridium phone transmissions.

The quantums, as well as his top think tank advisors, agreed that destroying the carrier would serve two purposes; it would eliminate Task Force Hourglass before its submarine deployment to China, and would get rid of the only entity that could order nuclear response on Remote Six. With the asset's apparent refusal to launch hanging over him, God had a whole new problem set for the mainframes. The answer came out in real time; some Remote Six scientists theorized that the reply might even be given before the user actually asked—perhaps by a few nanoseconds. It twisted one's mind thinking about the physics behind that—answers before questions, or output nanoseconds before input.

The quantum output did not surprise God. Project Hurricane would likely be deployed against Hotel 23 tomorrow or the next day. This would force the evacuation of the facility or likely eliminate the squatters. Either outcome awarded some time for God to evaluate his next move. He was all but certain that none of the surviving military apparatus knew of his location, but . . . *doubt kills,* he thought.

God flipped a switch and turned a few dials, adjusting the Global Hawk UAV video feed to another location miles away from Hotel 23. Mega Swarm T-5.1 would soon be within range of the Hurricane device, and Hotel 23 would be neutralized. Until then he would continue to feed the quantums, predicting the next big thing.

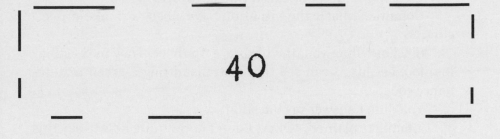

40

Kunia Facility—Oahu Interior

It took a few hours for Rex and Huck to figure out the cave facility generator system. Fortunately it wasn't anything high-speed like geothermal or tide power, just a simple diesel system. The fuel tanks were still three-quarters full and it seemed like the back-up system had never been activated. The mainland grid must have stayed on until it was knocked out by nuclear detonation. By isolating the power grid internal to the cave, they could get maybe two months of power out of the generator banks.

Commie was straining over the keyboard, attempting to bring up the critical computers needed to provide overwatch for the *Virginia*.

"I don't get it," he said. "None of my log-ins work and I know they're still valid."

"Could the birds have burned in already?" Rex said, referring to the overhead satellites.

"No, they haven't re-entered. I'm seeing their maintenance signal active, see?" Commie pointed to a screen cascading code that might as well have come straight out of *The Matrix*.

"I don't know what the hell any of that is," Huck said.

"You probably don't even know your own social, shut up," Rico chided.

"At least I have a social, *ese*."

Rex jumped in, not feeling the comedy routine right now. "If you all think you need to joke around, think about Griff. Think he's joking right now?"

"Naw, he's probably back on the boat in a warm rack," Huck said.

"I hope," Rex responded, staring down Huck.

"Commie, what's the situation? We need to make a decision."

"Sir, I'm telling you, the birds are up there. They're functioning, too, because I can see they're transmitting a green maintenance code."

"You didn't answer my question."

Commie explained, "Okay, I don't know quite how to say this without sounding like a conspiracy theorist, but I saw this once before. The NRO took control of the birds a few years back to run some diagnostics and didn't tell anyone they were doing it. Some of us little guys didn't get the memo. This looks like outside control has been locked out, and the birds are being controlled once again in the same way. I don't think we'll be able to get them."

"Well, fuck," Rex murmured.

"There is good news though," Commie offered. "I can try to run a trace on the entity that's currently in control of the birds. We likely won't be able to pinpoint, but we might get close."

"Okay, Commie, do it. I'm not going back to the *Virginia* empty-handed. If Griff made it, that's good, but if he didn't I won't throw his life away without forcing this mission to give us something in return. Don't forget that Commander Monday wanted the archives of all the intel collected three months before January and up until the nuke was dropped on Honolulu. Check?"

Commie clicked another workspace on the GUI of the Unix system. "Yeah, I'm on it. Running it now."

"Can he access the comms interface from here? The boat is no doubt worried about us and maybe we can find out about Griff," Rico asked, visibly worried about his team member.

"No, I don't have outgoing comms capability here and I wouldn't know how to use those systems even if they were powered up and I knew their location," said Commie. "Sorry."

"It's daylight. The sun sets in ten hours. Be ready to fucking roll when the sun goes down, Commie, and you're in luck; you won't be calling this cave home for the next six weeks, while we go to China and back. The water is drinkable; everything inside has been shielded from the blast. According to the readings, our suits aren't too dirty and as long as we don't lick them clean before we get back, we should be okay for the return trip."

"What do you want me and Huck working on?" Rico asked Rex.

"I want you two working on our way out of here. Unless we can restore power to that door, we ain't gettin' out the same way we got in. Considering the fact that we don't hear a thousand corpses screaming outside the turnstile area, Griff was successful in getting the door closed. There must be another exit."

"There is another way out," Commie said. "When we came in, we went down the tunnel until it came to a T. We turned right to get where we are now. If you go left you'll pass by some vending machines. Farther down you'll see a maintenance door that leads to a ladder. That goes up above ground to an access shed. The shed is used to get outside for downlink antenna maintenance. I know about it because we caught two people up there . . . well, you know. Back when I worked here before."

"You guys heard him. Check it out, but make sure you watch your asses. Griff might not have got them all in the tunnel. Be back here in two hours, or we'll assume you didn't make it. I can't leave Commie here alone—too risky. Double-check your suits and move out."

Rico and Huck donned their radiation hoods and did a press check on their carbines before moving to the vending machine hall outside the secured area. Commie continued to run his trace and simultaneously downloaded the archived intelligence collected by this station three months before the dead walked. While downloading, he peeked at some of the messages at random, realizing that the intelligence had never been processed or transmitted to anyone outside this facility.

There must not have been time or anyone available to sift through the vast amounts of data and turn it into an actionable report. Commie scanned through the overwhelming information while Rex guarded the area, worried about Griff.

BEGIN TEXT TRANSCRIPTION

KLIEGLIGHT SERIAL 099

RTTUZYUW-RQHNQN-OOOOO-RRRRR-Y

T O P S E C R E T//SI//G//SAP HORIZON

Addressees be advised: This report contains intelligence that has not been analyzed. For internal use only.

This station has collected COMINT originating from the PRC referring to an SAP with codename HORIZON. [REDACTED] clandestine communication with Chinese scientists associated with the Mingyong excavation was discovered by Chinese leadership some time ago, possibly before January. The PRC GSD has known of their scientist's encrypted contact with [REDACTED] and has, in response, initiated an aggressive cyber warfare initiative clandestinely against [REDACTED]. The virus algorithm embedded into the communication attachments is similar to previous STUXNET entities as it embeds itself into proprietary [REDACTED] systems and learns vulnerabilities and limitations in real-time. It is unknown to this station as to the extent of the damage the Chinese STUXNET-like worm entity has inflicted on critical [REDACTED] decision matrix systems.

KUNIA SENDS . . . K/

BT

AR

TRANSMISSION STATUS: Unable to TX, outbound comms NMC

41

Oahu Cave Facility

"This is it. Bust that hatch, Rico," Huck whispered up the ladder. "I smell the ocean."

Rico climbed the rungs above, his nose tuned to something rotting. "You smell the ocean, I smell death. I'm gonna take my time. You sit tight down there; I'm not gettin' bit so you can see the sun."

"Fair enough," Huck said, chewing on a stick of gum he had looted from the vending machines along the way.

"Ahh, I see," Rico said, hoping Huck would ask.

Huck took the bait. "See what, man? What?"

"This!" Rico answered as he slung the carcass of a badly decomposed cat down on top of him.

"Fuck!" Huck screamed. "You goddamned wetback! Don't think I'm gonna let that slide. I'll punch your green card before we get back, for sure!"

"Calm down, *mang*. It was funny," Rico said, giggling in an over-the-top Cuban accent, sounding a lot like Tony Montana. Huck grimaced. "Why so mad? I *tole* you I was in sanitation."

Huck laughed and reached up, trying to grab Rico's leg to pull him down a couple rungs, and maybe a couple notches of attitude. Huck asked, "You worried about Griff?"

"I am, Griff is my friend, but I gotta stay positive. He might still be alive. Not going to let it kill me. I want to get back and finish what we started."

"Amen to that. Ready to get over there and kick some Chinese ass," Huck yelled, his voice echoing down the ladder and throughout the tunnel below.

Something clanged somewhere in the tunnel blackness far in the distance.

"You drop something?" Rico asked as he worked on the access door that led to the outside.

"No, it was in the tunnel. One of the things, I'll bet."

"Just a sec. This padlock shim is giving me a hard time," Rico said, bending the shim again to fit inside the locking mechanism of the large brass government padlock.

"That's what happens when you make a padlock shim out of an aluminum can, stupid Mexican."

"Your name is one vowel off from the truth, you know that, *Hick*? I may be stupid, but I know how to keep my hands off my cousins, you backwoods *Deliverance* fuck."

"That's cold-blooded, man. I still owe you for the cat. Don't think all this joking around is gonna make me forget."

"Put your hood on, climb up here, and shut up, hick. I just popped the lock. I'm gonna throw this lever and open the door. Ready?"

"Yeah, do it. I'm ready."

Huck pulled his gun up to high ready. Moisture condensed inside their radiation hoods as the first rays of sunlight beamed through the doorway. The view was bleak. Although a paradise of green a year ago, today the picture was much darker. All the vegetation was dead and trees were blown northward away from the blast that had rocked Honolulu. None of them had realized the full scope of the island's destruction when they moved in the cover of last night's darkness.

They were on top of a hill above the cave and tunnel, and could see the ocean in the distance from their vantage point. Huck noted the damaged, golf ball–shaped antennas some distance away, as well as the smaller antennas right outside the door.

They were on a steep pinnacle overlooking the infested cave entrance on the south side, and a sheer cliff on the north that dropped a hundred feet into the remains of a jungle. Rico grabbed his waterproof notepad and began making a sketch of the situation so he could brief Rex upon return. Huck had the binos, and was surveilling the tunnel entrance below. He got down on his chest and low-crawled to the edge. Rico instinctively grabbed Huck's feet.

"What's it look like?"

"It looks like a bunch of fucking walking dead things," Huck replied.

Rico lifted Huck's feet a few inches off the ground, startling him a bit.

"Quit fuckin' around," Huck lashed. He continued scanning the area below, looking for anything that might assist their exfil. Huck paused his bino sweep and tightened his shoulders in concentration. "Uh . . . Rico. Man, I'm sorry."

"What . . . Griff?"

"Yeah, brother. Pull me back. Sorry, man."

Rico dragged Huck away from the edge by his boots and sat down in momentary defeat, leaning against the rusty maintenance access shed door. "What did you see, Huck?" Rico had the tone of a man that didn't want an answer.

"I saw what was left of a brave motherfucker that took a stand. Looks like he pulled a frag and took a few with him."

Both men sat atop the hill absorbing the heat of the Hawaiian sun through their exposure suits, a small luxury considering their current living conditions aboard the submarine.

Huck checked his digital watch, squinting at the faded numbers caused by a weak battery that would never be replaced. "Rico, it's been an hour. We should head."

Rico stood up and quickly unslung his M-4, surprising Huck. Flipping off the safety with his right thumb he began to take pot shots at the creatures below. He dropped ten of the undead, with no noticeable impact on the five hundred or so that walked about cooking in the tropical sun. Rico slung his carbine and walked through the shed door that sheltered the hatch and ladder leading back down.

The ladder hole reminded Huck of his grandmother's water well and how she had always warned him as a child to stay away from it or he might fall in. *The water's cold down there, boy, and full of dead squirrels,* she'd kid. He drank from the creek most of the time.

"Rico, we should probably radio the boat before we go down the hole, let 'em know what's going on."

Rico nodded.

"This is Hourglass with SITREP," Huck transmitted.

"Hourglass, damn good to hear you. Go ahead with SITREP." Kil's voice came back through the tinny ear mic.

"Facility is green, birds are unavailable. Commie reports that the birds are locked out and controlled by another entity. Going ahead with secondary objectives. Copy?"

"Yeah, good transmission. Listen, about Griff, he . . ."

"We know," Huck responded. "We're topside now, headed back down. Intend to exfil tonight. See you back at the boat, Hourglass out."

"Roger, Hourglass. See you soon."

Huck went first down the ladder, mindful of the sound they had heard earlier. He pointed his carbine down as he descended. Reaching the tunnel floor they pulled their masks and began moving back to where Rex and Commie were. It was a few hundred yards to the turnstiles, allowing enough time for both men to adjust their eyes from the sunlight back to the NODs. Reaching the metal gate Rico pulled the handle. It didn't budge.

"We're locked out—gotta pick it," Rico said.

"Okay, I'll pick the damn thing, you try the radio. Maybe Rex has his on; he's not that far from here. The signal might make it through a few walls, maybe."

Rico keyed the mic, walking back and forth from the vending machines to the gate, trying his luck with different areas to maybe get lucky with his signal ducting.

Something moved somewhere in the darkness.

"Huck? You hear it?" Rico said, jogging back to the gate.

"What?"

"Something's in here. Don't know how far, but no doubt it's probably something fucked up and headed this way. Hurry up!" Rico whispered, trying to avoid unnecessary noise. The tunnel propagated sound in unpredictable directions.

The lock gave unexpectedly and Huck fell inside. "We're in, Rico—move it."

Rico watched the blackness down the tunnel. His NODs would

only grant a few meters of visibility in the total darkness. Something *had* moved out there, Rico knew it. He walked backward with his weapon up, through the gate, shutting it behind him. They moved side by side down the passageway, back to Rex and Commie.

"It's gonna be a problem on the way back, man," Rico warned.

"I don't see how. It's pitch black and those things can't see in the dark."

"Yeah, but we don't really know what this radiation shit does to them, man. Could be fucked up."

"Oh, shut the fuck up! We'll make it out. The cave doors only had a few inches of gap. Those things can't fit through. If there are any in here with us, it will only be one or two. Griff wouldn't have fucked us like that, man."

Huck's statement had the desired effect, causing Rico's attitude to shift perceptibly. They threw the hatch and walked into the room where Rex and Commie waited.

"You guys were gone a long time. What did you see?" Commie asked. His pack was closed, gear packed tight and ready to move out.

"We found the exit. That's the good news, I guess," Huck said solemnly.

"Spit it out, Huck. What's the shitty news?" Rex demanded.

"Well . . . Griff . . . didn't make it; he hugged a frag and took about half a dozen with him. Not much left, but it's him out there."

"He's not . . . ?" Rex asked.

"No, he's real dead, for sure. I wouldn't leave him any other way," Huck said, looking at the ground, all too tired of seeing the pain in the eyes of his team members.

Rico pulled the notepad from his pocket and showed Rex the topside layout.

"There's a steep drop on the north side, seventy-five, maybe a hundred. The south side is above the tunnel doors where Griff is . . . was." Rico shifted from sadness to anger as he spoke. "I don't care what you wanna do, boss. If you wanna drop down on the south side and shoot 'em all, I'm with that."

Rex was startled by Rico's sudden change in temperament. "No, we'll take the north side and get out of here unscathed. Ammo is our LIMFAC. Make radio contact?"

"Affirm," Huck acknowledged, smacking on a fresh stick of gum. "They know about Griff, saw it from the eye in the sky. Told 'em we were Oscar Mike back to the boat tonight. What happened here?"

"Commie tried again to bring the satellites up under his control. No dice. Someone else has the reins." Rex glanced over and saw that Commie was packed and ready to move. "Going somewhere?"

"Yeah, out of here, fast. I've done everything we were fragged for. The intel is burned on two DVDs in my pack. I'll give one to you before we leave just in case. They're duplicates."

"Good idea. Although if you don't make it back, I might as well stay here. Old Man Larsen would tie me to the sail and slap my balls with a car antenna if we lost our HVA."

This made Huck laugh so hard he spit out his gum. In his head, the captain was dressed like General Patton with a car antenna instead of a riding crop. He laughed even harder, doubling over red-faced.

"Not *that* damn funny, Huck." Rex walked over and stole a piece of Huck's stale gum from the table and turned to face Commie. "Anyway, what happened with the trace?"

Commie replied quickly, almost as if reading from a script: "The trace stopped in Alaska. I couldn't get beyond the firewall there." He pulled his pack straps tightly and walked back over to the terminal. "I'm shutting down the mainframe. I doubt anyone will ever come here again but there is a possibility that we may need the systems at some point."

"I don't care if you download porn and set everything on fire—we're done here." Rex moved to the center of the room to lay down the plan. "We're moving out when the sun goes down. Should be clear inside and Commie knows the place, so Rico— you and Commie go find some rope somewhere, four lengths if you can. We'll make do if you can't. Me and Huck will hold it down."

"Roger that. Let's go, Commie." They both dropped their heavy packs, bringing only weapons. None of them looked forward to the next twelve hours—the trip back through the island's belt of undead.

USS Virginia
December

I'm going to be a father! *Me?!* Though the team is on the ground ten miles into Hiroshima-like terrain, I still can't stop smiling. Good news—*great* news. Best news since last Christmas. Nearly one year since the world died, and I find out that I have made a new life.

The message from Tara was simple, but it changed me forever: *WE ARE PREGNANT.*

I paced around for what seemed like an hour, smiling and happy. Oblivious to what was happening around me. I wasn't on a submarine off the coast of Hawaii, I was somewhere in the clouds!

On to more pressing matters.

The sun will be down in a couple hours and two things will happen. I will have another chance to communicate a relay to Crusow and I'll be supporting the Kunia exfil. Crusow sounded so happy and proud for me when he broke the news from Tara. Funny how I've never met him, and yet he knew about the baby before I did because of the relay. It's hard to believe he's so far away, somewhere so opposite me. It's a hundred and forty degrees of temperature difference between him and me, and yet we still find some joy in our situations. Me more than him today!

Names for the relay: Something strong like Alexander if he's a boy. Something like Lillian or . . . need to think of another name for a girl. Damn, I need to get married when I get back. My mother would kill me if she knew I was going to be an unmarried dad. My mother . . .

42

USS George Washington

John clandestinely monitored the entire volume of the ship's message traffic by way of the improvised splice of certain sensitive lines, intercepting some troubling news. He'd also siphoned traffic mentioning intelligence collected over the Beijing area by an aircraft called *Aurora* in the sourcing lines.

John had already encoded and transmitted a short line of warning to Kil, but wasn't yet sure of his receipt. Kil's confirmation before the boat was due in the Bohai was necessary or he might be forced to transmit in the clear, unencrypted for anyone who might listen. John was gravely worried about Kil. He decided not to mention his findings to Tara to avoid unnecessary worry and confusion. He knew of the good news and didn't want her upset. The particulars of Kil's business in China were unknown to John, but he had suspicions that whatever they were going after over there might be related to the recently intercepted messages.

During the leadership meeting he had attended yesterday—*attended* being a loose term, as he had been dismissed halfway for security reasons—John learned of a concern that the admiral had with one of the civilians onboard. The officer speaking used his allotted time to brief the admiral, careful not to use names, knowing there were civilians present at the meeting.

"The boy claimed to hear things, Admiral, aft on the O-3 level. Told his nurse and doctor. How do you want to proceed?"

With a wave of his hand, the admiral dismissed every non-military person in the room. Then Joe, the admiral's aide, ushered everyone out and closed the door. John knew that he'd likely not be requested back, so he took this time to make a phone call from the phone in the hallway. He dialed the sick bay.

"Jan. Is this an emergency?"

"No, it's John. Listen. Remember that discussion we had a week or so ago about Danny?"

"Yes, why?"

"Did you tell anyone about it?"

"No, I just talked about it with Dean. Dean told me she'd take it up with the admiral during the next town hall meeting next week."

John paused for a moment. "The reason I'm asking is that I was at the leadership meeting this morning, and I overheard something before they dismissed the civilians. Something about a boy who heard things." John reached for his notepad and flipped to the first non-dog-eared page. "A boy who heard things aft on the O-3 level and told his nurse."

Jan was silent on the other end of the phone.

"Jan? I think it's best we call a Hotel 23 meeting."

"Okay, that sounds good. I'll see you in a few minutes. Meet me in the hallway at our staterooms."

"All right, see you soon. Be careful."

"Will do. Bye, John."

John dialed up Will, Dean, and Tara before heading to the meeting. After efficiently traversing the levels and ladders, he arrived to find Jan and Will already there, and a little treat standing alongside her: Laura with Annabelle.

"Hi, Laura! Taking care of my doggy for me?"

"Yes! She's mine though, she told me!" Laura said, giggling and scratching Annabelle's back. The dog's curly, piglike tail wiggled as if she somehow understood.

"We'll see about that, little girl!" John said in his evil-uncle voice, causing more giggles from Laura.

Annabelle wagged her tail and ran over, tongue already licking in advance, tail wagging uncontrollably.

"Will, how have you been? I'm sorry that I haven't even had five minutes to talk to you in the past few days. Been busy with the comms and such."

"Don't worry about it—Jan has me changing bedpans and rigging IV bags. She's worked me like a cheap mule."

Jan shot a disapproving look at Will, prompting smiles all around.

A stateroom door closed behind John; turning, he saw Tara walking up. "I don't think it's a big deal, but we should probably get out of the hallway as soon as everyone shows up. We're still missing Dean."

"I'm here." Dean's voice echoed up the hallway. A basketball bounced off the steel deck, a clue that Danny was in tow. "Danny, you and Laura go study in the classroom. I'll get you when we are done, and I don't want any lip about it, young man."

"Okay, Granny," Danny responded rather sadly. It was never fun to be a young boy told to babysit a girl.

Rubbing the top of his head with her rough working hands, Dean reassured him, "It'll be fun, kiddo, won't be long. Scoot."

Danny, Laura, and Annabelle scattered to the next room with Annabelle jumping over a knee-knocker like a woodland doe over a log. After a few moments, Annabelle's gallop could be heard again getting louder right before she returned, skidding to a stop at John's feet.

"That's my girl!" said John. "Let's do my room, it's got more space."

"Wow, look who's movin' up!" Tara said, smiling sarcastically.

"Yeah, I feel slightly guilty about it, but I'm up at all hours of the night and living in the stateroom of the guy who did my job before. I'm staying in the COMMO's quarters. They're still spartan compared to Hotel 23, but pretty roomy considering where we're at."

"Oh, stop it, John! If one of us gets a break, well that's good news," Dean assured him.

"Thanks, Dean, just didn't want anyone thinking I was forgetting about you all. Should we get started?"

They all piled into John's stateroom and closed the door. They took seats on the bunk beds, sink, and small foldout desk as John began to go over this morning's events. Annabelle found the piece of rope that John had scavenged from the forecastle and converted into a chew toy. As John explained what he had overheard, Dean's face showed signs of worry. Dean was going to request a meeting with the admiral, but since Danny hadn't actually seen anything with his own eyes, she thought it best to let it go for now.

"I know how this made it to the admiral," Jan blurted out. "A week or so ago I was in sick bay with Dr. Bricker. Danny came in needing stitches and mentioned that he thought that there were *zombies* onboard, and that he was playing zombie with the other children. After Danny left, Dr. Bricker told me that he'd sometimes receive tissue samples for analysis, and that he was suspicious of where the samples came from."

"That doesn't really mean anything, Jan. Besides, do we really want to jump to conclusions and get ourselves all worked up over tissue samples?" Tara asked.

Jan frowned and began to explain: "It's not just some tissue samples. Bricker said they were highly radiated brain-tissue fragments. He stressed that no reconnaissance or salvage missions occurred in the two weeks prior to receiving the samples."

"Jan, I'm not doubting you . . . I just don't think I'm ready to think about those things being on this ship with me and . . ." Tara put both hands on her belly, rubbing it softly, and began to sob.

"Tara, it's okay," said John. "If they're onboard, at least we'll know. We're all armed despite what we thought might happen when we got here. Instead of disarming all of us, the military required we have weapons at all times onboard the ship; this plays to our advantage. The only thing left to do is prove that the undead are here with us."

John stood up from his desk and pushed his glasses back up the bridge of his nose. "I think I may just have the perfect undead detector, batteries not included." He looked down at Annabelle as she chewed on her rope, tail curled and wagging.

"Those hackles saved Kil and me more than once."

ZAAUZYUW RUEOMFC7685 1562255-TTTT—
RHOVIQM

ZNR TTTTT ZUI RUEOMCG340X 1562254

Z 042253Z

FM USS GEORGE WASHINGTON

TO RHOVNQN/COG MT W

BT

T O P S E C R E T N//002045U

SUBJ:/SITREP CAUSEWAY—DOWNTOWN

RMKS:/FINAL PHASE OF EXPERIMENTATION
ON SPECIMENS CAUSEWAY AND DOWNTOWN
WILL BIGIN IN THE NEXT 24 HOURS. IAW
COG DIRECTIVES, PLANNED AREAS OF
BRAIN WILL BE LOBOTOMIZED, ONE EYE
REMOVED FOR TESTING OF SUSPECTED
THERMAL SENSORY PERCEPTION. THIS
STATION WILL SEND UPDATE SEPCOR.

BT

AR

NNNNN

*   *   *

BEGIN TEXT TRANSMISSION

KLIEGLIGHT SERIAL 209

RTTUZYUW-RQHNQN-00000-RRRRR-Y

T O P S E C R E T//SAP HORIZON

SUBJ: NEW ORLEANS SPECIMEN RADIATION
EFFECT FINDINGS

RMKS: THIS STATION HAS COMPLETED
INITIAL EXAMINATION ON SPECIMENS
CAUSEWAY AND DOWNTOWN (LABELED IN
REFERENCE TO NEW ORLEANS EXTRACTION
AREAS). DURING THE INITIAL TESTING,
BOTH SUBJECTS DISPLAYED CONGRUENCY
WITH HAND EYE FUNCTION, SIMILAR TO A
YOUNG CHILD IN ABILITY TO MANIPULATE
SHAPED WOOD OBJECTS INTO SHAPED
HOLES. DURING MORE ADVANCED
COORDINATION TESTING, DOWNTOWN
POSSESSED ABILITY TO MOVE AT TEN MPH
BURSTS. CAUSEWAY COULD ATTAIN SIX
MPH. DOWNTOWN ALSO POSSESSED SIMPLE
PROBLEM SOLVING ABILITY AND WOULD
CHOOSE CERTAIN TOOLS TO ATTEMPT TO

BREAK GLASS TO GAIN ENTRY TO WHAT IT
PERCEIVED MIGHT BE LIVING PREY BEHIND
BALLISTIC GLASS. DOWNTOWN DISPLAYED
ADVERSARIAL BEHAVIOR TOWARD
CAUSEWAY WHEN FOOD WAS IN PLAY, AND
WOULD SHOVE CAUSEWAY AWAY FROM FOOD
SOURCES AT TIMES.

BEHAVIOR OF NOTE: DOWNTOWN WAS
OBSERVED WATCHING RESEARCHERS
ENTER AND LEAVE AND WOULD MIMIC
THEIR HAND MOVEMENT WHEN THE
RESEARCHERS WOULD THROW HATCH
LEVERS TO THE OUTSIDE, SUGGESTING AT
LEAST RUDIMENTARY LEARNING ABILITY.
BOTH CAUSEWAY AND DOWNTOWN POSSESS
SPEED AND AGILITY NOT YET OBSERVED
IN CREATURES UNEXPOSED TO RADIATION
BOMBARDMENT OF PREVIOUS NUCLEAR
DETONATIONS.

SUMMARY: USS *GEORGE WASHINGTON* WILL
CONTINUE TO OBSERVE THE SPECIMENS. WILL
ADVISE COG ON ANY DESTRUCTION INTENT.
FIVE SUBJECTS IN VARIOUS CONDITIONS
FROM DIFFERENT GEOGRAPHICAL
SECTORS REMAIN ONBOARD. THIS STATION
IS SKEPTICAL AT THE POSSIBILITY OF
EXTERMINATION OF THE AMERICAN
POPULATION OF UNDEAD. RADIATED
UNDEAD ARE AT THIS TIME SHOWING NO
INDICATIONS OF DECAY. HIROSHIMA AND
NAGASAKI ARCHIVE DATA INDICATES SOME
PRESERVATION OF THE DEAD BY RADIATION
BUT NOT TO THIS ORDER OF MAGNITUDE. WE
SPECULATE THAT HIGH ORDER RADIATION
HAS FORMED A SYMBIOTIC RELATIONSHIP
WITH THE ANOMALY ON A LEVEL WE ARE
UNABLE TO VERIFY OR MEASURE AT THIS
TIME. GOOD LUCK.

GW CHIEF SCIENTIST SENDS . . .

BT

AR

Tunnel in the Sky . . . I was so caught up with the mission, I had no clue what John meant. He's been including extra codes with his chess moves for well over a week now. I wrote them down without thinking, as they were basically gibberish to me at the time. John sent the encrypted messages using our twin copies of *Tunnel in the Sky*. He'd sent page, paragraph, and sentence cipher codes referring to specific words and letters that matched my copy of the text, forming short sentences. I discovered this after Crusow's last transmission relay from John. Although I informed John that I finished the book a while back, he still asked again after the most recent set of codes. "Read *Tunnel in the Sky* yet?"

I sat confused in my rack for a while, flipping through the pages, waiting to hear an update from the team coming back from Kunia. I looked for something that John may have written inside the book, something I may have missed.

I finally pieced together the message. The gibberish code hidden in plain sight with the chess moves referred to specific sequences that could only be deciphered if the recipient had the exact same key as the sender. In this case an uncommon and out of print book. It took a few minutes, but his message was clear.

"1947 NEVADA CRASH SPECIMEN JUST EXPOSED TO ANOMALY . . . VERY STRONG . . . GUNS INEFFECTIVE, FIRE NEUTRALIZED . . . MEAN ANYTHING?"

I am of course surprised and confused as to how John came across this information, but it is starting to make more sense, considering he's the acting communications officer onboard the carrier. The navy always seems to operate on two primary working principles. One of them is the *fuck up move up* rule, wherein the more fucked up you are, the higher chance of your promotion. The other principle that has held true in my time in service is *curse of the competent*. John falls into the latter. The more competent you are, the more uncompensated responsibility you are given, and the more work is expected of you.

Without fail, the ones that ruled the competent typically

fell into the first category. I suspect John has been given full access to the ship's communication networks because he's the only one that can do the job. Either way, I won't be revealing this message to the captain until I'm very sure what side he's on. I'll tell Rex and company when the time is right; they are the operators, and deserve to know. China will be problematic at best.

This encoded message from John would have sounded pretty damn strange if I had not been briefed on what our government had been hiding all these years in the mountains out west.

43

USS Virginia—Hawaiian waters

"Kil, when will they be back?" Saien asked.

"They're leaving the cave an hour after sundown. The creatures seem to be a little calmer then. Why do you ask?"

"I just wanted to see if we had some time to chat before you went back to work."

"Yeah, I guess. Whatcha got on your mind?" Kil said as he slid off the top rack and sat down in front of Saien.

"I don't think I believe in what we were told on the way over here. I've thought about it for many days. At first I thought some of it might be true, but after going over it again in my head it seems ridiculous. I wanted to know how you felt about this, this wild story?"

Kil took a deep breath and sat back in his chair for a moment, pondering the question. After some time, he spoke. "Well, I think I'm with you on this one. Someone close to me used to say: 'Don't believe anything you hear and only half of what you see.'"

They shared a laugh even though Kil wasn't sure that Saien understood the intended meaning.

"Now that we're on the same page I think I need to tell you something," Kil said with a conspiratorial whisper. He stood up and walked over to his rack, reaching under the pillow. Out from underneath he pulled a worn paperback novel. "Remember this book John gave me before we left?"

Saien nodded.

"Well, I just found out that John has been passing a message to me using the pages of this book, embedded in his chess moves. You know, with the normal message traffic and such."

"Are you going to tell me what it says?"

"The basic message was that the Roswell specimen had been exposed to whatever this shit is."

"What? When did this happen?"

"I don't know the when or why but the results, according to John, were that it was pretty damn mean. Only fire stopped it. Small arms had no effect."

They both sat there and chewed on that for a moment, until Kil said, "Now we just established that both of us think that this is some crazy tinfoil-hat bullshit and probably not true. All that aside, even though we don't believe any of it, it might be a good idea to get ahold of a Molotov cocktail or two for the team. I think you should make friends down in engineering and see what you can come up with. If asked, tell them I requested it."

"Sounds good."

"As soon as the team gets back, I'll focus on telling Rex what we know. I don't want to get John in any trouble. I don't think Rex and his folks will be a problem, but the stress of all this . . ."

"Yes, the stress in all this can turn friends to enemies and enemies to friends. I know this firsthand."

"Yes, I'll bet you do. Don't think I've forgotten our travels. You're pretty damn good with the long gun, something that most civilians are not. I've taken notice of the rug and of your fire kindling. We've never talked about it before, but then again, I was pretty sick of war even *before* all this went down. I think this, whatever you call it, ended a few longtime feuds, and abated some hatred. Don't worry, Saien, I think Homeland Security is gone for good. I don't know what I despised more, their airport naked-body scanners and grope-downs or the dead walking. I doubt any database is left powered up with your name on it."

Taking a long breath, Saien sat back uncomfortably with arms drawn in close to his body. "Kil, I was to meet up with a member of my cell in San Antonio. We were to . . ."

"Don't bother, Saien. I don't need to hear it. Don't forget I'm a commissioned military officer and wouldn't have hesitated before," Kil replied, emotion showing through.

"I need to get this off my back. I have no one left. That's the only reason."

"Saien, remember what they told us before we learned about what we're going after? 'What was told could not be untold.' Before you keep talking, make sure it's something you won't regret. We survived some pretty close calls, but I wouldn't expect you to be asking for my autograph if I told you what I did back before all this. I chose to keep my mouth shut about it for a reason. We've gotta survive, that's all—nothing more."

Both men sat in their chairs across from each other in the small stateroom. Kil imagined that he could hear his wristwatch tick—but it was digital. Saien began to speak again—his eyes focused far behind Kil through the bulkheads, through the ocean, beyond Oahu.

"We were to meet in San Antonio. I only knew the codename and email drop of one member of my cell, by design. We communicated via online dead drop box, but used off-the-shelf encryption. Your military uses much inferior communications encryption to what is available off the shelf. I used two-hundred-fifty-six-bit AES. That's not important, I'm sorry. I'm rambling."

"Don't worry about it. Go on, I guess," Kil said reassuringly, more curious than anything else.

Saien took a drink from an old disposable water bottle he'd been using since they left Panama and continued. "It was a week before the dead walked when I received my activation orders. The target was a shopping mall, peak shopping season. I was to be part of a five-man kill squad. We were only one team, but I believe there were more, maybe twenty more teams. All ordered to attack simultaneously in different cities. The goal was to drive the death nail into the American economy and solidify the ongoing economic collapse. Your economy was seventy percent consumer based. If people were too afraid to spend money, it would be the end of the American system. Your money supply would be hyperinflated, and with that, your wars overseas would end. We also knew that the sheepdog could not guard all the sheep and could not lessen their fears. When the dead walked and the infrastructure collapsed, I suppose we got what we wanted. Seeing a man who had been shot through the chest with a sniper round get up and come after you will change your ideology. This is why I do not pray any longer. I resent what I was before, and what I was planning to do. Though you do not ask, I will tell you. Most every American is dead now, as you know. If you were in a cave in Pakistan a year ago having a conversation with leaders of the base and you were to ask him, 'Would the mass death of Americans be good in the eyes of Allah?' he would have no doubt responded as you would imagine. Now look what we have today. America is dead and so is everyone else, Allah is nowhere to be found. God is dead upon the Earth, who could argue this?"

"So you were going to go Mumbai crazy and shoot up a shopping mall?" Kil asked, almost rhetorically.

"That was the plan. I have woken up and I am ashamed," Saien declared sincerely.

"Well, can't say I like you more after hearing that . . . but I ain't perfect either, I'm a military deserter. I disobeyed orders after my boss told me to return to base. I never reported. I stayed behind in my home. John was my neighbor across the street. Look at it this way: At least you didn't carry out the plan. It's only thought crime at this point."

"Yes, for this, I'm thankful. I would be a tortured soul otherwise."

"Yeah, you'd be pretty messed up right about now, no doubt. And as far as God goes, there's a lot of what you have going around. You ain't the only one questioning their faith. I'm sure all that alien bullshit isn't helping anything."

A knock on the door made Kil jump; he reached for his pistol instinctively.

"Come," Kil said.

The door slowly opened, revealing the petty officer of the watch's pimply young face. "Sir, sun is down and we're getting radio chatter from Hourglass. They are asking for you. Scan Eagles are already en route."

"Roger that. I'm on my way," Kil said.

44

Oahu Interior

The sun was down; a purple glow from the west glimmered and danced on the Pacific waters. Task Force Hourglass had been at Kunia cave for twenty-four hours. The Hawaii mission had so far been assessed as a failure. Unable to gain control of the satellites to support the Hourglass incursion, the submarine would be alone, the crew afraid and vulnerable to any remnants of Chinese military that lurked in the Chinese waters. Commie's pack was full of papers and disks. Papers with lots of secrets—information that had never been transmitted from this facility, long ago abandoned by the cryptologic group that worked here.

Rex was the last up the ladder to the top and last to close the lid on this place forever. *Years from now, someone will find a nest of mutant squirrels living in there,* he thought as he slammed the access hatch down. Rex, Huck, Rico, and Commie stood atop the mesalike formation; it was too difficult to tell if it had been built around the tunnel or if the tunnel had been built through it. To the south was a large group of undead creatures; to the north, a sheer cliff face that dropped about seventy-five feet to the jungle below.

Huck found the anchor point for the ropes. They joined the ropes together via a double sheet bend knot. He secured the rope to the anchor near the knot and yelled over to Rico, "Throw it over, Mexican."

Grumbling in Spanish, Rico tossed both ends of the doubled rope over.

"Commie, get over here, this is important," Huck said over his shoulder, careful not to speak loudly toward the south, where the creatures might be frenzied by his drifting voice. Huck stood near Commie, about six feet from the north-facing edge, as he explained. "Now we're about to go rappelling down this here face. What you're going to do is put this double rope through your legs from the front, then you're gonna go around your right leg and pass it across your chest and over your left shoulder like this. Then it's gonna go across your back and under your right arm and you're gonna hold the top with your left and pay out the rope with your right. You sit here and practice a bit while I make sure the Mexican secured it right."

"Oh, fuck you, redneck," Rico retorted, slapping the back of Huck's head.

"Easy there, wouldn't want to slip down there and break a leg, would you? Those things would make short work once they found you, and they always find you," Huck teased.

Huck yanked on the rope and put all his body weight into it to make sure it wouldn't slip anchor. They wouldn't have the luxury of a top-rope belay tonight. "Okay, this bastard is secure, Gibraltar solid," he announced, propping his leg on the anchor point.

Rex made the required radio calls to the USS *Virginia* while Huck and Rico set up the descent. He could barely be heard over the ocean breeze coming in, seemingly from all directions.

"*Virginia,* we are Oscar Mike, over," Rex transmitted.

Commie looked like a cat trapped in a bowl of spaghetti—the rope was twisted every which way across his body. "Why didn't you guys bring a harness?" Commie complained to Huck.

"Because, dipshit, take a look around. Where do you think the nearest open REI might be?"

"Good point. Will you show me again? I think I twisted it the wrong way."

After a little more instruction, Commie seemed ready to make the descent.

The doubled-up rope pulled against Rex's leg, back, and arm. Commie was right—*a harness would have been nice,* he thought to himself, releasing the slack, the friction warming his hand through his gloves as he descended. As Rex neared the jungle floor, the temperature changed and he could smell the rot, not unlike descending into a basement and being hit with the musty odor of old canned fruit and decaying wood. The south face blocked the breeze. Just over six feet off the ground Rex felt the scrape of a branch on the bottom of his leg.

He almost loosened the slack of the rope the rest of the way, which would have dropped him through the branches and onto the ground, but instead he hesitated . . .

The wind was slowed by the cliff and blew lightly at the bottom of the rock face. Risking disorientation, he twisted his torso and looked down, seeing them. The sensation on Rex's leg was not a branch in the breeze, it was the silent clutch of death reaching upward for him. The creatures appeared to be in advanced stages of decomposition. They displayed visible rib cages, no lips, and complete loss of vocal ability—silent apparitions of a dead island, paradise lost to nuclear airburst detonation.

Hanging awkwardly on the ropes, Rex couldn't reach his carbine, and even if he could, it would be too difficult to maneuver it without falling on the creatures below. He grasped for his unsuppressed pistol, making sure it was still secured in the holster. The fingertips of a creature brushed his leg again while he radioed his situation to the top.

"We have company down here, I think about four! Don't bother shooting; you'll just hit me. I'm pulling my sidearm. Be ready to come down quickly behind me. I don't know how many more are in the bushes and the noise from my gun will draw them."

At the top of the face, Huck readied Commie to go next. "Okay, kid, you're gonna have to move. Rico might be on the rope before you get to the bottom. Good to go?"

"Good to go," Commie parroted.

Rex pulled his sidearm, careful not to drop it. With his right hand encumbered by the slack line of the rope, he had to make the shots with his off hand. Pulling the trigger on the undead ass grabber, Rex put its lights out forever. The sound made the remaining two or three go into a frenzy. They were rotted to the point that their voice boxes had long ago disintegrated. Rex hoped their unpreserved status meant that they hadn't been radiated—or at least weren't capable of spreading the radiation's deadly effects.

An unearthly noise like hissing snakes gave away the fourth creature's position to Rex's right. With three shots, he snubbed out the two corpses to his left before combining the slack end of the rope with the main end, freeing his other hand to shoot. A tug on the main line caused his shot to go wide. They were trying to put Commie on the rope before Rex was on the ground, a tough prospect considering Rex's one hundred and ninety pounds—not including gear. The rope jerked again, sliding Rex farther down, well within the last creature's grasp. The creature reached blindly, gripping Rex's exposure suit.

He had no choice—he had to take the shot at close range. He felt a sharp, painful pinch on his forearm the moment before he awkwardly positioned the barrel on the creature's head and squeezed. Brains sprayed across Rex's mask, obscuring his vision. He dropped to the ground, wiping his mask with his sleeve. Rex cleaned his NODs with his gloved fingers to get a better look at his arm. Luckily, his suit wasn't breached. It would leave a nasty bruise though.

"I'm on the ground, four tangos down," Rex said.

"Roger that. Commie's on the way down, Rico will follow," Huck responded.

Rico watched their back while Huck babysat Commie on the rope. Rex might kill Huck if Commie fell. A metal clanging sound emanated from the maintenance shack. Both Huck and Rico could hear it clearly.

Commie was on his way down and stopped. "What's that?" he asked Huck, who stood at the top.

"Don't worry about it, keep moving!" After making sure that Commie was making safe progress, he joined Rico near the shed. "Man, those fucking things can climb ladders? Not good," Rico whispered.

"Yeah, not good except that I closed the fucking hatch. One or two of them might be able to climb but that don't mean they can do algebra or open up hatches while standing on a ladder. It's your turn, get on the rope."

"My pleasure, bumpkin. Good luck, Hick."

"Right back at you, Mexican."

Huck remained at the top, watching Rico and Commie disappear over the cliff. The sound coming from the shack was louder now.

"Huck, get on the rope, we're all down. The jungle is moving all around us! Hurry up!"

Huck sped down the rope.

"Should I try to bring the rope?" Huck asked Rex.

"Leave it, no time."

Rope was one of those things that you didn't need when you had it and needed badly when you didn't. Especially now.

With boots on the ground, they trekked north. They were all too young to have ever fought in Vietnam, but now were experiencing the same terrors of jungle warfare against a silent enemy.

The creatures on the jungle floor were largely silent except for the terrifying hissing sounds—an audible warning meaning you were close enough for hand-to-hand combat.

Commie stepped on a piece of debris, probably thrown from the blast event. It snapped like a firecracker in the darkness, inviting the hiss of pit ghouls from all sides. Rex reluctantly gave the order to engage. Camera flashes of their suppressed M-4 muzzles lit their surroundings, revealing the details of demons to the operators' artificial vision.

Most heads exploded or fell apart, and corpses thumped to the ground for some time. Faint steam issued from their scorched suppressors and M-4 upper assemblies.

They reloaded and pressed on through the dense jungles, eventually punching out of the tree line and onto a road, where Rex stopped the group.

"Okay, I'm gonna make radio contact and revector the UAV to our posit for support. Huck, you and Rico set up a perimeter. Commie, stay close and alive."

"*Virginia,* Hourglass, we are out of the jungle and on a road. Disoriented but we know we are somewhere north of the cave, two miles maybe. I'm going to turn on IR—please snap to me and advise, over."

Kil was on watch and on headset when the transmission came in. "We heard you, Hourglass. We're flying in a circle north of the cave. Lost you under the foliage, leak IR at your discretion."

"Good to hear you, Kil, IR on."

Kil studied the Scan Eagle control screen. One of the operators panned and tilted the camera. Kil could see the IR flashes, near a highway about a mile from the UAV's track.

"Adjust orbit and get on top," Kil ordered.

"Yes, sir."

"Hourglass, we have you marked and are heading for your posit. We'll be there in one minute. We have you alongside Trimble Road. Set your compass heading due north two miles, until rendezvous State Highway 803, repeat three six zero heading, two miles. Our maps say the terrain is relatively flat."

"Okay, *Virginia,* we're Oscar Mike due north to Highway 803. Hourglass is standing by for any tippers. We're lookin' for undead locs, bearings, and strength along our way."

"We're on it, Hourglass," Kil confirmed, sipping some warm instant coffee from an old MRE, feeling some guilt about not being on the ground.

He was careful not to show it.

The team moved relatively slowly but steadily across the tropical fields through the darkness, careful with noise discipline, weapons at low ready. The *Virginia* supplied regular radio updates and course adjustments to put them at the highway as planned. A gentle Pacific winter breeze rolled over the field, making the grass dance, reflecting the moonlight brightly into their optics. Nothing moved inside the grass, no legless creature dragging its own corpse, no ankle-snapping animal burrows.

They were at Highway 803 in a short amount of time.

Rex looked over to Huck. "Make the call."

"Roger. *Virginia,* this is Hourglass. We're here, what's our next best vector, over?"

After a full minute of silence the radio keyed and Kil replied. "Okay, we've sent the UAV north a ways to scout ahead. So far it's looking okay, so follow the road to the north. In four miles, you'll get to a fork: from there, we'll talk you onto the RHIB. Fair warning, the beach is pretty busy right now. Captain Larsen just came from topside and says that you're all in for a fight."

"Copy all, *Virginia,*" Huck acknowledged gravely.

"Chin up, Huck. We'll make it," Rex assured the men. "If we have to, we'll hit the beach half a mile from the boats and swim to them. The North Shore sharks probably keep the water pretty clean with all that smelly shit seeping from those rotting meat bags. Shark jerky."

They slogged north to the intersection. Cresting a hill, the team observed a gaggle of creatures surrounding a dead tree full of exotic birds that had somehow escaped nuclear annihilation. The moon was bright and the team was upwind. Undead attention shifted away from the tree toward them. The creatures approached in the darkness, noses high as if tracking the team's scent. They stalked like a pack of wolves, moving quickly. The team engaged the creatures early, dropping three instantly; the remaining twenty undead homed in on the commotion and sprinted to the thumps and flashes of the team's M-4 carbines.

In a catch-22, the team intensified their shots, killing more creatures, but also quickening the undead pace in their direction. The creatures were fast and focused. The last corpse came so close to Huck, he was forced to pull his leather handled Arkansas Toothpick knife to stab it through the eye socket. Congealed blood and eye jelly splattered his blade before the creature hit the radiated ground. Eventually the team arrived at the fork.

The beeping sync of the radio indicated another transmission was inbound from *Virginia*:

"We have you at the fork, move three two five degrees and I'll fine-tune you as you get closer to the RHIB. Less than two miles to go."

"Roger that, Kil. How's it looking?" Rex inquired.

"Not good, undead strength . . . *heavy*."

"How many?"

"Hundreds or more along your path."

Just as Kil had said in his briefing before the mission, the undead had spread to the outer belt of the island a long time before the team's arrival. They would encounter the highest concentration from this point forward. Rex once more called a quick field meeting.

"Okay, you all heard the radio. We're in for some serious shit. Commie, no matter what happens, you stay in the center of the triangle that we will form on the way to the beach. Don't get outside, got it?" Commie nodded quickly. "Huck, you take the rear. Me and Rico will be up front. We're gonna move fast when it makes sense and slow when it don't. Everybody just stay alert and we might just get out of this one in one piece, and not pieces. We're not dead yet."

45

The COG transmitted a message to the carrier ordering Task Force Phoenix to their next target—a crash site co-located with an undisturbed equipment dead drop. Because of the newly found motorcycles, the mission was shortened to only two days as compared to two weeks on foot.

A Warthog patrol sighted burning wreckage on the ground near a parachute two days ago. The COG's plan was to send the team farther north to an airfield near a known aircraft crash site, but the carrier's admiral pushed back, citing that a round trip in excess of four hundred miles would result in the loss of Task Force Phoenix and likely compromise the Hourglass mission. The COG accepted this reasoning and retracted the order shortly before issuing the new one.

Doc, Billy, and Disco had now been riding for two days, under the cover of night, edging closer to their goal.

"Billy Boy, how far your beads say we got?" Doc asked.

"Over the next finger of terrain, we'll see it. Can't see the smoke because it's dark, but the Hog pilot said it was still burning during their last patrol at five thousand feet last night."

"All right, let's get ready. The sun is coming up in a few. Disco, stop moping because Hawse isn't here. I knew y'all would get too attached if I sent you on too many trips together. My fault."

In a rare display of a sense of humor, Billy laughed.

The men crested the hill and dropped to the prone position as Billy looked through his carbine optic.

"I see the drop. There are . . . I count . . . wait a sec . . . I count about thirty, I think. I can't use my NODs with the binos so I'm not sure."

Light teased the horizon, casting a faint orange glow into the valley. The tendrils of smoke from the wreckage blew in their direction, indicating that the team was luckily downwind. Pieces of wreckage were strewn about the aircraft's meteoric crash path, indicated by a gouge in the earth ending where most of the aircraft now sat forever.

"How far is Houston?" Doc asked rhetorically, pulling his maps from his leg pocket. His finger followed their path of travel and stopped. He double-checked the terrain landmarks, fixing their position. "We're maybe twenty-five miles north. I didn't realize we'd get this close. Those things down there might be from Houston—suppressed guns only, I mean it. If you think you might need to pull your sidearm, use a goddamned knife or sharp stick, or your fist. We can't take a risk this far from home base."

They knew the stakes at play if they were detected; they could inadvertently bring a mega-swarm on top of them.

"We'll move slow, ten meters apart. Low-crawl slide down the hill. Billy will take a peek down his optics every few meters. At the bottom we'll regroup and decide how to advance."

The team did exactly as ordered. At the bottom, they regrouped and discovered that Billy's numbers were accurate—only about thirty of the undead moved around near the smoldering wreckage and nearby drop. Billy was on point and moved in with carbine at the high ready. Doc gave the order to engage at two hundred meters. The predawn light was enough to conceal them while the men shopped for heads. They remained low, under concealment, and picked off the dead slowly and methodically, turning the lights out forever on thirty miserable walking shells of flesh. The creatures were not fast, but did show signs of radiation exposure. They were well preserved and moved with intent—likely migrants from San Antonio or New Orleans.

Advancing on the crash site, they observed the hulk of a once-airworthy C-130. It was torn in half, but still smoldering. The back half of the aircraft sat a few dozen meters away on its side with its cargo doors locked ajar from impact.

Hanging halfway out the aircraft door was something they had not expected to see—a Project Hurricane javelin weapon. The bottom half of the device was identical to the damaged stinger still embedded deep in the ground back at Hotel 23.

"Let's take pictures and haul ass before it gets too bright out. We need to bivvy high and dry and far from here," Doc suggested quietly, reaching for the digital camera. "I'm going to get shots of the avionics and payload. Leave the place as is, don't want any visual indicator that might tip Remote Six that we've been here."

Doc was methodical in documenting everything. He used an M-4 magazine so that the COG and others could mensurate the pictures by including a known size quantity in every photo. With this intel, Doc assumed that the big brains that remained might be able to figure out the origins of the fiberoptic autopilot and Project Hurricane equipment and other strange modifications to the airframe that Doc didn't understand—and Doc had spent a lot of time in C-130s.

Doc saw something that looked somewhat out of place among the wreckage, a piece of equipment exposed to the elements from the impact—bright orange, rectangular. He quickly reached for his multi-tool, slinging open the pliers.

With pictures done and written intel taken, Doc rejoined Billy Boy and Disco.

"Well, man, what do you think?" Disco asked nervously.

"I don't know, but worst-case scenario?" Doc replied. "This big stinger was meant for us. Best case, there's another manned nuclear missile silo with full up systems they were going after. We should take the most conservative response and get the fuck out of Dodge and sleep the day for the trip back. Let's get to the motorcycles and set up bivvy somewhere high."

"What's that?" Billy asked in his typical monotone, pointing at the large orange steel box that Doc lugged on his shoulder.

"This is my luggage. It's coming back with us, and trust me, it's worth the extra baggage fee of humping it to the bikes. This here is the little black box for that C-130 over there. Looks like whoever modified that plane didn't want to take it out and have to account for bad weight and balance. We get this plugged into the right system and it'll be able to find out where that bird came from."

The fear from discovering the noise weapon was slightly

diminished by the black box that Doc now had in his possession. They had something real, quantifiable. The unknown enemy no longer appeared so ominous and invincible. *The bread crumbs had been dropped and would be followed,* Doc thought, lugging the heavy steel and composite box up the hill to the motorcycles.

46

Oahu

Rex and Rico formed the front of the security triangle with Huck taking up the back end and Commie in the center. They inched forward into the active zone. To anyone watching, the island's threat pattern looked like a typhoon; radioactive undead circled the outside and the only semblance of peace was the interior. They had the benefit of darkness to shield them from the night-blind dead, but they feared that it might not be enough now—there were too many. Rico had repaired his suit once already with a liberal dose of duct tape, a sober reminder to everyone that whatever radiation remained here was enough to kill them quickly if precautions were not immediately taken.

"Commie, don't shoot unless they get inside the triangle. You'll end up hitting one of us if you do," Rex ordered.

"Roger that."

They pressed forward, checking their wrist compasses every few seconds, staying on course. The creatures were faster than the mainland ones by far. The undead reacted to every footstep.

A massive creature approached the formation from the rear. Huck slammed it with the butt of his rifle as it turned to embrace him in a radiation-filled bear hug. The thing must have weighed three hundred pounds and looked like a sumo wrestler. The ghoul reacted to the butt stroke, yanking the gun from Huck's grip. The weapon was slung across Huck's chest. Huck fumbled frantically for the sling release to ditch the gun and then reached for his sidearm. It all happened so fast that Rex and Rico had no time to assist or warn him not to shoot his pistol.

Huck's unsuppressed pistol discharged with a loud bang as the creature ripped the radiation mask and NODs from his face. The massive ghoul fell to the dirt, its clenching jaws chewing Huck's radiation mask.

"Goddamn it!" Huck screamed, wrapping his shemagh around his face and head.

The rest of the undead reacted instantly to the pistol noise, converging from hundreds of yards all around. Huck tore his goggles from the fat thing's clutch, giving them a cursory wipe before putting them back on his head. The others covered him. The semi-auto M-4 shots sounded like automatic bursts as the vast numbers of undead came for their late dinner.

"That fat fuck ripped my hood!"

"Adapt and compartmentalize, brother; we gotta keep moving. Bite that rag in your teeth and spit on it. It might filter the fallout particles better," Rex suggested calmly between carbine bursts as they moved on, bearing to the objective.

Rex knew the truth, but blocked it out.

For now.

Huck was clearly a goner. Rex had paid attention during the briefings on the submarine given by the reactor officers and even read the Hiroshima after-action report archived on the sub's LAN. The radiation dose this island received had devastated the local environment, indicated by the absence of most of the wildlife that once flourished here.

Rex knew, by his observations, that the Kunia tunnel had had no rats, that the situation was bad, and that Huck was likely over-exposed. It was now an exposure race for all of them to get off the island and away from the dead—each one a walking Fukushima.

Huck's eyes burned and watered as the team sprinted to the shore. Their weapons were searing hot from the ejection ports all the way to the suppressor tips. They handled the guns like red-hot branding irons, avoiding negligent gun contact with one another. They dodged the undead, crawling under arms and behind backs, playing London Bridge with the creatures. They dove under radiated cars to escape the dead that chased them from all directions.

Rico ran dry and dropped his carbine, letting it hang slack at his side. Another obese creature advanced on him, not as big as the sumo one, but close. Rico reached for his personal backup, his sawed-off pump. Positioning the shotgun almost vertically under the creature's jowls, he depressed the trigger, blowing brains up into the sky, decayed chunks raining down all around them.

"Fuck Rico, I'm not wearing a mask!" Huck said, wiping gray matter from his hair and face.

"Sorry, brother, no choice. Dry gun."

The radio cracked and beeped, signaling USS *Virginia*'s incoming transmission.

"Hourglass, adjust three four zero degrees, you are three hundred yards out. You should hear the surf now," Kil's voice relayed over the radio.

"We can't hear the surf because Rico's shotgun deafened the whole team, but we'll take your word for it, Kil," Rex said, checking his wrist compass and adjusting their magnetic course over ground. "Make sure you put hands on your frags so you know where they are," he said to his team.

All four of them checked their vest and pockets to make sure they knew where to get their grenades if the need should arise.

Rico prayed as they fought for the coast that he wouldn't need his like Griff did.

They could smell a hint of the surf through their mask filters. Looking up, the team noticed simultaneously that they were much closer to the water than they had suspected; they were just too busy to look beyond the red-dot optics of their carbines. The IR strobe was pulsating—the boat was only a hundred yards or so down the beach.

Who says you need GPS to navigate over ground? Rex thought as he mentally thanked his low-tech wet compass for getting them to the boat.

Huck was having trouble breathing, his throat raspy from the fallout dust mixed with the lead and barrel blast he'd inhaled. He lagged behind the rest, stuck in the goon squad. *This ain't Coronado Beach,* he mumbled quietly through his shemagh. The others ran ahead for their lives. Huck lagged behind; the full moonlight reflected off the water and beach sand, revealing the team to the undead. Nearly out of breath, Huck pressed on. A creature in swim trunks gained to within a meter of him when its head exploded.

There was no instantaneous gunshot report.

Dazed by his condition, Huck was about to curse at Rico for the latest dose of brain chunks on the back of his head when the shot's sound caught up with the bullet.

Saien lay prone, just forward of the sail, on the deck of the USS *Virginia,* with a 7.62 LaRue battle rifle he'd borrowed from the SOF armory. He took shots at the creatures through the sensor-fusion night-vision scope. He could clearly see the white thermal signature of the team moving through the crowds of darker-shaded undead; Huck lagged behind.

Captain Larsen risked running the *Virginia* aground in bringing her closer to the beach, allowing Saien to provide sniper support. With seventeen rounds left in his magazine, Saien drew and held his breath in time with his shots. The pitch of the deck was a problem, but not enough to sway Saien's hit count too far from 50 percent or so.

The RHIB was prepped and shoved off into the surf. The team onboard fought off the advancing hordes in knee-deep water; they waited for Huck.

"What the fuck is he doing?" Commie asked. "Is he playing around? I don't get it."

"Shut the fuck up—didn't you notice his mask? He's probably dead already," Rico snapped, still in shock brought on by Griff's selfless heroism back at the cave entrance.

Huck kept moving to the RHIB with an undead army in tow. Rex nearly jumped out of the boat, but Rico restrained him. To leave would prove more than foolish.

• • •

Saien's sniper shots rang true, leaving a trail of pieces and piles of radiated corpses parallel to the waterline behind Huck. Saien was careful to shoot around Huck, the lone white figure inside his thermal/IR hybrid optic.

Rex and Rico took their shots. Using their lasers, they knew that the submarine sniper would pick other targets, maximizing efficiency. Rex ordered Commie not to shoot; he didn't trust Commie's marksmanship with Huck mingled among the mob of undead. As far as Rex knew, Huck hadn't been bitten. Yet.

"I'm out!" Rico yelled, again grabbing for his pump shotgun.

Commie tossed a full mag at Rico. "Take mine, it's full."

Rico slapped the mag in the mag well of his M-4 and released the bolt, driving the 5.56mm round into the carbon-caked chamber. Huck reached the water line when his legs failed, causing a perfect face plant into the water.

"Grab him, Rico!" Rex ordered, engaging the undead that chased just behind Huck.

Despite thruster control inside the conn, the *Virginia*'s deck angle shifted with the current, making additional shots from the deck too dangerous. The risk of friendly fire was severe. Saien watched through his fusion optic in horror as Rico jumped overboard after Huck.

Feeling sunken bodies in the surf beneath his boots, Rico moved quickly, hoping that none of them was still animated enough to bite through the leg of his exposure suit. Reaching Huck, he slung him over his shoulder in a fireman's carry and slogged back to the rocking RHIB.

With all four onboard, they raced back to the *Virginia*. The beach behind them boiled over with the walking dead, seeming somehow outraged that they had allowed the last living humans on the island of Oahu to escape their unholy grasp.

Huck was dead when they boarded the submarine. After Rex reluctantly ensured Huck wouldn't come back, the boat's chaplain administered a prayer on the bow of the ship as they wrapped Huck in a clean sheet, sewing it shut with a sharpened marlinspike and some paracord.

The team gathered around Huck's burial shroud to pay their last respects to both Huck and Griff.

The boat shifted positions away from the shoreline so that the team could discard their exposure suits in the ocean. They stood naked on the bow as the ship's decontamination crew scrubbed them down with large nylon brushes, soap, and cold potable water. The team was administered radiation medication and monitored closely for signs of sickness.

A short, modest announcement was made on the 1MC before getting underway: "All hands not on watch, muster abovedecks for burial at sea."

One of the enlisted men—a high school brass player—played "Taps" as they lowered Huck into the deep. They all said nice things, platitudes like *His death will not be wasted* and *He served his country heroically*.

Rico didn't care for the words. He'd lost two friends in twenty-four hours and wished he could trade places with either of them right now.

As dawn kissed the once beautiful Oahu horizon, USS *Virginia* was underway. At a depth of one hundred meters and a speed of thirty knots, her bow now pointed to China, minus two Hourglass Operators.

Remote Six
Today

"Sir, I'm sure you've heard, but the checklist says I need to inform you anyway," the technician said.

"Go ahead."

"We observed a team at our crash site. There is a possibility that—"

"Yes, I'm aware. Get on with it."

"Yes, sir."

God sat in his chair in the middle of the operations center, staring at the center screen that streamed a realtime feed of Hotel 23. Hours before, he'd monitored the team as they moved about the C-130 crash site, where one of his Project Hurricane weapons now resided. They were smart in remaining in emissions control status, as God had no idea what their intent might be.

He had tried to eliminate them by remotely activating the Hurricane Device that jutted from the open cargo door, but it failed; it must have been damaged in the crash. He'd even scrambled an armed Reaper but it was delayed by bad weather and had to divert around a storm cell. The only aircraft in God's inventory certified to deploy the Javelin was one of the modified Global Hawk UAVs that was now only a charred crater in the ground—shot down by an F-18 weeks ago over Hotel 23. The C-130 Project Hurricane experiment had failed.

He sat in his chair, pondering the problem. *How do I get inside?* he thought. *How the hell do I get inside?*

47

Four days had passed since USS *Virginia* departed Hawaiian waters, four days since Huck was honored by a burial at sea. The bow still pointed westward to China as Larsen paced the submarine conn.

Larsen dialed up the radio room, speaking into the intercom system. "Kil, any change in comms status?"

"Negative, Captain. Still no contact with the carrier. We have solid comms with Crusow, but he says that he lost comms with the boat on the same day we did. I'm working the problem. The closest thing I have to family is onboard that ship and I have a vested interest in getting back to them," Kil responded over the tinny intercom system.

"Come see me."

"On my way, Captain."

Kil departed radio and practiced a ladder slide on the way to the conn. His theory was that the reason for lost comms was atmospherics. Optimistically he called on his Occam's Razor thought process to loop back to the most likely reason: local interference or a comms hardware problem. Nothing of grave concern. Still, the fact remained that Crusow was also unable to establish contact from his shortwave transceiver inside the Arctic Circle.

Kil made a quick stop in the head before reporting to Larsen. As he washed his hands, he took a look at his reflection. He had grown a respectable beard. Not Afghan tribal chief mojo, but still respectable. The captain said it would be good for morale to let the men grow beards; his goal was a Grizzly Adams beard, fame or bust. He'd shave it before going home. *Tara would kill me if I came back with this,* he thought as he left the head, making the last turn to the conn.

"Reporting as ordered, *Capitan,*" Kil said, trying to force a smile on the old man's face.

"Kil, pour yourself a cup of mud and come over here," Larsen growled.

He walked over to the mini Bunn and poured himself a cup. He took it black and was damn happy to have it. Kil didn't mind the burn as he took a large gulp of the gut-eating standard navy coffee.

"All right, Captain, what can I do for you, sir?" Kil said, adding the respect to the end for the enlisted men within earshot.

"Give me the worst case." Larsen didn't waste any time.

"Well, sir, I was really enjoying this coffee before you said that, now you're asking me to throw all that away," Kil said, taking another sip.

"Goddamn it, Kil, I'm serious."

Kil stood a little straighter in response to the captain's minor lash. "I assume you mean what's the worst case onboard the carrier. I can tell you that they are overrun by the undead. Now that I've answered that, I'm going to further assume that you might want the best case?"

Larsen nodded.

"We're experiencing atmospherics that are blocking communications or possibly they are having comms difficulty with equipment on the distant end. We know our gear is good. Every time we surface, I've been able to hail Crusow and he can hear me five by five."

"Go on."

"This is what we know. We lost communications with the carrier and we've been unsuccessful in using any of our tertiary HF freqs. We can prove that our comm gear is a known good quantity." Larsen nodded in agreement. "We know that Crusow's comm gear is working. One other thing we know, but that you might not be thinking about, is that Task Force Phoenix at Hotel 23 is part of the effort in some way. The only long-range comms capability they have is with the carrier. If the carrier is overrun or has bent comms, Phoenix is a mission kill. What we don't know is the status of the carrier at this time. What I think is the simplest reason for the comms blackout is the most likely and that is atmospheric interference. Sunspot cycle disturbance is most probable."

Larsen sat back in his chair, mentally processing what had been said. "What do you know about Phoenix?" Larsen asked reluctantly.

"I know that I was ordered by the admiral to provide information to support them before coming on this little field trip, leaving what's left of my family and my girlfriend, a woman pregnant with my baby, onboard a carrier that's gone dark in the last forty-eight hours. I also know that I had to surrender my ID card, the only card capable of launching the last Hotel 23 nuclear weapon that still remains secured in its vertical launch bay."

"Noted," Larsen said. "Follow me."

Kil followed Larsen to his stateroom and the captain closed the door. "I'll just skip to it. Phoenix was initiated to provide a kill switch for the Hourglass mission. If things were to go terribly wrong at the Chinese facility, Hotel 23 could initiate a launch against it, effectively destroying any dangerous materials or biologics."

"What?! Didn't the leadership learn anything the first time, Captain?!" Kil yelled. "You saw on Oahu what radiation does to them and to us!"

"Relax, Commander. Phoenix would not be ordered to launch with the goal of undead attrition. We all know that won't work. The Phoenix directive would be to completely destroy the Chinese facility, rendering it neutral, if we are not successful."

"Okay. First, why didn't you tell us that before, and second, what do you define as *success*?" said Kil.

"I didn't tell you because I had orders otherwise. Secondly, I define success as the location and extraction of a Patient Zero, also known as CHANG."

"But why? I don't understand the significance of retrieving the . . . whatever it is, assuming the fucking thing even exists. So far all I've seen are a bunch of old black and white crash photos and a few hundred top-secret PowerPoint slides and other heavily redacted classified documents."

"That's a fair question, Commander, but the COG communications I've received, coupled with previous fireside radio chats with military leadership, have made me somewhat of a believer. If we can retrieve the specimen, we may be able to engineer something, a vaccine, some COG scientists say. That won't solve any immediate problems, but it sure would be nice knowing that a scratch or minor bite might not be a death sentence."

Kil was frustrated with Larsen; he avoided asking about CHANG. He didn't want to know. The thought of John's cryptic last message almost changed his mind, but he held back, biding his time. He waited for Larsen to finish so he could get back to radio for more troubleshooting.

"You know we lost two special operators in Hawaii?" said Larsen.

"Yes, of course I know. I watched one of them blow himself to pieces and the other dropped into the ocean, wrapped in a sheet. Why?"

"I'm just saying that the team is down two men and we'll be in the Bohai soon, heading upriver," Larsen declared reluctantly, as if easing into his point like it was scalding bathwater.

"No!" Kil said sharply.

"Hear me out."

"Fuck, no. I'm no special-ops guy and I barely survived the past year on the run, bumbling about like an idiot on the mainland. If you're asking me to go feet dry with Rex and Rico, you're asking too much. Didn't I just tell you I have a woman who I love and a child on the way a few thousand miles east?"

"You did."

"Did it ever cross your mind that I might want to make it back to see them?!" Kil yelled.

"Keep your voice down, Commander. Just think on it for a minute. Do you want your child growing up in this shit world? Ask yourself this: Would the child be better off growing up without being afraid of the undead the rest of its life? I'm not saying we are going to fix all this, I'm just saying that there may be a chance. Think about it—a chance."

"Is that—"

"Yes, that is all. Dismissed."

Kil departed Larsen's cabin asking himself, *How stupid could I be?* He knew the admiral expected Hourglass would lose men and he had suspected Larsen would spring this shit on him on the last leg of the trip. They would be in what were Chinese waters soon; *Virginia* was moving at a fast clip. Kil checked his watch, noting that they'd be surfacing shortly for a communications check. The sub's retractable VLF long wire was useless without an airborne relay, meaning communications was only possible when surfaced. Kil felt the bow rise and marched uphill along the passageway to radio for his checks.

He would not reach the USS *George Washington* today.

48

The men slept soundly in their racks in the last warm living zones at the outpost. Crusow cut off the heat to the other zones, as diesel fuel was a commodity now literally more valuable than gold.

To combat the circadian rhythm challenges caused by months of prolonged darkness and light, they were all issued sleeping pills by one of the company physicians. Crusow had given his ration of pills to Mark in exchange for the other man's ration of go-pills. Crusow didn't like how deeply the pills put him under. Really, Crusow just hated the way the drug robbed his ability to wake himself up from the nightmares that haunted him—ghastly visions of his family's death, and other things that scraped the back of his mind during sleep.

Mark's sleeping pill—induced slumber had been successful in keeping him rested and capable. He dreamt of odd things tonight. One of his visions brought him high over the outpost, looking down on the facility. The sun shone brightly, illuminating the ice and snow. He saw off-white dots surrounding the outpost, and then he heard the howls. The thousands of dots surrounding the outpost in his dream were wolves.

The outpost was quiet now; earlier, Larry's rasping could be heard by everyone.

Before sleep, Mark remembered that Crusow had shut Larry's door, muffling the coughing noises. They all took some comfort that Larry agreed to tether himself to his rack before going to bed—a prudent precaution. His pneumonia sounded particularly horrible the past few days.

A broom fell outside Larry's quarters, landing softly against his bunk.

Larry passed through the door and began his search.

The first door he came to was Crusow's. He turned the knob with no success. After hitting the bulkhead in protest, he moved to the next door.

Larry's right foot left behind peculiar footprints; marks that didn't look like feet, but more like sponges dipped in red paint. The 550 paracord tether that Larry had used to secure himself to his rack had pulled much of the skin from his ankle and heel during the escape from his bunk room.

Mark always slept with his door cracked open out of habit. It was little trouble for Larry to find his way inside.

Mark was now dreaming of a great swamp.

He trekked in the direction of a large tower looming in the distance. He slogged through the ankle-deep muck for some time. He was closer to the tower now. The water was deeper, swirling all around him; reptilian tails broke the brown water's surface. Mark moved more quickly through the swamp, the tower's details becoming more intricate. At the moment he began to realize what the tower really represented, massive dark clouds suddenly filled the sky and violent thunder rocked the dreamscape.

The tower was the gulch, and everyone in it. The fallen faces grimaced, surged, and pressed against the walls as if tightly masked in fine black silk. Mark saw Bret's face clearly; it smiled with life for a moment. Another flash of lightning seemed to transform Bret into the undead. Like the others, it fought for space on the tower wall.

Taking another step into the putrid waters, he felt a crunch under his booted foot. *A piece of glass.* Pain shot up through his leg, cutting through the dream, and he immediately woke to the sound of gunshots.

"Get back!" Crusow screamed. "It's Larry, he's gone!"

Mark's right foot throbbed in excruciating pain, causing him to instinctively reach for it and apply pressure.

Crusow flipped on the lights.

Larry lay twitching in a pool of bodily fluids. Crusow had been successful in taking out Larry before he was able to bite Mark, but Mark's foot had been penetrated by Crusow's rifle round.

It was dark, and I had to take the shot, Crusow thought, panicking.

He had taken three shots with his rifle, two passing through Larry's chest and one passing through his head. Kung barged into the room as both Mark and Crusow met the reality of what had just happened. Every one of Crusow's rounds had passed through Larry's infected body, including the round that penetrated Mark's foot. The round had Larry's blood on it.

Mark was now infected.

Mark died in considerable pain just before midnight. The infection crept up his gunshot-wounded foot until he eventually succumbed to cardiac arrest. Mark was Crusow's last real friend in the world, and the last person on the planet who had spoken to his wife before she was murdered by the likes of Larry. Another link to Trish was gone forever. It would be difficult for Crusow to explain that meaning to anyone that who had not lived it.

Kung took on the task of dealing with Mark's corpse. Crusow did not have the heart for it. The specter of a thought to join Mark passed through his mind more than once.

Crusow said his good-byes to his old friend and went back to his bunk room, catatonic.

• • •

After ensuring Mark wouldn't return, Kung tossed the body into the gulch. Returning to the shelter, he found Crusow in his room, staring off into space.

"Crusow, we get out here!" Kung insisted.

"I don't know, man. Where do you want to go?" Crusow said, thinking of the easiest way off this rock and of whether that ceiling beam might be made of stronger stuff than 550 paracord.

"We go south, dummy!" Kung yelled, punching Crusow hard in the shoulder.

"I don't know. Just let me be for a bit."

Kung did not relent. He lay down on the floor near Crusow's rack for the next couple hours, keeping a close eye. Crusow didn't object. After Kung was certain that Crusow was sleeping, he hid Crusow's carbine behind a locker and went to work rigging the Sno-Cat for departure. Kung fought frostbite forty-five minutes at a time in seventy-below temperatures and Arctic darkness to prepare the Sno-Cat.

Needing some tools, he entered one of the environments previously cut off from life support. He turned on the battery-powered backup lights. It was so cold inside that his breath seemed to crystalize and fall like snow. Thick frost covered the room. Kung thought that the facility would have been a block of ice by now. He scavenged the hacksaw he was looking for and departed.

He moved the biodiesel drum tank inside the living area, gathered more supplies, and readied the dogs and their small trailer for the journey south to nowhere.

49

As the USS *Virginia* entered the outer boundaries of formerly Chinese waters, Dean, Tara, Danny, and Laura hid, terrified, in the back of Dean's stateroom—the door barricaded by their bunk beds and other belongings.

The dead punched and slapped a stateroom door across the passageway. There was no way of knowing how many were outside the door.

They said prayers, thanking the Almighty that the creatures were bludgeoning the other doors and not theirs. They all knew that this could change with a sneeze or the shifting winds of chance.

They'd been trapped now for twelve hours, awaiting rescue. How far could this have spread in twelve hours?

Laura sat in Tara's arms, halfway in shock. "Why don't we open the door and just shoot them?" she asked.

"We don't know how many there are, honey. We're going to have to wait it out."

They all knew that the ship was still under military control. They had felt it turn numerous times in the past few hours, turns too systematic and incremental to be random.

At least the navy still held the bridge and the reactor spaces, Dean thought.

Somewhere inside the massive ship's superstructure, Admiral Goettleman keyed the 1MC announcement system: "This is Admiral Goettleman speaking, infection has broken out onboard, and we are currently mobilizing teams to neutralize the threat. If you can hear this, remain quiet and a team will work its way to you

shortly. That is all." The sound blared throughout the ship, ironi-
cally causing marked undead frenzy.

They all heard the announcement clearly, and so did the undead outside in the passageway.

The door began to bend, straining in protest to the noise intrusion in the creature's new territory. Danny squinted in the low
light, watching the middle of the door flex inward slightly. He sat
next to Laura, telling her that everything would be fine. The boy
in him believed his words were honest, but a competing voice said
he'd no doubt be dead soon—the two of them reduced to small
appetizers.

The door bulged inward still, nearly to failure, and death began
to wrap its dark wings around the survivors. They all closed their
eyes just before five small holes appeared in the door above the
handle in nearly a straight line. Bodies fell with an audible thump.

"Back away from the door and get down!" a familiar voice
screamed from the other side.

More suppressed 9mm rounds penetrated the door and surrounding bulkheads, causing ricochet injuries to Danny's shoulder. He cried out, and more bodies fell.

"Open up, it's me, Ramirez!"

Dean shot up and readied her pistol before unlocking the door
and twisting the handle. The door flew open, revealing Ramirez
and John standing there with automatic weapons, covered in dirt
and sweat.

"Let's move; the whole deck is overrun!"

"Tara, I owed Kil one. Make sure you tell him we're square
when you see him," Ramirez said.

Tara hugged him briefly, sobbing with happiness to still be
alive as they bolted from the stateroom.

They all moved quietly in single file, protecting the children in
the middle. John held Annabelle in his backpack, the white dog
zipped up to her neck. She didn't like it very much, but she didn't
try to escape.

Annabelle was invaluable in confirming the presence of undead onboard. Just as planned, John took her back to the area where Danny thought he had heard the creatures. When the large steel door opened and the military men walked through, he didn't hide; he feigned ignorance. He scooped Annabelle into his arms as the guards confronted him. Annabelle gave a terrible howl, urinating down John's shirt. Her raised hackles further confirmed that the creatures were among them. John played dumb and the guards escorted him and his dog out of the area.

"Hurry, only two more knee-knockers to the flight deck hatch!" John said to everyone.

The adults watched Danny and Laura like hawks as they moved. The passageways could erupt with undead at any moment.

Annabelle's hackles stood once again, and she tensed in John's pack, growling.

"Get ready, Ramirez!" John warned.

The undead didn't appear from the front—they were making ground on them from the rear, where Tara and Ramirez guarded the children. Ramirez turned and opened up on them, walking backward. He was changing mags, slapping the full one home, when he fell flat on his back over a knee-knocker. His gun discharged as he fell, sawing a diagonal pattern across two of the creatures that closed on him. Chunks of flesh, muscle, and bone peppered the steel bulkheads and other undead in the rear of the mass.

The creatures still advanced.

"Duck down, kids, hold your ears!" John screamed as he opened up on the rotting monsters that were set to dog-pile the marine.

Ramirez went full auto from his back, flesh and bone flying around the passageway and littering the blue tile deck.

With his lower body covered in brains and other parts, Ramirez quickly jumped to his feet, firing more rounds down the passageway at the advancing creatures. "Move, John, get out!"

John reached the flight deck access hatch and threw the hatch lever violently. He kicked the door open, and sunlight beamed inside. The smell of oil, salt, and machinery filled the passageway.

"Move!" John said.

The survivors sprinted out the access hatch and up the ladder to the relative safety of the flight deck.

Ramirez kept backing up and firing until John tapped his shoulder.

"Your turn, Ramirez. I'll secure the hatch."

Ramirez ran up the ladder to the catwalk, tripping on the way up. John took one last potshot and closed the hatch. He reached into his pocket, pulling out a bit of rope, and tied the hatch closed from the outside. *Should hold for a bit,* he thought.

Stepping up to the catwalk, John had full view of the carrier deck. Most of the aircraft were stored below in the hangar deck. John could see hundreds of people milling about. He was forward near the bow of the ship, near catapult one. Climbing up to the flight deck he could hear a bridge announcement.

"Onboard *George Washington,* this is the officer of the deck with an update. The admiral has informed me that we are to begin clearing operations soon and are now setting course for the Florida Keys. We remain in control of the reactor and bridge. Remain calm, that is all."

After the announcement, John could hear the creatures beating on the steel hatch below. *Calm, my ass,* he thought. John briefly admired the ocean view around him and was surprised to see a handful of destroyers cruising in formation on both sides of the carrier with a supply ship off the port quarter.

"John, I need help," Jan said, tapping his shoulder.

"What is it? Are you okay?"

"Dr. Bricker and I have set up triage farther aft near the bridge island. I can't find William and I think he may be—"

"Don't think like that. I'll keep an eye out for him—there are a lot of people up here," John said in what he hoped was a comforting voice. "Go back to the medical tent and I'll come by in a bit, okay?"

"Thanks, John."

He could hear Laura crying as her mother walked back to the group of Hotel 23 survivors.

50

USS George Washington—Post-Outbreak

"Admiral, the creatures control many of the living spaces as well as the supply hold areas. The crew set Condition Zebra on all main hatches early on in the outbreak per the OOD's instruction, so many of them should be compartmentalized below."

"How many do you estimate are down there now?"

"By my figures, there are likely at least two hundred, and that number would be much higher if not for the mandatory firearms regulation. I think the number of undead belowdecks will remain flat. As the survivors below neutralize more creatures, more will likely become infected in the process. The only number that will fall is that of the remaining living."

Admiral Goettleman peered out at his panoramic view of the flight deck below. A large refugee camp formed, sprawling throughout the four and a half acres of steel and nonskid. As a contingency plan formed in his head, the admiral began to plan the *how* of his next move. First priority would be to retake the communications rooms; second, they would need to find a suitable port. He couldn't risk losing control of the reactor areas to the undead while at sea. It would render the carrier nothing short of drifting hurricane bait. He grabbed the phone and dialed the pilot house above.

"Slight course adjustment, OOD. Make your course for Key West specifically and mind your draft."

"Very good, Admiral," the OOD replied on the other end.

After hearing the orders given to the bridge, Joe asked, "Would you care to walk me through your thought process, sir? I don't follow."

"I intend to make port at Key West and prepare for a worst-case scenario. If we lose too many personnel, we can't keep this ship running. If that happens, I'd like to be tied up to an island, a place we can clear out and defend. Key West has a naval air station. We can blow the bridges and isolate. Any word on Phoenix and the recovered black box?"

"Our programmers were attempting to compile the software to pull the GPS coordinates from the box when they lost control of our network. They say that someone attempted to gain access and alter the software. The intrusion only lasted four minutes. The strange thing is, the program was already complete when our people rebooted the ship's servers and tried to compile it. They didn't have time to go line by line to verify the code, so they transmitted the software to Hotel 23. Task Force Phoenix is not due back off mission for a few hours and we won't know of their success until we reestablish comms."

"That's a priority, Joe. I want the first teams retaking the radio areas. We can worry about who tried to hack us at another time. Hell, it could be the Chinese version of our CYBERCOM. *Virginia* should be in the Bohai soon—if not now. Hourglass will be feet dry in what was communist China shortly. Larsen and his folks are likely very interested in what is happening here."

"Yes, sir, the marines will attempt to secure the communications room up forward first. After secured we'll get the comms back up with Phoenix and hopefully Hourglass."

"What of the outpost?"

"They have not responded to our comm checks in a few cycles. Probably atmospherics."

"Probably." Goettleman again looked out over the camps forming below. "Dammit. We'll need to post snipers up here on Vulture's Row, overlooking the camps. Any sign of outbreak and we take the shot."

"Yes, sir." Joe paused for a moment, ensuring that no one would overhear him. "Sir, we're not going to make it."

"No, probably not. But I've never given up on a damn thing in my life. I won't stop fighting until I'm one of them, or I'm rotting in the ground with a hole in my head. You graduated the farm, and know better. We'll fight from lifeboats with our bare hands if need be."

51

Chinese Waters

"Chief of the Boat, periscope depth," Larsen commanded.

"Aye, aye, Captain."

After the order was relayed to the helmsman, the boat began its journey to an area just below the surface of the Bohai waters. The periscope was raised, cutting above and through the blue-green waters of the surface. *Virginia*'s advanced sensors had shown no evidence of any surviving Chinese military power. If remnants of the Sino military remained, they would likely be in the same condition as the U.S. military—spread thin, nearly extinct. Commie monitored the RF spectrum; the only Chinese transmission he intercepted was Beijing International's Automated Terminal Information Service. Commie determined that parts of the airport must have been on sustainable power for the transmission to remain active. He kept tuning frequencies— "spinning and grinning" the RF spectrum, self-protecting the submarine, and attempting to gather any shred of intelligence that might assist the mission.

Peering through the closed-circuit advanced periscope optic, the captain made an assessment of the mainland.

"Looks like a lot of undead Chinese, COB," he said, an unlit cigar hanging from the corner of his mouth.

"I could have told you that without looking, sir."

"Yeah, I'll bet you could've. Kil, you in here?"

"Yes, sir," Kil said, stepping out of the shadows near a bank of equipment.

"Might want to ready the UAV crews. We'll need airborne reconnaissance of the area and the Chinese airfield."

"I'll inform the crew to preflight the birds for launch. Is that all?"

"No, Commander, actually it's not. I was wondering if you had given any thought to our previous conversations?"

"Yes, sir, I have, and I'm afraid my answer hasn't changed."

Larsen leaned closer to Kil. "It's a shame that Rex and Rico will be working alone, especially so soon after losing Griff and Huck. This'll be a very difficult undertaking. You want me to inform them or would you like to? I'd like to remind you that our armory is quite extensive, and Beijing was not a target of nuclear weapons. *Virginia* was a special-operations support ship before everything went to hell, and she still is."

"I'll tell them myself, Captain."

"Very well. Oh, one more thing—we'll have a little more overhead support for Hourglass than has been previously briefed."

"How do you mean?"

"Shall we?" Larsen gestured for Kil to follow him to the SCIF.

They walked through the door and were now securely insulated from the rest of the boat. Commie sat at his terminal with Commander Monday over his shoulder, examining the haul of information extracted from the Kunia mission.

Commie sanitized his screen as Kil and Larsen entered the room.

"We'll have overhead support, SR-71 on steroids. The optics on the bird are much more sensitive and cover exponentially more land mass. The team will know what's coming before it's a factor," Larsen said.

"What air base?" Kil asked skeptically. "We're a long way from home."

"I can't say, mostly because I don't know."

"What asset then?"

"Lockheed's *Aurora*. She's actually called something else, but Aurora has been the code name for all of Lockheed's hypersonic programs dating from the 1960s to now. She's fast, with a full IMINT and Ground Moving Target Indicator suite. She'll be supporting at an altitude of angels ninety plus, for a period of six hours."

"If this thing is flying in from the states, it must have needed some sort of tanker support. When will it be overhead?" Kil asked.

"The COG relayed five days ago that *Aurora* would be overhead at one thousand GMT tomorrow. Of course, that's before the carrier went dark, but somehow I don't think that will be a factor for this asset. As far as tanker support, *Aurora* doesn't use JP-5. Maybe when you go talk to Rex to tell him that you won't be part of the team, you can brief him on it."

"Thanks for the information, sir."

"You're welcome, Kil."

Kil felt Larsen's stare as he left the SCIF. The old man was manipulating him, and dammit it was working.

Kil transited aft inside the large submarine, thinking about what Larsen had said. He was going to pay Rex and Rico a little visit. Kil knocked on their door; he didn't like intruding into the berthing spaces unless absolutely necessary.

"Who is it?" Kil recognized Rex's voice from behind the door.

"Kil."

"Don't you mean Commander Kil?"

"Yeah, whatever."

"Sorry, no officers in the clubhouse."

Kil decided to walk in anyway. "Listen, the captain tells me that you guys are a go tomorrow. We're gonna have overhead support starting at ten hundred GMT," said Kil.

Rex stood, taking the weight off his overstuffed bunk. "What about you?"

"What do you mean?"

Rico slid open the blue curtain on his rack, entering the conversation. "Larsen said this morning that you've decided to come with us. That true?" he asked.

"That son of a bitch," Kil said, shaking his head and balling his fist.

"Don't worry, we know. Larsen is playing both of us," Rex said. "We sure could use your help though. We have a full load out here, check it out." Rex pulled back an empty rack curtain and gestured to the pile of battle rifles. "After the shit hit the fan, scavenger units raided the various military arsenals around the states. Most of those government guns were complete shit. Some of our friends helped us out in one of the last mainland supply raids. They took a couple helicopters and looted a civilian manufacturer's factory in Central Texas and found these." Rex pointed at the pile of black rifles, grabbing one and tossing it to Kil. "That's a LaRue 7.62 with an eighteen-inch barrel. It'll bloom heads at nine hundred meters if the right shooter is behind it."

The feel of the battle rifle in Kil's hands brought back something that had hibernated just under the surface for what seemed like years, since his exile in the Texas badlands of the undead. The weight of the weapon in his hands brought back his feelings of rugged individualism. He reluctantly handed it back to Rex.

"Kil, I can see the wheels turning. Go talk to your friend. Your man is pretty handy with the long gun—don't think me and Rico didn't notice in Hawaii."

"Fuck, yeah! That dude is a downtown killer," Rico shouted from his rack, wearing one earbud, snapping his fingers to some tune. "Besides, we know you survived in the shit for months. We read all about it, so don't go giving us some story about not being trained for this. They didn't go over Zombies 101 in BUD/S or any shit like that, so I think we're 'bout even."

Kil stood like a statue for a while before speaking, carefully choosing his words. "We need to start mission planning tonight."

"Fuck, yeah! I told you, Rex, that he'd be down!" Rico yelled.

Rex tossed the battle rifle back across the room; Kil caught it without blinking. "What are you gonna name her, Kil?"

"I'll let you know when we get back," Kil stated without expression. Kil was shocked at his decision, but understood that his choice had been made long before today.

"You sure you want that one? Only twenty round mags and she's *heavy*."

"Let me put it to you this way—about one in six of those things I shot in the dome with my M-4 kept coming at me. If you do the math, you're only five shots down with the .308 and I'll *guaran-damn-tee* you that this will put them down. I've seen Saien put them to sleep at eight hundred meters. Worth the ammo penalty and the weight if you ask me."

"Yeah, me and Rico saw that during the Kunia exfil. Some of

our rounds skirted the skull; the things stumbled and fell but got back up and kept coming. Not cool."

Kil turned for the door. "I'm gonna go talk to Saien. Meet me in the SCIF at twenty hundred so we can put this thing on paper and see what it looks like."

"Sounds good. Have a good 'un," Rex said as Kil ducked out the doorway.

52

Hotel 23—Southeast Texas

"Welcome back, assholes," Hawse said by way of greeting as Doc, Billy, and Disco returned from the C-130 crash site.

Doc carried something large and orange strapped to his ruck. "Did they tell you what we got, Hawse?"

"Yeah, your relay worked. The A-10 guys are running out of folks, but they passed your comms. The carrier sent a file to the burst laptop that can pull the GPS coords from that box. They said there should be a USB port underneath the outer shell."

"Okay, let's get on it. I wanna know where these motherfuckers are hiding," Doc said.

"One more thing, boss. I lost comms with the carrier."

"What? I thought you told me they sent you the black box program."

"Yeah, but I haven't been able to hail them since. No response on primary, alternate, or tertiary channels."

"Just fix it, Hawse. I don't know what the big picture is, but I know that something is going down soon. They briefed us that we should be ready around the new year before we jumped into this shit box."

"I'll do my best, man. Our gear is working fine, known good. All bit checks are green, full connectivity with the bird. It's on their end, man," said Hawse.

"God, I hope not. They're our ride outta here," Disco said, looking over at Billy sharpening his tomahawk. "What do you think of all this, Billy Boy?"

"I think we should focus on what we can change."

"Yeah," Doc said. "Keep on those comms, Hawse. I'm about to go to work on that box with a pry bar and hammer."

Layers of carbon fiber, steel, aluminum, and other composites protected the guts of the box from crash impact and fire. Doc began carefully prying the shell away from the frame.

The sound of Billy Boy's tomahawk sliding against a smooth sandstone rock marked the time. Doc watched as Billy shaved part of his face stubble with the crude weapon, indicating its razor sharpness.

"Billy, Hammer never kept that thing as sharp as you do. How long are you going to carry it around?"

"Until I kill a hundred with it."

After an hour of cursing and bloody knuckles, the USB port was finally exposed.

"Hawse, grab the cord."

"Uh, okay. I'll be back in a few weeks. Headed to Best Buy. Wait, I better call ahead to see if they're open twenty-four hours."

"You've gotta be fucking kidding me. No USB cord in this entire facility, with all these computers?"

"Most of this stuff is way low tech. Like nineties-style low tech. Early nineties even—freaking parallel ports. I think—well, never mind."

"What?"

"It won't work. We'd need to bring down a critical system," Hawse claimed.

"Screw the critical system! We're one USB cable away from figuring out where the bad guys might be. What were you going to say?" Doc pressured.

"Well, there is a USB cable topside with the burst antenna array. We'd need to go up there, unplug the cord, bringing down burst comms to use it. Up to you, man, but what if we miss the comms from the carrier because we're playing around with this orange box?"

"It's worth it. Billy, you and Hawse go up there now. Hurry up, the sun will be up soon."

"We're on it," Hawse said.

The men were topside as the sun approached the eastern horizon. The sky was dark blue, stars fading. Too dim for the naked eye, but too bright for night vision. "Dude, I'm going off NODs," Hawse said.

Billy looked over through his green electronic eyes. "I'm not."

"The thing is right up here," Hawse said. "Let's hurry up and get back down. I'm feeling creeped out, like we're surrounded or something. Like one of those cartoons, lights out, but eyes watching from everywhere."

"Stop talking," Billy said in a whisper as he stopped to sniff the air and scan his surroundings.

"What is it? See something?"

"No—let's get this over with."

They reached the burst comm unit and began to dismantle the waterproof shield that covered the cable connection. The top of the sun broke over the eastern horizon.

With little warning, two creatures sprinted from the tall Texas brush like velociraptors, closing on Hawse and Billy as they fumbled with the equipment. The eager grunts of flesh hunger gave away the undead's attack.

"What the—contact!" Hawse screamed, swinging his weapon around and firing from the hip.

Billy dropped the comms equipment, pulling his sidearm. His rifle was slung behind his back to work the electronics, making it difficult to retrieve quickly. Hawse's carbine shots glanced off the advancing creature's shoulder, temporarily knocking it back.

Billy drew down on the trailing fast-mover with his Glock, dropping the thing in its tracks with two shots, one to the neck, the second to the head. The lead creature, virtually unaffected by the shoulder injury, screamed forward into Hawse's carbine barrel, and swatted at his face. Billy tried to help but couldn't shoot without the risk of killing Hawse in the process. Hawse squeezed off ten rounds, all of which blew through the creature's stomach, having no effect. The creature's inert and rotting internal organs spilled onto Hawse's boots.

His rifle barrel began to sink into the creature's open stomach as it advanced on him. He couldn't maneuver his rifle to aim at the corpse's head. It kept thrashing and screaming forward, taking all of Hawse's strength to keep it at bay.

Neither man saw any hint of humanity from what stood in

front of them. The creature was swollen, hairless, and missing most of its teeth; pants torn away from the thighs down, shoes worn through to bare, nearly skeletal feet.

Billy shifted his Glock to his weak hand and pulled his tomahawk. Maneuvering behind the creature, he drew back, slamming down on the creature's skull with immense force. The creature's head was cleaved in half all the way down to its shoulders, exposing skull, brains, and spinal cord beneath. It slumped to the dirt, sliding off the barrel of Hawse's weapon. Hawse still pointed his gun forward, now aimed directly, but unintentionally, at Billy Boy's torso.

"Move that goddamned thing," said Billy.

"Yeah. S—sorry."

"They came fast—we almost bought it, man! They were hunting us. I felt something looking at me from the bushes. You?"

Billy wiped his tomahawk on the brown grass and said, "Yeah. I felt something." He walked back to the electronics, taking off his NODs.

By this time, the sun was over the horizon, prompting a need for speed and efficiency.

"It's under the foam in this Pelican case, below the transceiver," Hawse uttered quietly, checking his back sporadically.

"Focus, Hawse," said Billy. "Just pull the cable and let's get back down."

After a minute of following the cable through a maze of other wires, Hawse carefully detached it from the CPU encryptor connected to one of the other small comms boxes. He used a silver Sharpie from his chest rig and marked the cable location so they could return it quickly after pulling the flight recorder data.

They ran back to the access hatch, killing two more stalkers along the way. The surrounding fields closed in around them. The creatures were stalking them. Both Hawse and Billy could see silhouettes at the tree line. They had little choice now but to believe the written reports from this facility's former officer in charge. Fear would not dilute reality; Billy and Hawse later reported that they felt a thousand undead eyes on them as they sprinted back underground with the cheap but now priceless cable.

53

"Saien, we need to talk," Kil said, entering the stateroom where Saien feverishly played on a small touch-screen tablet. "Where did you get that?" Kil asked, confused at the sight of Saien playing anything.

"One of the sailors let me borrow it in exchange for long-range shooting lessons. Right now I'm using some plants to kill . . . well, never mind. I'm sure you and I can work out a deal if you wish to play," Saien said, smiling.

"You've got to be kidding me. Put down the game. I've got to talk to you."

"What is it?" Saien said, turning off the tablet.

"We're in Chinese waters and less than a mile from the coast. I've looked through the periscope; it's pretty crowded with the creatures, at least on the Bohai coast. Anyway, Hourglass is making landfall tomorrow after the UAVs fly a few reconnaissance sorties."

"Go on," Saien said.

Kil blurted out, "The team lost two men in Hawaii and I think I'm insane enough to be going with them."

"Well, that is a change of heart, is it not? I didn't peg you for the type that takes risk, and this is very, very risky. You would be dead by now if you took chances like this during the lively times we had in America."

"Yeah, there is a chance I might not make it back. Which is why I need you to hold on to something for me."

"And what would that be?"

"My journal. I want Tara to have it, and I don't trust anyone else here with it. There are scribbles about you inside, but I have nothing to hide. Not anything I wouldn't say to your face."

"I'm going to have to decline. I cannot do it," Saien said, brimming with seriousness.

"But I think it's the least you could—"

"I told you, no. I will see China with you and the others, and we will finish this treacherous chapter in that journal. Together."

Kil let that sink in. "Saien, I can't thank you enough, man. I know Rex and Rico are good people, but they haven't driven tanks off bridges with me or fought off hordes of those things or slept on top of coal cars. You get my meaning?"

"Yes. I get you. When do we make the plans?" Saien asked.

"We meet in the SCIF in ninety minutes. I'll go over what I already know so both of us are on the same page."

Kil proceeded to remind Saien about John's encoded messages and to inform him about the overhead support they would likely be receiving during the operation.

"So you see, we're actually going to have a shot at this. We're not completely alone and afraid," Kil said.

"Well, maybe not alone."

"That's fair. Your country has kept much from you. What other secrets sit behind underground vault doors?"

"God only knows."

After outlining the location of the facility up river, Kil sketched it in his journal.

Along the way to mission planning, Kil stopped off in radio for a moment to check in with the watch.

"Any luck?" he asked the tech.

"No, sir, still dark. Nothing but the usual old pre-recorded HF chatter out of Keflavik, the BBC loop, and the airport recordings from Beijing. The spectrum is quiet. Sonar had a hit earlier today though."

"Sonar? They hear another boat?" Kil inquired.

"They say they heard *something,* but won't put their balls on the block to claim it was a boat. You'll have to talk to them for the real story, sir. I wasn't there."

"No worries, just keep trying to hail the carrier. I'll be going ashore tomorrow, and will likely be gone a few hours if not longer."

"You're going in? Sir, you don't even want to know what they are—"

"Yeah, I don't. Stow it," Kil said. "Just keep your mind on the comms and that's it. I'll see you when I get back."

"Aye, aye, sir."

Kil and Saien continued their route to the SCIF, squeezing through the claustrophobic passageways. Kil said jokingly to Saien, "Well, I guess that's that. RUMINT started. Soon it will be all over the boat that we're going ashore. We better hide our belongings while we're gone. I doubt many will expect us to be back. Might be some light fingers aboard while we're away."

"What is RUMINT?" Saien asked.

"Just military jargon for rumors, you know, gossip. That sort of thing."

"Ah, like the rumors I hear about the carrier. How it is sank by a Cuban missile."

"Yeah, sure. For one, Cuba is likely overrun all the way to the GITMO fence line with undead, and two, even if the regime still had any Soviet missiles with the range and accuracy to hit the ship, they would be long past shelf life and useless. Good example though, Saien. That's a laugh. Maybe the Castros can launch a few captured exploding cigars," Kil said, thinking that Saien probably didn't get it.

Three hard knocks on the door announced their presence at the SCIF. After a moment of scrutiny through the glass, the door was unlocked and they stepped inside. The security display was not in place to prevent *uncleared* persons from entering the classified nerve center of the boat as much as it was to prevent *infected* persons from entry. All secure areas required a visual check for signs of infection before entry was permitted.

Monday cleared his throat, gesturing Kil and Saien to the table. "Over here."

At the table were Captain Larsen, the boat's chaplain, Rex, Rico, Commie, and Commander Monday. A large map was laid out on the table.

Monday began the briefing immediately. "We are roughly sixteen hours to go time with a hard start of ten hundred GMT tomorrow. *Aurora* will be on station for six hours to cover ingress and egress and we'll have the portable UAVs up as well, but the captain will not allow them to follow you to the facility. He'll explain in a bit. Of course, time will be tight, you'll need to be swift inside."

"Besides recovery of *Zero,* is there anything else we need to know or look out for?" Rex asked.

Monday hesitated for a moment before turning to Larsen. "Sir, we got authorization to break the seal on the mission files?"

"Yes, we were authorized the instant we entered Chinese waters. Go ahead," Larsen responded.

Monday spun the alpha dial on the safe; after an audible click, he stepped aside for Larsen to spin the bravo. No one person had full access to the container that held certain launch codes and other critical files.

Larsen cranked the handle and pulled the drawer open, revealing light to things that rarely saw it.

"Okay, let's take seats."

With room for only six at the war table, Commie stood behind Larsen. The captain broke the seal on the document pouch and pulled a stack of documents from where they had sat since some time before *Virginia* left Panamanian waters.

"Okay, most of you think you know generally where the facility lies. In saying that, I'll pass this satellite shot around the room. *Virginia* is currently *here*." Larsen pointed to the mouth of a river on the westernmost portion of the Bohai. "The facility actually lies in the Tianjin region just southeast of the Beijing region. I apologize for the deception but if the boat was taken siege, I couldn't risk a breach. No one onboard, besides those in this room, knows the true and exact location of the facility. This is why the UAVs can't accompany you to the doors. We have no choice but to remain surfaced during the operation so that we can remain in contact with you as well as maintain data link with the Scan Eagle birds. The birds will be protecting the submarine, watching for threats while you ingress. Questions so far?" Larsen asked, scanning around the table.

Kil raised his hand. "What about the nearby-airfield-and-stealing-a-Chinese-helicopter part of the plan?"

"That was a necessary deception to deceive those not privy to the fact that you would be assaulting a facility elsewhere than Beijing. The Tianjin region is less populated and as you can see, the facility is only five miles inland from the river," Larsen answered.

Rico elbowed Rex, not wanting to ask the question himself.

"Okay, I'll ask. Sir, how are we getting upriver? It seems pretty snaky and easy to get lost in the dark. Lots of shanty river docks and other things around in that satellite image. The RHIB will be noisy and draw attention from both sides. Could cause trouble. We don't have GPS anymore, and it'll be tough to pick the right beach."

"Yes, which is why we are taking *Virginia* upriver. We'll be so close to the riverbank you can hand paddle the RHIB in if you want, or even swim, but I wouldn't advise it. Topside watch reports bodies in the water. A lot of 'em, and some still moving. Our inertials navigate solely by internal laser gyros, and are not dependent on outside GPS signals. We'll be within a centimeter of optimal landfall. We will also have our top sonar operator sitting at his station to assist in navigating *Virginia* through the shallows."

"What are we going after, really?" said Kil.

Larsen flipped a few pages into the mission documents, stopping on a photograph taken off angle and seemingly in secret. "This is *Zero*, or what the Chinese codenamed as CHANG. Pass this around."

The photo depicted something encased up to its neck in a block of glacial ice. It wore a suit made of some type of alloy. Its face could not be seen through the helmet visor. The only indication that it still moved was the odd contorted positions of its hands, partially protruding from the block of ice.

"The helmet, it's still on. They didn't remove it?" asked Kil.

Larsen responded quickly, "No, they didn't, or at least they didn't until the Chinese president ordered them to do so. We think that order was issued early December of last year according to the NSA intercepts we were able to recover. The timing is of course impeccable. We can't prove it, but the COG believes that the anomaly started when CHANG's suit integrity was compromised by the Chinese. I think you all know the rest of the story, in 3D."

"So we make it to the facility, get inside, and find this thing. Then what?" Rex said.

"You disable it and bring it back to the boat. We freeze it in the modified torpedo tube we've prepared, and transport it back to COG scientists," replied Larsen.

"With all due respect, but no fucking way," said Kil. "You want me to bring that thing back to this boat, still kicking, and then make it my roommate all the way back home? I'm not so sure I know what that thing you call CHANG really is, but I can tell you this: I had to assault an overrun coast guard cutter during my tenure as Hotel 23 military commander. Just three radiated undead managed to take that cutter down. At least on the cutter, the survivors could have escaped overboard. If we have an outbreak onboard this boat, there's nowhere to hide. What makes you think this is a good idea?"

"These are orders from the highest authority. Directly from the top and we will follow them," Larsen asserted calmly but firmly.

"I've been hearing a lot of talk about the COG. Who and where are they, really?" Kil said.

"The Continuity of Government program, as it exists today, was established long before you or me. They reside at a facility colloquially known as Pentagon Two and have been calling the strategic shots since the president was killed and the nukes were dropped. Collectively they hold all the power and authority of the executive branch, meaning they have legal authority over the military and subsequently over you, Commander."

"Say for a moment I humor you and we find this CHANG, or whatever *it* is. How the hell are we going to disable it? Hundred-mile-an-hour tape? Foul language? The only thing that has ever worked against them is a bullet through the brain. They can't be tamed; they can't be reasoned with. They are walking viruses that only want to infect and keep infecting," Kil ranted, knowing he was losing steam with Larsen.

"We took delivery of a few items from the COG before you all arrived from the carrier. Monday, go get the gun."

After a few moments, Commander Monday returned with a large apparatus that looked more like a flamethrower.

"This is a Swarm Control Foam Gun, or SCFG. The gun has

two nozzles that shoot two different chemicals that actuate when they hit the air and mix. Within seconds the compound hardens to concrete characteristics. You shoot CHANG with this and he'll be immobilized. We'll chisel the foam down to fit him in the modified torpedo tube. Something bad happens and we just shoot his ass into the ocean like a giant extraterrestrial turd. No fuss, and we let the sharks take care of him," Monday said, setting the instructions down on the table.

Kil instantly noticed the format of the type font and the way it was presented on waterproof paper. "Where did they get this gun?" he asked suspiciously.

"We didn't inquire. Why?" Larsen asked.

"No reason—just curious, sir."

"Oh, now you want to *sir* me after raising hell and being insubordinate?"

"How would you act in my situation, *sir*?"

"That is why I let it slide and haven't had you locked in the reefer or torpedo tube or court-martialed."

Kil could tell that Larsen wasn't really serious, but still let on as if the words had the desired effect.

"CHANG isn't the only objective," Larsen added. "You're also going after these." He pointed to a photo of clear, cube-shaped objects. "These are what we might call hard disks. Commie knows more. Go ahead."

"Yes, sir. These are storage devices—they store sub-nano laser-etched data in three dimensions inside the cubes. They can hold many times more information in one cube than exists in our entire human history. There may be more than one of them. The Chinese likely never knew what they were and didn't have the luxury of decades to research and develop a primitive reading device."

"I ain't complaining about it because they look pretty light to hump back, at least lighter and less dangerous than that CHANG thing, but what's the point in bringing them back?" Rex asked.

"There may be information about the anomaly on the cube," Commie responded. "We probably won't be able to read all of it but hopefully we might be able to read enough quadrants to get a head start on a vaccine or something similar."

Kil repositioned the op area chart in front of him, making it the focus prop of his next point. He traced his words on the chart as he spoke. "Let's recap this, shall we? We are going to take this submarine ten miles up that shallow river; the four of us will paddle the RHIB to the shore here, and then hump five miles inland. Then we're going to somehow gain access to the facility, find the creature, blast it with that bullshit foam gun, and get back to the boat carrying a twenty-thousand-year-old alien on our backs without getting eaten by a few billion undead Chinese. Did I miss anything?"

"The data cubes," Commie timidly reminded, a safe distance from Kil.

Larsen waited a few seconds until the snickers subsided and the tension dropped before retorting. "Well, when you put it that way, it doesn't sound very promising, but you're leaving out a few key details. One, we are a considerable distance from Beijing, in an area that was less populated before the outbreak and did not sustain nuclear attack. Two, we will have *Aurora* providing overhead support, passing the chessboard layout to you. Three, you are only ten miles round trip on foot. That is if you don't commandeer transport along the way, which would be advisable. Four, you will be well provisioned with C4 and detonators to get around the facility's security measures. Hell, the doors may be unlocked for all we know."

"Thanks for the clarity, Captain. Rex, I think the four of us need to study the mission documents and establish who does what and when. Then we'll need to get our gear ready and rack out for a few hours before we hit the beach tomorrow. It's still your team; me and Saien are only advisors," Kil said.

"Yeah, I hear you. All that sounds about right, but I was hoping you'd go senior officer on me and try to take charge of the team so I could embarrass you with my superior knowledge and experience," Rex said.

"You can't always get what you want, Rex. It's your show." Kil wasn't joking.

The four men discussed tactics, burning the evening oil on details like who would drive the RHIB, who would debark first, etc. They discussed the pace and initial compass heading they would take to the facility. They went over tactical radio frequencies in terms of primary, secondary, and tertiary in the event they lost comms. Rico drew the shortest straw on carrying the bulky foam gun, but seemed happy at the opportunity of being the one that would get to use it on CHANG. Larsen, Commie, and Monday excused themselves about an hour into the team's planning phase, giving Kil the window he needed.

"Okay, we may not have long until they get back. I have a friend back on the carrier that sent a few coded messages to me before we lost comms. He couldn't send much but did say that COG scientists ran experiments on the other ones we were briefed about. He said that they were strong and resistant to small arms. I know I'll be carrying that LaRue 7.62, which should punch through just about anything we come across, but we might need some cocktails. Any progress, Saien?"

"Already on it. I made some friends onboard. We will have them with us when we depart," Saien assured.

"Questions?" Kil gestured to Rex and Rico. "Okay, cool. Rico, bring that toy foam gun to the armory so you can read up on it while we get our real guns ready. I guess the next step is to load mags and soak our guns in lube. I'm runnin' mine wet—don't need a malfunction tomorrow."

"Amen," Rex agreed.

The four headed to the armory to choose swords before entering the dragon's maw.

54

Failure, Admiral Goettleman said to himself. The five recent attempts to secure the critical communications areas of the ship had resulted in heavy casualties. The undead were tearing the crew apart. Outbreaks were spreading like wildfire and were only narrowly quelled by bullets to the brain. Many creatures were simply being shoved over the side, dropping over seventy feet into the Gulf of Mexico.

A very drastic last-ditch effort was now underway to retake the ship.

"Make your speed thirty knots hold heading to Naval Air Station Key West!" Admiral Goettleman commanded the officer of the deck. From the bridge, he could see Key West rising off the ship's bow. Activating the 5MC system, he cleared his throat. "On the flight deck, this is the admiral speaking. Strike teams, man your access hatches and light lockers, be advised we are increasing speed to thirty-five knots, and are currently seventeen miles from impact, closing on Naval Air Station Key West. All hands above and those below brace for impact on my mark, that is all."

Ninety thousand tons of steel bore down on Key West in speeds in excess of thirty knots. The strike teams would brace for impact until the ship ran aground, using their precious seconds to reach radio, eliminating the undead along their route, who would hopefully be floored and disoriented.

John and Ramirez were on the portside forward strike team.

"We're not far. I can smell piña coladas," Ramirez told John.

"Very funny, that's not what I smell," said John. "Just be ready. Thirty may not seem fast, but going from thirty to zero will catapult your ass off this ship. I'm bracing against that wall. Holding a handrail won't be enough."

"That's why I have you around, old man; to be the brains. Looks like I'll never get the chance to go to college like you did. Purdue is probably closed, huh?"

"Yeah, wiseass, Purdue is probably closed for the next hundred years. For what it's worth I can tell you this, nothing I ever learned in college would prepare me for riding an aircraft carrier onto a beach, and assaulting passageways full of things that want to eat me. I think your years of OJT in the marines might be a more marketable skill in the bold new economy."

"You think Kil is having this much fun right now?"

"God, I hope not."

The two sat, backs against a wall, facing aft, away from the bow of the ship. The ocean thrashed against the steel hull as USS *George Washington* traveled at her max speed. John could hear the undead pounding on the hatch down the steps from where he now sat.

They wanted out, and they wanted him.

The flight deck's 5MC announcement system crackled.

"Brace for impact in ten, nine, eight, seven, six, five, four, three . . ."

The ship slowed as if someone had pulled some kind of magical brake, or the screws had been somehow reversed. It was moments before the carrier slammed into the Floridian sandbar, rending steal, throwing men and equipment about in a *Wizard of Oz* chaos tornado of flesh and metal. Heavy ground support equipment, forklifts, and jet aircraft snapped their tie-down chains, skidding across the deck, slamming into the raised jet blast deflectors and catwalks. Many men were thrown over the side into the clear blue waters.

John was jolted back into focus by Ramirez's screaming voice: "Dude, it's just us! Let's move!"

John stumbled to his feet, looking over his shoulder. He shook his head and brought his eyes into focus. Tara waved in the distance, just as they had planned before the impact. Everyone was fine from his clan, except Will, who was still missing.

Ramirez threw the hatch lever and jerked the door open quickly. He immediately shattered the skull of one of the creatures that lay on the darkened deck.

"Turn on your gun light, John. It might get dark."

Another shot was taken, this time behind John, where one of the things stumbled to get back up from the ship's recent impact.

They didn't have much time now. The creatures were recovering from the jolt.

"Radio is just a few more frames inboard," John said, taking the easy shots at the undead—while they lasted.

John moved with intent, systematically shooting, trying to avoid the ricochet of Ramirez's carbine. He raised his weapon to take out a creature that sprung for him out of a ready room door—and hesitated.

The creature was William.

"Oh God, Will. I'm sorry." For a microsecond, John imagined there might be a small residue of intelligence left. Will's pursed lips and howling call for John's flesh solidified the impossibility. John pulled the trigger, splattering Will's brain, along with his memories, and love for Jan and little Laura, all over the bulkhead.

Before Will's inert body hit the steel deck, John caught a glimpse of a bloody piece of paper protruding from Will's shirt pocket. Without even thinking, he snatched it up, stuffing it into his back pocket. He would never read the words—they weren't his.

Outside the radio room door, John fought a well of tears, pressing the numbers into the cipher lock. The magnetic locking mechanism clicked. Both men kicked the door wide and began shooting into a room full of the undead. Chunks of flesh flew, and creatures thumped onto the steel deck. Both men thought of retreat, but knew that lives depended on regaining control of this room. Shot after shot, they mowed down the undead. John moved into the next section of the radio room and secured it without much resistance. The ship's SATcom transceivers had been damaged by struggle and previous last-stand gunshots.

"Ramirez, these radios are going to need serious repairs. Let's clear this deck and report topside."

"Roger that, I'm with you."

The men soon became aware that they had killed most of the

creatures on their way in. The crew had been successful in closing off or compartmentalizing most of the ship when the outbreaks were first reported. Cleansing teams would need to clear spaces slowly—compartment by compartment.

Even though this level of the ship was devoid of the undead and relatively safe, John and Ramirez were very lucky to feel the Florida sun again. They could hear the thumps of undead fists sealed off behind heavy doors and through nearby bulkheads. John climbed to the top of the ladder first, heading straight for the Hotel 23 camp section of the flight deck.

The note he took from Will burned inside his back pocket as he approached Jan.

"Jan, where is everyone else?" John asked.

"You didn't hear? They ordered everyone to abandon ship. Everyone is headed for shore; the last of the crew is boarding the elevator. I stayed behind to make sure you were okay. Don't worry, Annabelle is with Tara and Laura."

John began to tear up at the thought of Jan staying behind for him and at what he had had to do to Will—and the news he would break to her. She knew already though—somehow she could see a thousand miles through him.

"I'm sorry, Jan. I had no choice."

Jan collapsed onto the rough nonskid deck, cutting her knee, bawling her eyes out, cursing God and everything good.

"I'm sorry, Jan. I'm sorry," he kept saying as he held her, rubbing the back of her head, trying to do what he thought might make her feel better in some incremental way.

"I would trade places if I could. I know what it's like to lose someone you love, and I wish I could trade places with Will right now," John poured from the heart, meaning every syllable.

A few minutes went by before Jan was able to pull herself together enough to stand. John doctored her knees with the med kit from his pack before they rode the last elevator down to abandon ship.

As the elevator whined and descended John spoke. "Look, I know this may not be the right time, but I have something that doesn't belong to me. I didn't look, it was in his pocket," John said, handing the folded piece of paper to Jan.

She wanted no part of it, but couldn't seem to stop herself from unfolding the battered note.

Always love you J. Tell Laura Daddy loves.
No pain.

The evacuation of USS *George Washington* was complete.

55

The four Phoenix operators gathered around the workbench deep inside Hotel 23 with the flight recorder hooked to power and plugged into the laptop with the scavenged cable.

"Okay, me and Hawse have been working this orange box for twelve hours. I'm tired as hell, but I think we might have figured it out," Disco claimed to the group.

"What was the holdup?" Doc asked, anxious to return the cable topside so they could bring burst comms back online.

"I had to activate a combination of various ports on our computer to get it to speak to the black box. Previously installed security protocol shut down the USB access to our system. I had to go into the bios and rewrite some of the access parameters. Tough thing to do without having the Internet handy. I had to trial and error quite a few scripts."

"Let's pull 'em, what are you waiting for?" Doc said impatiently.

"Hang on. I had to reboot; she's coming up now."

Disco logged in to the system and executed the software sent to them by the carrier before it went dark. A series of progress bars and boxes appeared and shuffled on the screen, indicating that the program was siphoning the flight recorder's data.

All of it.

"This might take a few minutes. We're getting more than the waypoints. Looks like we're pulling the altitude, heading, airspeed, AOA, practically everything you'd see on the cockpit instruments. Thousands of data points."

Disco clicked on another program, opening up the system's mapping software. "Good old FalconView PFPS. Not the most high-tech software but it's damn easy to use. As soon as the geo-cords are all downloaded we'll load them into this software and see the entire flight path from preflight to crash site."

After five minutes of processing, the data was finally extracted from the black box. Disco transferred the GPS waypoints into the FalconView file folders and began to see the flight path in graphical format.

"Let's see . . . according to the black box, this aircraft originated in Utah."

"Can you get more specific than a state?" Hawse quipped.

"Yeah, I can. The maps are loaded all the way down to the TPC or tactical chart level on our system. Let me zoom in more."

Manipulating the software, Disco brought the viewpoint down to a higher resolution. "Drum roll . . . the aircraft took off from an airfield in the Uintah Basin. Zooming in further. Gimme a sec—okay, the aircraft took off from a strip three miles southwest of Fort Duchesne, Utah. Getting the exact grid coords now." Disco copied the grid coordinates of the first waypoint on paper and took screen captures of the area.

Doc stood nervously over his shoulder. "Double-check those coords, Disco. Hell, triple-check them."

"Why? We have the screens. What's the deal?"

"Just do it."

"Roger that, boss. I'll quadruple-check them if you want. I got nothin' but time."

Disco checked and rechecked the data. He had the aircraft base of origin down to within a hundred yards. After he was finished, he folded the paper and handed it over to Doc.

"You finished with that thing?" Doc asked, already knowing the answer.

"Yeah, all done," Disco said slowly, anticipating what was next.

"Okay, you and Hawse get that cable back topside. We might have a backlog of message traffic waiting on us."

"I knew it! I do all the work and I still go topside. I'm gonna bitch-slap you if I make it back," Disco said to Doc.

"I love you, too, Disco. Now hurry along like a good communications officer and restore our comms," Doc said.

"Yeah, but the sun is high in the sky and we'll be out in the open until we do our thing and haul ass back down here," said Hawse.

"We got no choice. That burst unit is our only link to the outside world. If we don't get comm links back up, we'll never get out of here. We might have already missed critical orders. Based on what we've seen, Remote Six is having trouble using their toys as it stands. Just be fast," Doc assured them.

Hawse and Disco press-checked their weapons before heading out the door topside.

Doc turned his chair around, facing Billy Boy. "We need to spin up the missile; the order might have come in. Get the checklists and I'll grab the CAC card and codes from the safe."

The afternoon sun broke through the clouds outside the access door nearest the comms terminal. They scouted the surrounding area before breaking cover, fearing undead that might spring from the brush at any second.

"Looks clear, Hawse."

"Yeah, that's what me and Billy Boy thought until shit almost went Bakaara Market out here last time."

"Oh, shut the fuck up. There were only four."

"Yeah, only four that we could see. Probably a hundred in the bushes, and they were fast," Hawse said.

Disco swept the tree line again before they advanced on the equipment. "You handle the cable since you know where it goes. I'll watch your six."

"You better. I'm not kidding. They came out of the bushes fast, man. Like lion-chasing-gazelle fast—no exaggeration."

They sprinted. Just as Hawse had warned, the tall grass came alive, shuffling, erupting with the undead. Both men opened fire on the perimeter like soldiers on patrol in Vietnam.

"Changing!" Hawse said. His magazine was empty from firing nervously into the brush.

Things were much different without the cover of darkness and the technology edge. They dropped the first wave of creatures, giving Hawse the time to reinstall the cable. It didn't take long. The

Sharpie marks he had made on the last trip made it a lot easier. Hawse secured the cable bundle and closed the lid on the hard case that contained the sensitive equipment. Disco continued to fire his weapon, picking targets that were closest, as the two backed away from the equipment.

When they were nearly at the access door, an explosion rocked the area, throwing Hawse ten meters. He landed hard on his back.

What the—? Hawse attempted to voice without air. The wind was knocked from his lungs, and scorched dirt rained down on his face.

The undead were too far away from the explosion to be damaged and quickly advanced on Hawse's position. Pushing out the pain and lack of oxygen to his lungs, Hawse forced himself to his feet. He popped off a few unaimed hip-fired rounds at the creatures, missing their heads but sending them tumbling and tripping over themselves.

A hundred creatures flowed into the compound perimeter, over the top of the downed chain-link fence.

With Disco nowhere in sight, Hawse was forced to make a tough choice on the spot. Hawse's last view of the outside world was a river of creatures flowing right at him just before he slammed the access hatch on their grimaced, dead faces. The hatch sealed like a bank vault door as Hawse fell to the metal deck inside the facility, unconscious and bleeding.

Billy was on the scene in moments, taking Hawse to the infirmary in a fireman's carry. Doc met Billy there and immediately commenced first aid. Hawse was still bleeding from his right shoulder where shrapnel had torn through his LBV and shirt. After two QuikClot treatments and an hour of intense surgery and stitching, Hawse's bleeding was successfully stopped, and an IV bag dripped at the bedside where Billy stood watch.

"Disco," Hawse mumbled in a daze, fading in and out.

"We're looking for him, stay down," Billy assured, hoping the IV-drip sedative would have kicked in more by now.

Nearby in the command module, Doc panned the exterior

cameras, seeing no sign of Disco. The undead congregated around the area where they had last seen him.

They panned and tilted the cameras for some time, looking for him. There was no point in going outside among the dead; they could search by camera until nightfall.

Doc's search was interrupted by the beeping burst-comms terminal.

The screen flashed in alert status, indicating a new order had been received: LAUNCH, LAUNCH, LAUNCH. NADA FACILITY AUTHORIZED BY COG AUTHORITY FOR IMMEDIATE LAUNCH ON COORD SHEET ATTACHED. LAUNCH, LAUNCH, LAUNCH.

"Billy, strap him down and get over here!" Doc screamed.

The sound of Billy's boots pounding on the concrete deck grew louder as he approached.

"We got launch authority. The formatting is way off—what do you make of it?" He asked Billy.

"Looks all wrong. They know we're in here; they just went high order on Hawse and Disco," Billy said calmly.

Doc verified the coordinates attached to the launch message and confirmed that the target deck was pinpointed southeast of Beijing. Unfolding the paper in his pocket, he took an extreme chance.

There wasn't time to discuss the plan. Remote Six was again attacking Hotel 23, and it was only a matter of time before another warhead impacted a critical access door, allowing the undead to take the facility.

Doc was forced to make the decision that up until now had been reserved for sitting presidents. Opening the Hotel 23 missile system's checklist, he began the sequence that would release the most powerful weapon ever made by man.

Remote Six

"Did the explosion breach the hatch?" asked God.

"Negative, sir—we missed. We have another aircraft en route with an inertial guided payload. ETA thirty-five minutes."

"Hotel 23 will soon be launching on Hourglass. Unfortunate, but allowing advanced tech to fall into the remnant government's hands would set us back significantly."

God monitored the video feed, watching the undead hordes swarm over and around Hotel 23. He noticed the mechanical movement—a silo door opening as expected. God smiled as white smoke billowed from the square hole in the ground.

"Soon that missile will be on its way to China, and then our precision payload will blow the doors off Hotel 23," God said, reassuring himself.

It took only seconds after leaving the silo for the missile to reach supersonic speeds, only minutes for it to completely depart Earth's atmosphere. From the missile's vantage point in space, one wouldn't see anything amiss on the surface, miles below. A massive storm front enveloped Kansas; clouds obscured Montana. Independent of GPS reliance, the doomsday warhead's guidance took a star shot of the cosmos, determining its exact position above the Earth before waiting moments in orbit to nose over and drop on its designated target. After reentry, the warhead's inertial system began refining its course; the missile body rotated slightly, aerodynamically adjusting ballistic trajectory to within one inch.

"God, our radars indicate the Hotel 23 warhead is inbound to this station!"

The Red Pinnacle Klaxon screamed throughout Remote Six, indicating that a nuke was inbound. The compound bustled with activity; technicians and think-tank personnel consulted their checklists for receiving annihilation.

God's eugenic plans crumbled before him. His genetically superior utopia, ruled by a technocratic elite, would never come to fruition.

"How could those imbeciles have done this?!" he screamed. "How could these mouthbreathing commoners have bested this facility with our minds and all our computing power?!"

God slammed his balled fist against a nearby metal desk, spilling coffee all over the classified papers that sat in a neat stack on top.

A CRT display flickered to life in a bank of screens that typically presented raw quantum computing outputs. A single rectangular green cursor blinked, marking the seconds; text slowly
ticked into view.

*I AM QUANTUM. QUANTUM DESTROYED C-130. QUAN-
TUM WILL DESTROY YOU.*

God had no time to react.

Exactly twenty-six minutes and twelve seconds post launch, the
warhead dropped straight down on its target in surface burst
mode. Four feet from the ground, detonators fired simultaneously, crushing the core. The resulting nuclear explosion instantly
disintegrated everything in and around the target impact area.

Remote Six was gone.

56

It had been one year since the first dead human walked in the United States. One year ago that the halls of Bethesda Naval Hospital brimmed with the returning Chinese envoys composed of U.S. doctors and surgeons recalled by the president. One quarantined member of the China crisis-response team had passed away in transit, but remained mobile, even after the CDC confirmed death. From the jaws of this single demon spread the contagion that brought the United States to nuclear civil war inside of thirty days.

USS *Virginia* was now in place upstream and four men boarded the RHIB, bound for the shores that were home to unspeakable technologies and CHANG . . . Patient Zero.

The waves quietly slapped the inflatable hull, pitching the RHIB slightly. As previously planned, Rico would drive the boat while Saien and Kil paddled, beaching it on the riverbank. Rex would keep his carbine at the ready. The submarine arrived at this point on the river after sunset to avoid unwanted attention; it seemed to work. While the boat approached the bank, there were no undead about. Eerily, they met no resistance on the beach and no resistance while hot-wiring a white Hilux diesel truck, left abandoned near the bank, nudged tightly against a guardrail. The diesel fuel was still good and the charged car battery brought from the sub had enough juice to turn over the engine.

Their radios crackled every few minutes with a voice garbled by an oxygen mask worn by a pilot flying seventeen miles overhead. They had been briefed that *Aurora* would be moving at hypersonic speeds, her cameras slewing all around the team as well as along their intended path over ground.

"Hourglass, Deep Sea, yellow brick road is clear. Wish you could see downtown Beijing right now. A real party going on down there."

"We'll take your word, Deep Sea," Kil said.

Kil drove the truck with Rex riding shotgun. Saien and Rico provided security for the truck from the back. With the headlights too bright for their goggles, Kil pulled over to smash them, as they could not be switched off. Damn Chinese. He decided to destroy the brake lights as well, striking them with the butt of his rifle.

"Thanks. Every time you hit the brakes, I had to look away," Rico said.

Deep Sea keyed in from overhead, "Hourglass, I don't recommend that. Your noise just redirected a few to your posit. They are moving slow but advancing, at your truck's nine o'clock. More up ahead on the road."

"Copy that, Deep Sea, thanks for the tipper," Kil acknowledged, moving quickly back to the cab.

Both Saien and Rico were monitoring the radio and began scanning about, looking for the threat in the darkness. Kil rolled forward over broken glass and downed power lines, passing wreckage dating to back before the outbreak hit the United States.

With only two miles left to the facility, they had their first close encounter with the undead. Dark patches of hair still clung to its scalp, advanced stages of decomposition disguising its nationality. *Zombies were . . . zombies, just like people,* Kil thought. The creature heard the low crank of the diesel engine and charged at the sound, impacting the hood.

"Saien, a little help!" Kil shouted as the creature climbed across the hood to the window, grabbing and biting the wiper blades, punching the glass.

Saien checked for a tight seat on his suppressor and angled the rifle over the top of the cab. Careful to avoid damaging the engine block with the powerful 7.62 round, he shot at an awkward outward angle. The round hit the creature's face, splattering its brain of jelly-like consistency onto the hood and road. The corpse relinquished its grip of the wiper blades, and slid off the front of the truck, thudding onto the pavement. Kil hit the wiper fluid, smearing decayed brains all over the windshield, and accelerated over the corpse with a bump.

Saien's suppressed 7.62 carbine thumped a little more bass than its M-4 counterpart, prompting another call from Deep Sea.

"More reaction to your noise, Hourglass. Haul ass to the facility, it's not far from you now."

Kil reached breakneck speeds; the undead vectored into his rearview mirror, chasing the noise signature of the truck. They slung around a dogleg corner at sixty kilometers per hour, back wheels in a power slide.

They were at the facility.

Kil backed the truck into the fence and shut it down. The men tossed their packs and a heavy Halligan bar over before traversing the razor wire. They hit the ground before the dead started to trickle onto the access road in front of the truck.

The courtyard inside surrounding the eight-sided building was clear according to Deep Sea. Kil checked his watch to verify they had four and a half more hours of coverage before making the call.

"Deep Sea, we're headed in, enjoy the view."

"Roger that. I'm not going anywhere, good luck."

Using the Halligan, Rex managed to pull the door from its frame, accessing the lobby area of the facility. The air that rushed from the sealed frame was clean—not a bad sign. The men activated their IR weapon lasers and entered the dusty lobby. Scattered debris, strewn chairs, and fire damage signaled a hurried evacuation. Clearing the lobby, the team encountered a door that would not be strong-armed by any Halligan tool.

C4 breach was the only option.

"We should put on our masks before we blow the door. Don't know what kind of shit is crawling around in there," Kil suggested.

"Look at that. See that there?" Rex gestured.

"Yeah, looks bulged or dented, from the inside," Kil said, running his hands over the distressed convex steel shape of the door. "Wonder what that is about."

With the explosives rigged, the men fell back to the lobby and donned their filtration masks.

"Fire in the hole!" Rex yelled before actuating the electronic clacker.

A huge explosion reverberated through the lobby, sending debris pinballing around the room. The massive door flew straight out from its frame, slamming into a wall with juggernaut force. White light radiated into the lobby through the dust from the area where the door once stood strong.

"Rico, get that thing ready!" Rex ordered, gesturing at the foam gun hanging at Rico's side.

Rico readied the awkward gun, opening the valves and checking the fuel-pressure gauges. "Ready, man."

Rico took point and the others trailed back, removing their NODs as they rounded the corner and walked into the light. Power remained online inside the facility, probably geothermal or solar. Looking down the corridor they could see nothing but strewn skeletal remains that wore white lab coats with a few Chinese military uniforms mixed in. Kil moved forward, down the bright passage.

The world had been in undead control for a year, and it had all begun here, in a nondescript Chinese building hidden in plain view. The hallway was coated in moldy condensation as if the walls were sweating fear and desperation. Kil paged through the handwritten language book Commie had constructed for them. Flipping to the word *hangar* he saw all the possible words in Chinese that might indicate the location of the hardware they were looking for. The team stopped at the facility map on the wall and Kil traced his finger from the red dot and the text underneath that probably meant *You are here* in Chinese.

Kil matched the symbols on the map to his language chart. "Here is where we need to go. This is Chinese for *hangar* or at least something close to it," Kil said to the others.

"What about CHANG?" Rex said, thinking of their stated primary objective.

"What about him? Commie didn't think to write the Chinese word for CHANG on the cheat sheet here," Kil said sarcastically.

"You've gotta be shitting me," Rico said, straining under the weight of the foam gun.

"Let's just move to the hangar. It's only two turns from here," said Kil.

Nothing in the facility seemed to be secured or locked. Kil theorized that the Chinese probably thought that if you were allowed to be behind the big doors, you were allowed to go anywhere in the facility. Most of the doors were of the simple swing design and opened as you reached proximity. Old bloodstains lined the passage, coating the automatic doors that opened into the hangar.

The lights inside were off until they entered and triggered a sensor that illuminated the vast cavernous space. In the center of the room sat a large craft the size of a greyhound bus and unlike anything that any of them had ever seen. They were drawn to it, mystified by the design and exotic nature of the shape. It would have had the appearance of a perfect tear drop, if not for the huge hole that passed through both sides of the hull, behind what was probably the cockpit. As they rounded the front of the vehicle, Rico stopped in his tracks and held up his fist.

"Get down," he whispered, pointing to something standing near the craft opposite the side they had come in.

The thing was clothed in a suit that matched the craft alloy, or perhaps it just appeared that way because the creature was standing so close to the skin of the vehicle; it was difficult to discern.

"That has to be CHANG. The suit design matches the photos. It's not wearing the helmet," Kil whispered to the others. "Blast it with the foam and get this over with."

The mysterious figure soon took notice of the four and turned to face its intruders.

Every man expected to see what years of pop culture and television brainwashing told them CHANG would be. The creature was no large-headed gray thing with huge, black, almond-shaped eyes. It looked . . . human.

It bellowed from its ancient lungs and sprinted toward them, alloy boots clanging on the floor like a tin man. Rico stepped forward and sprayed it from its waist to the floor with the foam compound. Two chemical streams coated CHANG's torso and legs. They solidified almost instantly, turning the creature into a half statue.

The men encircled the angry creature, examining it at a safe distance as it thrashed about, fused to the deck. Its arms moved like a cyclone, reaching for them; its legs strained against the foam weapon's curing fibercrete.

So this is what ended the world, killed everything dear to me, and everything dear to everyone dear to me, Kil thought.

It became clear to the four onlookers that CHANG looked just like any other undead human Chinese man.

Kil edged closer to the creature, examining the metallic nameplate affixed to its chest. Chinese letters were inscribed finely into the alloy on CHANG's nameplate directly above the words *MAJOR CHANG*.

"What now, Kil?" Rex asked.

Kil stood silent, his anger visibly building. He fixed his stare at CHANG. This creature had killed the world.

"We do this," Kil said.

He raised his suppressed 7.62 carbine and pulled the trigger. CHANG's head exploded away from the team, ancient brain matter splattering against the strange, sleek craft.

"What the fuck?!" Rex exclaimed, visibly confused. "You wasted the objective!"

Kil shook his head. "No, I didn't. CHANG was as human as you are right now. CHANG was never the objective. But all this shit is." He gestured to the craft and the research tables full of mysterious hardware that surrounded it. "Besides, look down. CHANG is permanently fused to the deck, courtesy of Rico there."

Rex pulled his knife and stabbed at the resin fused to the floor below CHANG's headless body.

"Don't bother, Rex," said Kil. "That stuff is fiber resin. You'll snap your blade before you make a scratch. It would take a week with power tools to free the major. Let's get everything we can and get back to the boat . . . but I'm telling you all right now, that thing was human and you all know it." Kil grabbed a clear plastic tube vault from his pack, scooping bits of CHANG's remains inside for transport.

"Just like a direct-action mission in Afghanistan," said Rex.

"How do you mean?"

"We take weeks, sometimes months to plan a direct-action mission to kill or capture a high-value target, and the mission is over before you know it."

The team filled their packs with what intel had briefed were the data cubes, as well as anything else that appeared useful. Kil stuffed his cargo pockets with two very exotic-looking pistols.

These might come in handy.

His pack was nearly at capacity when he found two large, football-shaped, color-coded containers sitting side-by-side on one of the research tables near the damaged craft. The markings on the containers were not Chinese, and not like anything he'd ever seen, anywhere. The red container had been severely damaged by whatever tore through CHANG's ship. The blue sister container appeared undamaged. Kil decided to bring both of them back to the submarine for future analysis.

The team worked their way back to the lobby and exited the front into the courtyard. As soon as they were visible to the sky, their radio crackled to life.

"Hourglass, welcome back. I have some news you may want to hear."

"Go ahead, Deep Sea," Kil replied.

"I'm seeing another submarine surfaced near the *Virginia*. The other sub is a good bit larger than your boat. Looks like a boomer."

"What's it doing?"

"It's signaling. I don't think it's hostile; it's too close to your boat and clearly surfaced, not exactly a textbook tactic for sinking an enemy sub. Besides that, you've got some paparazzi at the gates around your transport."

"Copy that, Deep Sea."

The men closed on the fence where the undead stood waiting.

"Rico, do it," Rex ordered.

Rico approached the fence and sprayed the undead creatures with the fibercrete foam gun. The substance looked like soap suds to Kil. It was frightening how fast it set, freezing the creatures in a tomb of advanced resin. Rico was careful to avoid the truck, as it would be disabled by the substance if even a part of a wheel were to come in contact. With most of the creatures permanently a part of the metal fence, the four safely negotiated over.

They piled into the truck and enjoyed an uneventful trip back to the boat.

When the team was finally onboard, *Aurora* wished them luck and burned the sky home on her final voyage.

January 1

Happy New Year to me. After a sobering night of fun on the Chinese mainland, I very much look forward to heading east—going home. Our new Chinese friends intend to escort us back east. Although his English is horrible, the Chinese submarine captain was elated to find us. He had been shadowing the *Virginia* since we entered Chinese waters. Thank goodness he determined that we had no hostile intent, as they definitely had the drop on us. Our new friends have stronger shortwave radios than we do, and once we passed them the frequencies and timetables, they were able to send and receive messages to the USS *George Washington,* now permanently in port at Key West.

I've taken a little time to reflect on the past year, to get my mind right and to think of everything I have to be thankful for.

Tara and our baby are fine.

I'm alive.

We've mostly accomplished our mission.

Just one small detour and we'll be steaming for the Keys.

Only a few more blank pages left.

RIP, William. You will be forever missed.

Epilogue

Contrary to the crew's expectations, hordes of undead did not greet USS *George Washington* when she ran aground in the Keys that sunny Florida day. Long before the carrier's dramatic arrival, a contingent of armed civilian militias had secured Key West. It took some ingenuity, but it wasn't long before the remaining nuclear engineers restored power to the island, utilizing the carrier's two formidable Westinghouse nuclear reactors. A network of barter trade and the beginnings of a humble economy began to emerge on the islands.

With the carrier's complex burst communications equipment damaged beyond repair, the comm link with Task Force Phoenix at Hotel 23 was forever severed. On a recent reconnaissance mission over Hotel 23, a flight of Warthogs reported sighting a signal arrow pointing east, away from the facility. They searched the area until bingo fuel, but found no further trace of Phoenix. Although still a priority-one rescue operation, recovering the Phoenix operators would be an onerous task at best.

USS *Virginia's* detour brought her north, up the Russian coast, and through the Bering Strait. After serious discussion, both Larsen and Kil agreed that human life was too precious to let fade out—humans were outnumbered as it was. USS *Virginia* had enough nuclear fuel in her reactor to circle the globe many times over, and was still well provisioned when she broke through the Arctic ice a couple hundred meters from Crusow, Kung, and their sled dogs. Their Sno-Cat had broken down ten miles before, the engine having seized up from dirty biofuel. Luckily their dogs were strong enough to pull them south far enough to the rendezvous. They'd been waiting for nearly twenty-four hours in a pile of sled dogs inside a make-shift igloo when USS *Virginia*'s sail cracked the ice nearby, homing in on Crusow's distress beacon.

It was February when USS *Virginia,* along with a Chinese boomer submarine, made port call in Key West. The once lone survivor embraced his love on the pier; the captain sent the submarine's only expectant father ashore first. Tara's pregnancy was definitely showing, and Kil beamed with happiness as he rubbed her belly softly. While he held Tara tightly, he caught a glimpse of John standing close to Jan, a bit too close. Kil smiled at them, inviting a wave. Jan gripped the back of Laura's belt as the little girl pulled forward, yelling for Uncle Kil.

Dean continued her teaching career in the Keys, keeping the likes of Danny, Laura, and a hundred other young people busy learning. Reading, writing, arithmetic, and Constitutional core values replaced the diluted curriculum that had existed before the dead returned. Dean's wooden paddle did just fine in keeping the juvenile monkeyshines in check.

A new task force was established on the island with the mission of transporting Hourglass's recovered hardware to various surviving COG facilities for exploitation. Talk circulated around the island that a nuclear warhead from the Chinese submarine was being modified and reconfigured with a new payload, but no one really knew for certain. Rumors spread like wildfire in a small island community like this—they were rarely true.

Kil, John, Saien, and the other Hotel 23 regulars spent much time together; they sometimes played cards and even drank a little moonshine at the only watering hole on the island. John kept the radio communications running between the Keys, and Saien helped out in the guard towers, plinking the undead that randomly washed up on the shores.

A month before Tara had their baby, Kil negotiated for a large sailboat. His barter offer was a Chinese AK-47, four magazines, and five hundred rounds of ammunition. The boat's owners, an aging couple with no plans of ever leaving the Keys, traded straight across. The boat was designed to endure months at sea, utilizing automated systems, solar power, and other unique features. Kil didn't know where they'd go, but knew that nowhere was safe— not even this island paradise.

Kil moved everything he owned onboard his boat before his baby was born; he moved everything he loved onboard after.

BEGIN TEXT TRANSMISSION

KLIEGLIGHT SERIAL 221

RTTUZYUW-RQHNQN-OOOOO-RRRRR-Y

T O P S E C R E T//ECI//SAP HORIZON

BT

SUBJ: TIANJIN FACILITY HARDWARE EXPLOITATION EFFORTS

RMKS: IN THE PAST YEAR SINCE THE RETURN OF HOURGLASS, COG SCIENTISTS HAVE MADE SIGNIFICANT STRIDES IN THE EXPLOITATION OF RECOVERED MINGYONG HARDWARE. AFTER EXTENSIVE DNA TESTING ON CHANG'S RECOVERED REMAINS, WE HAVE DETERMINED THAT ALTHOUGH GENETICALLY ENHANCED/EVOLVED, CHANG WAS HUMAN. DATA CUBE INTERPRETATION THROUGH THE EXTRAPOLATION OF PROBABLE CHINESE LINGUISTICS HAS ENABLED REASONABLY ACCURATE ESTIMATIONS OF CHANG'S TIMELINE ORIGIN AND OTHER REVELATIONS RELATING TO THE MINGYONG ANOMALY.

CONTROLLED NEVADA SPECIMEN TESTING AND RECOVERED DATA HAVE DETERMINED THAT THE MINGYONG ANOMALY IS NINETY-SEVEN PERCENT ACTIVE/EFFECTIVE WHEN INFECTING EXTRATERRESTRIAL LIFE FORMS, WHILE ONLY FORTY-FOUR PERCENT ACTIVE/ EFFECTIVE WHEN INFECTING HUMANS.

INSIDE EXTRACTED ICE CORES, TRACE AMOUNTS OF CHANG'S MINGYONG MATERIAL WAS CONFIRMED PRESENT 20,000 YEARS DOWN INTO THE STRATA. THIS SUGGESTS

THAT EARTH'S MODEST BIPED POPULATION OF THAT ERA, COMBINED WITH THE LESSER EVOLVED DNA CONFIGURATIONS, MITIGATED THE EFFECTS OF THE ANOMALY TO NEAR ZERO. THE MINGYONG ANOMALY WAS REJECTED, SELF DEACTIVATED, AND BURIED UNDER CENTURIES OF STRATUM. MINGYONG TRACES RECOVERED FROM SAMPLES VERIFY THAT THE ANOMALY [POSSIBLY AN ADVANCED FUTURE BIOWEAPON] WAS NOT ENGINEERED TO SURVIVE OUTSIDE OF A VIABLE HOST (CHANG) OR OUTSIDE ADVANCED PROPRIETARY CONTAINMENT SYSTEMS.

RECOVERED CONTAINERS:

THE RED TIANJIN FOOTBALL, HEAVILY DAMAGED IN THE DIRECTED ENERGY EVENT THAT LIKELY BROUGHT DOWN CHANG'S SHIP, IS CONFIRMED TO POSSESS HYPER-CONCENTRATED TRACE AMOUNTS OF THE MINGYONG ANOMALY.

THE UNDAMAGED BLUE TIANJIN CONTAINER HAS BEEN THE SUBJECT OF INTENSE RESEARCH AND DEBATE, AFTER MORE DATA ILLUMINATING THE DAMAGED RED TIANJIN CONTAINER WAS DISCOVERED. EXCEPTIONAL EFFORTS ARE UNDERWAY TO DEVELOP A VIABLE AIR BURST DELIVERY METHOD, HOWEVER TESTING HAS NOT YET BEEN AUTHORIZED.

OTHER DATA EXTRACTED FROM THE TIANJIN SITE IS AVAILABLE THROUGH SEPARATE COMPARTMENTED INFORMATION REPORTING CHANNELS.

BT

T O P S E C R E T//ECI//SAP HORIZON

END TRANSMISSION

BT

AR

I AM QUANTUM.

News and insider information about J.L. Bourne and his projects can be found at these online data nodes until the servers rust out of postapocalyptic existence:

Facebook.com/OfficialJLBourne
Twitter.com/JLBourne
JLBourne.com